***Childwold*** is a work to remember her by and, simply, one of her best pieces of fiction yet. . . . There is great similarity between this book and her 1970 National Book Award winner, *THEM*."

—*Detroit Free Press*

"Joyce Carol Oates's best book. . . . No other book by this author has quite the magic of this one."

—*Cleveland Plain Dealer*

"In *CHILDWOLD* she demonstrates the virtuosity that puts her in a class whose only other present-day occupant is Vladimir Nabokov . . . its main theme is so reminiscent of *LOLITA*."

—*Cleveland Press*

"Miss Oates enchants."        —*Associated Press*

"There is no experience comparable to an Oates novel. . . . Oates has a story here, and a good one, but she is much more than a storyteller. This book is enthralling. It is a sensual pleasure."

—*Houston Chronicle*

# Childwold

## Joyce Carol Oates

FAWCETT CREST • NEW YORK

*CHILDWOLD*

THIS BOOK CONTAINS THE COMPLETE TEXT OF
THE ORIGINAL HARDCOVER EDITION

Published by Fawcett Crest Books, CBS Publications, CBS
Consumer Publishing, a division of CBS, Inc., by arrange-
ment with Vanguard Press, Inc.

ISBN: 0-449-23450-9

Printed in the United States of America

10   9   8   7   6   5   4   3

*For John Ditsky*

Every man's condition is a solution
in hieroglyphic to those inquiries
he would put. He acts it as life,
before he apprehends it as truth.
　　　　　　　　　—*Emerson*


We are not the readers but the very
personages of the world-drama.
　　　　　　　　—*William James*

# One

THAT final year of my life, I often dreamed of Evangeline in her attic room, asleep in her high wind-rocked moon-haunted bed, in that rotting farmhouse on the river: my teeth grinding as hers did, my voice guttural and sleep-stricken. My knuckles bled, I must have been gnawing at them.

I dreamed of her muttering in her sleep words I would never hear, her child's face contorted, her hair a fair curly aureole about her head, the small fist of her heart beating hard and steady, steady, though I should cease to exist.

The moon is a stone. The moon is nothing but rock. You must think of it that way, but without weight, weighing nothing: that way you can't think of God.

One idea pushes the other away.

Sleeping at the top of the house, you are likely to be wakened by the wind, the threshing of the walnut tree just outside the window, the moaning in the silo. You are likely to be brushed by the moon's light. The wind seems to blow it into the room. It shines through the narrow window, a miracle that it can find you, in the dark, past the trumpet vines that have grown over the screen. You are awake. You haven't been asleep. Someone was groaning God don't let, God help us, God please, begging God in her sleep, rubbing her knuckles against her teeth, but it wasn't you—you've been awake all night.

The moon is a rock but it doesn't weigh anything. It has no light of its own. You could lie flat against its surface, arms and legs stretched out, face pressed against the rock; it would be something to feel, to touch—it helps you to think of something solid to touch, like the boulders and rocks and stones and small pebbles by the river, things you can touch, grasp, be certain of, pick up if they're small enough—throw out into the river again. But God: God can't be touched. No wonder people laugh. If you think of God you want to ˆpray; your throat hurts with the need, like crying, you want to cringe and whimper and beg; you hate the sounds of your own wheedling voice, God help us, God don't let; you hate the desperation, God please, God help Momma, help all of us; it drives you wild to hear yourself, you sound like your sister June whining for attention or like the baby or Momma that night she was hurt so bad.

The moon is a stone, the moon has no meaning, the light that falls across your legs has no meaning, like the headlights of cars or trucks you can see in the distance at night, out on the highway. There are night birds—there are crickets in the grass—hundreds and hundreds of sounds. One of the apple trees creaks in the wind, you can hear it plainly, you can hear a barn owl nearby, must be in the hay barn, swallows and pigeons in there too, and mice, and rats—saw a water rat down by the river the other day—should have thrown something at it but maybe it was a muskrat—anyway it was too quick, swimming under the dock.

Around three in the morning the baby will start to cry and Nan will get up to feed him and then it will be quiet again until your grandfather goes out, leaves the house by the side door, tells the dog to be quiet. You can hear him though he thinks no one is listening, he thinks he is alone, five or five-thirty and everyone else asleep—the big ugly falling-apart house jammed with sleep.


A pheasant, a male pheasant, starting up suddenly: deliberate surprise. Saw me coming, waited for me. The noise of their wings—always a surprise.

Reminded me of—?

Something opening its wings, so broad the sky is darkened—the clouds and the mountains run together, the division between them lost. Wings opening, spreading. Must have been a dream. The hawk I nailed to the barn
11

door last year, wings spread, neck broken. In the dream I was victorious as in life. The bird was an old woman, a silly old woman with a trembling neck, her skin a thousand wrinkles. I shouted at her to go away, go away, old woman, what do you want?—get on away from here!—and there was no danger.

The world is best at dawn. The human mind is best then. Singing to myself, under my breath, feel very good this morning, better than I have in weeks; the pheasant was beautiful, knocks your eye out, their beauty, flapping of wings a good sound, no danger, there is danger sometimes with hawks if you show weakness, otherwise they keep their distance, know who owns the land. . . . The world is best at dawn, before the sun gets too hot. Late summer, harvest: too hot. Seventy years ago the misery of that first harvest—working in the fields with the men—beside my uncle, wringing wet, head aching, such heat, tomatoes the worst, agony of that morning and afternoon and early evening, almost fainted after lunch, never dared complain. . . .

Old woman, I said to her, not afraid for a moment, old woman, you can go to hell, eh?—go back to hell where you belong.

"Oh you pests, you pests! Look what you're doing!—*Stop* that, Davy! Didn't you hear me?"

She would have slept later than seven-thirty, she would have liked to sleep until nine, but it was impossible, it was just impossible, every morning something happened to wake her up and of course she couldn't just chase the children out of the room and go back to bed and sleep. Once the day began, it began: three of the smaller children climbing in bed with her, noisy and silly, and the dog barking out in the driveway, and—her hearing was so acute these days—the old man in the kitchen downstairs, fumbling around, must be sweeping something up—had he broken another glass? He would sweep up the pieces and make no mention of it to her, not a peep out of him, as he hadn't mentioned the other glasses and that nice china cup and a plate or two, and the fact that at least a third of one of those four-ounce jars of ground black pepper had
12

fallen into the fish chowder he was making last week—the top must have been loose and he didn't know any better than to shake the pepper directly into the pan, and afterward he claimed he had spooned it all out and there was nothing wrong with the chowder. But everybody's mouth was burning: and then the nerve of him, to get peeved at *her*.

"Go away now and let me get dressed, don't knock the pillow onto the floor—the floor isn't clean—aren't you listening to me? June, leave Chuckie alone! I saw that! Do you want a spanking first thing in the morning?"

They bounced and giggled and burrowed beneath the covers. Arlene swatted at them, pretending to be frightened—she drew her legs out and squealed for them to stop. Davy tunneled all the way to the foot of the bed and tried to push his way through to the floor, but of course his head was caught in the bedclothes; one of the other children grabbed his bare feet and tickled them. What a commotion, what a kicking and screaming! It was no wonder Arlene never got enough sleep, no wonder she'd be dragging herself around by late afternoon. And those circles beneath her eyes!—in the bureau mirror she caught sight of herself for an instant and it was quite enough, thank you, she didn't need to inspect that face any more closely. She stood heavy and sluggish and contemplative before the bureau, head turned away from the mirror, eyes narrow, stale with sleep, blinking rapidly. What day was it? Which day of the week? What was the date? Her mouth tasted like hell. Her rayon nightgown was ripped beneath one arm. And look at the room, which she'd tried to straighten out only the day before—And what were the children doing, bouncing on the mattress like that? She grabbed one of them, she cuffed another on the side of the head. The bed was practically a wreck already, couldn't they see?—were they trying to break the springs?

They ran out, laughing and squealing.

"Goddam you pests! I'll catch up with you! I'll warm your rears!" Arlene shouted.

And there is Laney slouched in the kitchen doorway, eating a piece of bread with elderberry jam smeared on

13

it. She won't sit down for breakfast. She *won't* take time for breakfast. It's whole wheat bread, the last of the loaf Arlene bought from old Mrs. Arkin just yesterday, and that's at least better than the white bread most of the children gobble; but she should sit down at the table, have something warm, and at least a glass of milk. But no. Don't even bring up the subject. There's Laney, catlike, arrogant, holding herself apart, eating fast as one of the little boys, as if it was just something she wanted to get over with. Pretending not to be aware of her mother. One glance at Arlene's face, and that tiny hurtful wincing, that flicker of pain and dread and exasperation—that's all! And dressed in an outfit that couldn't be more ridiculous —her usual soiled blue jeans and a cheap, thin jersey blouse from Kresge's, an ugly off-yellow, and the imitation velvet jacket with the brass buttons, wine-colored material already wearing out at the elbows and cuffs; but of course she imagined herself stylish, like her girl friends, like those pretentious pathetic loud-mouthed girls at the high school. What an outfit! And her shoes—thick-soled squarish ugly things, like combat boots, laced up with red plaid shoelaces. "For Christ's sake, Laney!" Arlene cried. "Can't you sit down at the table? Can't you get out of everybody's way at least?—Look at her standing in the doorway, so stuck-up! In her best Sunday clothes!"

She stared toward the window, ignoring Arlene. Like one of the cats, sly and self-centered and so quiet sometimes Arlene couldn't hear her walking around, even on the stairs to the attic or in her attic room; when she did condescend to speak, her voice was low and husky and surprising, the voice of a mature woman rather than that of a brattish scrawny fourteen-year-old dressed for school in an outfit that just amazed Arlene, it was so absurd.

"Look—are you really going to wear *that? That?* To school, to town?"

Laney glanced at her, her eyes narrowed.

"I wear whatever I damn well please," she said.

"I'd like to see you again as soon as possible. Tonight? I could pick you up after school, could drive you back home afterward. . . ."

"No."

"My pretty Evangeline. . . ."

She turned away, annoyed. Wouldn't let me touch her or even look into her face. "My name is Laney," she said coldly. "But I don't want you to call me that either—not even that."

"What should I call you then?"

"*Nothing!* Leave me alone!"

Trembling, his body trembling with—

He was so—

Could hardly speak at times, his teeth chattering, his eyelids fluttering—

One Saturday night in Port Oriskany, eighty miles from his family's farm in Childwold, Vale Bartlett walked into a lakeside tavern and saw, at once, his gaze swinging instinctively to her, his mother standing at the bar in tight-fitting red slacks, laughing, her head thrown back in a parody of good humor, her fingers closed upon the forearm of a tall, big-bellied man with thick dark hair and a plaid sports shirt and a braying laugh as loud as hers.

The rage began in him again, began so violently he was terrified he might faint—

On a raised platform at the rear of the tavern two men and a woman were singing above the din, strumming guitars. Vale turned away from his mother, turning as if to judge the entertainment. He stood with his hands on his hips, legs apart, knees slightly bent; his head jerked in time with the music.

*You know I'm the one 'n' only one for you*
*So why do you treat me so darn mean 'n' cruel*
*Why break my poor old heart the way you do*
*When you know how lost in love I am with you—*

Vale was with a girl named Molly, just a girl from the cannery who thought she was better-looking than she was; he had not forgotten, and was not going to forget, the way she'd stared at the scars on his face, stupid and rude and scared and in awe, the first time they had met. He gripped her arm. He pulled her along, protesting and laughing and picking at his fingers. The woman at the bar was hidden from view. The man beside her had become two men, the twangy music was louder and more desperate because no one was paying it heed, maybe the woman in the red slacks was a stranger after all, hair tied back in a kerchief the way Vale's mother never wore it. He had no time to ponder; the rage built to a tremor, the girl giggling and picking at his fingers was going to learn, the little bitch was going to learn, he hadn't enlisted in the United States Army and been shipped around the world and back and discharged honorably just to be stared at by a little bitch like that, doused in perfume, her breasts loose in a bright orange sweater, calling him *Vale* in a breathless wheedling voice as if they were lovers in a movie and everyone was watching. He dragged her back through the crowd at the door, told her they weren't staying in this dump—the music was lousy—he couldn't stand it—they could have a better time on their own.

You're hurting my arm, Vale! Jesus!

Then walk faster, he said.

Awake before dawn. Summer, winter. Hard to sleep. People walked through his sleep now, murmuring, speaking of him as if he were absent or paralyzed or dead. That white-faced angular man—a stranger—melodic voice—sudden smashing of the table, the sideboard, the cut-glass bowl—a quirt he'd brought in from the stable—must have been his father, his dead harmless hated father, whom he had not seen in seventy-three years. Seventy-three years! —A horse-trader, a bankrupt, a drunkard, it was widely known—had no more feeling for his youngest son Joseph than to send him off to America, an undersized boy of ten, to cousins in Boston who would treat him like trash and who would finally ship him farther west, when the child labor laws overtook their part of the world—poor semi-mute Joseph taken on by a distant cousin or uncle, Lenehan, who had a few acres of good bottom soil in the Eden Valley and was bitterly, angrily childless.

He did not hate his father. Did not remember hatred. Had been afraid of him—everyone was—the rages, the drunken tears, the sudden affection—a childish man,

16

Joseph understood now, not to be held accountable for his cruelty: after all, he had died at the age of forty-one and Joseph, his son, was now eighty-three years old, old enough to have forgiven, to have triumphed. The face grew vaporous, faded, did no harm. His mother he could not remember, had never remembered well. An apron, a swollen belly, boiled eggs, prayers and the rosary and the little plaster holy-water font in the bedroom, shrieks of anger, disappointment, pain—shrieks of laughter—But where was the face, why could he not summon any face—seeing instead the face of his wife—seeing it and forcing it away. His mother's name had been Nuala. His father's name, Robert. The Hurleys of the village of Watland, forty miles from Galway. Names, words. He did not remember. His pain he did not remember, or his fear, or his hatred. Nuala: faceless. Young enough to be his daughter now. Granddaughter. An apron smeared with something—blood?—a grunting struggle with milk cans—Joseph helping her, the two of them straining together—odor of manure—glinting green-black flies—but her face, her face?—and the odor of the marsh, the wild grasses, the bog lilies, the peat—the wintry rain—the hills that were mountains worn down, unlike the mountains in this part of the world: here they were still noble, covered with pines, a few of the peaks even snow-topped. He did not hate his poor broken dead father, he did not hate the priest who had gripped him by the shoulder and shook him hard, saying he would come to no good end—why had the man touched him, what had he done wrong?—could not remember. No hate, no rage. Worn away. Faded. Forgotten. Except there was a tortoise-shell comb on the bedroom floor, he saw it suddenly, his mother's or his grandmother's or an older sister's; yes, he saw it clearly, he stooped to pick it up—to examine it closely, stealthily—

Grandpa!

Then it was one of them calling to him, scolding, impatient. He blinked. Raised his head. One fumbling hand wiped something wet from his chin, quick so she wouldn't see, and he assessed the situation and saw the cause of alarm: a child splashing in the chicken trough.

Yes, yes! I see! I see perfectly well!

The woman fussed over the child—women were always fussing over children, one had fussed over him, he had relented and allowed his face to be washed, his hair to be combed, he had tried to eat the soft-boiled eggs meant to fatten him, and then they had cast him out—out upon the great rocking Atlantic—seasickness that had nearly killed him. This sharp-voiced young woman scolded her child, scolded him, for a moment he not only couldn't recognize her but actively refused to recognize her, then he got to his feet, not at all feebly, and came down from his shady perch, and asked if he could help; knowing there was no damage, no real trouble, the child was only wet and muddy, the mother was only exercising her dominion over the child and over him, quick to fuss, to exclaim. Ah, it was his granddaughter, not his daughter: his oldest granddaughter Nancy: the gray-green eyes set close together in the tanned, rounded face. She was not his favorite granddaughter, but he liked her well enough.

I must have dozed off—

It's all right, Grandpa. It's nothing.

—Did he hurt himself?

It's nothing! Only a little dirt.


The moon is gone, the sky is all the sun's, thinly overcast and glowing hard and hot. You ran from the jeering Wrezsin boys, you shouted back over your shoulder at them, bastards, ignorant bastards they are, you wouldn't let Brad touch you, you sat hunched up against the car door while he drove to Yewville taking the corners too fast, swerving, saying nothing. Momma says people are always telling tales about the Bartletts, always telling lies, lies, Laney, she says, pulling you around to face her, don't you give them anything more to talk about, do you know what I mean? . . . because we are as good as anyone, we are as good as anyone on earth. Momma's face all bruised, the left eye still bloodshot, stitches in the eyebrow and part of the forehead, a witch, an ugly witch, sewn up with black thread, and she and Nan were streaking each other's hair yesterday, silvery-blond streaks in brown, Laney, she says, touching you, rubbing your neck so that you jerk away, I
18

love you all, I don't intend anyone to break the family up, I can get money, I can get more from the county, we're eligible for more, we shouldn't have to beg, we're as good as anyone, if your father were living. . . . You jerk away from her, you want to slap her. Stop! Shut up! She only loves the little ones, loves the babies, loves Nancy's baby best, she forgets you are her daughter, she thinks you are a woman like her, she tells you things you don't want to know. *One little, two little, three little Bartletts . . . four little, five little. . . . And another one on the way.* You ran from the Wrezsin boys before the schoolbus was in sight. You climbed in Brad's car, shaken, your face swelling with hate. You hate them, hate them, you would like to kill them, Wrezsins and Arkins and Krassovs, everyone who knows you, knows your family; Brad tries to touch you, you turn on him and deny it: that your mother is pregnant again: and he whistles and makes a face and says Jesus Christ, honey, I never said she *was.*

Horrendous stink. Eyes rolled back into the head, swollen black tongue protruding, neck raw-rubbed, broken, its rope burns aswirl with insect life, teeming in the heat of late August of an endless summer, unrecognizable face aswirl, ateeming, humming with activity, swarms of flies, colonies of maggots, unrecognizable creature, no one's corpse, stink of rot and excrement, no no no, hanging from the beam, dead weight, weight of the dead, heavy as concrete: no no no no No. No one's corpse.

Six days' beard. Melancholia. Filthy bare feet. Liquor, stale rye bread, peanut butter. Suicide impractical in this heat. Endless summer, endless Augusts. Forty Augusts. Pascal too ascetic, Thoreau too boyish, Father's old Bible simply boring when not hilarious, Kierkegaard perverse, wordy, disappointing, pigeons and mourning doves on the roof, owl-like calls, soft moans, coos, murmurs. Decades of gray-white droppings. Centuries. Crusted hard as cement, centuries, Augusts, torpor, Kasch the son of Kasch, an exposed oaken beam, rope, rope burns, some bleeding, much inarticulate screaming. Impractical. Beam might break. Termite-riddled, so old. Dust. Filth. Spider webs and tiny husks of insects, decades old. Suicide too much effort. Too sensational. Headlines KASCH THE SON OF KASCH, then oblivion. Pigeons, mourning doves, squirrels on slate roof the only witnesses. Pointless. Suicide demands an object, the infliction of pain on that object. Revenge. Reflection of death in survivors' eyes. Guilt-stricken. Corpse swinging at the end of the rope, fingers clawing at neck, only pigeons and mourning doves and squirrels, a cruel jest, no drama, anticlimactic, wouldn't be found for days. Horrendous stink. No glamor. Survived by Miss Leita Kasch, seventy-seven years old, lifelong resident of Yewville, innocent aunt of the deceased, climbing carriage-house stairs panting, holding her frail side, worried, violating nephew's orders never to visit, smells the odor, pauses, white-withered face aghast. No no *no*. Cannot. A cruel jest. No one's corpse.

Staggered downstairs. Ran. Vision of faceless corpse, flies and maggots and heat, Aunt Leita and the director of the museum and a Yewville policeman in the doorway aghast, aghast, the stink a good joke, a way of completing the summer. *No.* Do it to someone else! Bring someone else back to the room! Liquor, a blow to the head, the rope, the beam. Grunting. Heavy. A full-sized creature impractical. Better a child? A child. Boy, girl: no matter. Perhaps girl. Girl. Kasch delirious with excitement, ecstasy-pain, oblivion. Kasch the son of. Perverts lonely too, like everyone else. No no no no. Really, no. Must direct the mind elsewhere. Pascal declares: *All our dignity consists, then, in thought. By it we must elevate ourselves, and not by space and time that we cannot fill. Let us endeavor, then, to think well; this is the principle of morality.*

Staggered into the world, six days' drunk, aghast at the heat-dazzle, the riches. Yewville. Friday evening, eight-thirty, sun still hot, glowing-orange, strange to be in a body, navigating a body, resurrection of Fitz John, world shifted on its axis and sun too close, voyager, pilgrim, home town forty years after. Bring someone back to the room. No. Yes. Have never. Not yet. Hanging impractical, awkward, no good tying knots, would require—wouldn't it?—a slipknot—never learned—no summer camp, no instructions. A girl: yes. Someone. Spied on them often enough, down by the river. Girls, boys. In park, in cars. Laughter lifting out of darkness. Ah, what pain!—tinge of needle-sharp exquisite pain. Laughter, giggling, girls' voices. Bottles broken. Beer cans thrown into river. Dark. Fireflies. Gently glowing, on and off and on and off and on, heartbeats, pulsing of wrist, invisible. Kasch invisible. Maniac. Pervert. But lonely: lonely. Bring someone back to the room. Horrendous stink, must be something spilled, sunk into floor. Rodent droppings. Can't blame. Aunt Leita not welcome, no one welcome, no cleaning maid, no one. Experiment. Spiritual. Retreat from maya. Retreat from desire. Experiment in progress. Hilarious results. Where I lived and what I lived for. How I lived. Why. Find a girl and bring her back to the room. Ecstasy of pain. Hers. Yours. Must be innocent. Yewville streets crowded, Friday night, smells of exhaust, hot dogs, hamburgers, chili, mustard and relish, popcorn in Fast Billy's Arcade, spilled beer, streets and sidewalks noisy, migrant workers yelling, drunk, burned black by sun, happy. Where I lived, what I lived for. I returned to Yewville, scene of my birth, because I wished to live deliberately, to retreat from history, both personal and collective, I wished to look inside my soul, to look slowly and thoroughly and lovingly, I wanted to live deep and suck out all the marrow of life, as the saying goes, to drive life into a corner and reduce it to its lowest terms. Am I not noble, am I not original, squinting weak-eyed into the sun, savage picture postcard, the two-lane bridge and the Eden River and the orange fiery glare, ah lovely, lovely, this is why we live, I'm not cruelly jesting, I am quite serious, returned to Yewville after twenty years' absence, father and mother dead, way cleared for exploration of self, memory, soul. Noble. Time-honored. Mystic. Buddha sitting in lotus position, one hand pointing into the air, airy consciousness, the other pointing to earth. Must not forget earth. Must not float free. Must not kick free. Swinging from beam, nails clawing at rope, termite-riddled beam creaking on the verge of collapse. Cruel jest. No. *No.* Wished to drive life into a corner and reduce it to its lowest terms, whether it is of the Devil or of God, we'll see, we'll get there first. Experiment. Seagram's. Kasch the twenty-year-old prodigal son, twenty years' wandering, genius, immense plans, colossal galaxy-wide plans, now staggering through Yewville half blind.

Perfume from woman, passing close. Leaning against a man, a boy-man, the two of them laughing. Odor of nuts, popcorn, candy. Is it a festival, a street fair? No. Friday night. Crowds, swarms. Young people, adults, children, the tottering, the staggering, the half-blind. Many drunks. Many. Five days picking fruit in the valley, Friday night, wages, beer, wine, cotton candy, bright-dyed hot dogs and bright-dyed pickle relish. Bad section of town. Worse than I remember. Eleven taverns on Bridge Street alone. Drunk in doorway of bus station. Asleep, dead? Kasch without his glasses. Tottering blind. Inner eye: interior wisdom. Must have faith. Experiment. Gang outside a billiard parlor, teasing girls. Girls young. Very young. Motor-cycles. Noise. Migrant worker, white, slapping woman—wife?—in alleyway. Screams. Roar of motorcycle. Fan from restaurant, sickish, grease, heat. Must stop for a beer—Riverside Inn. Throat parched. Dehydrated. Seagram's and rye bread and peanut butter. Have mercy.

Sun now setting, now gone. Relief. Dusk. Old man on curb, one shoe off. Singing. *She pushed a wheelbarrow through streets broad and. . . .* Lively old boy. Enviable. Bingo hall, electronic bingo, *seven days a week,* $1500 jackpot, beer belched up, gas, for a deadly moment danger of vomiting. But no. Recover. Charming Kasch, sloe-eyed. Balding. Young-old man. Wishes girl, wishes girl to slide arm around waist, nestle fingers in damp-hot flesh, lean together laughing, smirking. Suicide impractical. Pointless. No one to survive, no one to lament, no one to feel horror. Only Aunt Leita. Deaf. Innocent. Maiden lady seventy-seven years old, father's aunt, Father dead, estate leased to county, mansion a museum, Kasch decaying in the old carriage house and who's to care?—a nuisance, that boy. Suicide unknown in Yewville. Knives and guns used to kill. Game, fish, people. No subtlety here. City of child-hood, populated now by strangers, girls and boys pawing one another in public, music amplified by record store, a new generation, newer and newer, country boys with side-burns and silky shirts open to the navel, farm girls with soot-blackened eyes, transparent blouses, tiny breasts and

22

tiny nipples, tight blue jeans, bare feet, clogs with wooden heels, shrill delighted laughter, motorcycles passing in slow stately dignity, a police patrol car turning the corner. Sense of expectancy. Excitement. Drive life into the street, taste it, smell it. Be dazzled by it. Boys and girls hunting one another. Men hunting, single men, alone, prowling, careful not to stagger. Friday night. Drama. Glamor. Single movie house, marquee dismantled but film playing, not yet closed down, Paul Newman starring, gangs of boys out front. Music. Horns. Exhaust. Girl in pink slacks. Nearsighted Kasch, blinking. World rainbowed, seen through water. Street lights blurred. Expanded. Girl in pink slacks materializes, walking this way, unescorted, looks good, shall I buy a six-pack of Stroh's, shall we drift to the river, shall we make our way back to my flat, shall we climb the stairs, arms about each other's waists, white blouse, ruff, tucked in tight, parody of schoolgirl, pink nylon slacks, shoes with pronounced heels, thick teased strawberry-blond hair, men staring, someone in parked car staring, Kasch alert, Kasch stroking stubble on face, Kasch's myopic eyes seared with the effort to see. Old boarded-up Wilberforce Hotel, relic of grandfather's heyday, girl nearly collides with farmer's family, kids with ice cream cones, boxes of popcorn—Curleys Nuts—the fattish sunburned wife carrying a giant brass-colored panda with button eyes—girl striding on by and emerging into Kasch's field of vision, a woman his age at least, wearing a synthetic wig, coarse-skinned, small over-bright eyes fixed on Kasch's face, fixed on Kasch's stare. Nothing attractive about her at all. Would you like . . . ? Hey, mister. Hey. Nice night, isn't it? . . . Okay, you bastard, then fuck off. Get lost.

Hurried retreat. No time for dignity.

Escape: crossing over to Main Street, legs numbly performing, the woman's derision floating after but ignored, ignored. A small galaxy of women sneering and guffawing at Kasch, hell packed with them, pointing out his blemishes, his failings, his small private accursed hopes. Okay then, fuck off. Fuck off, mister. . . . Main Street almost deserted. Stores darkened. End-of-summer sales, red banners in show windows, old-fashioned façades

23

—stucco, limestone—something grim and soiled and pathetic about downtown Yewville, even the newer stores tawdry, mean. They are building shopping malls on the highway, a gigantic one north of the city, another one planned to the south. Must catch up with the rest of the country. Yewville, meager city of my birth, once a lumber town, a trading post, an important stop on the river. Great-great-grandfather's fortune, in lumber. My namesake, Fitz John. Made his fortune and built his mansion and ran for Congress and won and ran again and lost, anti-Republican in 1860, dangerous stand, provoked a mob—so it is said—into threatening his life, fire-bombing his elegant house. Copperhead, they screamed. Traitor. My namesake, stubborn reckless man, ridiculed Lincoln, almost alone in this part of the state defended the South's position: not out of sympathy with slavery but because he believed the South had the right to secede from the Union if its people wanted to secede. Nearly killed, beaten badly, on crutches the rest of his life, eccentric, courageous, maybe a little crazy, refused to leave Yewville and spent years rebuilding the house, though there were more threats made against him; finally completed it: a stone mansion, a stone monster, as fireproof as the builder could guarantee in the 1860s. And it was never fire-bombed again, never touched. My birthplace, the scene of my childhood, best forgotten. Too dark, interior woodwork overwhelming, a circular banister, high ceilings, stately columns and doors that weigh a ton; a fortress, a mausoleum. I never think of it. I have detached myself from my personal history. Now it is signed over to the county on permanent lease, now it is known as the Kasch Memorial Museum, a dingy pretentious place for exhibits of Indian culture, rocks and minerals and "authentic" costumes of the past, old yellowed newspapers, fossilized heroics. I never go there. Never. There is also a library that bears my family's name, on a side street here, not far from the high school: I never go there either. Sydney and Elvira Kasch, my parents, in ecstasy over their own self-importance, their generosity of spirit; small-time nobility; what else could they hope for? Impressing the neighbors with their charity, giving so much away only because they owned so much.

Inherited so much. Still, the estate is considerable even now: stocks and bonds and property in the city, not sure where—Main Street?—probably one or two blocks, at least—unless it was sold years ago and no one happened to tell me. And this street, Millgrove: familiar name. Slopes down to the old mill, and the lot the Loblaw's grocery store was built upon, our property, our investment, the first "supermarket" in this part of the world and very successful. The country people would come in streams on Saturdays to wander through it, women from the hills and their gangs of children, fascinated, frightened, in awe of the piped-in music, the boxes, cans, bottles, miracles in packages, the farm produce—heads of lettuce, and carrots, and asparagus above all—that was so *clean*. Down at the market, the farmers' market where everybody haggled over prices, everything was dirty; flies buzzed and settled on one's face and arms; the dirt floor stank, turned to mud as the long Saturday progressed, open at five in the morning and closed sometime around eight at night, raucous, lively, mind-boggling, doomed. Anecdotes about the supermarket: that the big bunches of bananas held gigantic hairy spiders, that a child had been bitten and died on the spot and it was hushed up, or that a farm woman had traversed the aisles fearful of the check-out counter, had spent the entire day in the store until her family came to get her. . . . Loblaw's now closed, the building razed. Parking lot in its place.

Friday evening, stores darkened on Main Street, still a "good" part of town; life elsewhere tonight. Father & Son Shoes. Woolworth's. Yewville Ladies Fashions. Grady's Dry Goods. Montgomery Ward. Berardi's Diner. Kresge's. Menton, Abel, & Klein's Dept. Store. First National Bank and Trust. YWCA-YMCA, good cobblestone building, quite old. On a side street the old Rialto Theater, marquee advertising discount furniture. Old Post Office building, red brick, Army-Navy-Marine Recruiting inside, up the wide stairs and to the right, remember posters. Impressive posters. Exciting. Kasch denied the privilege of self-sacrifice, Kasch's heart broken: asthmatic, half-blind, a tendency to migraine. Dissociation from classmates, from my generation, from a certain segment of my generation . . . a certain segment of history. My fate. Would probably have been broken into pieces by the Army, by the collective; had wanted, in fact, to join the Marines; must have horrified my parents, amused others who knew better. Brave pitiful Kasch, intelligent eyes blinking behind his glasses, perpetual adolescent not knowing how to arrange his expression, what to do with his hands. Now I am an adult, one of the adults of the world. Now I am one of those in charge. . . . But where is she? Where is the girl? Intersection empty. Drugstore open, doors wide open. Girls and boys loitering. So young. Policeman at curb, lounging against seat of motorcycle, exchanging remarks with two young girls. His face a blur, I can't see his face, my own face is a blur, rapidly receding. An adult. One of the adults of the world. Middle of the journey of what is known as life. Obstacle course. Series of experiments. Where is she, where does she await, the perfect victim. . . . Not one of those girls, so shrilly gay. Both smoking. Another joins them, appears to be no more than thirteen years old; the patrolman grins, grins knowingly. A communal mood. I am invisible.

The old City Hall: Greek Revival. 1899 cornerstone. Revolutionary War statue, scabby lawn, a movement in the darkness—human figure lying there—pawing at the ground for a moment, then lying still again. Hello, I will cry, are you anyone I know? Do you need help? Are you a form of myself? Are you ill? Dying? . . . Life is elsewhere.

A skinny young man, bare-chested, lay in Boston Common years ago, at early evening, groaning, groping for a bottle that had rolled from him. People passed by, people hurried by. Help, do you need help? No, they hurried by. Eyes averted. Occasionally staring. A fascination about them, the dying that lie at our feet. I hurried by also. I felt a pang of terror—something about the young man's contorted, babyish, yet almost intelligent, almost *profound* expression—something about the position of his body, the way he had twisted himself around, one arm extended, one filthy hand groping for the bottle that no one would roll to him. No more than a yard from the sidewalk. He lay there groaning. We passed by, quickly. He lay groaning, dying. Lies groaning, dying. I lay beside him, self-conscious in my expensive clothes.

Where is she, where are you?

From dust thou comest, to dust thou shalt return. Must hurry.

*By merest chance* (he noted afterward) Kasch turns not back toward Bridge Street but strolls aimless and harmless-appearing down another street, toward the river. *By merest chance.* Infinite universe, infinitely expanding, Principle of Indeterminacy, *merest chance,* in one direction the maggot-swarming corpse with that idiot's tongue, in the other direction a ninety-five-pound angel, gray-eyed, fair hair curly, aureole about her head, small pursed lips, small hard breasts, suntanned, lovely, the breath knocked out of Kasch, an exclamation torn from him. Torn.

Prowling by river, by overpass, train trestle, boarded-up mill. Weeks ago. Had seen, had spied. Had imagined. Girls, boys. Boys, girls. Lovers. Cars parked on riverbank, behind tavern. Car radios, laughter, breaking of beer bottles on bank, on rocks. Summer. Endless summer. Water tower. Gang of young people. Someone diving into the dark, dark water. Cries, applause, shouts, laughter. Beer cans flung after. Curses. Kasch prowling behind bush, pulling at pursed lips, rubbery drooling lips, Kasch the monkey, Kasch the spiritual pilgrim, in retreat from the world, driving life into a corner, there to suck its marrow and taste and assess and transcend. Experiment in progress. Experiment temporarily failing. Where I lived, what I lived for, knees trembling, piercing pleasure, a girl's groan in a nearby car, silence, the waited-for throb, throbbing, oh my God, as always it is, it can't be, cannot be, it is overwhelming, a blow, an annihilation, the girl's voice lifting after, liquid, near-inaudible, Kasch trembling sweating shivering, water tower in silhouette against moon. On his way back Kasch confronts another solitary wanderer spying on the lovers, disheveled, silly-drunk, a man in his fifties, a bum, but still human enough to be embarrassed. Stumbles in other direction, discreet.

Tonight no one else. Grass wet. Steep hill, leveling off at river. Moon behind clouds. Opalescent. Park bench, figures, girl's voice raised—anger, alarm. Five, six, seven people. Very young. Envy of youth, no, jealousy of youth, no, no wish to be that age again, aghast, relive it all, hideous, could not bear, the exuberant plans, the failed marriage, former wife adrift upon the void mouthing memories of Fitz John, sad smirk, hideous to contemplate, cruel jest. Why didn't I kill *her?* Too late. No passion. Lost. No envy of those young people, not even the boys pulsing with life, lusty-limbed, genitals, bellies, muscled arms and shoulders and thighs, flicking hair out of faces, quick-eyed, not-nearsighted, the girls groaning beneath them, the girls clutching their long thick hair, heroic of face, even their pimples and bumps and scars heroic, for through their loins the future throbs. No envy. No jealousy. A slight yearning, perhaps. No more! That and no more! Desire to creep closer, to spy, to see, to know. To throb in unison with. Grovel. Drool. Pant. Shudder. No more, not a bit more! A ring of mean-eyed flush-cheeked devils observes, grinning, chuckling, tittering like monkeys, ringed about the ceiling of whatever squalor Kasch has sought refuge in, eyeing him in bed, in his bachelor's bed, squirming hotly in his unjealous lust, goading him onward, on to the most vile conclusions, Kasch groveling in Kasch, no lover but Kasch. Tonight the lovers are gone, their cars elsewhere. A harsh note to the children's play. Someone is drunk and angry and someone else is frightened and angry and the others are laughing, the others stand about laughing, rude jocular hearty, good-natured, the girl is saying Stop, stop! goddam you stop! One of the boys is tugging at her, she pushes against him, there is laughter, there is always laughter, Kasch thinks it is time for him to leave.

Kasch thinks clearly: It is time for him to escape. Time to exercise prudence, discretion, wisdom.

Wanting only a voyeur's pleasure, not a hero's. The pulse of, the throb of. These young people play rough. A boy sitting on a picnic table, feet on the rim of a wire trash barrel, yelling something incomprehensible—a beast's glee. Other boys, overloud. They are drunk. They are drugged. Packs of them in Yewville, packs of them in Boston, in Los Angeles, even in London—a phenomenon new in poor Kasch's lifetime. Glassy-eyed, wide-grinning. The girls as well. Wild and despairing in their laughter, no transition between the sounds of frantic joy and those of fear. The girl who is being bullied—maybe she is enjoying it? Maybe, Kasch thinks, she deserves it?

He stands watching, cringing. Stands behind a tree like a figure in a cartoon.

Stop—don't—*don't*—

He will leave. Tiptoe away. He must leave. A voyeur, not a hero; not a martyr. Came to the town of his birth not to fulfill himself in action, in time, for he had been attempting that—with bitter, bitter success—but to retreat, withdraw, stand permanently on the side of life. No involvement. No rebaptism in the waters of the world, no beginning again. He will simply walk away. He will—

Instead he hears himself shouting. He hears his voice, loud and high-pitched and strong. What is he doing! What will happen! But there is no time to think: he shouts down at them, waves his arms wildly. He shouts: Police! Hey! Officer of the law! Just a minute, you—

Then he is running, running at them. He is actually running. Still shouting, still waving his arms. Police! Stay where you are! His voice is shrill but stronger than he has remembered. The group breaks into individuals, suddenly. It has no power. No strength. One boy turns and runs at once, in silence; fast as a deer he runs! The boy with his feet on the trash barrel gives it a kick and jumps away and the barrel overturns and rolls along the path. Action is uncoordinated, panicked, rather comic. Kasch is comic but no one sees. He runs down the hill as if not in fear of his life and the young people scatter. He is daring all. Risking all. Kasch the poet, Kasch the pervert: now Kasch the hero. In the forty-first year of his life. In the middle of the journey of. He runs.

The boys run along the riverbank, two girls follow, there is frightened drunken laughter, and then silence, and

he and the other girl, the weeping girl, are alone. . . .
The moon shifts suddenly. Kasch's eyes are throbbing and
his heart so agitated he is afraid he will faint.

What were they doing to you? he asks. Are you all
right?

The breeze from the river has not yet driven away the
odor of sweet smoke, and the odors of beer and wine.
The girl, very young, stands with her face hidden, hands
pressed childishly against her face; her breath comes in
long shuddering gasps.

*Come along with me,* Kasch will whisper. *I can take
care of you. . . . Come.*

Vale broke his way through waist-high ferns. They were
strange: so tall. He hadn't remembered them that tall.

He stepped over fallen logs. There were a number of
hazel bushes—he remembered them, though they seemed
out of place—had made fishing poles from them, hadn't
he?—he and his friends. And there was the giant anthill
his grandfather had burned out with kerosene, years ago,
when Vale had been a child. The ants had run out frantically, in all directions, and Vale and Grandpa Hurley
and Billy Arkin and maybe someone else—he wasn't
clear about it—had tried to stamp them to death. Get
them! Get them!—But they were so fast.

Get them!

He heard shouts. He heard explosions.

No, it was quiet except for the river. He pushed forward
through the vegetation. It was a little larger than normal
but it was familiar. He wasn't lost. He was in his own part
of the world. He knew the names for things here.—Wasn't
that an explosion? No. He was alone. It was quiet. He
plunged through the hazel bushes and found himself on
the riverbank, where he and other boys had fished; so he
wasn't lost. Spiny perch, rock bass, smallmouthed bass
they had caught. Sometimes carp—garbage fish—no good
to eat, but exciting to haul in.

Momma said: Look here, hon, I'll be happy to fry
them up for you if you gut them outside—okay? Throw it
to the cats.

He wasn't lost.

. . . Smiled slowly, remembering an enormous snapping turtle he had caught in a marsh by the river. Had pounded it to death. Rocks in both hands pounding, pounding. The son of a bitch had fought like an alligator! They were vicious things, deserved to die, could snap your finger off, snap the entire hand off!—deserved to die. He had smashed it with rocks in both hands, while the other boys cheered, Vale hand over hand pounding it to death. The shell had cracked—both shells. Inside, the crepe-fleshed reptilian body writhing and the long neck darting out and the jaws snapping, the small yellow eye maddened with terror. Take that! I'll kill you! Bastard! Fucking filthy bastard! . . . Vale panting, wheezing. My God what a mess. Blood, entrails, shit. How old? Centuries. The boulders splattered with it, Vale's clothes and arms and face splattered, drew his arm roughly across his face, careful to wipe his mouth.

He isn't lost. He is back home.

Woke and slept and woke again, his snoring abrasive, loud as a wasp's buzzing. Hangover. Hadn't eaten the night before. Woke and found himself fully clothed except for his shoes—where were his shoes?—found the bed empty, called her name but there was nothing, no one. Molly? Hey. Hey there. Sat up and his head pounded. Saliva ran out of one corner of his mouth. In a panic he remembered—he was back in the hospital. Air-lifted from Hué City. Wire strung throughout his body, holding him together, delicate-pulsating currents of electricity holding him together, voices whispering and encouraging him— you will be perfectly well again, you will be perfectly well again—can you hear us?—Vale Bartlett?—can you move your eyelids, Vale?—can you hear? But there were trucks outside. The place vibrated. It was the De Sales Hotel, $3 a night, $18 weekly, a few blocks from Lake Oriskany. He remembered. He knew.

He laughed with relief. How far he had traveled, sent around the world in his handsome uniform, how well he had performed, an act of exceptional courage, they said, now he was back home or nearly, and perfectly well again. Perfectly well.

Molly! he shouted.
Molly where the hell are you hiding!

Now it had hold of him. Now it took hours of walking, and fishing, and weeding in the garden, and fuss with the grandchildren, and chores about the house, to burn it away.

Something spreading its wings—opening them fanlike to darken the sky—the landscape dimmed, the mountains faded into shadow—the need to move his arms about, wave them wildly, to get everything clear again.

Eight acres. Some good bottom land, a dense woods, fields and pastures gone back to weeds, briers, saplings— he ached to clear them—muttered aloud, the wish was so strong, so bitter. Like a cow begging to be milked. Eight acres, nothing farmed, only a kitchen garden for him to work; in his prime he'd owned two hundred fifty acres, along the river and far to the southeast, to the Yewville Road, he owned it still, it was really *his*. He knew it all. Had worked it all. It was his: people still spoke of the Hurley farm and they meant that land, all that land, down to the Yewville Road and the village of Marsena.

Eight acres. He checked his property every day, some-times twice a day. Before breakfast and after supper in the warm months. In the afternoons he slept in his room at the rear of the house, next to the kitchen; slept from about three o'clock to five, if the pain in his legs and hands wasn't too bad. Sometimes in his light, wispy sleep he walked the farm, what remained of the farm, examining his property. There were fences that needed repair, there was flood damage in the lower fields; sometimes he threw the covers irritably aside and jumped up and dressed hurriedly and went to the barn and saddled his horse and rode out. . . . Must check fences, must look up his stock, what had the rain done, had there been a windstorm, had the rain frozen to hail, were the cattle sick, what was the meaning of this tangle of briers, these gigantic cutworms threading his vision, the perplexing midday eclipse of the sun. . . .

The old man, Lenehan, sitting in the horse barn, arms limp on his thighs. Not glancing around when Joseph's shadow fell across him. Frightening, the old man's silence, taking it so hard. Who had died?—the old woman? Joseph too had wept, Joseph too missed her. But it was easy to forget: a winter and a spring and a summer. But the old man sat in there, his back to the horses, ignoring them, unaware of them, shirt sleeves rolled up and long gray underwear exposed, overalls not quite snapped shut, manure drying on his boots.

What's wrong? Joseph said in a whisper.

When his uncle did not look around, Joseph backed away, escaped.


What's wrong? his favorite daughter asked.

Arlene drying her hands on a towel and tossing it onto the cupboard counter. Arlene thinner than he liked, and her face still bruised, faintly plum-colored, orangeish, sallow, but she wore lipstick. Must be going to the village or to town.

Are you going to the police about that, are you going to the sheriff? he asked.

She stared at him. Blinked. Pa, we're on our way to visit Mr. Krassov, don't you remember?—you've been after me to drive you in. Don't you remember? Aren't you ready to go?

He had forgotten but didn't show it; never let a flicker of surprise cross his face. —I asked you about the police, honey. You know I asked you about them.

I *told* you. I told you a hundred times!

She walked out of the kitchen, made the floor shake, throwing her weight on her heels. Angry. Moody all the time. She would not go to the police and he didn't want her to, not really, didn't want that kind of trouble, didn't want any kind of trouble with people in town—people who didn't know them and weren't sympathetic. Nancy didn't want her to go either. Only Laney—Laney was the one. But Laney was just a child, didn't know how things were, didn't have any idea. —Still, his voice rose peevish and old-womanish, he heard himself scolding his daughter as if these words were expected of him, or were a way of disguising how she'd crept up on him and taken him by surprise in his own kitchen:

You know how people talk around here! You know how they must be talking about us, laughing at the Hurleys behind our backs—You *know* what an insult it is to me—

Three years old you were, so the story goes, walking along the bank above the river, Momma up at the house and Pa in town, your cousin Gretchen supposed to be watching you. And Vale and Billy Arkin down at the dock, fixing it from where the ice had broken it that spring, and you hid behind some tall flowering weeds to spy on them— and the water was roaring so, the waves roaring, heaving thrusting roaring water, a gull was trying to walk on the water, sinking and then darting up immediately, its long bent wings flapping, and then sinking again, claws outspread—it was the same water, the same pounding waves, the same noise you heard at night when the windows were open, but now it was louder—in and through and up and down and in every direction, pounding in your ears, in your head—You called out to Vale but he couldn't hear, you started to run down the steep path to where the boys were, and something shot away before you—a snake, you claimed later it was a snake, but really you didn't see it, it might have been only a clod of dirt you kicked yourself —and suddenly you were falling, screaming, falling—then you were in the water and it was hard when you struck it, and very cold, and it was as if someone had grabbed hold of your head playfully and pushed it right under—

Vale saved your life. You loved Vale, love Vale. You think of Vale, before he left for training camp, before he was sent away: you remember being embarrassed, saying good-by, squeezing his arm while Momma made such a fuss and was crying like a baby, you remember getting ready to say *Once you saved my life, I'll never forget*— but it was just Vale, big-shouldered, grinning, his front teeth discolored and his skin slightly pitted, Vale with his brown eyes, bleached-out brown-blond hair cut short for the Army, it was just Vale with everybody crowding around and joking, Vale a little drunk, and you didn't say a word: you didn't say a word.

They killed him. Where he was sent. They killed him, he was dead, he disappeared, someone else was shipped back, Vale died, Vale had been smashed, his face wasn't put together right, the two halves did not fit, the new teeth were too white, like porcelain, it wasn't Vale, Vale died, was sent away in a gigantic jet plane and never came back: and you never said a word.

She took her hands away from her face.

My God, I said. . . . God.

A perfect face, an angel's face. In the uncertain moonlight her skin was like pale china, translucent china, my mother's and grandmother's white chinaware; held to the light, it yielded its fragile nature, you could see your finger passing behind it: such beauty! In the moonlight the face had no color, the eyes were merely dark, set in their shadowy sockets, the small parted lips were colorless, the small, slightly snubbed nose quite pale. My God, I said, a child, a girl, a perfect little angel. Her cheeks were damp, her eyes were filled with tears. My words were torn from me.

—But you're—You're too— How can you let them touch you, you—?

Faded shorts cut from blue jeans, cut ragged and high on her thighs, and a blue halter that tied around her neck, leaving her thin midriff bare; her feet so small I could have cupped them in my hands. An angel, weighing no more than ninety-five pounds. Her small breasts quivered, her curly hair seemed electrified with emotion, she stood for a long moment staring at me, her hands still raised as if framing her face. . . .

The child reeked with wine, that cheap red wine that turns my stomach.

"That noise! . . . turn it off, will you?"

"I like the radio. I . . ."

"Turn it down, then. Sounds like cats squawling."

Driving the car Earl had given her for her birthday back in April. She had turned on the radio at once; didn't want to be alone with her thoughts. Always thought of him in the car.

"The best music of all is nothing: just silence."

"Oh Pa. . . ."

He seemed irritable today, uneasy. Would never admit that going to town upset him. Had gotten into a habit of shaking his head and frowning, drawing the corners of his mouth down, meanly down, so that tiny dentlike wrinkles appeared in his cheeks.

"*Oh Pa,*" he mimicked.

She turned the radio down low; then she turned it off.

"That's as sure as hell a lot better," he said.

She glanced at him. In a way she enjoyed his grumbling, his bad moods; it gave her a chance to cheer him up. Unless he was in a really bad mood, or had had too much to drink. . . . She was his favorite child, after all. Always had been.

What a surprise, though, to look at him suddenly and see how aged he was now! Sometimes, when she wasn't prepared for it, she felt so bad she could cry. Eighty years old, eighty-two years old—or was it eighty-three already? —his head trembling sometimes, hands trembling, joints ugly and swollen with arthritis. His bad knee worse than ever, making him limp; maybe he should have a cane or even crutches—but of course he wouldn't hear of it: pretended nothing was wrong. (A horse had kicked him many years ago, had smashed the knee bone pretty bad. Never grew in right again.) Oh it was sad, so sad! Arlene hoped he wasn't in terrible pain. They said arthritis was terrible, and the way he coughed and wheezed sometimes must have hurt him, but he wouldn't talk about it—never talked about his health to anyone. Refused to see a doctor. Men didn't talk about such things, he said.

If a man started talking about his health, he said, that was the end of him: carrying on like a woman. Might as well turn over and die at that point.

Arlene couldn't help it, she was proud of the old man. At his age, after that heart attack some years ago. . . . He was still going strong, wasn't he? . . . and in her opinion still rather handsome, with thick white hair, surprisingly thick, and bushy tufted eyebrows, a strong mouth. He didn't wash very often, though, and Arlene dreaded bringing up the subject. His temper tantrums! His whining exasperated voice! Accusing her of trying to boss him around, trying to take her dead mother's place. . . . His neck was a mass of wrinkles that crossed one another, edged with dirt; his fingernails were always black, and even the webby spaces between his fingers were grimy. He did shave, though, once or twice a week, and asked her to wash his hair for him, maybe twice a month. Of course she washed his clothes, though it was sometimes a struggle to get them away from him, and he didn't like her in his room, changing his bedclothes, so sometimes the sheets were filthy when she finally threw them in the washing machine. He smelled of old clothes, of the barnyard, of tobacco, of stale spilled food, of onions—which he chewed raw—his breath sweetish-sour. His teeth must have been rotting, he hadn't gone to a dentist in years; Arlene remembered him pulling a molar with a pliers, years ago, then showing the tooth to her, showing the bloody little roots and making a jab at her with the pliers. Now it's your turn, Big Eyes! Hey! Gonna get *you* next!

Sometimes his teasing had frightened her. And his stories about killers and kidnappers and arsonists, strange people who lived up in the mountains, and gigantic beasts, black bears and killer moose, mountain lions, rabid foxes, wolverines, wildcats. Crows that could peck your eyes out, hawks that could swoop down to claw at you without warning. Big Eyes, he used to call her, sitting her on his knee. Pretty Baby. Pretty Girl. . . . Telling her about things he claimed had really happened, strange murders, acts of revenge, lovers who wandered after their deaths along certain stretches of road, cemeteries that weren't safe after dark, the covered bridge on the Marsena Road that was haunted (thank God the rickety frightening thing had been torn down a few years ago: Arlene had always dreaded it) by the spirit of a nineteen-year-old boy who had drowned in the river there; and there were wailing ghost-babies, in wells and cisterns and old barns, and even a ghost-baby that had caused the death of a living baby by pushing it aside when it tried to nurse, and there was nothing the mother could do . . . a tale that had particularly frightened Arlene as a child.

But the stories were just stories and she had loved to

hear them; she knew very well they weren't real, and anyway, they had all taken place in the old days, before she was born. Everything had happened then, everything big and alarming and worth talking about! The really bad storms, tornadoes, hurricanes, blizzards, floods, droughts, invasions by insects. . . . He just liked to talk, liked to talk to *her*. Arlene had been the baby of the family, the lastborn of the six children who had lived. Her mother must have been at least thirty-eight when Arlene was born, and she had never been well. So sad, Arlene's mother dying when she did, only a few years later, and Carrie having to take on so much responsibility before she was really old enough. . . .

Arlene's father had had a heart attack in his sixty-ninth year: a mild one in the morning that he had ignored, telling no one about the pain and the shortness of breath, and another, massive one at noon, after he'd been out in the fields for hours. Working in the heat, stubborn, defiant, working alone, and then returning to the house for his usual big lunch and collapsing halfway through it. . . . How horrible, Pa clawing at his chest, gasping, wheezing, groaning in pain! Arlene had been terrified. And afterward she saw that he was aged, aging, her father was actually an old man now; the unbelievable was taking place, the unthinkable, there was nothing she could do about it. He was ashamed of himself, ashamed of being bedridden. He would not talk about what had happened. Never really spoke of it, except to allude to his "trouble." But he had changed, subtly and irreparably. Blustering and noisy and strong-willed as ever, yet often weak, petulant, anxious. His skin got finely wrinkled as an old glove, the nostrils seemed to enlarge as if the flesh of the nose were shrinking; stiff gray hairs protruded from the nostrils, and from his ears . . . so stiff they seemed like small wires, not ordinary hair. (Arlene had to get his permission to clip those hairs from time to time when they became too prominent—but careful, careful: he was still vain about his looks and could fly into a fury if she said the wrong thing.)

Bad-tempered as Earl in certain ways. But not so mean.

Today he wore his dark blue gabardine suit, his only

suit, shiny and baggy from many years of wear—twenty-five years, at least; and a white shirt that had gone a little yellow from repeated launderings; and a black string tie Arlene had given him some Christmases ago, which gave him the appearance of an old rancher. He looked good, didn't he? In spite of his frowning? An attractive healthy tan, anyway. And his head not trembling so much, as it sometimes did when he was fatigued. . . . Yes, she thought he looked good. For a while lately he had seemed quite well, certainly liked to wander around the countryside and fuss in the garden, even in the heat of August and September. She couldn't talk sense into him, didn't even try; it was hopeless. He *would* work in the kitchen garden. There was hoeing that had to be done, he said, and it was his garden, his little kingdom. The children could help, but it was really his. He wanted credit for the produce, she supposed, and it kept him from grumbling bitterly, as he had for years, about not being a real farmer any longer. Radishes, carrots, cucumbers, sweet corn, beets, cabbage, onions, eggplant, peppers, muskmelons, potatoes, strawberries, green and waxed beans, lettuce, celery, even a few boxes of peanuts that had turned out quite well, and of course tomatoes: so many tomatoes! Bushels of them, bushels, more ripening every day; what was she supposed to do with them all? As many as the family ate, more ripened, even began to rot. They were delicious, they were wonderful plump red tomatoes, but no one could eat them all, and there weren't really enough to make it profitable to sell them in town, and canning was a nuisance, an old-fashioned nuisance, Arlene just didn't have time for it any longer. . . . He seemed hurt that she didn't can very much now, only pears and sweet cherries, which the children loved.

As if he were following Arlene's thoughts, he said, ". . . should have brought something along, some pears, maybe; maybe even a melon. . . . He'd like that, he would have liked that. But I never even thought of it."

Arlene agreed.

"So forgetful, a goddamned nuisance to myself," he mumbled. ". . . Is it too late to turn back?"

"Pa, of course it's too late," Arlene protested. "Why, we're almost there! Look, see where we are? —We're almost there."

You went with whoever it was, he said Come along, come with me, you were shivering in your shorts and top and no shoes, and feeling a little sick, suddenly exhausted; Come with me, he said, his voice kind, soft, his hand brushing against your arm so the hairs tickled and you drew away, drew away so he would know but at the same time not be insulted. You were a little high, a little sick. Not really sick. You were trembling because of him shouting—the police!—and running down the hill—thank God it wasn't the police, they would remember you from the other time, in June, three patrolmen with nothing better to do than creep up on you and your friends, drinking beer and wine at Cranberry Lake, the bastards creeping up as if it were a game and then calling out to you All right, kids, all right, over this way—come on! The bastards.

Can I help you, can I drive you home? Would you like to come to my place, wash yourself, your face is slightly dirty—you've been crying—is there anything I can do for you? Do you need somewhere to stay?—How old are you?

Quizzical, gentle, kind. You liked him. You wondered if he knew your father. Needed a shave, wearing wrinkled clothes, shirt open, sleeves rolled past his elbows, but not a workingman—not a farmer—not with that voice. Kasch, his name. Kasch. You think he's lying: What? Kasch? Kasch is the name of the old mayor, the name of the library, the museum— He pulls at his chin, rubs the stubble nervously, but he isn't lying: he really is a Kasch.

You walked the mile or so to Indian Trail, where the museum is, but you didn't go in the front way—the iron gates were shut—you went with him along an alley, to a back gate, which he opened; it wasn't locked. Do you live in the museum?—is this where you live? You begin to laugh. Nobody lives here!

You wondered if you should go through the gate with him.

In comfort and squalor and anonymity I live here, in the
40

carriage house, he said; I live alone. . . . See? This building here.

Must have been after midnight. Fireflies, crickets, cicadas. The air smelled wet. The lawn was hilly and dark. Suddenly you wanted to cry, the smell of pine needles was so strong, and the damp night air, and the fireflies that are always a surprise, going on, blinking, disappearing, like at home, like the fireflies you would be seeing out your window at home; and the crickets and cicadas almost as noisy as in the country. You wanted to cry because the man was so polite, because he wasn't going to hurt you.

Up these stairs, he said. Go first.

A cobblestone building, old. The stairs were steep, the light was dim. Where do *you* live, he asked, is it far?

You told him you lived in the country. You had missed your ride home, had been supposed to ride back with a friend but she left early, went to a movie and wanted to leave right after that, and you didn't want to leave so soon, you'd met some kids and were having a good time—it was a nice night and everyone was having a good time.

How old are you? he asked.

Sixteen, you said. Which was not true but maybe he believed it. —Sixteen.

What were they doing to you, those boys?

Oh hell, it was just that one—he was just fooling around. I can take care of myself.

It made you nervous, how he stared at you. Closed the door and stared. You yawned, then you wanted to cry again, then a ticklish sensation began and you wanted to laugh, then you discovered mosquito bites all over your legs and began to scratch them, scratch them hard—a trickle of blood ran down your leg and down your ankle and onto his floor.

It's a good thing I came along, he said, standing there watching, not knowing what to do. They seemed like an unpleasant bunch.

Oh they were just fooling around, that guy was just fooling around, he didn't mean to hurt me, none of them would hurt me—wouldn't dare. You looked around the room, hands on hips. Never been in such a place before.

Piles of books on the floor, a table cluttered with papers, a ratty old horsehair sofa worse than Momma's, a floor lamp with an old-fashioned fringe shade, crooked, a bed with a carved headboard reaching halfway up the wall, looked like mahogany, like Grandma's old bed kept in the barn, the bed she died in and nobody wanted—and a beautiful crocheted bedspread draped over it, Momma should see it, you couldn't help running your hand over it and telling him how nice it was. On an old rocker by the bed there was a braided-rag-rug cushion, so old it was faded almost colorless, but it was pretty too, you had to go examine it. Momma taught me to braid things, to embroider and knit and crochet, you know, and do needlepoint—but that takes too long—but we don't do those things anymore, there isn't time. Oh God the messes I used to make!—knitting a sweater for one of my baby sisters, y'know, and by the time I got done it was so stretched, looked like a goddam tent, it was too big for *me* even and for Momma even, I guess we gave it away to one of my aunts—I got better at knitting afterward, but never do it anymore except sometimes in the winter; I knitted my brother Vale some socks for cold weather, for him to wear in the Army, y'know, but I don't know if he did, I don't know if the package got to him—we insured it at the Post Office too but what the hell? What can you do?

He turned another light on and was very nervous, walking around, drawing the shades. They were old and cracked. There were dead bugs on the windowsills and on the floor. You were rubbing your eyes. So tired. Too much wine. A cigarette would wake you up, where were your cigarettes? Jamie had them. Jamie had them.

—wouldn't dare hurt me, you said, because I'm a Bartlett; because my brother or one of my cousins would hurt *them*. The other side of my family's the Hurleys. —From Childwold.

That far!

It isn't far in miles, you said, a little annoyed, it's only about fifteen, but the roads aren't much good—

Childwold, he said. Childwold. . . .

You sat on the arm of the horsehair sofa, suddenly

42

tired. Could curl up here and sleep. Sleep. Back home Momma might or might not be waiting, might, might not; Nan was probably out at Ephim's, getting drunk, having a good time, better that than lying in bed half the day and saying she wanted to die, wanted her and the babies and *him* to die, and Grandpa would have been asleep long ago —got drowsy after nine o'clock these days. Then you remembered that Momma wouldn't be out with Earl, things were changed between them, you knew very well she wouldn't be with him, must have known, but the thought struck you and hurt, and you heard again Jeannie saying you'd better come home with her, her brother was driving back right away, how the hell are you going to get home, Laney, what the hell are you trying to do? I could telephone Momma, you said. I could stay with Aunt Esther. I don't know: I don't give a damn.

*Childwold,* the man repeated. Struck hands lightly together, palms of hands. Stared at you. Dark-haired, long pale mourner's face, big eyes, reminded you of the dog's eyes—so brown, moist, shining—and his chin narrow, a shadowy cleft to it. Momma's age. Did he say he knew your father? Couldn't remember. Lots of friends in Yewville, your father was well-liked, Mr. Decker at the high school knew him and asked after the family, how was Vale, wounded, was he, but back home again . . . ? A terrible thing, that war. Terrible. Your head felt light and hollow and you were afraid you would be sick.

No, I didn't know your father, the man said slowly. No.

Do you know Momma? Arlene Hurley?

No. Sorry.

Maybe I better telephone Momma, you said suddenly. Before she worries.

I don't have a telephone.

Don't—?

You looked around the room, saw the beams across the ceiling, the spider webs, the exposed nails. Something was buzzing in your head. The man took a step toward you but when you turned he hadn't moved—not a bit. He was extricating something from a drawer, he raised it to his face, smiled at you while adjusting a pair of glasses. The light struck their lenses like a wink.

43

I don't give a damn, you said, drawing your arm across your nose, if she worries or not; I don't give a damn about her.

He showed you where the bathroom was. You closed the door but it didn't catch. It didn't lock. You ran water, turned the faucet on hard, squinted at yourself in the cabinet mirror. Oh! Laney! Jesus Christ! Pink-orange lipstick smeared around your mouth and chin and onto your throat, mosquito bites on your shoulders, sunburn marks where the halter cut in, and your collarbones showing, and your breasts the size of a baby's fist, that small: and the hollows around your eyes dusky, like death, like you'd been awake three days in a row. Hair frizzy from the damp. Temperature in the nineties that day. Staring at that little bitch Laney, meeting her eye to eye, you felt the jumpy elation in your blood drain away and you were sober again and your mouth tasted like crap and you thought: I won't even cry. I won't bother.

But in the other room he hadn't taken off his trousers, hadn't turned off the lights, was sitting now in the rocking chair, leaning forward, elbows on knees, chin on hands, smiling, watching. Do you feel better now that you've washed your face? he asked. You look better. . . . You're very beautiful.

Your face went hot. Oh shit, you said.

Oh, the children, the children—!
The house galloping with children—!
Momma says there was a father, always a father, each one of us has a father. But it's a game; who is he? where is he? . . . Long ago when we went to church (you don't remember: you weren't born yet) there was Daddy nearby, back in the churchyard; we rode with Duane Stickney who did the mowing for the church, one of those big grass-cutters like a tractor where there's room for a driver and a passenger, two passengers if they're small. There it is, there's Daddy, he's buried under that! That marker! *There!* His name was Lyle Bartlett. Not everyone could remember him but Momma could remember him, except she kicked off her shoes as soon as we got in the car, away from church, and pulled off her hat with the straw flowers

and said Thank God! that's enough of that for one week. And no fighting in the back seat, you kids—hear? None of that. No tears, no bad thoughts, it's Sunday and Sunday dinner, rhubarb pie and elderberry pie and tarts your Momma baked for you, and a nice man is coming to take us on his boat at Cranberry Lake, if it's big enough for us all, and anybody who makes trouble or whines or belly-aches or pinches or kicks is going to stay home—you hear? Enough is enough for one week.

She didn't always go back into the cemetery to see Daddy. Enough is enough, Momma said. She made a yodeling noise, half singing and half groaning. . . . I just can't cry anymore, she said.

Mary Ellen has a different daddy, we were teasing her, and Chuckie too, and Nancy's Louise and the baby Dennie —not the same daddies as ours—it's a secret, who. We know, but you don't! *We know, but you don't!* Which was a lie, but got them squawking so Momma poked her head out of the shower stall in the corner of the kitchen and started yelling: Who's the guilty party? Who's behind this? I been listening to you all along, you little brats! Vicious brats! If Granddaddy was here I'd get him to paddle you, he knows how, he hasn't lost his touch! One of the little ones had made a mess on the floor, wet in his pants, and was sitting in it; Laney came in and grabbed us and shook us hard and Momma said for her to change the baby's diaper, long as she was downstairs. Then Momma turned the shower on harder and pulled the curtain shut, so there was nothing for Laney to do but clean up the mess with paper napkins and get the diapers out and change the baby right there on the kitchen table, her face all screwed up. Who's your daddy? we were asking her. Do you have a daddy? Is it all the same one? She threw the old diaper into the paper sack and mopped the baby up and sprin-kled powder on him and bent down to blow on his chest and stomach so he giggled and kicked, and she looked up at us smiling: we all got the same daddy, she said. So shut up.

Big-bellied gut-stuffed Tuller: his loud deep laughter, his wide mocking eyes, the gold signet ring on his left hand, the gold stretch-band wrist watch, his habit of tapping on the car horn as he drove, his bad temper, his big tips even at lunch counters, the way he cleared his sinuses, the yellow clot of phlegm spat out gleaming like a bright coin on the earth. Pardon me, lady! he would say to Arlene. Suit yourself, Arlene would say, a trifle hurt.

Earl was still a good-looking man. Forty-nine years old, high-colored, a tendency to puff and pant and suck in air noisily; and of course he snored—like an airplane revving up, Arlene teased. His eyes were a most unusual blue. They fairly started from his head, even when he wasn't clowning, and his nose was broad, slightly flattened as if someone had pressed it in, and there was a perverse rakish pinch to his upper lip, so that his lips did not quite meet and his teeth always showed. Earl Tuller! He collapsed in a chair, big and brutal and sprawling, liked to unbutton his shirt, slip his belt out a notch or two or unbuckle it altogether, lean his head back and sigh so that his cheeks belled out. Yet he dressed with care, spent money on his clothes, sent away for custom-made boots with two-inch heels and insisted Arlene do the same, he'd pay for them with pleasure. I like to see a woman of your size, with legs like that, parading around in boots. High heels, the higher the better. Makes your ass stick out the way it should.

Some people, Arlene said, coloring, should watch their big mouths.

He slapped her bottom in front of the children and even in front of the old man. He tickled her, helping her with her coat. And the coat!—Persian lamb from special order at Menton, Abel, & Klein's, Yewville's only decent store. He was crazy about her, liked to gobble her shoulders and breasts and belly and thighs and between her thighs, couldn't get enough of her, he claimed; it was a good thing she was built generous as she was—his former wife, that sad sick gal, hadn't enough meat on her to go through a grinder. But that was ancient history! Ancient history! He pinched Arlene so hard, sometimes her buttocks showed black and blue for days.

And he ran his big hard grasping fingers through Laney's head of curls, not minding her scowl and deathly-mean look, and joked with poor Nancy about her absent sky-minded boy Prentiss—her husband, that is, out at Pilot School somewhere in Kansas, it was said, and going to send for her and the baby and Louise any week now, and teased her beet-red with an almost tuneless song he droned in her ear—

*Gonna drive me crazee—*
*If you ain't my babee—*

*Gonna drive me crazee—*
*If you ain't my babee—*

*Gonna drive me crazee—*
*IF YOU AIN'T MY BABEE—*

And he tickled and wrestled with the boys, except for Ronnie, who was too big—at twelve, Ronnie was getting on toward Vale's size, and like Vale was developing a quick whippish temper—and brought presents for them, dolls and small handbags for the girls, softballs, bats, footballs, an inflatable green dragon for playing in the river—which was torn away from the little boys and lost downstream, their first outing—and bicycles that looked to be second-hand, so Ronnie and Laney judged, examining them; for it was known that Earl Tuller had a brother-in-law in Derby who bought and sold bicycles. Himself, Earl owned and managed a roadhouse on the Yewville Road, and a big modern twenty-five-lane bowling alley just outside town, and it was rumored he owned parts of other businesses, a gas station right on Main Street, another gas station in Marsena, and vacant land, former farmland, he was acquiring cheap as the old farmers sold out or died, and their heirs were quick to sell, wanting only to escape the foothills and the small old farms slowly dying one by one in the Eden Valley. That was Earl Tuller!—wonderfully good-looking when he smiled and his heart showed in his face, in his gaze, turned fully on Arlene.

He was so good with children!—she loved that in a man. Lyle had been nervous with his first- and second-born, almost as if he were afraid of them, or intimidated, or resentful; Earl squatted down and moved right into their world, thighs straining at the material of his trousers, his smile wide, boyish, sincere. Maybe he teased them a little too much, but they liked it most of the time—they liked *him*. There had been other men, one or two others, maybe three, maybe even four since Arlene's husband's death that New Year's Day—a five-car accident, a pile-up on the highway because the road had frozen icy-slick in a matter of minutes—maybe even five men, if you chose to count Ephim Johns, which didn't seem necessary; he and Arlene had known each other since grade school. But these other men were intimidated by the children too. Quiet around them, and fluttery-eyed, anxious to escape, to get Arlene away from the house and alone. Even Chuckie's father, even Mary Ellen's! Such cowards. Liars. Two years ago this very month there'd been the baby boy who had died, a few days' life in the hospital and then death, and Arlene had been crazy with grief and still could not quite believe it—how had it happened?—her labor so effortless, the easiest so far, and yet the baby—Jonathan, she had named him—had died without ever coming home; his heart hadn't been properly formed, the doctor told Arlene, looking at her as if—or was she imagining it—it was *her* doing, *her* fault—served her right, the life she led. And that poor baby's father hadn't been any-where near, not within a hundred-mile radius; the bastard. But Arlene hadn't expected much of him.

So Earl was a surprise. Earl was a wonder. She loved him, she squeezed his shoulders and ruffled his hair, he was just an overgrown boy himself, playing with the children, pulling the smallest ones in their wagons, crooning to the baby—Nan's baby—lifting Mary Ellen above his head so that she squealed and kicked, a tiny writhing animal, her lovely copper-colored hair curlier even than Laney's, squealing terror and delight—if only he were Mary Ellen's father, and lived with them here, and everything would be set forever—

"You sure got a way with children," Arlene told him. "Those kids—they think the world of you."

"I think the world of *them*."

"Their life hasn't been easy. . . ."

To which he didn't reply.

He's like the County Welfare, Arlene heard Ronnie snicker to Laney, and wanted to slap his insolent face except it was beneath her dignity, eavesdropping on her own children. Not quite, Laney giggled. No food stamps.

He gave her no cash, none. Or very little. Maybe thirty dollars, maybe fifty now and then. It wasn't that kind of relationship and he wanted her to know. He thought highly of her; he respected her; she wasn't like the women who crowded around him in Derby or up at Port Oriskany, smelling the fine expensive leather of his boots and belts, the fine expensive soap and shaving lotion he used so liberally, and of course they noted the car he drove—that was the first thing. Arlene wasn't like that at all. They had met the summer after that poor baby had died, and Arlene not yet recovered from the grief, ten pounds lighter than usual, not looking her best, and still Earl had been struck by her, had come right over to her table and dragged along a chair, inclining his head to hers so they could be heard over the music, saying afterward she had looked so mournful he hadn't recognized her at first—then saw it was Arlene Bartlett, Arlene who should have been laughing and having a good time, who surely deserved a good time; so he had come directly over to cheer her up. And he had.

He was somewhat inclined to be jealous, but that was only natural—a big husky good-hearted man like that, a man's man, not tolerating any fanciful behavior. He told her, he was direct. He was always direct. Didn't warn her, or threaten her, just told her, allowed her to know that he wouldn't stand for any—couldn't guarantee what he might or might not do if there was any—Did she understand?— she did. Nothing infuriated him so much as people laughing behind his back, and they surely would at the least provocation, and he *couldn't* guarantee what he might or might not do if Arlene lied to him. Did she understand?

"Why Earl," Arlene said, hurt, "I don't lie to anybody. Honey, it isn't in my nature to lie. . . ."

"Nor in mine either," he said.

For her birthday he presented her with a Buick Royale to replace the rattletrap eyesore with the rusted bumpers and one missing fender she'd been driving for years, and everyone in the house including Grandpa Hurley ran out into the drizzle to stare and exclaim: What a surprise! Nothing like it in memory! It had four doors, a "sun roof" that slid open easily, air conditioning, a radio, an adjustable steering wheel, a fan with three speeds, cushioned seats like sofas, leather and inlaid designs, recessed lights, a defrosting mechanism for the front and rear windshields, the locks on all four doors were controlled by a master switch at the driver's seat, and it was a proud bronze-gold—nothing like it in all of Childwold, was there? It was last year's model, never driven before, a bargain—so Earl said modestly, in order to deflect Arlene's gratitude—he couldn't resist. Oh she loved him, adored him! Threw her arms around him in front of all, and in the rain! Her face crumpled, joy and grief and utter astonishment broke her; she wept, staggered away, found herself standing in the mud of the rutted driveway not knowing what was happening, who she was, or why, or when all these miracles were taking place—not knowing if this was life itself, such an astonishment; like those hours of sweaty straining labor that could result in anything—anything at all.

Of course he drove the car when they were together. And checked it, examined it. A nick on the front left fender—a blemish on the chrome handle of one of the doors—a bit of tar picked up, so Arlene nervously explained, on that awful Marsena Road the county had just tarred and done such a smelly sloppy job on: these things Earl noted at once, and they did not please him. "Jesus Christ," he muttered, going red in the face, having discovered an actual two-inch scratch in the handsome bronze finish one day, "what are you trying to do, woman, kill me?"

The September heat-haze!
No end to it, driving and dreaming, time swinging backward and forward, now this way, now that—the strong scent of hay, so powerfully strong, sun-heated, sun-glimmering, the haze bright with butterflies, with bees, trees emerging laden with fruit—sour red cherries, big black sweet cherries, pears, apples, peaches, elderberry
50

bushes weighed down, birds struggling in their branches at the side of the road: everything thick with invisible life, teeming with invisible life: what are you doing here, in this place, your quick mind darting back and forth . . . ?

No end to it. Dreaming, drifting. Now this way, now that. You sleep and you wake—downstream. Leaves heavy, motionless. Haze. September. The intense butterfly-dotted heat-haze, September, harvest, birds beginning to gather, flocking in the stubbled fields—so early, so early!—grackles, cowbirds, red-winged blackbirds, starlings—and, underneath the currents of invisible life, insect life, droning of thousands, thousands, perpetual sleep in their frantic activity, mating laying of eggs hatching of eggs larvae cocoons wriggling forth life mating death eggs mating death-cocoons, death wriggling forth, you own all the land from the Eden River to the Yewville Road and the village of Marsena and all the dreaming drifting warring life within it, it's yours, no debts, no mortgage, owned free and clear on this day of April 16, 1921, the teeming invisible life within it subservient to you, thousands, millions, frantic insane perpetual buzzing—like the river's ceaseless motion—the heat-haze lifting, at the side of the dusty road two children selling sweet corn and big red plump tomatoes and pears still green and McIntosh apples, please stop, please buy, barefoot and pleading and you wave and get no response from them, no recognition, don't they know their daddy rents from you, lives on your land, don't they know who you are . . . ? Should have saddled a horse to ride across the fields, along the creek trail, could get to the Krassovs in half an hour; Josef and Joseph sitting out back of the woodshed drinking blackberry wine, Mrs. Krassov's blackberry wine, drinking and talking and laughing and singing, complaining of the heat, the drought, the sons and daughters who didn't work hard enough, the cost of commercial fertilizer, everything changing—had to have a head for mathematics now, calculation; instinct wouldn't help, something new and ugly wriggling forth, markets middlemen distribution warehouses trucking companies trucking unions cost of tractor gas cost of feed for stock cost of oil repairs new tires

51

hired help in the fall costs swinging this way, that way, you slept and you woke and it was in the midst of a bitter combat: why shouldn't you and your family work for forty cents an hour, winter and summer, fourteen hours a day, why should the government subsidize you go dump your produce in the river go blow out the brains of your stock through their bawling mouths nobody cares nobody gives a damn, there are dealers, men in white shirts, corporation farms, city planners, the county zoning commission, the county board of supervisors, tax assessors, sewers to be laid outside Yewville and taxes to follow, a new high school and taxes to follow, a new grammar school, thousands and thousands and thousands of dollars, nobody cares, nobody gives a damn, why shouldn't you work for forty cents an hour you own your land you love what you are doing, why should you begrudge the strangers in the trailer courts and their children their many children their gangs and packs of dirty children, the schools are for them, the future is for them, why are you so murderous, why would you like to take the shotgun along trotting across the sun-struck fields tilting your hat to shelter your eyes, no one has forced you to sell your best land, rich dark bottom land sloping down to the river. Josef Krassov is worse off, Josef Krassov is badly in debt, you can sit together out back of the Krassovs' woodshed that stinks of kerosene, Josef on a smooth-worn milking stool, Joseph on the bench beneath the old walnut tree, drinking blackberry wine, waving the flies and yellow jackets away, singing—fox fire burning all night long, swampfire burning on my grave—the old collie whimpering in his sleep making halfhearted clawing motions, poor old Sam, the grandchildren grew up and got bored with him, he dozes now by the walnut tree waiting for you to scratch the back of his bony skull, fox fire burning all night, swampfire burning on my grave, a long way yet 'fore I can rest, nobody asks *Am I happy? Am I unhappy?* gauging their lives the way the young do now, happy, unhappy, in love, out of love; you wake to the surprise of their rough raw young voices, their noisy ignorance, you wake in the midst of their battles and can't make sense of them and can't believe

52

they are real, don't they know the heat-haze will settle over them, the hills will be alive with white and yellow and orange-and-black butterflies, their shouts will be drowned out by the insects' droning and singing, don't they know, don't you know—?

What was he doing?

Wolf's Head Lake, the sandy parking lot, those black flies around the trash container. . . . You ran back to the car to get something and there he was, an old man, you'd never seen him before but he seemed to know you, seemed to be angry at you, at *you*. What, why . . . ? You stared. You were too surprised to be frightened.

He was babbling, his voice was high and reedy and accusing. No sense to his words. No sense! He crouched between two parked cars, an old man your grandfather's age, your grandfather's size, you were eleven years old, you couldn't believe what you were seeing, that old white-haired man with his pants unzipped, shaking his thing at you, at *you*, so ugly, red, flopping, rubbery, like a balloon nearly depleted of air—so laughable! You stared, you couldn't move. At first you thought he was accusing you of something, he seemed so angry. But how was it your fault, what had you done? What had *that* to do with you?

Then you ran away. You ran.

Ran.

Now you see them sometimes, watching you in that queer, veiled way: unsmiling, grim, resentful, hard, hating. Why, you want to ask them, why? What has it got to do with me? . . . They watch you, they watch the other girls. Not all men, but some men; in fact, quite a few. Why so angry, so hateful? *You'd better watch out, girl,* they seem to be saying, *you'd better run! This thing can hurt you plenty!*

I stood to the side. I observed. My heart was filled to bursting; I was a pilgrim but I stood to the side—for as long as I could bear it.

Kasch, the demons muttered, what will happen to you? Falling in love: falling under an enchantment.

Enchantment. A chant, a litany, a sacred recitation in others' voices—demons or angels, who can judge? *Childwold,* the girl said, her voice low, almost hoarse, throaty. A grown woman, a prematurely aged woman. A child. Her head at my shoulder, her body small, light, the bones heartbreaking, so frail. She washed her face and reappeared shivering. There were inflamed mosquito bites on her shoulders and legs and one long puffy bite on her throat. Prematurely aged, dirtied, used, wise. That throaty voice. Those clear gray eyes. Her head came to my shoulder, she was so small; a child. *Childwold,* she said.

That night I grappled with her and overcame her and snapped her fragile bones in my heated love, in my generous lust. I tore at her mouth with my own. I tore at her tiny breasts, her thighs. She did not resist—not much. I overcame her. I threw myself upon her from a great height and was transported, grappling guzzling whinnying groaning, excruciating pleasure, my brain turned to jelly, to liquid, hot and searing and violent, violently discharged—fiery liquid, searing the very air. The image of what I sought danced from me and teased me, the curls on her forehead damp, clotted, her fine light eyelashes clotted, I heard her voice echoing in my skull that night and many nights thereafter, a litany, a sacred chant, the words of which were so beautiful I woke weeping—

Childwold
Childwood
Childwide
Childworld
Childmold
Childwould
Childtold

You woke in terror but there was nothing—nothing—only rain on the roof so close overhead, and the *ping* of the first of the drops caught in the basin at the far end of the room where the roof was starting to go bad. And you loved rain, loved to sleep beneath it, loved the sound of the wind and the trees and the rain, loved to sleep secret beneath it while the vines outside your window rustled and

54

you put your mind to the river behind it, eased your mind into the soft reassuring sound of the waves; no danger at all, no danger up here, not even in floodtime: your grandfather had been wise to build the house on this high grassy knoll.

There were times you woke ready to defend yourself, ready to scream, but there was no reason; no reason. The first of the roosters crowing, or a bird in the chimney or in the trumpet vines rustling against the side of the house, or the dog barking, or someone driving by out on the road, and you woke startled, wondering what it was, who it could be—who would be driving on that narrow old dirt road this time of day? The rustling of the vine was dry and rasping and comforting and the wind came from the mountains, always cool, always blowing the stale heat-haze away, only wait a few hours and the weather will change, it's one thing you can count on here; so people said again and again and you said it yourself and it seemed to be true. You slept lightly and woke and slept and woke again, and the pattern of light on the sloped ceiling was always different, the moonlight faded and daylight began, the room was secret and cave-like at the very top of the house; in summer there was a shifting patchwork of shadows on the walls and the ceiling as if you were lying underwater. Like butterflies' wings, the delicate trembling shifting shapes, like the minute slow-darting motion of fish, the scattering of maple seeds blown wide and whirling like snow, you lay there content, warm, secret, safe.

There were times the fear was for nothing, a child's nightmare, and there were times you heard them downstairs, heard a voice raised, then the awful silence, the silence thick in your ears, and another voice and then silence, silence. In the other house, so long ago, your father still alive, the heavy footsteps, the banging of the screen door, your mother calling out—an argument, or teasing?—and the car starting in the driveway and the screen door banging again, your mother out there in her nightgown, her voice raised but the words inaudible. Teasing, teasing. You didn't know. You pressed your hands to your ears and counted to one hundred, then to two hundred, then you were asleep and everything was

55

changed, and in the morning Nancy might ask if you'd heard all the commotion last night and you would barely remember—sit there blinking, blank. When he died your mother screamed. You were seven. It was so long ago, it was best forgotten. There are things best forgotten, Momma says.

Out in the driveway, in Earl's car, they sat talking so loud you knew they were drunk and didn't care. Earl was new: you liked Earl. Momma liked Earl. Before Earl there had been a man who looked younger than Momma, but who was almost bald, and never came into the house; drove up the drive and tapped on the horn and waited. He was married, somehow you knew he was married, maybe one of the kids told you at school. Hey Laney. Hey. Little girl, hey. That new boy friend of your mother's, guess who he is! Earl and Momma sat out in the car and their voices came up into the night, rising, punctuated by Earl's racking cough and his throat-clearing, you couldn't always hear the words and didn't want to, didn't want to. Angry sibilant voices. Adult voices. There was mention of someone named Brickner, but you didn't know who Brickner was, and Momma was laughing and protesting, and after a while the car doors opened and closed and Momma came inside and Earl with her, now quiet, tiptoeing, and in the kitchen she must have made coffee for him. You stood at the window for a while leaning out, your bare arms out, watching the lighted rectangle far below on the grass, the kitchen window, not hearing any voices now and thinking maybe it was all right, maybe you could go back to sleep, you had to get up in a few hours—had to go to school next morning. Maybe it was all right. If he married her—if he came here to live—maybe it would be all right.

Momma said how she loved that man, how she couldn't get enough of him. Talking over the phone to her friend Judy Wreszin. Momma said how he came along in time to save her life—a strong proud *good* man—like there weren't many of, these days. Practically an extinct species, Momma said.

Last time, though, when you woke it was because of

Momma out in the yard, Momma crying and whimpering. Oh, my God! My God! You woke and got out of bed and started down the attic steps. You knew what had happened, somehow you knew; in the dark you ran down the narrow smooth-worn steps and didn't slip, you ran to the closet where the guns were—only two of them now—and got the .22, which is always kept loaded—the shotgun isn't—and you called out Momma! Momma!—so she would know you were there and would help her. The door wasn't locked; is never locked. Momma was screaming and you got to her, helped her inside, you said Momma it's all right, Momma what happened, it's Laney, what happened, is he out there?—is he out there?

Dear God, God—

The blood on her face!

You thought he had damaged her eye, her poor eye—you thought he had smashed her face—there was blood everywhere—her nose, her mouth—blood down the front of her ripped dress—Momma crying, holding onto you, crying Laney, Laney, don't let—

Is he there? Is he out there?

Laney he's going to kill me, he says, says he will kill me—I came home alone—I cut across fields—was afraid to go on the road—he's crazy, crazy-drunk—they had to pull him off me—he wouldn't stop, wouldn't stop—at first they just stood there, they were too cowardly to interfere—stood there gaping—I ran and he caught me and slammed me against some people and against the wall—he wanted to kill me—I didn't do anything, Laney, I swear—I didn't do anything—someone was fooling around—I don't even know who—fooling around at the bar and put his arm around me and kissed me and it was nothing, Earl didn't even care, didn't mention it, and then later on he said something about it—about that man—about him and me, did I know him from before, was he one of my boy friends?—and I told him no, I told him no, but he got angry, got angrier, got so drunk and mean and called me names for everybody to hear and I didn't do anything, Laney, I swear, I didn't do anything, didn't know that man but he wouldn't believe me—He's going to follow me here, Laney, he's going to kill me—he said he would kill us all—I never saw him so drunk, so mean—Laney—

Momma stop, please. Momma. My God—

Laney I never did anything to provoke him—

Now the house was lit up and everyone was crowded in the kitchen, all but the smallest children, Momma please! Momma! Now Nancy was there to help, to wail along with Momma, the children were wailing what is it, what happened, what is going to happen, blood on the linoleum and splashed on the table covered by oilcloth and on the three-legged wobbly chair and on the counter and on the stove, the top of the stove, smeared on the rusted burners, such a racket, a hallooing, a din of sea-thickened voices, the river rushed into the downstairs through the opened windows carrying all before it, such a din, such a tide, an earth-quivering sickhearted tide, you ran pushing them aside though they clutched at you weeping:

On the porch you stood, clear of it, stood out there with the rifle picked up so long before, teeth gripping your lower lip, sweat on your forehead, you stood on the porch in the dark waiting, waiting, the trembling was so bad you had to lean against the railing, waiting for him, for the headlights of his car, you paid no attention to the damp night air so fresh and the moon cricket-loud and the peepers frantic for life and the night birds that never sleep and the waves rising to the bridge and the dog yipping and whining and Momma still crying in the kitchen *I never did anything, I swear I never did anything to provoke*—

The boards were splintery and strong beneath your feet. You waited. Finger on the trigger as you'd been taught; you waited. Are waiting. You were trembling and the trembling got worse but you stood there with the gun, watching for the headlights that would be his, his, that would come from the east, turning off the dark Marsena Road onto your road, which looked lighter in the night because it wasn't paved and wasn't tarred, you waited and saw how you would run out to meet him before he got anywhere near the house and the people inside, you would run out in the dark, the cinders in the driveway have never hurt
58

your bare feet, you would run bent over to the very end of the driveway to the mailbox to the high grass, you would not hesitate, when the car slowed and you saw his face you would offer no greeting, no warning, you would not call him by name, you would raise the rifle and fire, and fire again, and run to the car and fire again, again, bringing the barrel of the rifle up against him—

You were trembling, stooped over the pain of your bowels. You are trembling. You died, are dying.

You died.

*Two*

CRUEL, very cruel! As only the brain-besotted know, the most foul of jokes, a young full-blooded gelding, an even-gaited glossy-coated high-stepping chestnut gelding, groomed and saddled with care, with love, ridden to death, sides heaving, lungs bellowing, eyes starting out of his head, ridden in the blast of late-summer heat, through swarms of honeybees, through a furnace of sun, ridden sweat-slick and foaming at the bit, up and down the tangled overgrown unfamiliar hills, out of the sunshine and into the briers, into the ten-foot-high snowdrifts, terrified of sheet lightning, forced to ride into it, rearing, plunging, screaming, your knees gripping his sides tight, your body bent over his, face against the stinging mane— cruel, very cruel!—whoever touched him with the tip of his whip—sent you riding—buttocks rising from the saddle, red-welted, raw—thirty-five years old in late sun-splashed summer, riding along the easy riverside path, one, two miles, three miles, an easy trot, beware of copperheads sunning themselves on those flat white rocks, the sun makes them lazy and defiant, power in poison, a bite on the inside of your elbow—remember?—fifteen years old you were and swollen and near death, head rocking and pounding, voice a high-pitched wind—beware of pheasants and quail starting out of the grass, the horse's heart and your own, none too strong, beware thunderous rain-bellowing harrowing storms, hay-rotting, wheat-smashing, the most cruel of evils: act of God. The river alongside is heaving, thrusting, smashing, pounding, toppling head-on southwesterly, which is your direction also, trotting cross-country, across your own staked fenced
62

cleared planted beloved land, rushing from the mountains in the east, carrying all before it, hallooing rowdy cruel unreadable: atop your favorite (and costly) horse, you follow the lane—wheatfield, cornfield bordering—the woods to your right so proud, the open meadows to your left—sun and shade dappled like butterflies' wings slowly opening and closing, opening and closing, dappled like stray cautious fishes, minnow-sized, flitting across your path and across your burning face—how cruel, whose joke, how will it end, whose whip, whose shout set you in motion, the gray pockmarked Atlantic heaving and the universe swirling like your guts, why, he's an orphan!—an orphan!—youngest of twelve and set free upon the mad rushing tide, set off with a kick of his father's and a sob of his mother's, soiled white apron raised to hide the shame, so tumultuous a ride, thirty-five-year-old husband, father, lover, dark-haired, even-gaited, cruelly deluded, everyone watching and whispering as the handsome animal begins to falter, the eyes rolling blind in the head, teeth snapping for the bit, legs longing to rear, hoofs longing to crush, the whinny hideous because it is so humanlike and so sane: ridden in the blast of summer heat to the knee-high waters of autumn to the first blizzard of the year, plunging through the uncleared briers and the dunes of snow, no help, no sympathy, the land mocks but is silent, there can be no reply, riding to a friend, a friend's face, a friend's hand raised in greeting—a circle in the wilderness, lighted—tended—friends' faces, friends' linked arms, one house opening into another, rooms opening warmly into rooms—the human world where you are named and prized and even envied: but the ride ends abruptly, you stagger and would faint, the horse has been ridden to death beneath you and falls away and you are standing feebly, knees shaking, swarms of dots in your vision, you feel the face pushing through your own, the other's face, *his,* pushing through your healthy ruddy skin, you touch yourself in awe, in astonishment, groping to cover every patch of pain, and find your friend equally ravaged, unrecognizable, an evil-smelling sallow-faced bony creature propped up in a chair, a palsied hand reaching uncertainly for your own—

"Why, Mr. Krassov," says the white-stockinged woman, "isn't this a nice surprise—isn't it—a visitor—two visitors: come closer, he's looking at you, he's listening: see! And such a nice day, isn't it, a nice day all day, morning and afternoon, come closer, here, shake hands, here, don't shy away—"

Cruel, very cruel! Cruel!

Half her face smeared in blood. A tooth loose, the upper lip cut. She spat out blood. She taunted him: You can't. You don't know how. You aren't a man. You're nothing. You don't know how. You're no good. He struck her and she crouched and grinned though it seemed her nose must be broken, the breath was haggard, horrible. You don't know how, you're not a man, you're nothing, there's nothing there, a woman can't feel you, a woman doesn't know you are in her, there's nothing to you, nothing there, nothing— He seized her by the shoulders, by the throat. Shook her. Shouted. He was going to cry, the agony was so great: he was going to collapse upon her. Her nails dug into his hands. Her face was contorted. She staggered and he fell upon her, his feet slipping. He lost hold of her throat, his hands fumbled at her waist, her hips, she slapped his face again and again methodically from side to side slapping, the cheeks slapped, hot, bright, scalding—

You're nothing. You don't know how. You can't. You're not a man. There's nothing there. There's nothing in you. Nothing.

End of year approaching. Winter solstice approaching. I don't want to hurt her—not again.

Farthest point of the sun's retreat: life most difficult at this time, world sinking in snow, in glittering dangerous ice. The other day it was summer and now it is winter, icebound, interminable.

The girl with the heart-shaped face, the thin shoulders, gray eyes, bite-ridden legs. Her ribs showing, undulating beneath the translucent skin. I hurt her didn't I. Hurt her badly. Made her acknowledge me. Oh the grief of it, the nausea of triumph, the afterhurt of pleasure squeezed from another's body. She writhed, kicked, groaned. Squirmed. Put up an excellent struggle. Wiry-bodied, a healthy young animal, her breath somewhat fouled by cigarettes and cheap wine. My love.

I follow her everywhere. I spy upon her. The world is sinking in snow, innocent deathly snow: the lovers by the river are gone, forgotten. I have no need of them. I follow her along the street, the snow muffles my footsteps, I am invisible, but her fair bobbing head catches the sunlight, the pale winter sunlight, and she cannot hide from me. My angel, my soiled angel. I reached up into your small tight body, didn't I, I jammed myself up into you, didn't I, and we are bound together forever, forever, forevermortal, the two of us. My lily of the snowfields. My broken one. On your wrist dirt raised itself in rolls, in tiny wormlike rolls, teased into being by my thumb. You are dirty and I would lick you clean.

Yawning and shivering she lay back against the car seat and I drove her miles and miles into the night, into the hills. Into the foothills of the mountains. We might have driven forever—through the night and into the next day— I would not have cared. My dear one! My trusting one! Everywhere my eyes darted she was open, achingly open, she could not have resisted me for a moment. A child. A daughter. Asked me did I know her father? No, no. Her mother? No! Never.

But you seem to know me, she said.

One of my sweaters around her like a cape; sleeping beside me; trusting. Long drive in the dark. Long drive. Trusting. How has this come about, how dare she sleep. O Charon! The river we crossed, the rattling old-fashioned bridge, built high above the water in terror of spring floods, old, rusted and old, the hilly darkness into which we drove old, discomforting. A maze of dark roads. Her murmured directions: my fear we should be lost. The meager city of my birth, population 30,000, left behind. Friday night has evaporated. On Bridge Street are they sleeping, the citizens of my soul? In postures of absolute abandon, rest, peace. Only I am awake.

The moonlit dry highway. The narrow blacktop road.

Woods on either side, trees overhanging the road, branches brushing against the windshield of the car. Have I driven this way before? Am I expected? Woods opening to fields, cornfields. Odor of earth, wet, vegetation. The girl stirring beside me, murmuring something I cannot hear. Home? Taking me—? We turn off another road and the houses we pass are dark. Houses, barns, outbuildings passing in silence. I am driving cautiously. I am a cautious person. We are in the foothills of the Chautauqua Mountains and the air is colder here, the moon and stars brighter, I feel that I am expected, I cannot be lost. . . . The village of Marsena: Bethel Pentecostal Church, prominent sign. White-glowing houses. Darkened windows. A half-mile long and the country closes in again. Night.

Road giving way to road, ascending, narrowing, a one-lane wooden bridge, sharp turns, the headlights illuminating junglelike bushes, saplings, briers, vines. A long hill, must use brakes; slip into a lower gear. Heart pounding, though I am not afraid. Of what, afraid? I am not going to be implicated. Not going to be involved.

Village of Childwold. Population 800.

In awe of the tense moonlit beauty of this place: the road that has now leveled and straightened, the small white houses, the enormous feed mill built close to the road, hulking, darkly complex. Strong smell of grain. Another large building, its metal roof glowing in the moonlight; a long veranda, wooden posts: broad front windows darkened. There is a school, a small brick building the size of an ordinary house, set back in a weedy yard. There is a church, Methodist. A grocery store. A few more houses, set close to the road, behind them the hills rising at once, and then the country again—another narrow bridge and the country again. *Childwold,* sang the voices, *Childwide, Childwood, Childwill, Childwoe.*

A newly tarred road and the turnoff onto her road, *hers.* She is awake. A mile in, she whispers. Awed by the darkness as I am. There is a farmhouse, a long dark lane, front yard a pasture, fenced. Big trees. There is an odor of rot, of fungus, of scum; a marshy area to our left. Grasses high in the ditch. A pair of eyes glaring at me—cat?—picking up the headlights of the car. A ravine, the
66

sound of rushing water, small rocky stream into which things have been dumped—I catch sight of an automobile on its side, seats dragged halfway out into the creekbed— then the vines close in again.

You can let me out here, she whispers. Has folded my sweater neatly, laid it on the seat between us.

I stop the car and for a moment can't see any house— on one side there is total darkness, a woods, on the other side a dark lane leading back between two fields gone to weeds and saplings. A mailbox, its flag pointing down. Aluminum. Letters painted on its side too blurry for me to read.

Home?

Home.

By day a nightmare of a place: one of those old farms gone bad, one of those Valley farms I had heard about, good rich soil it no longer paid to cultivate, buildings run-down, neglected. But this house was larger than most farmhouses in the area. Must have been quite a place at one time, a big ungainly wood-frame box with a peaked roof and old-fashioned lightning rods and a wide sagging veranda that ran the full width of the house, now cluttered with things—chairs, an old sofa, bicycles, children's toys, cartons, clay flowerpots. Peeling paint. Rotting shutters and shingles. The front steps leaning sharply to one side. Once white, now badly in need of paint, unevenly weathered so that it looked both monstrous and insubstantial, watery-gray. The sun grew stronger, the sun pounded and pounded, I stared at the old house and could not understand why it fascinated me so strongly: big flopping ungainly place, like a slovenly woman, ill-proportioned, blatant, uncanny. There was a chimney, a stone chimney that had begun to crumble at its top; vines grew thickly upon it and upon part of the house. There were birds around the chimney—swifts, swallows?—making quite a racket. One of the small barns was built directly onto the back of the house, a custom in this area, as it is a custom in northern New England, and it now sagged away from the house, or the house sagged away from it, as if their separate foundations had shifted. Connected to that barn,

67

perpendicular to it, was an enormous barn—really enormous—as large as any barn in the Valley—with old lightning rods glinting in the sun, prim and fussy, though part of the roof had caved in. Once painted red, now badly weathered. There was a silo, there was a corn crib, the remains of a windmill, a chicken coop and a chicken yard, a rabbit hutch, and other old buildings; everywhere were high grasses, saplings, overgrown bushes, wild flowers, trash. My senses whirled. I left the car and walked up the driveway. I was invisible. To my left was an old pasture; its barbed-wire fence was still fairly substantial. In one corner was an old tractor and some farming equipment, dumped, forgotten, surrounded by tall mustard weed. To my right was a badly eroded patch of land, red-clayey, in which hollyhocks and sunflowers and tiger lilies grew wild and lovely. Savage burst of color! My senses whirled, I was intoxicated, I could not turn back, though a dog had begun barking somewhere near. . . . Look, someone had whitewashed a few big rocks and set them alongside the cinder driveway, but gave up after doing seven or eight of them; for some reason that touched me. I stared, I was lost in contemplation, no one could see me from the house, no one could know who I was, no one could stop me. . . . Several old cars without tires, partly stripped, doors swung permanently open, dumped years ago in far corners of the sprawling yard, beneath trees. Jays and blackbirds making war this morning in the remains of a pear orchard. Crickets, and gulping hoarse sounds that must have been frogs; from somewhere near came the pungent odor of water, warm stagnant water, the rich odor of marshes, marsh grass, sun. I was invisible. No one could see. I was not going to turn back.

Ah, the size of the house! Like a small hotel or a mansion, very nearly the size of my parents' old home. A wreck now. Must have been too large for these people to maintain. The shingles were badly rotted, the chimney would not last another winter. On the second floor was a broken window, mended sloppily with plywood and black masking tape. On several of the first-floor windows was that cheap translucent plastic material, used for insulation by people who can't afford anything better; it was ripped and fluttering. So many windows, so many faces! . . . but I was invisible, I was not in danger.

Around the house were many flowers, but many weeds as well: a jumble, a dizzying jumble of colors. Poppies, Queen Anne's lace, cosmos, sweet peas, morning glories, trumpet vine, peonies, marigolds, tiger lilies and hollyhocks and sunflowers tall but looking ravaged, and roses in various stages of breakdown . . . wild currant, honeysuckle, snowberry, elderberry. There was no order, no order I could determine. In the weeds were broken toys, abandoned sleds with rusted runners, an old tricycle, old tires, those lightweight plastic bottles that milk now comes in, rain-soaked and sun-parched newspapers and magazines. A universe of trash, of beauty. A universe of smells. From the pear orchard came the odor of fruit, and the odor of heat and decay. From another direction came the odor of open fields, of sun beating on grain, on corn. I could see, behind the house, a vegetable garden: must have been a half-acre at least, and well weeded. Enormous tomato vines, and lettuce, and carrots, and other plants I could not identify. The dog was barking angrily.

The quality of the light here!—piercing, almost cruel. Cruel. It magnified everything. The trees were giants, the hills seemed to quiver with life, the mountains in the distance were tremulous, my own shadow was about to break from me and dance with frantic joy. The birds shrieked, their shadows too danced upon the grass, beneath the sagging veranda something squirmed, taking shape, the air smelled wonderfully of hay, of old manure, of flowers, of fruit, of ditchwater, of marsh grasses and cattails—it sang with invisible insects, insects everywhere, brushing against my face and glancing away, crickets and grasshoppers and bees and cicadas and small white butterflies. A dog rushed at me, yelping. A mongrel, mostly Labrador retriever with long floppy ears and a long ungainly tail, coarse black fur splattered with mud, dried mud. It clawed in the dirt, circling me, barking frantically; its eyes were nearly closed and its ears were laid back.

No no no no—

No—

Beneath the veranda a child's head appeared; then another. Someone giggled. At the door another child appeared suddenly behind the screen and called to the dog. You, Butch! Be quiet! Quiet! . . . I approached the veranda and the dog gave way, growling deep in its throat. On the old sofa on the veranda was a plaid blanket, and scattered across it were empty Coke bottles, a spoon, a copy of *True Romances* and a copy of *Reader's Digest* and what must have been a Sunday feature magazine, in bold primary colors. . . . Three small children scrambled out from beneath the porch, giggling. One of them clutched a scrawny tortoiseshell cat. Butch, goddam it, shouted the boy at the door, fair brown-blond hair like the girl's, the girl I sought, not so curly as hers, Butch, get 'round back of the house and shut up! —Mister, what do you want?

Behind him stood another child, peeking under his arm. And then a woman appeared and pushed them away and came out onto the porch; she stared at me rudely. Yes? Yes? What? She carried a baby in the crook of one arm, her blouse was partly unbuttoned, her tight, faded orange slacks were stained, her hair was up in rollers, her face looked shiny, as if rubbed hard with a rag. I saw that she was young—hardly more than twenty. Her gray-green eyes were set close in her healthy, chunky face.

A girl of about six ran out onto the porch and hid behind the young woman's legs, sucking her thumb, staring at me. The young woman scolded her. Nobody's going to bite you, cut that foolishness out! Mary Ellen!

I smiled, I held out my hands to show that I meant no harm, that I was lost, I was no danger. It's going to be a hot day! It's been, now, four-five days in a row, so hot! The young woman smiled; she smiled easily; her face was broad, her jaw strong, teeth big and white. She stood with one hip higher than the other, the baby resting comfortably on the hip; she smiled, she gave me directions back to the main highway; her eyelashes were pale, almost white, but her eyes were strong and clear and pretty. I stammered. I wanted to ask—wanted to beg—heard myself saying how strangely weak I felt, hoped it wasn't my heart, I had been driving for so long, lost, down one dirt road and onto another, and onto another—and—

She led me inside, murmuring. She held the screen

door open, her arm long and sturdy and tanned. A big girl, big-breasted, wide-hipped. She was barefoot and each of her toenails had been painted scarlet.

Children's toys on the floor, children's clothes, shoes . . . more newspapers, magazines . . . too much furniture crowded in the living room . . . a worn, frayed, colorless rug . . . a pedestal floor lamp, bright brass . . . a television set with a small screen . . . doilies, embroiderd or crocheted, on the sofa and the chairs . . . a ripped plastic cover on a new-looking armchair; odors of milk, food, a faint odor of urine, of diapers. She returned with a glass of water. Tepid water in a jam glass, her hand brushing against mine, my senses brimming with gratitude, with love, my eyes brimming with tears. Thank you! It's so kind of you. Noise on the stairs, another child, a boy, clattering as if he wanted to break the stairs, but the young woman doesn't notice—doesn't hear. We talk about the weather, the long drive back to town, the bad condition of the road here—so dusty!—and the other roads, recently tarred, aren't much better—the county is run by crooks, people pay high taxes and get nothing in return, did I know they'd been snowed in for four days last January?—and then the snow-plow left a ten-foot-high bank of snow by their driveway, the bastards! We talk, we fall silent, the telephone rings in another room, two rings, silence, two rings again; she is impassive, undisturbed, asks if I'd like more water, if I feel better now, would I like a Coke, would I like, maybe, a beer?—the telephone rings again and I must have looked nervous because she said it was a party line and not their ring. My heart is beating, gulping. My smile is lopsided. Through a window I see a sunflower spying upon us, its big coarse homely beautiful head bobbing my way, and the baby squirms on the young woman's hip, staring at me, tiny mouth open, tiny white teeth, one arm snakes toward me and I am astonished by the small fingers, the small perfect heartbreaking fingernails. —Your baby, I say softly, fumblingly, your baby is so—Oh, he's a nuisance, a terrible nuisance, she grins, cheeks dimpling, he's a devil already, keeps me up half the night—He's so beautiful, I say, and the girl rolls her eyes and blushes and laughs, a farm girl's laughter, surprised

71

and loud and slightly embarrassed. I ask about her husband and her smile contracts and she shrugs her shoulders. I have made a blunder, I am ashamed, I see the wedding band on her finger and a diamond engagement ring, an intricate, raised setting for a tiny diamond, ludicrous, pathetic, touching, and I say again that the baby is beautiful and she tells me all babies are, she loves babies, wants to have a dozen of them; it runs in the family, she giggles, my momma's the same way. We are standing close together. We are perfectly safe. There are children on the porch, there are children in the kitchen at the rear of the house, there is the baby on her hip. . . . My name is Nancy, she says suddenly, boldly.

She brought me a can of beer and brought one for herself and we sat, the two of us, on the veranda, on the sofa, talking, and the dog drew near, cringing, and finally licked my hand and lay with his chin on my shoes. We talked. She talked. Her mother and sister were gone, gone shopping in Marsena, her grandfather was out fishing with some of the kids, she was lonely, her girl friends were scattered now, two of them married and gone to live in Port Oriskany, another gone to Yewville, working as a secretary, she was lonely, her husband was in the Midwest, in a training program, he was doing very specialized, difficult work, he was a hard worker, she was going to pack up and join him in a few weeks, it was lonely here, she was lonely, she loved her family, the baby's name was Dennie —Dennis; her other child's name was Louise, that blond girl out by the swing, wasn't she cute?—and that little girl she was playing with, that little girl was Louise's aunt, wasn't that silly?—a little five-year-old baby somebody's aunt!—she thought that was very funny; she laughed; she tapped the can against her big front teeth. She got along real well with her mother, not always with her sister—that is, her fourteen-year-old sister, who was at a bad age, always in a bad mood, crabby and secretive and smart-mouthed, and not as cute as she imagined herself; and there was her grandfather, she got along real well with him, and most of the time with her brothers and sisters; but she was lonely, there wasn't anybody to talk with, did I live in Yewville?—was I married?—did I have any children myself? . . . We sat together for some time, we talked, I wanted to touch her, my heart thudded, my senses whirled, I became invisible once more.

In the De Sales Hotel one night there was commotion down the hall and Vale, who was trying to sleep, got up and went down the hall to rap on the door. No one answered. It was quiet. He stood in the drafty hall in his underwear and yelled and pounded on the door, but no one answered, so he went back to his room and back to bed, where he slept, being quite tired—he had a job now, he worked from eight in the morning to four-twenty in the afternoon, loading and unloading for one of the river-front warehouses. Sometime during the night, he didn't know when, he didn't have a watch, didn't have a clock either, just woke and slept according to instinct, was proud of his ability to know when to wake, when to jump out of bed and begin the new day, sometime during the night there was a rap on his door and he muttered Who is it, or Go to hell, and tried to sleep again, but a few minutes later there was another rapping and somebody shouting words he couldn't comprehend; so he turned over onto his back and his eyes shot open, wide, and he heard himself think clearly *Somebody's going to get it* and his belly contracted with the tension, and in another minute his bedclothes would be soaked—he sweated so easily now, after the trouble in the hospital—so he thought he might as well get up, and ran out into the hall, and ran down to the other room where the door was now wide open, and five or six—or seven—maybe more —men were in there, some in their underclothes, some dressed, one of them trying to take hold of Vale's arm and plead with him: Mister! Young man! Have mercy! A doctor, can you get us a doctor? No one's awake in the hotel—Vale pushed the old bastard aside, peered into the room and recoiled at the stench, a room no larger than his and all these bums crowded into it and one of them naked on the floor, pot-bellied, skinny-chested, arms and legs outflung, such a sight, such a disgusting sight,

73

Vale's lip curled and he muttered My *God*. Nothing disgusted him as much as these old alcoholic sons of bitches, puking on the stairs and in the lavatories, hanging about the waterfront streets, skulking in doorways and in alleys, sitting with their feet in the gutter—no, nothing disgusted him quite so much, he had to push the old guy aside again, jab him with his elbow to make him keep his distance: There's been an accident, you see— We need a doctor but the manager is off duty— It was an accident, only an accident— No one is to blame— Vale went to the naked man and stood with hands on hips considering him. Did he know him? Had he seen him? Never. An elderly man. White stubble. Finely wrinkled skin, milky eyes, flabby mouth. Ugly. Ugly. Stank. All of them stank. Thin white hair, delicate veins at temple, oversized ears, oversized nose, the nostrils especially wide as if the nose had shrunk with age, drool at mouth, neck ravaged and filthy and reddened—wounded?—chest flat, sunken—belly swollen—genitals slipped between his flabby white thighs, tiny, secret, disgusting. Vale gave him a prod. Hey wake up, you stinking son of a bitch! Noticed the blood seeping about the neck but poked him just the same. Wake *up*. What the hell do you think this *is*. One of the men was trying to leave and the others were detaining him and there was a scuffle and an elderly man in his underclothes sank to the floor weeping and Vale gave the naked man a sharp kick in the ribs but the body was heavy—heavy. Stinking sons of bitches, Vale said, all of you. Don't you know people have to sleep, people have jobs, there are people even in this shit-house who have jobs, I have a job, it doesn't pay much but I have a job, I work at the dock from eight till four-twenty, I had to join a union, I pay union dues, I pay taxes, the government deducts my taxes from my pay check, they don't pay me enough, I need my sleep, I need to recover, I'm twenty-three years old and just beginning, you bastards won't let me sleep, you deserve to die, the police should break your heads open and dump you in the lake, I need my eight hours sleep and you're depriving me, I'm going to complain to the management—

He pushed them out of the way and went back to his

room and slammed the door and locked it and went back to bed and took many long cautious breaths to calm himself, because he was easily excited, had a quick temper, of the family he was the one with the quick temper, his father had been mild-mannered except when drunk, and his grandfather mean enough but slow to lash out. He had a quick temper, his mother said. In the Army he'd gotten into trouble a few times but was well-liked, he was always well-liked, wherever he went people liked him, men and women both, he was handsome, had always been handsome, except now for his face, but that was attractive in a way, he believed it was attractive, seen in a certain light with his head at a certain angle it was attractive, girls went for him, girls always went for him, liked to stroke his hair and the scars, fingering them lightly, stroking caressing loving, there were always girls, there were many women, what was this place?—Port Oriskany—many women here and he would meet them all eventually, but now he had to sleep, had to sleep, and he lay on his right side as usual with his shoulders slightly rounded and his knees raised toward his chest and his legs tucked in and his arms crossed, though he had to be careful or the right arm would get numb and awaken him, but he didn't sleep, didn't sleep, he shut out successfully the noise down the hall—now people were on the stairs, now doors were opening and shutting—but still he couldn't quite sleep and it irritated the hell out of him: that job, and not enough sleep. And every night there was some disturbance. The night before, an enormous fly buzzing him, and when he snatched for it in the air it flew to the ceiling, and when he dragged a chair over and tried to swat it with a newspaper it flew lazily to a far corner, and when he went there it flew down to the bed, to the very pillow, and he had yelled at it and chased it and broke into sobs at one point, so cruel was the predicament. Another time, the week before, the eve of the first day of his new job, out on Front Street a man and a woman had been screaming at each other in Italian, and Vale had lain in bed praying for them to stop but they hadn't, not for quite a while. And another time. . . .

Then someone rapped on his door again and he

shouted Go to hell! Goddam bastards go to hell! and a man told him it was the police, open up, and Vale swung his legs out of bed and grabbed the lamp and threw it at the door, shouting for them to fuck off, he needed his sleep, he had a job and needed his sleep. But they didn't go away. Eventually they broke the door in and Vale, in his underclothes, sat sulking against the headboard of the bed, his arms folded. He told them he was a Vietnam veteran, wounded and honorably discharged, the holder of a medal, he had a job in the morning, he knew nothing about the old bastard with his throat slit, he wasn't going to answer questions, he wasn't a witness of anything, he knew his rights.

You'd better come along with us, the sergeant said. Better get dressed.

I'm not getting dressed. I'm not going anywhere.

Son, you'd better get dressed. A man has been murdered just down the hall—

So *what!* Vale said in disgust. He asked the sergeant for a cigarette. He made no move to get up. Another policeman appeared in the doorway, gun in hand. I'm not getting dressed and I'm not going anywhere, Vale told them both. I know my rights.

We're taking everyone in this dump down for questioning, there's been a man murdered tonight, you'd better cooperate; better get dressed.

You'll have to carry me to the station house, Vale said, stubbing out the cigarette. He lay sullen but limp, not resisting.


Oh, the children, the children—

In the big hay barn, in the old horse barn, down at the river, down in the beech woods where the boys had their shack—under the bridge, down behind the schoolhouse, back of the old McCord lane where there was such a jungle now, and in the deserted McCord house, and hitch-hiking on the highway (though Momma would be very angry if she knew)—with the Carmichael children one winter day making war on the Gelfant boy, throwing snowballs and iceballs: shrieking, shrieking, crazy with excitement, with sheer meanness!—Gonna kill you, we cried, hey, better run like hell, dirty old crazy old freak, dirty old crazy old ugly old freak—and he ran, how he ran!—oh he ran, ran!—clumsy red-faced puffing whimpering—beginning to cry: how we howled with laughter! *Freak! Freak! Freak!*

One of us hung back, didn't chase him across the fields, one of us stopped halfway up the hill above the river, breathing hard, feverish, suddenly tired. Sad. Funny, was it?—the Gelfant boy was a moron, they said—adults said—coarse-skinned, slow-moving, nasty nasty nasty— threw rocks at ducks on the river, even at ducklings, killed rabbits, cats, was suspected of having killed at least one dog—so people said: funny, was it, to see him run like that?

Sad.

One of us went to stand above the river, snowsuit damp, snow inside boots, mittens wet, nose running—one of us stood and watched the dark narrow strip of water between the wide, chunky banks of ice, swift-flowing, not yet frozen, strangely quiet. . . . Those shouts, those snatches of laughter! Oh, the children were lively as squirrels, quick and mean and frantic as cats gone wild!

*Freak, freak! Freak!*—their ringing fading wintry-sad cry. . . .

How I wanted this, how I wanted you, what I wouldn't have given for this. . . . No price is too high for this, for this.

In her sleep she dreamed of her lover, of Earl, of a man who resembled Earl, the dark hair on his chest and belly cross-shaped, thick, bushy, his muscles still hard beneath the patches of soft flesh, gripping her tight. His legs were short in proportion to his body but they were lean and strong and muscular. His chest and belly were fat; she did not mind, did not notice. Folds of flesh now at her own waist, pockmarked bunches of flesh on her thighs, too-white, and the drooping breasts, the scarred abdomen, she did not see, did not comprehend. I love you, I love this, don't leave me, come closer, come deeper, how I wanted this, how I wanted you, how I love you, her arms wrapped tight around him, legs wrapped

77

tight around his buttocks, heaving, grunting, don't leave me, I love you, I love—Earl or someone who resembled Earl, sometimes only the body itself, the feel of the body itself, faceless, gone lean and hard pressing into her, penetrating her, filling her, so that she began to sob with the relief of it, hours in the labor room and her backbone ready to break and the mattress soaked and her lover nowhere near, hundreds of miles away, Smitty his name, a salesman from Derby who traveled throughout the county with samples for hairdressing salons—shampoos, sprays, bleaches, hot combs, hair nets, hair driers— freckled, gangly, nearly bald, innocent-appearing, weeping in her arms because he would hurt his wife so very, very much when he told her that he loved Arlene and planned to marry her; the pregnancy, the whispers, the dirty looks, Pa ignoring everything, her sister Carrie on the telephone twice a day, how could you!—how could you, again!— and Arlene with her hands resting on her swollen stomach, utterly content, staring at the fields, the barn, the silo, the flocking birds, the tumult of flowers in the front bed, the woods, the hills, the mountains, the clouds, the sky— ah! when the baby kicked, how perfect the world became!

Her lover entered her and filled her deeply, powerfully; she touched her belly and it was full, hard, swollen, she shivered with dread, with excitement, her lover had no name, no face, his body had flowed into hers, there was nothing left of him now but the baby inside her: inside her: she gasped at the realization: it was inside her, secret, dark, warm, living, inside *her,* she had it now and would not relinquish it until the very end, until it was time, months and months and months of pleasure, Arlene moving through the world with another world held inside her, the two meeting in her, in her flesh and blood and bones: how perfect both worlds were! People were jealous of her, other women were jealous of her, her own daughters were ashamed, let them think what they pleased, she did not care; how she wanted this, *this,* how she loved it, her entire body filled and throbbing slow with life, it did not matter that the men deserted her, that they died, killed themselves in car wrecks

78

and had no insurance and no savings and no thought of her —it did not matter: only this mattered, and she had it.

Then she woke. And everything fell from her. The sensation of pleasure in her loins, the great swelling joy in her stomach and chest, the conviction that she was happy again as she was meant to be happy. She woke, it was over, there was no baby, there might never be another baby, she would live the rest of her life like this, empty, yearning, sick with yearning, ashamed.

You walked along the riverbank on mild winter days, thinking of Kasch. Thinking of him smiling, reading to you from his books, asking if he might touch your hair, your hand.

You laughed. Unhappy, wild. You lit a cigarette and the wind blew the smoke away; you stood on the bank above the river, kicking down bits of dried mud. Below you was the beach, the hard-packed sand. Pebbles, rocks, several boulders, part of a gigantic log washed ashore years ago. The dock your brother had built, now nearly gone. Two posts remaining, a few boards at the shore. Wind. Waves. Gulls. The water winked and glittered harshly. You threw the cigarette out into the river.

But I don't feel anything for you, you told him. Not that.

I can wait, he said.

His eyes hooded, shadowed behind his glasses; his smile melancholy, a little mocking. The wildness grew in you, the desire to laugh. Laney, for Christ's sake! Laney! —If I could help you out with anything, anything, he said softly, if you needed money—

No. No money.

Laney saved from drowning years ago, Laney hauled out of the river by her brother. Lost balance on the path, stumbled, fell screaming, fell into the incredible rough water, sinking, choking, losing consciousness. Carried downstream. Turned violently around, arms and legs spun, eyes open, terribly open, the sky overhead a frantic blur, and then the water closing in again, mind going blank, black, expiring. No no no no. Oh no. She died but Vale plunged after her and swam and saved her, hauled her out, the two of them panting, sobbing, Laney in her brother's arms, Vale staggering to shore. Laney was bruised and bleeding and badly shaken, but all right. No need for a doctor—doctors were expensive. Momma took care of her. Momma knew how. What a bad girl you were, Momma wept, running along there, haven't you been told, what if you had drowned—? Oh, you poor baby! Poor little baby! Momma bundled you in blankets, sat you in the kitchen with the oven door open, fussed over you, fed you warm milk and oatmeal cookies, then washed you right in the kitchen, still with the oven on so you wouldn't catch a chill. Washed your hair too and dried it in a big warm towel, hugging you, my sweet little baby, darling Laney, the prettiest little girl—don't you ever do that again, you hear? Vale saved your life today.

She had spat water, horrible muddy water, had coughed and choked and cried. Later, they teased her— without Momma or Daddy knowing, they teased her about swallowing a mouthful of dirty water, didn't she know that sewers and drains emptied into the river upstream, and cattle did their business in it, what did it taste like, little crybaby? Vale heard them and told them to shut up. One of them talked back and Vale slapped his face, hard.

You remember that as if it had happened to someone else.

You told Momma you were gone a long time and had died, had gone to a new place. Not just going to sleep, but to a new place. In the water. Momma listened to you and shook her head and laughed, and fussed over you and kissed you, but she didn't understand. Little curlylocks, she called you. She hugged you warm against her, she loved you best, you loved her best, the two of you were together all the time except for when she came home with the new baby, with Ronnie, and even then she kept you close to her, the two of you fed him and bathed him and changed his diapers. So you told her about dying. You told her all your secrets. I was gone a long time, you said, and I could see Vale coming after me, and I could see myself turning round and round in the
80

water, and I wasn't afraid, I just watched it happen. I saw Vale run into the water and I heard him shout and then he started to swim after me, and I was watching, I wasn't afraid, there was water in my mouth and my eyes but I was outside the water too, watching. I saw Vale's arms coming after me and his face so close I wanted to cry for him but I couldn't, I wanted to say his name but I couldn't. I felt sorry for Vale, he was so scared. Billy was on the dock, then he was on shore running along, but I couldn't hear what he said. He was scared too. It happened so fast but it was spread out too, it took a long time, I fell asleep in all the time it took, and I wasn't afraid, I went to a place that was all dark, like under the covers at night, and warm, and I came to the house here and Momma! Momma! because I wanted you to come with me, and you weren't in the kitchen, and I saw you through the window in the garden, trimming the hollyhocks, and I said Momma—and you looked around but didn't see me and then I started to cry and then I was out of the water, Vale was carrying me to shore, I was safe, I wasn't going to drown, I threw up all over myself and Vale and he let me down on the beach and almost fell down next to me and it was all over, Momma—but it was another day, it wasn't the same day. It wasn't the same little girl.

You walked along the old path, hands in the pockets of your jacket. That little girl, this little girl. Who? Which one? Up at the house Momma is probably fixing supper. Momma heavier this winter, doesn't go out, Momma snapping at you and Nancy and Ronnie, Momma loves the little ones best, even Nancy's. You walked, walked. Mallards on the river—seven, eight, nine. Five males and four females. Across the river a wild field gone to weeds. Old McCord property. Sold for taxes and not farmed and the McCords—Ginny McCord in your class at school—living in a trailer outside Yewville. One girl, another girl. Ginny McCord. Jean Carmichael. Your cousin Alice, your cousin Irene. The retarded girl, Mary Zinner. Girls. Laney Bartlett. He told you you were beautiful and you laughed, embarrassed. He said he would not hurt you. He was lonely, he said.

Yes, you told him. I know.

But you don't know, he said, a note to his voice that surprised you because it was rather mocking. . . . You *don't* know.

Momma is lonely, Momma needs a man, needs to sit out in the car with a man, arguing, kissing, smoking cigarettes, passing the time; needs to sneak him in the house when she thinks we're asleep, needs to be loved. *Your mother is a . . . D'you know what your mother is . . . ? Stuck-up bratty Laney Bartlett, d'you know . . . ?* The Zinner girl crowded near you, whispering, her breath stale, her teeth discolored. *Little stuck-up Laney Bartlett.* Lonely, was she; lonely; no friends, no one to sit with on the school bus; attached herself to you, though it was obvious you didn't like her. . . . Miss Flagler, the girls' gym teacher: calling you into her cubbyhole of an office. Small, swarthy-skinned, alert, close-cropped black hair like a boy's, sardonic, mocking, "witty." In the yearbook, Miss Flagler is one of the "wits." Dark green shorts, white shirt, white woollen socks and gym shoes, favored only a few girls each year, those who are good at sports. You're one of them: good at basketball despite your size, good at volleyball, excellent on the trampoline and on the rings and ropes and mat. Like a cat, you are; the other girls complain, half-seriously, that you're double-jointed. Miss Flagler likes you, called you into her office a few weeks ago, asked what was wrong—circles around your eyes, bad mood all the time, sitting out half the gym classes? You shrugged your shoulders. She was nice and then she got irritated with you, lost her patience, told you to shape up or you'd be sorry. A few days later you had cramps, were sitting out the class, she directed a few sarcastic remarks your way and the other girls laughed, even your friends laughed, you tried to ignore her. Alluded to Laney being "delicate," Laney being "made of glass." You ignored her that day, but the next gym class she picked at you again, smiling that smile of hers, the bitch, the monkey-faced bitch, getting the girls to laugh at you until you shouted Leave me alone, leave me alone . . . ! And then she got angry, she told you to go to her office, to sit in there and wait, not to change your clothes but just wait in there. You ran out, you ran to your locker; you were going to change your clothes and leave school; then you decided against it, you were ready to cry, you didn't know what to do. . . . You went into her office and sat in the chair in front of her desk and waited, waited for twenty minutes, and finally Miss Flagler came in and closed the door and sat down and sighed, as if in disgust or exasperation. Still, she didn't say anything for a while. Then she accused you of being snippy and uncooperative and insolent, and you said nothing, you didn't even look at her, you were pulling at a loose thread on your shoelace; then she said she should really send you to the principal's office and have him deal with you, and still you didn't look at her, your eyes welled with tears, your mouth went hard and bitter with the effort not to cry. She asked you what was wrong: was it your family, your mother . . . ? Was it something about home . . . ? You told her no. No. She asked whether you were in any kind of trouble . . . ? You told her no. Your face went hot, you wanted to shout at her to leave you alone. Well, she said, drawling the words, I've seen you hanging around on the streets with some rough-looking characters, I've heard there's a bunch of you that does a lot of drinking, Laney Bartlett's mentioned along with them, that's the name I've heard; of course I could be mistaken. You pulled at the thread, untied the lace and retied it, your temples throbbed with blood but you said nothing, didn't give the bitch the pleasure of replying. Finally she changed her tone and said you could leave, the first bell had already rung, you'd better hurry, you could skip your shower, and she touched your shoulder and then gave it a little squeeze and you drew away from her and whispered, Don't you touch me! Don't you put your fucking hands on me!

. . . You heard the words again, you pressed your hands against your warm cheeks, hearing, not hearing, not believing.

Why did you say that to her, Kasch asked. The poor

woman. . . . I don't know her but she sounds sad, she sounds lonely. . . .

I can't help that, you said.

He began laughing. What was so funny, why did he shake his head from side to side like that? . . . He's like her, you thought; just like her.

I can't help any of you, you said.

They were telling Joseph about the Death-Angel.

When the body is waked, they said, the Angel is always present. He's there. He's listening. You can see him out of the corner of your eye but not head-on; you can see him in a mirror, but you must not try. He's ten feet tall. He's black. His wings are black, the spread of them is fifteen feet, there are big long black feathers on the wings, like a hawk's, but bigger. The quills are sharp, like knives. Sometimes, after the funeral, when the room is cleaned, a woman will find one of the feathers—sometimes just a pin-feather—and she knows what it is right away, and doesn't touch it with her fingers, and doesn't tell anyone about it. If she did, the Angel might return and take her with him. He would return and take her with him. He doesn't go far—he's always waiting.

On the way to the cemetery the Angel flies overhead, but you mustn't try to see him. If you close your eyes almost all the way and look out through your lashes, sometimes you can see him—but you mustn't try. If he sees you, he will take you with him. That always happens. Old Miles, you know, he saw the Angel at his wife's funeral, that was why he collapsed there in the road—right there—and he died a few weeks later. He should have known better but he was out of his mind, he'd been drinking for days. Do you understand? You can look at the Angel at your risk, but if he happens to see you—you're finished.

The Death-Angel is very tall, Joseph, do you know how tall? No, taller than that! Taller. Higher than the roof, even. There are eyes all over him. Not just the eyes in his face, like yours, but all over—in the back of his head, in his chest, on his back, at the tips of his fingers. The eyes are always open. They see everything. They see *you*. God sends the angel and only God can recall him, but sometimes God forgets, and the angel hangs around the house and in the barns, and that's why, when one person dies, the stock almost always sickens: they can smell him, the horses and dogs especially. . . . He has a hundred eyes, a thousand eyes. They never sleep. They never blink.

He sat facing Josef and the Angel of Death hovered nearby, but of course he did not turn. He did not believe in such nonsense.

He sat facing Josef trying to make conversation, but Josef did not respond. His old friend had been shrunk by the doctors and nurses, his fluids drained out by the tubing, this was a boring old man with a pale skull that looked dented, and watery-milky eyes, and his mouth without his dentures was caved in. Josef? Josef? Joseph sat facing him stubbornly, hands on his knees, Joseph Hurley in his best suit, in a shirt and a tie, paying a visit to the nursing home on Manitowick Avenue. A stroke, and another stroke, it was said, and his heart so weak, and kidneys failing, and now he was propped up in bed with his mouth collapsed to one side, nerves in his face twitching, but not in response to Joseph's voice.

"Pa, we might as well go," Arlene said.

She put away the handkerchief—she'd been wiping her face behind his back. Crying. Couldn't help herself. Forty years old and still a baby, built husky and broad in the hips, a strong-limbed woman, and good-looking, and able to run a household big as theirs, but still a baby; she cried at least half-a-dozen times a day.

"Pa, we might as well go!"

"We been here only ten minutes, honey. We only got here."

"Pa, he can't hear you, he doesn't know we're here. Mr. Krassov? He doesn't know we're here. . . . Pa, I feel sick. I think we'd better leave."

"Go wait in the car then. I'm all right."

"He can't see you or hear you, Pa. He—"

"Honey, go wait in the car," he said, waving her away. "I'm his friend, not you. He don't give a damn about you anyway."

Did a dance in the street once, Boylston Avenue, spider-thin then, silly arms and legs flung about, so gay; frantic festive dance because the curse was broken, I was in love; was loved.

Did a dance in the apartment, clowning to make my Laney laugh, serious cynical frightened little girl. I was heavier now by twenty pounds. Laughter unconvincing. On the phonograph I've carted everywhere with me, on my fruitless travels, a Louis Armstrong record from the forties, pure liquid notes reaching higher and higher.

Broke into a dance because it was unbearable—the tension.

Kasch undresses the girl. Waxy and sullen her face, sullen her young greeny-ripe body. He kneels before her. Kisses her belly. Her instructions are to clutch his head to her, her fingers caught in his hair. Her instructions are to groan, to bend over him, to rake at his back. But she merely stands there. She stands there. A small perfect statue: exquisite, adorable. He embraces her. He weeps. It has happened before like this, but still he weeps. The experience is always so brutal.

The girl fights him when she realizes what will happen. She gasps, claws, fights like the sinewy desperate animal she is—but she is no match for him—she is too small, her bones snap like dry sticks, she is nearly weightless, there is nothing to her. He throws her down. He scrambles over her, greedy. So little flesh to her, he seeks it blindly, bites and tears at it, his head snaps back with the frenzy of his passion, in the rhythm of an instinct millions of years old. He does not dare hesitate, does not dare glance up. He knows the possibility of our presence; he imagines he has seen our shadows out of the corner of his eye. Blindly he burrows, tearing at the girl, his body convulsed by long racking shudders.

A note on the queer, ugly, disturbing, maddening, marvelous depravity of the young: those girls I see on the streets late at night, hanging about the doorways of taverns, in and out of cars, glancing at me with no awareness of me —of my stricken awe. So many of them, and so young! Mine is the fairest of all, I want none other, but they are nevertheless everywhere, aren't they? Marvelous. Terrifying.

In one of my seldom-consulted books I read that the adult human being resembles the embryo of the ape. Marvelous too! Perhaps a clue. I read that certain species become played-out, overspecialized, they lose their vitality and must sink into the chaos from which they arose, unless evolution can go back a few degrees and retrace its steps and make a new beginning in a more hopeful direction. . . . A man named Garstang, a dubious theory of recapitulation, *paedomorphosis,* whereby the organic universe can revitalize itself indefinitely. The biological clock can be rewound, there is sometimes an escape from the cul-de-sac of evolutionary "progress," it is a hideous possibility because it involves sexual maturation at the juvenile stage. . . . The animal is ready to breed while still displaying, it is said, juvenile or larval characteristics: often the adult stage is never reached. It is not necessary. And so the species is rejuvenated because it squeezes out the overspecialized adult stage.

Paedomorphosis: the shaping of the young.

We become increasingly infantile, primitive, in order to survive. But not "we"—*they!*

Murderers, and so innocent. So lovely. So purposeful, squeezing us out. . . .


"No. It's a lie. Somebody's been telling you lies. I don't want to talk about it."

"Look at me. Look over here, Laney! Do you want your face slapped?"

Laney muttered something Arlene could not hear.

"I want to know where you were yesterday if you weren't in school."

"I was in school. . . ."

"You weren't! And a damned poor liar you are."

"Go to hell, Momma, will you? Go to hell and leave me alone."

She threw the book down and it fell off the edge of the bed and onto the floor. Her face had colored, she was defiant, cringing, small as a child. Arlene stared at her. . . . Fourteen years old? Only fourteen? But she had to remember, had to force herself to remember, that she herself had been married at the age of fifteen and had had her

87

first baby by the age of sixteen; and Nancy had started going out with boys even before her thirteenth birthday.

"What a thing to say to your own mother," Arlene cried.

Laney was sitting on her bed, sideways; now she took hold of her ankles and bent forward, rocking slightly, forward and back, in misery. ". . . Sorry," she muttered.

"If it was Brad or one of the other boys. . . ."

*"Brad or one of the other boys!"* Laney said. "Momma, for Christ's sake you don't know those kids, you just don't know; don't talk to me about them."

"Brad always seems, always seemed . . ."

"He's all right. He's fine."

". . . but a man that age, in his forties, they said, and you go to his apartment with him. . . . Laney, my God, why didn't I know anything about this, why didn't somebody tell me before? . . . Why didn't you tell me?"

She looked at Arlene coldly. Those wide gray eyes, those strong cheekbones . . . Arlene stared at her and saw the girl's father, the girl's dead father, and heard his low, almost hoarse voice: "Why should I tell *you? You!*"

"What do you mean by that? . . . Talking like that to your mother, your own mother. . . ."

She had not come into the room. She stood in the doorway, breathing hard. A telephone call from a woman who lived in Yewville, a few minutes questioning Nancy—who claimed to know nothing, who claimed that Laney told her nothing, nothing about her life—and she had run upstairs, and up these narrow, steep stairs to the attic, clutching her side like an old woman. Panting. *Laney, you bitch, you little lying bitch, how dare you.* . . . She had opened the door without knocking. No one came up here, Laney wouldn't allow anyone in, had her little kingdom in the attic, her secrets. There she sat on her bed, in the red flannel bathrobe Arlene had made for her, in her woollen socks, a book in her lap, a pencil in one hand, her thin shoulders hunched with alarm and her expression cautious and empty. *Bitch,* Arlene thought, *don't you look at me that way.* . . .

"Why did you say that, what you just said?" Arlene whispered. Her side did hurt, she was pressing it and

88

fingering the small roll of flesh: she was still out of breath. ". . . You looked at me as if you hated me."

"Just leave me alone, Momma. Nothing in my life has anything to do with you."

"You *do* want your face slapped. . . ."

She stepped forward and Laney ducked, crying out, but of course she didn't slap her—Arlene hadn't slapped Laney for years.

"Why, you're going to break my heart!" Arlene exclaimed, as if it were a truth she should have recognized long ago. Then she sighed and looked around the little room, and could not help but admire it, and said: "Now I know why you're always hidden up here, away from the rest of us."

Laney shifted uneasily. She ran both hands through her hair. "Not from you, Momma. From the kids. I have to have a place they can't spoil, don't you know that? You must know! . . . I didn't mean what I said just now, Momma. I'm sorry."

"Oh I know, I know how sorry you are," Arlene said lightly. She was about to cry. She had begun crying, but would not acknowledge it. She crossed her arms and studied the room, a single tear running down her cheek, ignored. Of her own mother's doll, handmade, with a painted porcelain face and a tiny rosebud mouth, rouged cheeks, faded blue eyes and flattened yellow curls, dressed in a bridal gown with brittle yellowed lace, given to Laney as a child and now propped up against her bureau mirror, she said: "Nice! Sweet." She liked the way the mirror was placed, so that it reflected the window; in the day it would make the room lighter and would make it appear larger. But the mirror was old, the lead backing had started to spot through, leprous, cloudy; she saw Laney's small pale face in it, slightly distorted, and she shuddered. "This hunk of furniture is so old, must be a hundred years old . . . a wonder it hasn't collapsed by now. . . ." On the bureau top were glass figurines that Laney had been collecting for years: ballet dancers with full skirts and elegant high-stacked hair; cats of various sizes, with graceful curved tails; and horses, and birds, and elephants, most of them from the five-and-ten, a few of them from the gift departments of better stores. There was a plastic-backed brush and mirror set, mock tortoiseshell, with the initials *EAB* in a flowing dark brown script—for Laney's full, regal name, the name on her birth certificate, was Evangeline Ann Bartlett; there were snapshots framed in cheap metal frames with cardboard backing—Arlene and Lyle and the children, Grandpa Hurley, girl friends of Laney's, aunts, uncles, cousins, Laney herself, a child of ten or eleven, holding a kitten in her arms and grinning into the camera. *That* was the Laney Arlene knew.

Though the room was small and the walls sloped on either side, Laney had managed to cram many things into it—the bed and the bureau and a small rocking chair and a set of bookshelves at the foot of her bed. On the crude floorboards, which had been painted green, was a hooked rug, now rather dirty; it had once been bright red. The colors in here! Arlene did not really approve. Everything seemed too intense, almost frantic; it reminded her of photographs in glossy magazines, where rooms were displayed because they meant something, had some secret hidden meaning, and were not shown simply to give pleasure. There were floral designs and stripes and patches of color, like the pieces of a jigsaw puzzle. Small throwpillows from the dime store covered in satin, corduroy velvet—in odd colors like puce, purple, saffron, and gold; a yellow-and-purple striped pillow on the rocking chair; a bright green curtain half pulled across the doorless closet at the far end of the room. On the walls, on nearly every inch of wall space, were so many things that Arlene could not begin to absorb them all: cutout photos of flowers, of tropical and desert flowers, of mountain peaks far more splendid than those in the Chautaquas, and of lakes, rivers, falls; photos of strangers' faces, people of all ages and colors, none of whom Arlene recognized; several old sepia-colored pictures that must have come down through the family; a large daguerreotype of a group of people gathered about the steps of the Methodist church in town, all of them beetle-browed and stiff, and rather ludicrous in their solemnity; and old Christmas cards and birthday cards and Valentines, beginning to curl at their edges. So much, such a profusion, poor Arlene's eyes blinked rapidly and she shook her head, not understanding. *To Our Little Darling On Her Birthday:* a coy curly-haired miss beneath a fringed parasol, smiles and dimples, an orange kitten at her feet. . . . So much, so many things, what did they mean? She found herself staring for some time at a glossy photograph of a Monarch butterfly, magnified many times, so that the creature's dark-glinting body and antennae and eyes, and the black veins of its wings, were rather monstrous. ". . . So many things!" Arlene murmured. Laney had been saying she was sorry, her voice raised slightly, whining, but Arlene preferred to ignore her, examining this strange room. Well, it *was* a kingdom. It was Laney's own, and nothing else in the house could compare. Outside it was windy and snowing but in here, in this ark of a room, with two space heaters plugged in, it was warm, cozy, inviting. Arlene would have liked to sleep here herself. Would have liked to crawl under the heavy quilted covers with her daughter, her dearest, prettiest daughter, and sleep, and let the snow blow against the window all night, and never think about getting up.

"Well," she said slowly. "Well. . . . Is it awful for you, honey, to be poor?"

"What? Why do you say *that?*"

"I don't know," Arlene said, almost embarrassed. "It just came to me. . . . But is it bad for you, does it bother you?"

"We're not poor," Laney said. She had been scratching at her head and she looked disheveled. "We get along all right. Next year I can get a job, we'll have more money. We're not poor *now*. Vale might get a better job, he said something about a training school or night school, going to college, and he'll send money, and . . . and . . . We're not as poor as some people, are we? We get along all right."

"I was thinking, the other girls at school, some of them, you know, their fathers have good jobs . . . you know, it might be . . . I was thinking you might be embarrassed or ashamed or . . ."

"I'm not ashamed of anything," Laney said flatly.

"Yes, you've always been so sweet, you've always been my good girl," Arlene said in a queer, pleading voice.

Then she stopped. She must bring up the subject of that man, Kasch, that man Laney was rumored to be seeing, she must return to that subject and yet she dreaded it, dreaded losing her girl again. ". . . so easy to get along with most of the time, I know it's hard, so many kids and you and Nancy stuck with a lot of the work, and Vale gone, and your father dead, and Grandpa so weak now . . . needs looking after. . . . And I know, I know you've been worrying about me, I know. . . . And. . . ."

She faltered and was silent

In the old mirror she caught a reassuring glimpse of herself: the bruise was gone now, she was pretty again, and normal-looking, except for the scar in her eyebrow and forehead, which could be disguised easily enough with eyebrow pencil and bangs brushed low.

"This man," Laney said carefully, "this man somebody told you about . . . he offers me money, but I don't take it. He offers to buy me things but I tell him no."

Arlene stared at her helplessly.

". . . I always tell him no, Momma, I don't want anything like that from him. He's a friend of mine, Momma, just a friend. I mean that—just a friend."

"A friend . . . ?"

"A *friend.*"

"Laney, a man that old? And you? It's . . . it's not right."

She sat on the edge of the bed, suddenly exhausted.

Laney leaned over to pick up the book from the floor; she handed it to her mother. "He's strange, he's very sweet . . . he talks to me for hours, and I talk to him. . . . I can't explain. He's just a friend. There's nobody like him. Grown-up people don't talk like him, I don't have any, you know, any friends who are adults, it's very . . . it's very strange, I can't explain," she said, laughing nervously, "sometimes he scares me and at other times he, he's just . . . he's just so funny. . . . That book is his; he lends me books."

Arlene opened the book at once and leafed through it.

". . . Just a friend, isn't married, doesn't have any family . . . lives alone . . . is very kind . . . Offers me money but I. . . . Momma, I hate being questioned and *thought* about, I hate people talking, just you don't listen . . . don't believe them. You always tell me, Momma, don't you, not to believe what I hear? So I don't. I don't. Now you owe me that too, Momma," she said softly. "I have a right to my own life."

"I thought this was a schoolbook," Arlene said. "I thought . . . thought you were doing homework."

"It's just a *book,* Momma. You look so white!"

Arlene turned pages and came to a passage marked in blue ink and read, her lips moving silently—

. . . I only know myself as a human entity; the scene, so to speak, of thoughts and affections; and am sensible of a certain doubleness by which I can stand as remote from myself as from another. However intense my experience, I am conscious of the presence of and criticism of a part of me, which, as it were, is not a part of me, but spectator, sharing no experience, but taking note of it; and that is no more I than it is you. When the play, it may be the tragedy, of life is over, the spectator goes his way. It was a kind of fiction, a work of the imagination only. . . .

Arlene reread the passage, frowning. She was angry. She was baffled, as if the words were meant to deceive her, sly and insulting. What did it mean! All those fancy words!

"What *is* this," she muttered.

"Momma, it's just a *book.*"

"It sounds crazy. . . ."

She tried to read the passage again but lost the meaning almost at once. She turned to another page, began another paragraph; but with Laney watching her, and her own feelings in such a turmoil, she couldn't concentrate. Such crazy complicated sentences! She closed the book and handed it back to Laney, who took it from her in silence, and their eyes brushed each other, and in that instant Arlene felt that she would never be young again: not only would Laney outlive her, and live a life she could not control, but Laney was already grown from her, slipped far from her, beyond Childwold. Her own daughter! She was reading this book, which was only a jumble of words to Arlene, and she treasured it, and Arlene could not follow her into it—could not understand, could not share. She

93

was angry. She was hurt. She saw Laney as a stranger might see her, and now she really began to cry.

"Momma, what's wrong? Oh Momma. . . . Momma, hey," Laney said, laughing, crawling over to her, "Momma, what *is* it? He's just a friend, I told you he's just a friend. I don't love him, it isn't like that, anything like *that*. . . . Don't you believe me? Momma, you're such a baby!"

"You'll have to bring him to the house," Arlene sobbed.

"Bring him to the house! My God!"

"Some Sunday, or at Christmas. . . . Unless you're ashamed of us."

"I'm never going to bring him here," Laney laughed. "Momma, where do you get your crazy ideas? Oh Momma," Laney said, her voice shrill, as if she too were going to cry, "please don't cry, hey, why are you crying? . . . I don't love him. I never will love *him*."

But she did cry, she couldn't help herself, and later that night, after eleven o'clock, already in her nightgown and robe, she went to the telephone and picked up the receiver, still red-eyed and still feeling bad, wondering who would be telephoning at that hour: and it was Earl.

The shock of his voice was so great, she didn't understand at first that he was calling from out of state, from Chicago. From a pay phone at the airport. He was on his way home, he said, and wanted to hear her voice and ask about things, and—was she there? could she hear? was the connection any good? She barely whispered yes. She held the receiver hard against her ear and shut her eyes. "Hello? Arlene? Honey? —You know I never meant no harm, honey. You know that. I wouldn't hurt you. I wouldn't hurt a woman. I don't hit women—I don't. I'm not that type. The type of man that does that—it's a criminal type, a depraved type. I got carried away. You know that. Can you hear me? Hon? I always treated you good, didn't I? Then there was that misunderstanding, but I'll make it up to you, I want to see you right away— soon as I get back— You know I never meant no harm, Arlene, don't you?"

She held the phone clutched tight, must have been

standing in a strange posture, her head bent; one of the smaller children came by, saw her and grabbed her leg and began whimpering. Momma, Momma? Who is it? Earl was talking quickly, his voice came loud and clear across the windy snowy miles, Arlene could not interrupt or put the receiver back, she stood there listening, stricken, "You *know* I never meant a thing," the voice said, "and I'm cutting down on the drinking—been thinking of you, hon, thinking of you all along—wanted to call before but just couldn't—I swear to God I never meant to hurt you—I wouldn't ever hurt you—don't hurt women—a man that even touches a woman, why, even if he's been drinking— why, a man like that—I just—You aren't mad at me, honey, are you? Mad at Earl? You know I always treated you first-rate, didn't I, there was never any complaint, there was just that one time—lost my temper, was working so hard that week—didn't always tell you the pressures on me, hon, so many goddam things to think of—payrolls to meet—you wouldn't understand how it is, Arlene. Look: I want to make it up to you. I'm going to make it up to you. Been staying with my brother out West, been thinking things over, and—well—let's get together first thing I'm back and settled—hon, are you still there? are you listening? I got a lot to make up to you, I know—"

"No," Arlene said. *"No."*

"What? —The thing is, we got to see each other in person; it's no good over the phone like this. I been thinking a lot about you, hon, and I sure am sorry—you must know I'm sorry—you know *me*. Look: there isn't anybody else, is there? There isn't anybody else? He'll have to talk with me too, if there is, you know what I'm like—I take these things seriously—I'm a serious man, honey, you *know* I am. Is there anybody else?"

"No. —But I don't want to see you," Arlene said.

"Hon, in a day or two I'll call—we can talk it over— we'll feel a lot better—"

"No!" Arlene said.

She hung up.

She waited for the phone to ring again, but it didn't ring: she carried the child back to bed and went to bed herself. But she couldn't sleep.

No, no you don't, she thought bitterly, greedily: no, none of you, never.

The fish head, the tail and the bone, broken, and fat salt pork, cooking slowly in the large kettle; and onion and potatoes and scalded milk; and crackers; and butter. Salt and pepper, of course. Don't boil! Stand over it with the big wooden spoon and don't let it come to a boil! . . . Here, taste it. Here. Is it too hot? Does it need more salt? Pepper?

Where is the ice-cream freezer? You crank it by hand, slowly; then, as the ice cream stiffens, you crank it faster and faster. Rock salt: the more salt, the faster the ice cream will freeze. But it won't taste as smooth. Take a quart of cream and scald it. Then you want sugar and a pinch of salt. Then you chill it and add some grated vanilla bean . . . or a tablespoon of vanilla if you don't have the real thing. Then you pour it into the freezer can and get going. No, it isn't too much trouble! It isn't. It isn't any trouble at all. That ice cream you buy in town, in the paper containers, that's just trash food . . . you shouldn't buy that for the children, you shouldn't. It's no trouble at all to make the ice cream my way. But where is the freezer? I can't find it in any of the cupboards . . . even on the highest shelf, where the old kettles and iron frying pans are, and the popcorn popper you got with those stamps, I can't find it. Where is it? Why is it gone?

Thick pieces of whole wheat bread, broken from the loaf by hand. A honeycomb, dripping liquid honey. Tiny link sausages. Eggs scrambled in butter. Pancakes with grape jelly, preserves made from the grapes out back of the house, along the lane. Big round waxy-looking damp-looking purple grapes! Burst one against the top of your mouth: isn't it delicious? And coffee, freshly brewed. And sugar and cream, our own cream, fresh this morning. And butter: spread thick on the pancakes. Blueberries sprinkled with powdered sugar . . . a few peaches, cut in quarters . . . a bowl of strawberries and cream, or is the strawberry season past? If the peaches are ripe then the strawberries must be past. Yes, their season must be past.

At harvest time it's important that everyone should be well fed.

We can seat fifteen at this table if necessary.

In 1927, that was the biggest harvest of all; we had fifteen hands then. Even Anna was working, in the morning when it wasn't so hot. Wanted to. I didn't force her.

Lemonade with ice. Iced tea as well. Coffee with a spoonful of ice cream in it. Delicious. . . . But it's cold now, it's very cold now, isn't it? I can hear the wind. There's cold air rising from the floorboards, these old floorboards, the linoleum doesn't do much good. All the roofs need repair. The barns especially. They're swaybacked as old doddering mules. Last summer there was moss on the old cow barn; and trumpet vine growing like crazy. Sunflowers and hollyhocks moving right in, and morning glories—them tiny white ones—and saplings all over. And briers. Maybe I will clear the place. Around the house anyway. Tomorrow I can shovel a little, Ronnie and me. It's good to keep active. Long as I have them fur-lined gloves, and the hat with the ear flaps Arlenie gave me, and overshoes, I don't mind the cold. In fact I like it. Always did. Ten degrees below zero it was one January, and with the wind blowing hard they said over the radio it was really forty below—which might be an exaggeration, eh?—and I walked to town and back just for the hell of it. . . . No, I guess we needed something at Wit's. I guess Anna was grumbling and so I got dressed and went out and bought it, and that shut her up. For a while.

Anna's hands: the fingers slightly squarish, the nails filed short and blunt. As big as my hands, they were. Her feet, though, were smaller than mine. She got up when I did though there was no need—could have slept till I got back from the chores—but she never liked to lie in bed. Quick, deft movements, almost brusque, surprising in a woman of her size. Even when she was pregnant—setting the table so fast, one two three four!—and half-a-dozen things cooking on the stove or in the oven—and me and the kids in her way—but she was fast, always silent when she was in the kitchen, never talked much or smiled if I joked. Didn't like my jokes, said I got in the way, only one

97

cook at a time, please; if you're going to make up fish chowder be sure the guts are well wrapped up and out at the dump, don't you leave that mess for me to clean up, don't you dare! In silence she set the breakfast things on the table. Now we were all there. The boys and me. Mason, the hired man. Anna and Carrie made breakfast and served it and cleared the dishes, and had their breakfast when we left for the fields. Sometimes I skimmed through *Farm and Home Bureau Reports*. . . . Weather forecasts, tables and graphs showing the rainfall, the inches of snow, statistics for this year and a year ago and ten years ago. Full-page advertisements: tractors, combines, milkers, threshers, fertilizers, feeds, sprays and spray equipment, pickup trucks, shotguns and rifles and fishing gear. At the table John and Herman and George and little Matthew, dripping grease onto his lap, and Anna poking him —mind your manners, you ain't a pickaninny! Carrie at the sink, in overalls like her brothers'. My other daughter, my favorite—where?—Arlene, where?

Ran away to get married. Fifteen years old.

Said she wasn't pregnant and she *wasn't*. Her and Lyle, they were in love. Lyle Bartlett. A twenty-six-year-old, his family half in the country and half in town, pulling out of the country, farm getting run-down, ugly sight to see. . . . No, wait. No. That's wrong.

No.

Not born yet.

She isn't born yet.

She isn't going to be born!

Anna's face composed, closed; looks at me the way she looks at the boys; waiting for us to eat and leave. Then she'll clear our places. Then she'll wash the dishes.

I can cast the net out again and again . . . I cast it out and haul it in and . . . and there she is, my Anna, scrubbing the oilcloth on the kitchen table, and even scrubbing the chairs, where the smaller boys dropped food.

Anna!

The last-born will be a girl. I know. I insist.

Prices are bad this year. The decade has gone wrong. There was good weather last year but the market was bad —might as well dump everything in the river. Washington,

98

D.C. Economics. Work for fourteen hours a day, work like slaves, like niggers, and see what difference it makes. The Bartletts going broke, that good land up for sale and nobody buying, nobody with money to buy. One hundred acres of mine sold: thank God there was a buyer. Shame, such a shame. But I will buy it back as soon as the economy improves. In the newspaper it was predicted. . . . In the *Farm Bureau* report it was predicted. . . .

The lettuce crop: that was our subject.

Anna, it was nobody's fault!

In New York City, in 1929, there were men who blew their brains out, rich important clever men, there were men who jumped out of buildings and killed themselves!—so how can you blame me, how is it my fault?

Old woman, go to hell! Go back to hell where you came from!

Cruel, very cruel. The lettuce. A freak thing to happen, though I'd heard from my uncle Lenehan about it happening once before. Did I ever tell you about it? . . . In 1934, it was. The worst year of all. Them acres along the river, planted in lettuce, prospering, a delight to the eye: and what happened but a thunderstorm come along one morning before dawn, before I was even up and dressed. Icy pelting rain, a full hour of it and more, and terrible lightning. Thunder so loud it went right through my poor skull. And then. . . . Did I tell you this? And then the rain stopped and the clouds blew away and the sun beat down, so hard it was like the equator, I swear, the sun beating down like crazy, Jesus God, I could feel it through my straw hat like spikes being driven in, and I knew what would happen and I ran out there through the puddles and just watched. . . . And the lettuce was cooked right in the ground, the heads burst open from the heat! Yes! The worst thing that could happen happened and I knew it would happen, because my poor dead uncle told me, and I just hung around and watched and was moaning aloud and practically sick from sunstroke myself. Jesus! Fields and fields of it. My beautiful lettuce. Cooked and burst and afterward rotted. Rotted.

But it wasn't my fault, was it?

Nuala. Anna. The brusque impatient movements, the

99

heat and comfort of the kitchen, the smell of scalded milk, the stained white apron. There was a wood-burning stove. It's gone now. It's stored back in one of the barns, last I knew. There was a pile of chopped wood, quite a high pile, and another out in the shed. Watch out for spiders! —Used to scare the baby, Big Eyes, pretending the spiders were going to get her and tickle her. More wood, out in the shed.

Nuala: forgotten. Dead. Father and mother dead in the west of Ireland and who's to care, to mourn? Not me. Not Joseph Hurley. Cast out onto the Atlantic, given away like a pauper's child, an orphan, a foundling. Youngest of twelve. Who's to care? No religion for me, thank you. No priests. No taxes and special collections, no monasteries and missions and convents to support, no thank you, no building funds, no prayerbooks, rosaries, Masses in honor of the dead, no holy days of obligation, no stations of the cross, no holy water, no blessing of the throat, no blessing of the house, no baptism for my babies, no first communions, confirmations . . . no extreme unction. And no purgatory. And no hell. No! None of that.

My philosophy is: this is the New World.

This is the New World, eh? You can feel it in your bones. Soon as you land on this side. There's different weather, different winds. Snow heaped up twelve feet. A hundred degrees in August sometimes. Mountains are taller here, capped with snow. The new is new, the old is old. I hated the old. Yes I did. Even before the War I said my good-by to it, I wasn't never going back. They wanted me to—I think. Wanted me to send money, anyway. Had plans to ship someone else over, my sister and her husband and her children, no thank you, nope, none of that. Never answered that letter and never regretted it.

I wasn't born here in America but I am an American in my bones.

You breathe it in, the air of the New World. Not the cities—I don't mean them. I mean the country. I mean *here*. You buy your own land, you clear your debts, you're *here*, where you belong. No religion here: just land. Fields and woods and mountains and rivers and lakes. Good rich soil. Did I tell you how big the farm was when I bought up the McInnis land . . . ? Yes. Two hundred and fifty acres. From the river down to Marsena, that was the Hurley farm, Hurley & Sons I planned to call it: going to have a sign painted on the hay barn, Hurley & Sons in big white letters. Or maybe red, I couldn't decide. And a new roof for the barn. And a new floor, concrete, for the cow barn. . . . But there was the trouble, nobody buying produce, and milk going sour, and fruit rotting, and strikes in the cities, and hunger marches, and the National Guard, and talk of war here at home . . . and one hundred acres were lost . . . and then the lettuce, and bad prices for the wheat; and Anna blaming me. She knew better but she couldn't help herself.

Once I came up behind her in the barn, she was bent over looking in the hay, looking for a chicken's nest—the chicken wanted to have chicks, wouldn't lay her eggs in the coop—and I put my hands on her waist and she started and cried out, surprised, and afterward blamed me: couldn't help herself, she said, crying, it just wasn't her way of life, her or her family's, to take things the way I did. Singing when I worked, figuring out pranks and practical jokes—like for April Fool's Day when I pretended there was a green lizard on Carrie's back—or hid the salt shaker—or rode over to the schoolhouse to tell the teacher the President of the United States was coming to Childwold and school was out for the day—just nonsense that I am ashamed of now: that wasn't her way at all. Firecrackers on July Fourth, or driving to Yewville to the movies or to Port Oriskany for a big boat show: not her way at all. There was one Joseph who was her husband, the Joseph she married and was proud of—in the company of her sisters, anyway, since she could lord it over them; that was the Joseph she loved. Then there was the other Joseph, the one she ran from, or was afraid of, or nagged, or fed in silence . . . the one she kept fighting and blaming. "Joseph" she called the one, like it was a name that belonged in the Bible. The other one she didn't call by any name at all—never "honey" or "dear" the way I heard other wives sometimes talking to her husbands, or my
101

own children when they got married. Ah, old woman! Always old! Old at the age of thirty! Joseph this, Joseph that.

Joseph, *no*.

No no no no no.

He's the one to blame.

Blame. Shame. Someone's to blame. A shame. Shame! —Who spilled this? Who made this mess? There were fish guts in the sink, rock bass guts and tails and heads. Who's to blame? Flies. The hole in the screen door. Should be repaired; the screen replaced. Hardware store. Witter's. No: they said Witter's was closed. Boarded up. A new place, then. Sometime. No hurry.

She blamed him, Anna did. Heavy-footed about the house, good with the stock, could pitch hay like a man; very good with the chickens. Hers. Laying hens, dozens of eggs, gray-and-white speckled hens, Rhode Island reds, white hens clucking and picking in the dirt, running free. Shallow depressions in the dust. Beds. A shame, the sicknesses on a farm. Someone's to blame. She went to church with the children and one by one they dropped away, sided with their father and wouldn't go; a lot of nonsense, it was, and he told them so, told the minister himself so one famous day, all that gibberish and singing and moaning and begging for favors—*that* was the shame of it, he declared, not his own attitude. If she wanted someone to blame, he shouted at her, why not blame her precious Christ?—and God the Father?—and what's-his-name, the Holy Ghost? And leave him alone.

She said it was his fault—his greed. His piggishness. Drunk and climbing all over her and not listening to her, and then it was too late, and she was pregnant again, and hadn't the doctor told them, warned them? But old Joseph didn't care, did he?—a pig, a besotted pig, manure on his boots and the cuffs of his trousers and beneath his fingernails, he mumbled bleary-eyed and apologetic but of course he didn't care, how could he?—just an animal, like all men. The doctor had warned her about her heart and when she had wept and said, But what can I do, what can we do, he snapped—Do what other people do! Your husband knows very well. And he did, he did. It was
102

only that one time, returning late from the Childwold Fireman's Picnic, a little high-spirited, singing, only that one time, and maybe another time when he'd forgotten . . . but she hadn't stopped him either, had she? Blame! Shame! If anything went wrong, if lightning struck the old dead elm that had been struck a dozen times already, up there above the river, why, the old woman would blame someone; would cast her eyes about to find someone to blame. . . . But she wasn't old, not always. Had been young. As young as he. Lustrous black hair, big breasts, hips, thighs, rather quiet, stubbornly shy, a bad habit at first of speaking so softly he couldn't hear her—but of course she was just a girl, his bride. Didn't know any better. Didn't know about men. He frightened her, he was so quick and coarse and jubilant, but she didn't start to blame him until much later, years later.

Go away, old woman—back to hell where you came from—

He drank because of his arthritis. And his eyes—they ached. The doctor had said they'd be all right after the operation. But they weren't all right. He knew. Pain pain pain. The incredible stabbing pains in his chest. The burst of light, lights. Where had he been? Safe in his home, at the kitchen table. What if—out in the fields? Deadly sun, heatstroke, death by dehydration. The poor Donner boy, what was his name, collapsed during threshing season, face flushed, chest heaving; they had poured water over him but he hadn't revived—boy in his late teens, a pity, a mystery, dying in a few hours like that, no warning, and his parents grief-stricken the rest of their lives: who was to blame, to blame? She blamed him about John. John running off, John enlisting in the Navy. But he couldn't tolerate the boy's fresh mouth. Sass. Set his teeth on edge, the boy's mocking smile after he'd been struck, that cringing doggish look to him, who's to blame for him, who's to blame he ran away? Never did his share of the work, though he was the oldest boy.

Nuala. Anna. Pearl. Arlene.

—His favorite child, did she know she was his favorite, his pretty one, his Big Eyes, his kitten? Did she know he had had to struggle for her, wading thigh-deep in his wife's hatred? Another girl, another daughter; it was time; he chattered and she told him to hush, in front of family she told him to hush, she was deeply embarrassed and angry, and when they were alone she wept and would have struck him, except he caught her wrists. Many nights she had him sleep in John's old bedroom. Herself, she went upstairs early, alone, while he listened to the radio and read the paper or magazines, or played gin rummy with his sons and Carrie, and he thought about the farm, the stock and the crops and the trucking problems and the rainfall, he thought about how much he'd accomplished, and then of how—of how it had been taken from him: since the twenties the nation had gone bad, it would never recover, he would never recover what he had lost: so he wanted a baby girl, a daughter. He wanted a baby girl. He didn't know why.

Upstairs her footsteps were heavy. She was heavy. Breasts, belly, thighs. Her face dragged downward. He played cards with his children, sometimes played Chinese checkers and Parcheesi, and he listened to her overhead, and never spoke of her—shrugged his shoulders and kept his expression quiet—she was his wife, after all. They should not have married, he shouldn't have married *her;* but she was his wife. . . . He crouched above her, his fingers gripping her bare shoulders. How she fought! Her face distorted, pale, wet. Groaning, she was, like an animal in its death agony, such a struggle, such grunting and heaving, his hands slipped away, could not keep their position. Her enormous pale chunky thighs parted—my hands could not keep their desperate grip—it was Joseph there panting, grunting—it was I—the woman's thighs parting, the vagina opening raw, red, glistening wet—a second face, it was, a second mouth, blood-smeared, racked. It was alive, it was in agony! Joseph stared. I stared. The patch of baby skull appeared suddenly, behind the sticky threads of blood. Oh! I clutched my hands to my mouth, astonished. Oh! God! God help, God don't let, God please be with us. . . . I pressed my hands to my mouth, not wanting to scream. I would not scream. Would not. The woman clawed and bucked and groaned and
104

panted like an animal, her head turning from side to side. The pillow had worked its way out, had fallen onto the floor. Should they tie her legs to the bedposts? Legs and arms? No, she would break the posts. Tremendous strength in her! The creaking of the bed, the creaking of the floorboards. There was the stink of a body, and of blood. Sweat-soaked sheets. Push! they cried to the woman. Push! Push! Yes! Now! Now! He's coming! He wants to be born! He's struggling to be born! Look at him —look at him—he wants to be born, he can't be stopped— Joseph's eyes rolled with panic and went dark, blind. He began to scream. There were lights, filmy lights, but he was blind; he could not see. He gave in and began to scream. Once started, he could not stop. Screamed and screamed and screamed. Oh! He was afraid, in mortal terror! And so angry! So angry!

He screamed and was born.

Sweet red wine. Sugary-sweet. Went right to your head so you had to cut your eleven-o'clock class. They walked you in the corridor, your friends, you were all giggling in spite of the danger, and there was Mr. Hogan himself, looked you full in the face and *knew* . . . but kept on walking, walked right past. The Yewville teachers want no trouble this year! No trouble this year! . . . Last spring one of the men teachers was beaten up in the parking lot, nobody knew who did it, nobody was telling. He hadn't come back this year; they said he and his family had moved away.

Nobody wants any trouble.

. . . Couldn't stop giggling, it was so funny. Everything was funny. Tommy Redding's girl friend took you to the first-floor john. Silly Laney. Silly face in the mirror. Shouldn't drink, she said, if you can't take it. . . . You told her you hadn't had much, anyway it was Tommy's fault. His locker was right next to yours and he kept a bottle there in a paper bag, and was always fooling around. It wasn't your fault. Why didn't she go to hell then? It wasn't your fault.

She ran water and soaked some paper towels and tried

to wash your face with them. Water ran down your neck, tickling. You couldn't help laughing.

You're going to get us all in trouble, she said.

Oh shit.

Two senior girls came in. Gave both of you dirty looks in the mirror. Girls from Yewville, bitches, think they're so superior. Bitches. Better stay out of our way. . . . They're afraid of kids from the country, afraid of farm kids. They hate you. Think you're just trash, just dirt. Think they're so superior.

Who the hell are you looking at? you asked them. You mind your own business—go on out of here and mind your own goddam business—

Laney, stop!

They'd better be afraid. They'd better. There was Vale, years ago. People still talked about him, didn't they, Vale Bartlett, and your cousin Amos Hurley, that knife fight at a graduation party a few years back; self-defense, the jury said. Self-defense. There was a jury, a trial, a judge. It was in the newspapers. People better stay out of your way, better not look down their noses at you, better not make up lies. . . . Suddenly you didn't feel well. One moment you were laughing and the next moment you didn't feel well. Something was wrong, something was going to happen. There was Kasch, but it wouldn't be his fault, Kasch wasn't to blame. No. Earl climbing in the window at night, up the vines and into the window, to strangle you . . . ? No. No. That was just a silly dream, a nightmare. You wouldn't have to kill him. It wouldn't happen. It would never happen, never. God wouldn't let it. . . . There was Momma lying on the sofa, her face still bleeding. A bubbly catch in her throat. Asleep. Drunk. Sick. She stank of liquor and vomit, her dress was ripped, the front of her brassiere showed and it was stained with blood. Momma, how could you let it happen! How could it happen! She had ironed that dress just the other day, you'd been in the kitchen with her, talking. Talking about nothing important. The kitchen was warm and nice, the nicest room downstairs, and Momma was ironing the dress carefully, her favorite dress, she sprinkled water on
106

it from the Coke bottle you'd painted bright red years ago at the Childwold grammar school, to give to her as a Christmas present; all the little girls and boys made their mothers sprinkling bottles, outfitted with corks, for Christmas. The two of you had talked and laughed together . . . about what? . . . what? Outside it was raining and you saw one of the cats, the tortoiseshell, the stray that had turned up one morning years ago and had been taken in, flea-ridden, one ear badly mutilated, you saw him in the garden in the rain, just sitting on his haunches in the tomato vines, and you called your mother's attention to it, and the two of you stared, amazed, wasn't it unnatural for a cat to stay out in the rain, even an odd battered cat like that . . . ? You laughed together, you laughed.

It wore off and you felt suddenly tired, though it wasn't even noon yet, the school day stretched out before you and had no end you could hope for; it came to an end, the fit of laughter, your cheeks and jaws ached from the violence of it. No, you would kill him first. You weren't afraid. Standing on the porch, the boards splintery and hard beneath your feet, no, you weren't afraid, no one in your family was afraid, people had better watch out for you. You knew how to use a rifle: you had hunted a few times with the boys. You had killed. You knew how to kill. It was easy enough if you didn't flinch and didn't investigate afterward; let someone else investigate, not you, your stomach would turn at the sight, you weren't afraid but you would rather not go hunting, you hated to hear Grandpa talking about the old days, the old hunts, skinning and gutting deer—you hated to see the remains of fish down at the river, carp and perch the boys didn't care to take home, and sometimes bullfrogs they had cruelly smashed on the rocks, and sometimes turtles, as if these creatures had insulted them in some way and must be punished. It made you dizzy, to think of how cruelly these creatures had been punished, and would be. No.

On your knees in the lavatory, forehead pressed against the porcelain sink. It was cold, it was hard and cold. No matter that the floor was dirty, you didn't care, you had to press your forehead against the sink, it was so cold,

107

hard, so good, my God it was good, Tommy's girl friend was trying to pull you to your feet but you pushed her away. You shut your eyes tight, you felt your face pucker like a baby's.

Please God don't let, don't let it happen, God, please, help us, don't, don't let. . . .

# Three

THE children dart into corners, into shadows; hide-and-seek in the deep crevices; your lips move in prayer, in play. Caught you! There you are! One of the children stares at you, her underlip caught in her teeth. You would plunge forward to kneel at her feet, you would stagger, you would cry aloud with joy—

Angels, demons.

Cannot see them clearly.

They sing, ringing me in, prayerful playful voices, all I can know of them is their voices, their high cooing exquisite litany:

*Childwold*
　　*Childwald*
　　　　*Childweald*
　　　　　　*Childweld*
　　　　　　　　*Childwild*
　　　　　　　　　　*Childwood*
　　　　　　　　　　　　*Childword*
　　　　　　　　　　　　　*Childworld*
　　　　　　　　　　　　　　*Childhold*
　　　　　　　　　　　　　　　*Childmold*
　　　　　　　　　　　　　　　　*Childtold*
　　　　　　　　　　　　　　　　　*Childcold*
　　　　　　　　　　　　　　　　　　*Childchill*
　　　　　　　　　　　　　　　　　*Chillwould*
　　　　　　　　　　　　　　　　*Choldwild*
　　　　　　　　　　　　　　　*Chilword*
　　　　　　　　　　　　　　*Chillwild*
　　　　　　　　　　　　*Wildwold*
　　　　　　　　　　　*Wildhold*

                    *Woldhold*
                  *Willchold*
                *Willword*
              *Willworld*
            *Willwould*
          *Willwold*
            *Wildchill*
              *Worldchild*
                *Worldchild*
                  *Worldwild*
                    *Wold*

                              *Chide*

                                    *Choose.*

---

In the beginning is the Word.

No things but in words, through words!—no-thing, nothing, that is not first breathed.

Many-worded, many-breathed Kasch, childless son of Kasch.

Laney, do you doubt me? If you doubt me you will cease to exist!

---

In her cramped little room high in this house I wept, I weep. She stepped out of my embrace. Steps. I clutch at her, I clutched at her and wept.

How could she doubt me!

What revenge I will take upon her!

No, I was not cruel. I was kind, cavalier, undisturbed, a model of serenity. Brahma, playing hide-and-seek with Himself in the universe, could not have been more impishly serene.

For example, I contemplated at some length the antique doll on her bureau, with its glazed moronic-blue eyes; I touched its frail, brittle, aged lace, its tiny veil. Lovely! I examined the cheap beaverboard walls and the photographs and the drawings taped on the walls, I took note of the Valentines, the Christmas cards, the birthday cards, the numerous snapshots; I examined the little pillows, some round, some rectangular, some glossy, some with small cheap buttons. The floral designs that clashed, the stripes and polka dots, the gay brave splashes of dime-store color did not escape my attention. I fingered the needlepoint cover on the rocking chair's cushion. So much, so pitifully much! I stroked the quilt that lay on the bed. I drew the curtain aside to examine the clothes hanging behind it on a wooden rail: a fair amount of items, though none of them very attractive. This is poverty, Kasch. This is poverty, my friends. The odor of, the feel of, the spirit of. And yet—

Yet—

That rectangle of light, a surprise, a sliver piercing my vision—yes?—what is it?—only the reflection of a window in the bureau mirror. I walked into it, into its wide glare. Its surprise. No Kasch, no peering self-conscious befuddled face in that mirror.

The sky faintly blue, faintly gray. The sky of one's soul. Leaves. A hilly field. Trees, hills, mountains. It was summer then, I smelled the acrid, abrasive odors of summer heat. My head felt heavy, my nostrils itched. No: it was not summer. It was winter. The sky swirled whitely, the wind rattled a branch against the roof, I could feel cold air edging in around the window frame, though some rags had been stuffed in place. Cold, so cold! They bragged of the mad cracking cold and the three-day blizzards in the hills. Cold, childcold, worldcold, worldwill, would. She kneels on her bed and looks out this window, into this patch of the world, I thought, greatly moved, for some reason pressing my hand against my breast as if to appease my heart. She stares, she dreams, she lives.

There were the photographs, the snapshots. Filled with people. Overfull. Souls, faces. Families. Children. I was not equal to them, I was not equal to her. Snapshots of children smiling. Adults and babies, babies in the arms of women, in the arms of children, smiling, spread out bravely smiling for the camera. I love. I want. I don't understand. These are the people who have children, I thought, who populate the world. I stared, stared. I touched an old sepia-colored photograph but it was useless, useless to touch it—what could I gain? These are the people. These.

The old mirror showed a glaring rectangle of light from

the window. It did not reflect my anxious face. I stooped,
I blinked, I was invisible. The mirror was adjusted for a
much shorter person. I touched it, turned it. The light
leaped up, the light framed by the window. I passed my
hand over the mirror like a magician and the girl appeared,
standing with her arms crossed, uneasy, restless, frowning.

So lovely here! Lovely.

Couldn't we—? Couldn't I—?

In the mirror her profile appeared delicate, the small
nose slightly upturned, the curls falling languidly over the
forehead. I was careful not to make any sudden movements. I recalled a painting studied many years ago, in
Italy, I think—a nineteenth-century face, ringlets, fair
inward-gazing eyes, the girl leaning out an opened window and—improbably?—a burst of light behind her,
framing her, haloing her delicate head . . . a painting in
an oval frame. I made no sudden movements. Desperation
had cultivated my cunning. In the painting the girl gazed
at me, toward me, into me, through me, because of me,
a near-vaporous glow of beauty, great staring blind-
looking lustrous eyes. She was leaning out the window,
one arm extended, the palm of the hand turned up, fingers
stretched toward the viewer. I wanted to press forward,
I wanted to touch my fingertips against hers—

End of the year approaching. Winter solstice approaching.

One leaps at life, one invents wildly. When I turned to
her she stood flat-footed, arms crossed, watching me with
that cool gray assessing look of hers. Small breasts prominent. A cheap Orlon sweater, dark blue, and the usual
blue jeans, faded and soiled. Nostrils pink-rimmed; a bad
cold. Lips refusing to turn up in a smile though I smiled
with love.

I will transform her: I will invent her.

I will write about her with devotion, abstracting from
her certain qualities I find poignant and eliminating others
I find vulgar. There is the undeniable beauty, the premature cynicism, the slight, boyish body that could become
merely lean, merely tough, in a few years. But she is too
strong-willed. She is too cruel. She smokes, she drinks,

113

she strides along the sidewalks of Yewville with the others, sometimes she links arms with one or two of them, she is crude, she is vulgar, she is doomed. The cheap pretensions of this carnival of a room, this tiny desperate kingdom, are moving enough—but perhaps comic; perhaps she deserves to be merely pitied. I will emphasize her loneliness, her isolation. Her sensitivity. The dead father, the slatternly mother, the household of children, the stink of poverty, the fecund brainless terrifying countryside, beauty as accidental here as ugliness. I will make her less attractive but less hard. I will soften her by breaking something in her—that cautious, lidded gaze. Weaken her eyes, perhaps. Like my own. I am jealous of people with perfect vision—why should I not be jealous, why should I be ashamed of my jealousy? Her eyes weak, weakened by scarlet fever in her early girlhood, six long weeks of near-death, her heart weakened also, and she is constantly aware of . . . aware of death. Or I could make her eyes slightly crossed. Very, very slightly. So that one could hardly tell, though one would, of course, sense something not quite right in her gaze. Lovely! Lovely. . . . Or she might have broken her leg very badly some years ago, a fall from a horse, the poor bone beneath the knee broken in four distinct places and never mending right, so that she limped, could not help limping no matter how she tried to disguise it, and in damp cold weather the leg ached dully with pain. . . .

No. She turned, got the item she'd come up here for, and was about to leave.

So lovely here, so lovely, couldn't we—? Could I lie with you on that bed, on top of the quilt, dear, could I hold you in my arms for a few seconds, for less than a minute, could I, could we, out of our vast lifetimes, could we not find time for—?

A flame of desire, of curiosity so intense it is physical. I must *know* her. Must see her naked, must penetrate her tight, stubborn body, her stubborn brain. Must know her completely, from the inside. That first glimpse of her on the riverbank, her hands pressed over her face, terrified, so vulnerable—and on the city streets, when I am hidden,

114

invisible to her, spying on her, floating in the air about her—

I wouldn't hurt you, Laney, I said softly.

You're not going to get a chance to, she said, unsmiling.

Earl telephoned again and came to the house, and Arlene and some of the children hid in the cellar, that ugly dark dungeon of a place, like a cave, it was, with an earthen floor, an evil-smelling cistern, an old oil furnace, and boxes and cartons and toys strewn about; the only decent room was the one directly beneath the stairs, where the walls were hidden by shelves of canned fruit in identical jars, and the shelves had been carefully lined—years ago, it was true—with oilcloth. But they did not dare stay in that room, it was too near the door; they crept to the farthest corner of the cellar, following the weak beam of Arlene's flashlight. Not all the children were with her: Ronnie was out, Davy was out, June was spending the day at Carrie's, where there was a girl cousin her own age, Laney was in Yewville, Nancy upstairs dealing with Earl. She told him he wasn't welcome, stood at the door and refused to let him in, refused to accept a heavy poinsettia plant he had brought for Arlene and that, finally, he left on the porch after Nancy closed the door on him. Earl Tuller! Ruddy-faced, larger than anyone remembered, in a camel's-hair overcoat, his thick dark tufted hair fringed with snowflakes, his eyes squinting and watery as if with utter, profound bewilderment. Where was Arlene? Why did she hang up the telephone when he called? What was wrong? He was sorry—sorry—God knows he was sorry—what more could he say, what more could he do except apologize and ask to be forgiven? He struck himself on the breast, on the thick lapel of the overcoat, and his breath as he argued with Nancy was hot and brandyish—what more could a man do? Hadn't he always treated Nancy's mother like a queen, except for that one time?

He left. Drove away. The danger was past.

They talked of nothing else for hours, for days. The children peeped out the front windows, crept up into Laney's room—forbidden to them—to get the best view

115

of the road; Arlene made Nancy repeat her conversation with Earl again and again, until it seemed that she knew every nuance of his argument, had seen every twitch and frown and grimace. He had said nothing about the car!—not a word. There it was in the driveway, bronze-gold, handsome, imposing—and he hadn't said a word.

Arlene fingered her face, her eyebrow, absent-mindedly. The children chattered. One of her sisters-in-law, George's wife, called. She could not resist telling her about Earl. And a friend called the next day, a Wreszin, and Arlene could not resist telling *her:* they talked for forty-five minutes; Arlene went about dazed and glorious, her head ringing with advice. She listened, but remembered nothing. She listened attentively, desperately. But remembered nothing or did not really hear, a part of her mind fixed upon the sound of his voice, his anxious bullying *Arlene? Honey?* that she heard sometimes in her sleep.

When they did not talk about Earl they talked about the car.

She had to get rid of it—give it back to him! Give it back to the son of a bitch. —That was Laney's argument, bitterly put.

She had to get rid of it, her father agreed. It was a gift, it meant there was love, good feeling, she'd have to be friendly with him if she kept the car, wouldn't she?—so, he supposed, she had to get rid of it.

Why the hell give it back to him? It was hers, it was *theirs*. It was for the whole family. —Nancy spoke loudly, drowning the others out. Wasn't the car for the whole family, hadn't Earl said—that day last spring, right out there in the driveway for everyone to hear—that the Bartletts needed something better than their ten-year-old battered Chrysler, which looked about as trustworthy as the junked autos scattered around the place?—old rusting lopsided chassis, partly overgrown in warm months by weeds, partly covered in the winter by snow, the oldest of them being a Studebaker hulk, weatherworn to the point at which it was colorless. Why should the Bartletts beg rides with their neighbors, Nancy wanted to know, why should she have to walk all the way to the Arkins to ride with one of them into Childwold, why should they be stuck out here in the country, trapped, why shouldn't they drive to town in that handsome new Buick? They were as good as anyone else, she said. They were as good as anyone else.

So they argued. Laney fled upstairs, shouting. Nancy paced about the kitchen, self-righteous, whining, tried to get Grandpa Hurley to agree with her, in principle, that they were as good as anyone else and it was time people stopped feeling sorry for them or laughing at them or spreading dirty rumors about them. In the end Arlene put on her coat one morning and went out and drove away and was gone until midafternoon . . . when she reappeared in a car no one had seen before. It was a Pontiac Tempest, not a new model but one in fairly good condition; it was lime green in color. The Bartletts swarmed around it, amazed. The grandfather shook his head gravely, but the others, most of them, were quite pleased, liking it as well as the Buick, though it hadn't a sun roof. Arlene said it would do. She needed a car, she *would* have a car, and this one would do.

Momma, Laney pleaded, what—what is this? What happened?

She had driven to town and explained her situation to one of the salesmen at the place Earl had bought the car, a man she had known, though not well, but then she knew nearly everyone, didn't she, and he had been sympathetic, and had given her not only the benefit of a trade-in on this car, "more reasonably priced," it was, but some actual cash, since the Tempest was less expensive than the Royale. And so it had worked out quite well. She was pleased. She did not care to talk about it.

But Momma, Laney said, you were supposed to—
Supposed to what! Supposed to *what!*
The car wasn't yours—

But they all turned upon Laney then, telling her to shut up, to mind her own business, what did *she* know?— Nancy giving her a shove for putting on such airs, thinking she was too good for the rest of them. That car had been a gift, a present free and clear, and it had been given to Arlene for the family, for everyone to ride in, and if Laney didn't like the way things were, she knew what she

117

could do—snippy little bitch, Laney, in enough trouble of her own.

I hate you all, Laney cried. Oh God how I hate you all. . . .

There was a big black boy six feet four at least, taller than Vale by quite a bit, with a head of crazy frizzy hair, and a slow, chilling smile, and an aluminum hook for a left hand; he told tales of how his stomach had fallen out one day in the jungle and his platoon had left him for dead, but he stuck the guts back inside and crawled after the others and got a lift in a helicopter after all, and here he was; his name was Fitzgerald. There was another boy, Johnny, who had a Purple Heart, like Vale, and who had been over there for two years, just a farm boy, like Vale, from farther west in the Valley; he had a broad sweet empty freckled face, the freckles were unusually large and pale; even on his earlobes there were freckles, and on his arms and legs. He had been badly trampled, and hospitalized and then sent home, after some sort of party— a free-drink evening of some kind. He missed Vietnam. He was lonely. He was a friend of Vale's, but they hadn't much to say to each other. Fitzgerald, too, was a friend. They rarely talked. They traded stories, mixed stories up, got things confused. There were other friends of Vale's, but these boys were his buddies. They went around together.

Fitzgerald got Vale to enroll in the GI Educational Program at the college, where their way was paid, and they went three nights a week to a course called English 01 taught by a woman, Miss Carlson, and when Vale received his first theme back he saw that it was graded D—, and the woman had written in red ink *I found this very moving but you will need help with grammar and spelling, etc*. He crumpled the paper and threw it into the bitch's face. No, he controlled himself. He read the comment again and reread his paper as best he could. His handwriting was hard to read. . . . The boy with the aluminum hook was making signals behind Miss Carlson's back but Vale ignored him and waited until the rest of the class was gone, and talked with Miss Carlson seriously

118

about his prospects. She took the paper from him and frowned and seemed to be reading it again. She wore glasses; her eyes were big and slightly protuberant. Her hair was cut short. Shorter than his. She was about five feet three. She reminded him of one of his father's sisters —his Aunt Esther—but not much, just a little. He didn't remember his Aunt Esther. He hadn't thought about her for years. When Miss Carlson spoke to him he had to drag his mind back and for a few seconds it didn't come; he just stared at her and waited.

The content of your paper is very, very moving, she said, blinking at him, I realize you've suffered a great deal, you've been through so much, that terrible war . . . that terrible war. . . . I'm here to help you. We are here to help you. Your writing is very moving, Mr. Bartlett, but there is some confusion in the chronological sequence— for instance you mention training camp on the second page, and you talk about a sniper, and when you were wounded, and when you quit high school, and when your father died, and. . . . Your theme lacks unity, you will have to learn to compress and condense, you will have to learn to emphasize certain *ideas,* do you see, and your spelling and grammar . . . well, you will profit from practice, and have you gone to the bookstore yet to get the *Handbook?* That will help you a great deal, why, I consult the *Handbook* myself, it's invaluable. . . . She smiled at him, she liked him, he was pleased. Up close she was almost pretty. She was older than Vale, in her late twenties, he guessed. He took the paper from her. He blushed. Their hands touched for an instant. Her first name was Marjorie. He would ask her out in a few days. He would take her out somewhere and fuck her until her glasses fell off and her eyes rolled back in her head, and that would be that.

Went to the war, he did; 1919; lost in action, they said, and three of his letters came at the same time, all mangled and mud-splashed. How the women howled! So sad. Sad. His cousin Hendrix came back skin and bones, terrible racking cough, my God he was a boy of twenty-two or -three and looked like an old man—I hated to be in the same room with him, such a pitiful sight, he never once accused me of anything but I felt guilty just the same: never went myself. Knee bone shattered, one leg a little shorter than the other, hop-stepping so quick nobody could notice nor do they notice today; there are so many ways of disguising yourself. Never went to the war myself. Never went to any war.

Halfway regret it, I think. I think. . . . But no, shit: that's crazy.

Went to the war in 1919, Anna's cousin and his grandma's favorite, big long-faced blond boy, would have been handsome except for his broken-out skin. Poor Leonard . . . ! Saw him off at the Yewville station, the bunch of us, and I knew he wouldn't ever come back, knew it was a permanent good-by. Leonard, Lenny. . . . Had a guitar he fooled around with, or was it a mandolin, all vibrating and trembling like it was alive; tried to sing but his voice wasn't good, he hadn't any idea of pitch, couldn't carry a tune in a basket, as they said, but my God he kept trying, that boy kept trying, until his eyes just brimmed with tears. . . . Poor boy. Like a brother to me, a brother who went to die in France in my place. (What the hell is France? Where is France? Who gives a damn about—*France?* —That was what I shouted when the news came. Stomping around downstairs when the news came.)

Well, Lenny wanted to go and then he changed his mind, halfway across the Atlantic Ocean he naturally changed his mind, and wrote the damndest heartbreaking letters home to his momma. She read parts of them out loud to us, of course, so we knew them through and through, had memorized them practically, but she kept the whole letters for herself and wouldn't let anyone else even touch them. It was sad, it was real sad. . . . In his letters he was always asking about the farm: the stock, the dogs, even the cats and kittens. He asked if the boys were still swimming in the river, how the schoolteacher was getting along, if so-and-so had her baby yet, that sort of thing, it was all questions and no information about what *he* was doing, which we all wanted to know. After he died, those three letters were even worse, just asking about what we had for Christmas dinner, if we had sourdough biscuits, what kinds of pie, was there popcorn and fudge with almonds, was there any trouble getting the tree in the house, did Granddaddy get drunk and silly again, did he sing them funny songs of his . . . that sort of thing.

That boy just missed his family so! It was enough to break your heart.

When they said he had died I felt real bad, I don't know that I ever felt that bad before. Because I was, you know, a few years older than him; I should have gone to the war myself, maybe. Instead of him, maybe. But I didn't: because of my bad knee and because of the farm. How the hell could the farm keep going without me? Whereas Lenny wasn't needed as bad, *their* farm had all the hands anybody would need. . . . Anna let drop a few words, like she always done, not anything firm enough to really provoke me, she was just a girl then and loved me pretty much, I *think;* said she did, anyway. I did love her. Loved her for a long time. Years. I don't know.

But I was telling about Lenny.

So the next year came around and it was Christmas and on Christmas Eve one of Lenny's sisters came down with a terrible headache and scared everybody, and then she started babbling some language we didn't know, and throwing herself around, and crying, and then she sat up and started talking to Lenny: and that really scared everybody. Her eyes were open but weren't seeing anything. Her hair was all wild. She was sixteen years old, about, and always kind of strange, fainting spells and headaches and bouts of weeping, not a sturdy girl at all, though afterward when she was grown up she did real well for herself—had four boys and two girls—and snapped out of it permanently. But then she was awful strange, I was afraid of her, never knew how to act when she stared at me with those big eyes of hers. On that Christmas Eve she let out such a piercing yell, then was talking to her dead brother for, oh, fifteen or twenty minutes, sitting up on the parlor sofa where she'd been lying down on account of the headache, but now the headache seemed gone and she was just talking and talking, real fast, as if she was answering questions of his; but we couldn't hear any questions. It was the damndest thing, it was so scary. . . . I admit it, I was scared as much as anybody. I was actually trembling and broke out in a cold sweat. How the women and the kids were, you can just imagine. . . .

So that happened on Christmas Eve and when the girl came out of it she couldn't remember a thing, just looked at us, blinking, her face all sweat, her clothes all damp, and they took her away upstairs and fussed over her and put her to bed. We were all afraid, we didn't know what to do. I had the feeling Lenny was in the room with us. I knew he was there. But it was the damndest thing, what could you do . . . ? Looking around into the corners of the room, fixing the fire, trying to talk, bring things back to normal . . . making a joke or two like I always did (I believe I was the only *sane* member of that family), what else? . . . but if Lenny was there with us, he didn't speak. He watched us, maybe, but didn't speak. He might have felt sorry for the way he caused such a commotion.

Christmas Day was all right. I don't remember anything strange about Christmas Day.

So the year went by and the next Christmas Eve, sure enough it was the same sister, and she had a headache again, and everybody was real frightened, but she didn't pass out or go into a trance, just kept saying to her momma that Lenny was nearby, that he was "pressing" on her, she could feel something on the inside of her skull getting bigger and bigger, she was afraid her head would explode . . . kept begging Lenny to let her alone. It was the smell of fudge and popcorn and evergreen needles that drew him, she said. He missed us so! He wanted to come back but didn't know how. It was cold where he was, he couldn't ever get warm enough, he was so lonely, so sad, he wanted to come back and get into the room with us, sit at the table with us, but how could he do it?—because he had lost his body, you see. That was what she said.

I felt so sorry for him, I started to bawl. I felt worse than when they said he had died.

What can you do? —He was dead. He had lost his body.

So that happened, and the next Christmas Eve it was something of the same, but now everybody expected it and there was a lot of praying, kneeling down and praying, that sort of thing. They had the minister over. That discouraged Lenny, like any half-ass could guess, so he wasn't so strong that year and seemed sort of pathetic. I had the feeling (though I never *seen* him, actually) that he wasn't the age he was supposed to be, but had gotten a lot younger, so he was like a boy of maybe ten or eleven; this made me mad, because of course the family had done that to him with all the prayer and caterwauling, and the minister in the house, who wasn't anybody Lenny knew or cared about, nobody in the family. I can't remember his name and don't wish to. . . . So that Christmas came and went and the next Christmas it was something of the same, and the next Christmas too. He just wanted to come home, you see. It smelled so good in the house. It was so warm there, at least downstairs. I don't blame him, I don't blame him one bit. But I was disgusted with him so hang-dog like he had become, at least I had the sense of him that way, and wished he would show himself to *me* so I could cheer him up somehow and tell him to have a little pride at least. His cousin Hendrix was a pathetic sight. It was said they gassed him, his lungs was ruint, and his face was like a corpse's, and his voice very raspy and low and horrible to hear, like leaves rustling, and you would have thought Lenny might show himself to *him,* but he never did. In fact Hendrix was skeptical of Lenny. Didn't believe he was really with us on those Christmas Eves, said it was all crazy behavior, and stunts, and showing-off, but people said of Hendrix that he was jealous, just like when he'd been a boy he was jealous of the other boys if they got more attention than he did. . . . Later on he died himself. Got pneumonia and died. And never came back, either: not once. He had turned a little mean over in Europe, like a lot of them did, and didn't seem part of the family anymore. Maybe he couldn't help it. Anyway he never came back like Lenny did.

Then the years passed and things changed, and the older people dropped off one by one, and there were new babies, new kids, and the girl, the sister, grew up and moved away, down to the Alder River, and deliberately stayed away on Christmas, and Lenny didn't come back . . . oh, maybe he did come back, but it wasn't so strong, you couldn't actually feel him in the house. It was like he just looked in for a while but didn't care enough to come any closer. The house got fixed up. We put all that insulation in and fixed the roof and installed a good furnace. So maybe he didn't feel at home, didn't recognize it quite the same as before. The new babies, too, the young kids, lots of commotion and fuss because of them, and they didn't know anything about their dead cousin Lenny nor did he know them or feel comfortable with them. It was an awkward thing, I think I was maybe the most sympathetic of all even though he wasn't a blood relative of mine, and I remember going out to the barn (like we used to, sometimes, the men: for a little drink) and trying to talk to him, asking if he was nearby, could he hear me, would he make a sign to me . . . ? But nothing. Not a bit. Either he didn't give a damn about Joseph Hurley or he stayed close to the actual house and wouldn't come out to the barn, or he was losing heart, just kind of fading away. That seemed kind of sad.

Well, the last time he seemed to come near . . . well, that was a long time ago. I must admit. Before Arlene was born, surely. I had dreams about him quite a few times but didn't understand them. What a puzzle, them dreams! Christ! . . . Wish I could figure them out, don't you? Like somebody's trying to tell me something important but it's garbled up, like a jigsaw puzzle, and I *got* to fit the parts together but don't know how, just don't know the first thing about how to do it. Lenny appeared in a lot of my dreams but never had much to say. On Christmas Eve I sort of waited for him but the rest of the family—you know, they were younger now: they just laughed at the idea of Lenny coming—paid no attention or were embarrassed, just wouldn't talk about it at all. So he lost heart, he just faded away. . . . He loved us. But now we're mainly over onto that side with him, you know, crossing over one by one. His momma, his daddy, his brothers and sisters,

124

his cousins. . . . So naturally he would lose interest in this house, wouldn't he?

I wonder if I will be the same way!

A weekday, midwinter. Uncertain of the date. Still December? Still. Melancholia, affliction since adolescence, a week or more of it, gray inert octopus in the soul, drifting arms, drifting, cloudy, amorphous arms, tentacles, tiny suckers fastened onto the inside of my brain. In the mirror an unshaven grave heavy-lidded creature, my brother, my twin, pouches beneath eyes like bruises, bruised fruit, odor in here like damp rotting leaves, can't interpret, halfway enjoy, pleasurable; a mystery. Once I smoked with simple crude sensuous meditative absorption a blend of tobacco by the name of Dutch Cavendish, my former wife—whose name I do not recall—whose name I do not allow—liked the aroma of the smoke while she liked me and then hated it as she began to hate me and gradually I too hated it, hated the entire procedure, hated even the handsome pipe and the fact that it was a gift from her in the early days of our love, in the lyric tempestuous days, which should of course not be viewed from this midwinter midweek vantage point with cruel crippling irony —we *were* happy, we *were* in love. They were. Someone was. . . . Now the pipe is lost or broken or both; now I smoke cigarettes; now it angers me and embarrasses me to see, on the street, how very young my fellow smokers are, some of them children no more than ten or eleven years of age . . . perhaps younger. Pipe smoking was a meditative pleasurable waste of time and though it did not exorcise melancholia, it lifted my spirits; now that is lost, gone, broken, forgotten. We outlive ourselves. We look back and recognize no one.

Saw her the other day. Accident. I am afraid, I am not afraid, I am reckless, I am ill-dressed for these winter winds, my hair is too long, too shabby, my complexion both pale and red-blotched, I draw attention to myself, no, I am well-mannered as my parents taught me and innocuous, no one really notices me, *she* noticed me only

125

by an unfortunate accident. But I am afraid. I am afraid something will happen. . . . Walking with her friends, four or five of them, high-school students, loud, smoking cigarettes, bare-headed in this weather, all in jeans except for one of the girls—whom I've noticed before with Laney, a large blond girl with a big nose, a merry laugh, a red plaid coat, tan boots that come to her knees. Laney in a brown corduroy jacket, can't be warm enough, hands stuck in pockets, curls bobbing, perfect angel's face squinted against a cloud of smoke; tough scrappy undernourished sluttish creature. She glanced at me, I wanted to turn aside, go into a store, I must have looked guilty, shamefaced, she continued to stare at me as they passed, the noisy gang of them, one of the boys bumping an arm against me and not even noticing: then she nodded almost imperceptibly and shaped a greeting, but no smile, nor did I smile at her. She passed, I passed. A half-minute later she came running after me and grabbed my arm and said, You're spying on me! You're following me! This is the third time this week! —Give me five dollars, Kasch, she said, still gripping my arm and standing on tiptoe, her face uplifted, sneering, frightened, a baby's audacious face; and behind her, watching, her friends on the sidewalk, three boys and the big blond girl, staring, staring. I need five dollars she said, give me five dollars please, will you? I'll pay you back.

Melancholia: rather like a shadow, a literal shadow. Falling back from the future, from sometime in the future . . . but how far? Can't know. They laughed at me, are laughing at me. Laney among them. Pocketing the bill, running to catch up with the others, should have asked for ten dollars, for twenty, for a hundred; how could I refuse?

Her face intruding upon me, haunting me. Why, what, to what end, for what reason, an obsession that humiliates me, why, why me, why *this?* Fell in love with girls in my youth, and fell out of love. Fell in love with my former wife. And fell out. A year and eleven months of marriage did it: one day we were out, both out: we lived together for a while longer but that was it. But this time I feel dread, revulsion, I want to protect the girl, want to send her away from me, I shouldn't be alone with her, shouldn't touch her, shouldn't be wandering Main Street at noon and again at three-fifteen in the expectation of seeing her. Even her sister, big-boned friendly girl with her hair in rollers, sitting beside me so easily, companionably, I am lonely, I have no one to talk to, isn't it hot here, this has been a miserable summer, I am lonely, will you have another beer, do you live in Yewville, are you married?—I'm married and going to join my husband in a few weeks; in Kansas. Even the sister with her unexceptional face, her loud delighted laugh, even she intrudes upon me occasionally, I will drive out to see her, I will drive out this afternoon to Childwold to see her, I will ask her to divorce her husband and to marry me.

Came to Yewville, as I recall, to put my life in order. To experiment with solitude. *Via* negative. Asceticism. Alternative to suicide. Brought along my treasures, left the other books behind, filled this apartment with books I have dragged everywhere with me in the past fifteen years; and now I can't read them. Can't concentrate. On my best days, out of bed early and a half-hour of exercises, heaving and puffing, poor Kasch forty years old and twenty years out of condition, and then at the table by the window here, eager, expectant as a student, buoyed up by a sense of tremulous hope, as if God were about to speak, about to open one of the books to *the* page: but even then, on my best days, I read for only an hour at the most, and then the thoughts intrude, her image rushes in, I am miserable with desire, miserable with affection that cannot be discharged. . . . *Childwold,* murmur the voices, *Childwold Childwold.*

God speaks. In these voices. Haunting, tender, maddening. . . . But there is no God, there are no voices. These are phantasms in my brain, mere projections, shards of old desires, split-off fragments of my soul that yearn to coalesce, to be born. There is no God. I am not filled with God. I am pure consciousness trapped in time, in a body, I am unenlightened, I am dragged in a circle, I am helpless to fight free, I am licking the feet, the dirty feet, of the devils who dance about me, mocking me, I am prostrate before them, I am weeping onto their dirty toes, I would suck their toes, I would grovel in the dirt before them, I would do anything they bid me in order to be free. But there is no God, there are no voices. The girl is no one. I feel a slight paternal interest in her. I pity her. What she has told me of her family makes me shudder, with revulsion as much as pity; I don't want to meet them. I don't care about them. The sister, Nancy—the baby she carried on her hip: no. Hillbillies, nearly. White trash. My mother hated them, though she tried to disguise her hatred by being so generous, so broad-minded. I hate them too. I really do. I hate Laney's smoke-stinking clothes, her premature cynicism, her slight, almost dwarf-ish figure. I hate her fate—her doom. I am not involved with it or with her. The Kasches made their fortune in lumber, in pine and oak, they deforested many a mountain in the Chautauquas, they were neither good nor evil, they were selfish like everyone, less selfish perhaps than the other lumber barons in the state, less megalomaniac, less driven; I am not one of them, it is only an accident that I was born one of them, I might have been born anywhere at all, to any parents at all, and so I am not tainted with ancestral guilt: but even if I were, I would not be as guilty as others who have exploited the farmers in the Valley. I would not be as guilty as the corporate farms that are buying up their land so greedily. I am not involved with them, so God tells me. I know. There is no God. The voice is a delusion. I am not connected except by a stray, va-grant desire, an altogether contemptible lust. . . . Still her face presses against mine, something brushes near, I imag-ine someone is hurrying up the stairs as she did the other week, I sit alert, waiting, painfully expectant, the book be-fore me lies forgotten.

The works of Meister Eckhart, of Pascal, of Shake-speare, of Boehme, of Saint Augustine, of Thoreau, of Kierkegaard, of Rilke, and Nietzsche and Santayana; the Upanishads, the Bible, the Tibetan Book of the Dead. . . . Can't read, can't concentrate. I hear her tell me that her mother knows about us, someone telephoned, I hear her raspish indifferent voice saying she likes me, she *does* like me, but . . . but what do I want with her, what is the point of it? . . . Just friendship, I tell her. And laugh. And make jokes. And run my hand lightly through her hair, a fatherly gesture she cannot misinterpret.

*Their* high school is a low mean modern structure, grimly neat, factorylike, with a big blacktop parking lot and very little lawn, a half-dozen scrubby young maples and the usual evergreens close about the building. . . . *My* high school was a big three-story Gothic structure, brick, darkly maroon, windows high and narrow, roof covered with black rotting wet-looking shingles. Not far from the very center of downtown Yewville, near the Post Office: now razed, of course, and something dreary and new erected in its place. I remember elms and sycamores, I remember the rusty fire escapes, the peculiar half-pleasant stench of an unaired aging building. In my mind's eye I can see the narrow, poorly lit corridors, the old-fashioned molding, the battered baseboards, the rows of lockers, the blackboards worn to a filmy milky gray, the little foyer with its pretentious marble floor, its display cases for trophies and plaques. Years of my life spent there, in those classrooms, in those corridors, trooping up and down those stairs . . . now razed, gone, obliterated. My boyhood, myself: gone. I could, if I wished, summon back the high school; but I could not summon back that boy. He is not only gone, he has never been. *He* has never existed. A stranger, a frightening stranger! . . . he can make no claim upon me.

The school, the Capitol Theater, the lunchroom at the corner of Main Street and Algonquin, the YMCA where the boys took swimming classes once a week: frequented by someone with my name, my young face. But a stranger. No one I know. Fitz John Kasch: but not I.

I am closer, far closer to Evangeline than I am to that Fitz John.

How real the world strikes us, the world of the present moment, the world of daylight! Tactile, it is; palpable. Demonstrable. (Aquinas: Knowledge begins with the senses.) Yet once the world slips into the past tense, once

129

it shifts into "history," it is revealed to have been insubstantial; illusory; deceptive. And we, caught in it, are we not insubstantial as images in a film . . . ? A certain force, perhaps no more than linguistic habit, connects me with the Fitz John of those years, a boy in his mid-teens, but I have no true memory of him, no feeling for him. Pity, perhaps. (He was a troubled, vexed, ill-tempered, shy, yearning, bewildered creature.) Perhaps even sympathy. But he could have been anyone, anyone at all. Any stranger whom I might pass on a Yewville street with no more than a glimmer of recognition, a half-apologetic nod, a strained smile. . . . What force connects the two of us?

And if I refuse to acknowlege it . . . ?

---

No Laney then. Could not have loved her then. Not as I do now. . . . Girls like her, farmers' children, boys and girls from the hills: undeniably attractive. Crude, direct, scrappy, profane and obscene and quick to take offense; poorly clothed, cheaply adorned, a certain awkward style about them, a kind of glamor, wonder why . . . ? Their manner of talking, their bad grammar, filthy language, the danger of awakening their hatred: the boys were mean, even the girls could lash out with their fists if provoked. Prematurely skeptical, they were, distrustful of books and school and teachers, irreverent in ways that shocked some of us from the city; deformed adults, overgrown children, a threat to us, to me, yet strangely attractive, enviable, doomed as they were to quit school at sixteen or even younger and be swallowed up in the hills, in that slumbering vastness from which they came. . . . I glamorize them yet, I make of them something they are not, but why, why, when they make so little of themselves? . . . Anyway, Laney is not really one of *them*. She is my own invention, my own treasure.

*Existence involves changes and happenings,* says Santayana, *and is comic inherently, like a pun that begins with one meaning and ends with another.*

Unknowing, he stepped into the barn and there, beyond his own uncertain shadow, the old man sat, alone, alone as he never did, as no one on the farm ever did, several horseflies—gigantic black-glinting things—crawling on the back of his creased neck, on his legs, on his boots. His shoulders were slumped. His hands were empty. What is it, Uncle? What's wrong? No one sits like that, no one sits alone, the middle of the afternoon and hours of work to be done, no one stops, surrenders. . . . The old man turned toward him finally, eyes rapidly blinking, tearful, not quite in focus. But he did not reply. Did not seem to have heard, or to recognize his nephew.

Mourning his wife; in the stifling dark heat, in the familiar barn, alone, broken. An old man now. Broken.

*I'll never be that old,* Joseph shouted to himself.

The wind was making the car rock and you were thinking about the white gravestone, about the old cracked flowerpots and the withered wreath you had cleared away, last time, many months ago. You must go to the cemetery again—you must go soon. Brad was driving north of Yewville on the Derby Road and in the back seat Jeannie and her boy friend were laughing. You weren't drunk. You were not going to get drunk tonight. . . . The white gravestone, the sharp clear chiseled letters, the mound of grass, crabgrass, dandelion, wild mustard. Once, in the cemetery, you had noticed a swarm of birds, very small birds, darting and lilting in the bushes, small as hummingbirds nearly, and you hadn't known what they were, peering to make them out—tiny yellow olive-brown breasts, tiny strips of black on their wings and across their eyes—and your grandfather, who couldn't see them, who was almost blind then, identified them by their songs: spring warblers. Now it would be desolate there, now most of the leaves would have fallen, the grassy mounds of the graves covered with snow, with drifts and dunes of snow. Lyle Bartlett b. 1924 d. 1969. Drifts, dunes. White. Lost.

End of the year approaching, shortest day of the year approaching. New Year's Day. He died: you were thinking of how he died, how the car skidded, the other cars skidded, there were black ugly marks on the pavement, tire marks, and where the oil spilled in great flaming pools. There was an ambulance, there were photographers, the

131

sheriff and his men, even a fire truck. Near the Moran Creek Bridge. New Year's Day 1969, one o'clock in the afternoon, you were seven years old and many miles away, at home, in Childwold buried in snow, in silence, until the telephone rang. Momma screamed. Dropped the receiver and screamed. The headline in the paper: *First Fatalities of the New Year.*

Brad was talking loudly: maybe the Marines, maybe the job at Mason Construction, maybe to Derby where his friend Bob Dorsey was working, maybe to Port Oriskany. Couldn't stay at home much longer. Couldn't get along. He was drunk. He was a little high. The Derby Road was clear in both directions and there were only a few narrow strips of ice, hardly more than slush. He drove at seventy miles an hour. One hand on the steering wheel, the other on your knee, just kidding around, just friendly. Big warm heavy hand. Big knuckles. Just kidding around. Brad's dark hair in quills he had to shake out of his face all the time. Thick tangled eyebrows. Seventeen years old, quit school last year, owns only this car and a shotgun and a rifle and some fishing equipment and his clothes, has a job as a carpenter's assistant, is being laid off because of poor business, is laughing now at something Jeannie has said. Seventy-five miles an hour and accelerating. Gas pedal to the floor. You think of the skid marks on the pavement, of the melted snow and the black-singed grass, the pile-up, the twisted garish wrecks, the headlines and photographs. First fatalities of the year: all local people. . . . The white gravestone weathered to a queer oyster-white, a streaked gray-white, like the outside of your house; the Methodist church, the churchyard, drops of water falling from the trees though it had stopped raining hours ago, puddles in the paths, Momma complaining about mud on her new white shoes. Bartletts and Hurleys. Cemetery. Winter, spring, autumn. Summer. Winter again, and again. Gravestones with dates of birth and death: there was *Anna Hurley, b. 1901 d. 1941.* Your grandmother, a stranger, never known to you, Momma hardly remembers her . . . says she was always sick, always in bed, weak heart, weak lungs, not a real mother to her, died when Momma was only six. No memory, no face.

132

Made the rag-quilt on your bed. . . . Crows messing around by the fence, picking at something. The small birds driven away. What are they picking at? Better not look, Laney—you'll be sorry—come on. You didn't look. You never look.

Now Brad holds the steering wheel with both hands. He is up to ninety miles an hour. The highway is clear, there are no patrol cars, there is no danger. The four of you are silent. You watch the road, you feel nothing, you are thinking of the gravestones and the puddles and the old clay flowerpots tipped and broken, maybe smashed by boys playing in the cemetery; you feel nothing, you aren't drunk, you sit with your arms crossed tightly, afraid you will suddenly yawn. Brad is experimenting with the car. He passes a certain landmark—the billboard advertising *Farm and Home Insurance, Derby*—at eighty miles an hour, he accelerates, he notes how many seconds it takes to get the car up to one hundred. He has done this before, you have done this before. (One hundred six miles an hour is his record—the car just won't go any faster.) You hug yourself, you cross your legs. You hook your right foot around your left leg and sit there, staring, feeling nothing. You know this strip of highway, know every tree and field and billboard and house and barn and lane. You are afraid you will yawn. Your jaws ache with the need. You think of your father, and of the other men who have loved your mother, who have beaten her, hurt her, broken her. You think of Earl. Still you feel nothing. The wind is rocking the car slightly, the wind is making a terrific noise. So loud! . . . You think of Kasch, dark-eyed, self-mocking, lines on his face, sweet perplexed lines, creases; you think that you probably will not see him again. Brad begins braking the car now, at one hundred miles an hour.

The last time you visited your father's grave, many months ago, you stood self-conscious before it, bent slightly, both hands pressed between your knees. Wondering why you had come. Hiked the two and a half miles from home one day for the hell of it, cutting across fields, even taking a chance on an old half-crumbled dam, wobbly rocks a farmer had set across Yew Creek to make a drinking pond for his stock and hadn't gotten around to

133

fixing yet this year. Below you rapids, white water, some nasty scummy rocks, if your foot slipped . . . if one of the rocks came loose. . . . For the hell of it you went to the cemetery, alone, not telling anyone. Embarrassed if anyone should know. If one of the nosy neighbors should mention seeing you there to Momma or Nancy or one of the kids. Embarrassed, confused, even angry. Why were you angry, what did it mean? *Father:* what did that mean? *Lyle Bartlett. 1924–1969.* What did that mean, what meaning was there in anything, was there anything you could trust, anyone you could trust, who wouldn't betray you? No. You don't think so. You can't. You aren't like him, like your father—you aren't like anyone else. They can't understand you and you can't understand them. You are the most important creature in the universe, aren't you?—you know it's absurd to think that, but you believe it just the same. You have always believed it. You know it to be true. There is you, and there are the rest. You can't cry. You don't remember him very well. He was in town so much, he was at the store all day, until nine or ten at night, sometimes he kept it open on holidays, even, and on Sundays when it became legal to keep store hours on the Sabbath, he would even stay in town overnight in bad weather or when he and Momma had quarreled. . . . Then the store had to be sold, he owed money everywhere, there was more quarreling, more drinking, he moved out and Momma cried *Good riddance!* and Grandpa said he could never come back to the farm, but he did come back, things changed, he had a part-time job at a car lot in Yewville, he came out to the farm wearing a new straw hat with a bright red band—all the salesmen wore them, he said—and things changed again, and they quarreled, and made up, and quarreled again, and when you try to think of him he's mixed up with your uncles, with your mother's boy friends, even with Vale. You don't love him. You don't feel sad. . . . You are angry, though. Why does God make so many. The cemetery is filled, there are so many Hurleys and Bartletts . . . there are infants, women, men . . . strangers with your name . . . there are Wreszins and Arkins and Reveres and Ansprachs and McCords . . . like May flies, like grasshoppers, like tadpoles, like newts, like sycamore seeds, like milkweed, like battalions of clouds that pass overhead in broken clumps, in remarkable designs, unnoticed by anyone. Why did God make so many! . . . You don't believe in God, you know there's nothing there. You don't pray any longer. People laugh and why shouldn't they—you laugh yourself at such thoughts.

The car screeched and skidded and hurtled to a stop and Brad even put on the emergency brake as part of the ceremony. He flicked his hair out of his eyes. His skin glowed, he was breathing deeply. He said nothing, made no reply to something that was said to him, noted the mile indicator, and maneuvered the car around on the highway, to drive back to the second landmark—he would see how many tenths of a mile he had needed to stop the car. The car was in excellent condition, he said, but maybe the brakes weren't as sharp as they had been, and the tires not as new.

The car was in motion again, plunging forward. The wind wasn't so bad. Your friends were talking now, laughing. It was all right. Brad had done fairly well. It occurred to you that the dead had not really been alive—not really. Not the way you were alive now. How was it possible?—it wasn't possible. Even living people, other people, how could they be like you, how could they know what you knew, think what you thought? No. Even Momma. Even her. They weren't *really* alive as you were; they were different. It was a different thing, their dying. What happened to them wouldn't happen to you. *I won't die,* you think suddenly. *I didn't die. There's nothing to be afraid of.*

*Sunday, midwinter.* I examine the fragments I have collected, the notes scattered about the apartment in differing styles of writing: my own handwriting, more or less familiar, though not very intelligible, and handwritings that strike me as alien. This is one of my good days: up before dawn, exercise, an hour of meditation, a few minutes' genuine pleasure in attaining a kind of purity of consciousness—a break-through, as if to another level of being—but only temporary, only temporary, I will not boast, I will not cling, I will not expect it to return.

Pleasure also in the winter birds, fluttering in the evergreens or down on the snow, can recognize sparrows, juncos, cardinals both red and olive-red, another bird that is a grosbeak of some kind. . . . My Aunt Leita would know, would know all about them. Should I go across town to visit her—shouldn't I, should I—someday soon they will tell me she has died, noble old tough-fibered creature, and I will feel sick with guilt, I know Fitz John Kasch from many years of dwelling in his life . . . but if I do visit her, in that outrageous old nightmare of a house, I will be flooded with gossip, with complaints, with reports of her illnesses and those of her friends, and their operations, and their deaths, and their children's disasters and good fortune, and so forth onto all the generations that dwell in Yewville, for the old girl knows them all; or very nearly. Most disturbing of all I will be forced to speak again and to hear of my parents, and by that pathway I will be forced to contemplate my old, outlived life, which I no longer recognize and no longer claim. I repudiate not the past itself, not history, certainly, but the neurotic attachment to it, the emotional nets cast into it that impede spiritual development. For to the extent that I am Fitz John Kasch, with a specific history, specific desires and attachments (Oh, Laney! Oh, what folly!) I am deprived of . . . of. . . . I am deprived of freedom.

And yet there are conflicting views, are there not, my intuition guides me to a pile of books on the rocking chair, I spend a frantic fifteen minutes thumbing through one of them and come across this profound statement of Saint John of the Cross:

The soul that is attached to anything, however much good there may be in it, will not arrive at the liberty of divine union. For whether it be a strong wire rope or a slender and delicate thread that holds the bird, it matters not, if it really holds it fast; for, until the cord be broken, the bird cannot fly. So the soul, held by the bonds of human affections, however slight they may be, cannot while they last, make its way to God.

Chilling, lovely, irrefutable. I know, I know. . . . Yet elsewhere I discover that Saint John has also told us

> When the will, the moment it feels any joy in sensible things, rises upwards in that joy to God, and when sensible things move it to pray, it should not neglect them, it should make use of them for so holy an exercise; because sensible things, in these conditions, subserve the end for which God created them, namely to be occasions for making Him better known and loved.

*Use, make use of, occasions, so holy an exercise.* There is love, there is the girl, there are many girls, many women, many human beings. Kasch begins to salivate. Kasch is trembling. He recalls an admonition of Saint Augustine's that God is to be enjoyed by man and creatures only used as a means to God. *Used, use, enjoy, means to God, holy exercises, love, her face, her body, her arms about my neck, deliverance, God, no no no no no.*

I examine the fragments I have accumulated since June, when I came here to live. The early weeks' speculation and melancholia fall away, appear to be the jottings of a stranger; I had not encountered the girl until the very end of August. August twenty-fifth, in fact. But I force myself to read them. I read everything, reread, find a sinister hidden relevance to every notation, my head swarms, I know there is a pattern, the outline of a . . . of a face? . . . the outline of a life? . . . obscure, baffling, teasing. And then the anguished manic jottings of my "heroism" that night, my fall, my pride, my ecstasy, my shame. Six-days' drunk, I believe. Stumbling about looking for a—a rope? Sick. Ignorant. Plunged waist-high in the mud of ignorance, a beast, a stranger to me now, wandering hollow-headed about the streets of the city, the streets of the damned, peeping at would-be lovers, aroused to an act of "heroism" merely by circumstances, by instinct. Self-mocking. I do not trust anything save mockery in regard to my "generous" nature. Lending money to friends and acquaintances, staying up half the night giving drinks and food and advice to plaintive wrecked souls who might better have been served (so my former wife said, so others have said who presumed to sit in judgment on me over the years) by a kick in the buttocks. Kasch famous for his sarcasm and cruelty and cutting wisdom in one direction, and famous for his sloppy sentimental staunchless "generosity" in another. My wife was right about that, horribly right. The instincts of a hunting dog, she had, despite her affectation of rationality, her adoration of Bach, dislike of Mahler, loathing of Rachmaninoff, her rigorous hours —never less than six, sometimes as many as eight—of practice at the piano; and the way she wore her hair, the cold unwavering center part, the complicated twist at the nape of the neck; and the way she consented to make love—that is, to be made love to, if such a grammatical construction is correct. But she was right about that aspect of me. I think she was right. How she would howl with laughter, her serenity wonderfully shattered by simple therapeutic joy, could she know about the circumstances of my life now, my attachment to . . . to that to which I am attached at the present time. The bitch! Why didn't I strangle her that night! Staggering together across the bedroom, a frantic dance, my hands at her throat and hers striking, clawing at me, at my hands, at my face . . . her eyes rolling, her mouth ugly and contorted and. . . .

No.

I examine the jottings, the fragments. I am methodical. I am in no hurry. Eternity is in love with the productions of time, as Blake says, and I am in time, and in eternity, and in no hurry now. The woman is gone—banished. Fifteen years at least since I have seen her, a decade since I have even heard news of her. Remarried. They say. Perhaps. . . . So many handwritings! Such a confusion of voices, of thoughts. They are all mine and yet they are not unified. I want no unity, no false unity. I want no forced chronology, no lying emphasis upon one fact at the price of excluding others, I want nothing hypocritical and synthetic. In drama there are great events that bring time to a halt: there are catastrophic revelations that bring about insight, insights, wisdom, pity and terror and purgation (or so it is said). These revelations are always in the fifth act and they are always expressed in fine, careful language, in poetry. The past is illuminated by such magic, and the future is—the future is comprehended. Sometimes there is no future. But that, too, is part of the revelation. All is seen, all is known. In my most desperate year, just after the divorce, I dragged my wounded body to a psychoanalyst, a friend of a friend in Cambridge, and it soon struck me that the psychoanalytic model is that of the drama, the theatrical: one gropes for *the* memory, *the* symbolic experience, *the* revelation. And then there is the catharsis—the tears and gulping gratitude, the reorganization of the personality, the attainment of wisdom. False. False. Human life is far too muddled, too complex, too meandering. There is no single moment of comprehension, no key to one's relationship with anyone at all, such ideas are theatrical, hysterical, deadly. A common misconception I once wanted to write about in depth: that human life is centered upon and determined by events. On the contrary, the interior life constitutes the authentic life, and actions performed in the exterior world are peripheral. Reality is what I am thinking, what is thinking through me, using me as a means, a vessel, a reed, even, streaming through me with or without my consent; the interior life is continuous, unhurried, almost undirected, unheralded. Flow of thoughts, feelings, emotions, observations. Broken reflections. The glittering, winking look of the river. Surely our outward gestures are misleading, surely our deepest selves are mocked even by our good deeds, our charity. The sinister "self" that is photographed. Frozen in one attitude. A lie. An exaggeration. . . . Therefore I want no false unity in my life, in my temporal life, because it would be a lie.

I have lived too long with lies.

Arlene moved the poinsettia plant from the front window to a side window, where it wouldn't get too much heat from the furnace vent. It was a living thing, it had to be tended. The children were larking in the Christmas ornaments, unpacking the boxes from the cellar, noisy, almost out of control; every year Arlene was amazed herself to see how much they had accumulated—some of the glass bulbs and the tinsel streamers and the birds of felt and wool were very old, they must date back beyond her parents' time, must have been inherited from her great-grandparents, even, from people she had never known. . . . It amazed her, it intimidated her, to see all the things she owned, four boxes of Christmas decorations now, her responsibility, her mess to clean up after Christmas, and even now Davy was treating an angel made of a pine cone too roughly, and one of the little girls was chewing on a glittering golden streamer; and she had to slap Junie, who had been told not to plug in the bubble lights, not to play with them, but who was doing it anyway, on her hands and knees behind the sofa where the outlet was. Do you want to get a shock! Do you want to get electrocuted! —Three of the bubble lights weren't working anyway. The string of them had been a gift from, from, who was it, he had lived in Rockland, had owned half the town, a widower, yes, not long after Lyle's death when she had been a widow, had gone about thinking of herself as a widow, and people had matched her up with men like him: a good man, in his fifties. She could not recall his name. Or his face. It had ended abruptly, his spiteful daughter had told him about Gallanti, the engagement had been broken off and of course it was for the best, he was too old to handle the smallest children and would not have wanted any more . . . why, Chuckie and Mary Ellen would never have been born! that was an astonishing thought. A frightening thought. Ed Gallanti had managed the lodge at Cranberry Lake and she had liked him very much, had been a little crazy then, that year, but thank God it had come to nothing, he hadn't gotten the divorce, his drinking was worse than Earl's and his temper was worse, hadn't he half killed a man over on the lake, thank God it had come to nothing, and she'd gone on as she had, and now Chuckie and Mary Ellen were playing in the angel's hair, almost feverish with excitement; everything worked out as it should, Arlene thought suddenly. If only people could know it at the time. . . .

He worked now in the Superior Car Wash, located in the Superior Garage, adjacent to the Hotel Oriskany. It was the largest hotel in the city, quite old, with carpets that smelled of dust and rubber plants in the foyer that looked as if they were made of plastic. He was paid less than he had been on the waterfront but his hours were better and he wasn't so cold, and he met, sometimes, interesting people. He liked working with the different sprays, the soapy spray and the clear-rinse spray, and he even liked vacuuming out the insides of the cars, since sometimes he found interesting things there, which he pocketed before the vacuum nozzle sucked them up. His pay wasn't what he would have wished but occasionally he received tips. He looked forward to the tips and was disappointed when they were not offered. During Christmas week people were generous, though. That helped Vale's morale.

Arnold Brown tipped him a dollar and stood around chatting with him late one afternoon, and invited him into the hotel for a drink; Arnold Brown was a manufacturer's representative, he said, but did not explain anything further. In the Royal Lounge, at one of the marble-topped tables, he drank quite a bit and talked animatedly, telling Vale about his experiences in Korea. He had been in the war, in Korea. Vale listened, drinking martinis, Beefeater martinis that he had only recently learned to appreciate. He had heard some of the stories before, they had happened in Vietnam also, even the same wordings were familiar, so he knew when to respond. He either shook his head in disgust or registered sympathy. Sometimes he barked with laughter, like Brown. He had three martinis to Brown's four and that annoyed him—that really annoyed him.

In Miss Carlson's apartment he had drunk martinis, and she had sipped at one for a while. She had talked also. Not so animatedly as Brown but with many smiles, many movements of her hands. She was very nice. The apartment, on the twelfth floor of a downtown highrise, was

141

very nice. It looked out toward the lake, toward the better side of the lake, where the suburbs were; she was from one of the suburbs, she said. Her family. But she hated life there. She hated the narrowness of life there. Later, she had wept and was not so brave, she had lain unmoving, as if broken, sobbing, and Vale had used her bathroom and left. He couldn't get a refund from the college —they told him the government had paid his way, the government would be repaid if anyone was, but it wasn't likely that a refund was justified. After all, it was the fourth week of a ten-week session. Students were supposed to drop out in the first week only. Didn't he know?

Vale helped Brown leave the lounge, helped him cross the wide drafty foyer, helped him in the elevator and up-stairs in the corridor, took his key from his shaking fingers and helped him with the door, and, inside, walked him to the enormous king-sized bed and pushed him down. The man's legs were buckling beneath him anyway; he was only half-conscious. Vale put one of the pillows over his face for a while. When he was still, Vale checked his pulse—couldn't find it—probed with his fingers against the man's throat—located something throbbing there, so it was all right. He was breathing now anyway, he was obviously alive. There was no harm. Vale took most of the bills out of Brown's wallet, and his garnet ring, and his Accutron wrist watch; he unbuckled the man's hand-some leather belt and tried it on, but it was too big. He would have to jab another notch in it, probably it wouldn't look right. He stooped over Brown and probed in his mouth, thinking mildly of horses, or of something unclear, and discovered that Brown was wearing dentures, a bridge of some kind that came loose. He took it out. Four or five front teeth on a lightweight metal contraption, much simpler than his own bridgework, much lighter. He put the teeth in his pocket and left.

On the street, heading downtown, he felt quite good. It wasn't just the martinis. He would buy presents for the family—would go to one of the big department stores— would pay cash—would have the things delivered. River Road, Childwold. Mrs. Lyle Bartlett and family. Christmas presents. How the children would squeal. How he had

142

squealed and jumped about, years ago. *Love, Vale.* They would be very surprised. His mother would cry. How surprised they would be. How happy. He would drive down there for the day, for the big dinner, except that would scare them; he would scare them. It's just your face, Momma said, they'll get used to it, hon, they don't know any better; but it wasn't just his face, he knew it wasn't just his face, it was something else, he had gotten very angry at Ronnie and had hurt him, it came and it went, it flared up and subsided, he didn't know when it would come, or why, it wasn't just his face and his chest and his left shoulder; he'd be better off sending the presents and staying away, he would sign the card *Love, Vale* and they would be very happy, wouldn't they, and very surprised. He had meant to send them money all along but he hadn't been able to, so now they would be surprised.

After his shopping spree he went back to the De Sales where he had a room now on the top floor, and took the teeth out and examined them, and realized that they were incriminating evidence, and tossed them out the window into the alley below. He felt better. He felt fine. He slept for a while, on his side, arms crossed; his brain jumped and spangled with Christmas lights, Christmas ornaments, angels and stars and birds and tinsel.

Stark white walls. A faint odor of plaster, paint. Everything clean, bright, clear. Your vision wavers, you have never seen anything like the tall ferns in the earthenware pots, the size of small trees; you have never seen rubber plants before, so big, the dark glossy leaves so big, and that treelike plant with the variegated leaves, pale green with filmy streaks of white. The gallery floor shines, it is so highly polished. A kind of closely fitted hardwood you have never seen before. You are breathing softly, lightly. You walk lightly, hardly daring to make a sound. It is so unexpected, so lovely . . . ! You walk forward as if hypnotized.

Photographs arranged before you, a row of large photographs, placed slightly above your eye-level; so stark, white and black, so vivid, striking, unexpected. Others are here, the gallery is quite busy, you haven't time even to glance around. You step close to the photographs, you peer anxiously at them.

Sunrise in the Great Smoky Mountains: trees that resemble aspens, indistinctly arising out of shadow; splashes of light, gauze-like patches of light, so fine, finely grained, you stare in awe, without breathing, as if a clumsy move of yours could dislodge everything. Sunrise, trees, mountains, the remarkable delicacy of light, the blossoming of light in leaves. . . . You want to turn to Kasch, you want to cry out in amazement that you have never seen anything before, you have never seen the mountains before, though you stare out that bedroom window of yours every day of your life.

You know nothing! You've seen nothing!

And there are photographs of dogwood, life-sized; and of Canada geese in flight; of petrified wood in grotesque, anguished postures. You stare, you can't get close enough. You have never seen photographs like these. . . . Storm clouds that seem about to shift violently, to come alive. Oaks covered with ice, every branch and twig shimmering with ice. Pine forests, the tree trunks so remarkably straight, pencil-straight: immense boulders: decayed, partly toppled trees: abandoned towns in the Chautauquas: towns still living but small and dreary and pathetic, resembling Childwold and Marsena and the Rapids and Five Bridges and Frothing. . . . You half expect to see yourself on the street in one of these photographs. You stare, you don't want to move on, you cannot see enough, cannot comprehend enough. People move around you, strangers, you would ordinarily be interested in them, you are hardly aware of them, don't even overhear their conversations. The photographs pull at you, tug at you. Why, what is it, what is happening, what will happen . . . ? You are afraid you may suddenly begin to cry.

Laney Bartlett, wiping at her nose . . . !

Kasch is talking with someone a few yards away. The gallery manager. The two of them have never met, yet they seem to know each other. They are talking about the exhibit, about a diary the photographer kept that has just been published posthumously; Kasch has read sections from it in magazines but has not yet seen the entire book;

the gallery manager speaks enthusiastically of it and Kasch stands with him, the two of them strangers, brothers, Kasch tall and somber and cheerful and clean-shaven, his eyes crinkling at the corners, watching you.

A wall of faces: men and women and children, old, young, deeply creased, some smiling hesitantly, some frankly despairing, an elderly woman glimpsed through a window screen, face incredibly aged; a young mother holding up her baby; a girl your age, unsmiling, morose, not very pretty. There is another young girl scattering feed to chickens. There is an old man seated on a rumpled bed, staring impassively at the camera, hair thickly white, mouth level, stubborn, like Grandpa Hurley. Such people! Such faces! They are tough, strong, dignified. Unbreakable. Their beauty is so unexpected, such a surprise, the beauty in their plain hard open faces, their severe mouths . . . the beauty in their old, worn clothes, farmers' clothes, work shoes that look coarse enough to be made of wood or metal, women's dresses that are shapeless, baggy, soiled, children's shirts too small for them. . . . You blink tears away, you wipe irritably at your nose with a tissue. These people remind you of, remind you of. . . . But your own people, are they so dignified, so stubborn? Their faces so beautiful? You have never looked at them, you don't know. You have never really seen.

You move along to a wall of photographs of things no one values: shards of crockery on a rotting floor, frail, interwoven shadows cast by a snow fence, broken glass, spikes and screws tumbled upon the ground. Kasch comes up behind you, silently. You know it is Kasch. He stands behind you, looking over your head. What if he touches you, what if he rests his hands on your shoulders? You don't want to be touched. You wait, nervously, irritably; you don't want to be touched, especially not now, not here, in this place.

But he doesn't touch you. He seems to sense your feelings. You move along, he follows along beside you, studying details of gravemarkers in an old Chautauqua cemetery, debris carried along by the Eden River in floodtime, a partly defrosted stand of long-needled pine, more stark
145

patterns of light and dark, wood and snow, ice and sun, rock and earth and sky and water.

You are exhausted.

An hour in the gallery, an hour and ten minutes—and you are exhausted. Suddenly you feel hollow. Drained and emptied. The sensation is new to you, and rather frightening. But you don't want to leave. You want to see everything for a second time.

You hurry back to the first photographs, you don't care to speak to Kasch, not yet, not so soon, the sound of your own voice would be terrible to you in this place, there is nothing you can say about the exhibit that is right, nothing that would not be a kind of lie. . . . You want to see everything again, you're greedy, reeling with exhaustion though it is only noon.

How lovely, how unexpected, these photographs, the fact that a man existed who had taken them over a period of fifty years . . . fifty years! The fact that the gallery itself existed, with its clean white walls and its plants, the manager who seemed so friendly to Kasch, the other patrons, quiet and respectful. . . . There is a girl of about thirteen, with her mother; there is a middle-aged couple; there is an attractive woman, alone, in a thick soft russet-orange coat with a leather belt; there is a man of about fifty with a young woman who must be his daughter. Everything in this place has meaning, people have come here to experience the meaning, they know it is here, it has been deliberately and lovingly created and so they have come here, have journeyed here, knowing they will not be disappointed. . . . You find yourself watching the girl and her mother. Standing with your hands in your pockets, head slightly lowered, eying them, a little resentful now, bewildered, curious; you wonder who they are, whether they live in this village, Rosewood, this handsome suburb north of Port Oriskany, on the lake; you wonder if they are very close, the mother and the daughter, if the daughter can confide in her mother, if they love each other; you wonder if there is a father, if there are other children, if everyone gets along, what sort of house do they live in, where does the girl go to school, does she have many friends, boy friends, does she get good grades, is the family

146

rich. . . . But of course, of course they are rich: look at the coats, the gloves, the expensive leather boots, the smooth confident faces. . . .

You are faint with weariness, with hunger. Kasch wants to leave. There is still the danger of crying, you're almost angry for no reason you can comprehend, you don't understand, you are alarmed at your own emotions. Laney, Laney! He brought you here without knowing what it would mean to you, how deeply it would strike into you. Or did he know, did he guess? Out on the street you look back, stricken. *The Rosewood Gallery.* . . . You believe you will never come here again, you will never again get this far from Childwold.

You lied, you were good at lying. A sip of Kasch's drink, you laughed because it scalded so, it seemed to fly up into your nose, fumes leaping up into your head. You will have to lie, returning with the booklet he bought for you, the photographs, you will have to stand with your weight on one foot and your expression slightly weary, lying, a class outing, you'd said, because of Christmas, the entire class going by bus to a museum in Port Oriskany. You wanted to wear a dress for a change, and your good coat . . . and Momma was pleased, Momma actually brightened, saying she would fix that collar you'd wanted altered, and you could borrow her good gloves and not wear those filthy mittens you'd been wearing; it was a shame, she said, how a pretty girl like you goes around looking like hillbilly trash, like a little slut, no wonder your grades aren't any better . . . the teachers take one look at you and your friends, and that's that!

You reach again for Kasch's cocktail glass, playfully, but he moves it away. No. Not here. You're underage, don't you know?— do you want us both to be arrested?

We haven't done anything wrong, you say.

He laughs. He keeps the glass in his hand, raised. He is laughing and then his face shifts back, he looks sad, dark, mournful. What is he mourning, why does he do those silly little dances, all arms and legs, why does he drink Scotch from an unwashed tumbler, why does he smoke one cigarette after another but forbid you to smoke at all,

147

as if you'd listen to him, pay attention to *him?* A failure, he was; called himself a failure. But it set lightly upon him, he waved it away; it was you he wished to talk about, you he questioned, he could never come to the end of his curiosity about you, though you were embarrassed and irritated by him and wanted sometimes to tell him to go to hell. Spying on you, on the street! God! And everyone knowing, everyone laughing behind his back. The sales-clerks in the stores, your classmates, your classmates' parents—laughing behind his back. Momma knew a little. Momma knew certain things. You lied to Momma about this trip and she would probably find out, no one could keep anything from her for long, she had threatened to go to Kasch, to visit him in person, she had threatened to re-port him to the police—you were a minor, after all—or to the Yewville newspaper: Kasch was such a well-known name in the town, maybe it would get onto the front page! So Momma nagged and muttered and scared you but Nancy said, and you knew it was true, that Momma would never go to the police, never!—or to the newspaper—or to anyone like that, anyone in authority, especially in town. Hadn't she let that Earl Tuller almost kill her, and never a peep of it to the sheriff's office? And Earl hadn't been the first one either. So you were safe.

You are safe. You are with Kasch in a village almost one hundred miles from home, in a restaurant, seated across from him at a small table. You are safe but you feel weak, strange. You look at him, for the first time you really look at him, and he is homely and beautiful at once, he is making a silly joke, a silly face, he is beautiful, you feel the blood draining out of your head, a terrible wave of emotion comes upon you, you stare at him and can't hear what he says. . . .

Laney my girl, why so pale? You must eat. I must feed you. . . . You're only a child, I keep forgetting.

Birds in a big brass cage decorated for Christmas, the bars hung with holly and tiny red berries. The birds are real! The birds are real, singing sweetly, fluttering about, dipping and rising to their perches, parakeets, someone has said, and you stare at the spectacle in amazement—if only you could tell someone about this sight, a big bird cage with tiny warbler-sized birds of turquoise and scarlet and yellow and green, set in the center of a restaurant. There are people at nearly every table, well-dressed men and women, even a few children. Everything is so distracting, you want to look at everything, you want to overhear conversations, you want to approach the bird cage and look more closely at the birds and listen to their songs, which are partly drowned out by people talking. It strikes you as remarkable that people come here every day, that they eat lunch here every day, beautifully dressed men and women, so subdued, so unsurprised, so obviously enjoying themselves. . . . From somewhere overhead Christmas carols are being piped in. Medieval lyrics, Kasch says. Medieval, medieval. What does it mean, what do these things mean; your head feels hollow and light as if you'd been drinking, you are happy, you are so happy, clutching at the edge of the table, at the tablecloth, as if you were about to faint.

Like drinking wine, like smoking grass, like those red pills you used to take the year before, when everyone was taking them for fun: you feel so happy you are in danger. But you're safe, you know that. You're exhausted. You're starving. Kasch instructs you to take one of the rolls, don't you want a roll, and you take one out of the basket, embarrassed, not knowing why you are embarrassed, you are afraid someone will notice you're eating, you don't belong here and you're sitting at a table and eating, like everyone else . . . people might point at you and laugh. Laney Bartlett! One little, two little, three little Bartletts, four little, five little, six little. . . . Taunting, teasing, throwing snowballs. Green apples. Pears. Stones, mud clumps. One little, two little, three little Bartletts. . . . And another one on the way.

Once you begin eating, you can't stop. You spread butter thick on the roll, you're ravenously hungry, you've never been this hungry before. Kasch nibbles at part of a roll and orders another drink. A Manhattan, it is. He smiles and watches you eat and when your lunches are brought he only picks at his, watching you, amused, fond. He has ordered a mushroom omelette and a green salad

149

and for you he ordered an open-faced steak sandwich and French fries and a chef's salad with dressing of a sort you've never tasted before, so creamy and rich. You ask for catsup; you must have catsup. You are so hungry it frightens you. Salt, you want salt, you shake salt onto everything. Kasch picks at his salad, watching you. Would you like some of my omelette, he says, and you say yes, you've never had eggs that looked like that before, made in that particular way. The omelette is delicious. If only you could tell Momma! The steak is delicious, and the crusty rolls, and the French fries, and the salad, and the dressing. It takes you quite a while to eat—just cutting the steak with the knife, dreading some accident, takes a while. You must be careful, you must be gracious. People might be watching. Isn't that one of the Bartletts, some-one might say. Hillbilly trash. . . . If only you could tell Momma about the way the eggs have been fried, and about the salad dressing, and the parakeets, and the other diners, and how marvelous everything is!

Then, suddenly, you aren't hungry; you've eaten too much; you put down your fork and knife. But you haven't finished your meat, Kasch says, and don't you want dessert? No, no. God no. Your stomach hurts a little, you aren't used to eating this much, at this time of day especially. Most noons you hardly bother to eat—a sandwich you've brought to school in a paper bag, maybe an apple or a pear or a nice tomato in season, maybe you buy a candy bar, or a fifteen-cent bag of potato chips, and that's it, that's enough. You can't stomach the cafeteria food—they serve too much, and anyway it's too expensive.

No dessert, you're sure? —I was thinking of having another drink myself.

More Christmas carols, these are familiar, commercial, yet still quite nice. You are assessing yourself in the three-way mirror, embarrassed that the saleswoman is fussing over you, saying the coat is lovely, the color is lovely, but it would have to be shortened. The store has pink walls and a pink carpet. There are a number of Christmas trees, made of frosted glass ornaments piled on top of one another into pyramids. Your lips are chilled, you dread to meet your own gaze in the mirror, what are you doing here, what is the meaning of this, if the saleswoman knew who you were. . . . The coat is a very dark orange, with a brown fur collar and cuffs, soft, rich, lovely; your own coat is a skimpy cheap colorless thing, with ripped lining, now lying across a nearby chair. You can see it in the mirror. You can see Kasch, long legs crossed, in the mirror. Christmas, it will be Christmas soon, everyone is shopping, you've done your own shopping and wrapped your own presents, cheap little things; you're ashamed of yourself, your face feels numb, lips numb, if the saleswoman only knew where you lived, who you were . . . ! Kasch begged: Let me buy you something. Let me buy you something for Christmas. Can't I? Why not? What use is my money to me? What use is my life? —Speaking lightly, making fun of himself, pulling at his lip as he does when he is nervous. What sort of fur is this, you ask the saleswoman meekly. Mink, she says. Isn't it lovely? Lovely. Yes. . . . One little, two little, three little Bartletts, four little, five little . . . Eight little, nine little. . . . Teasing, chanting, stamping their feet, your own cousins started it years ago, Hurleys themselves, the first to sing the words, and then of course it was taken up by everyone at the Childwold school, by all six grades, and later on the school bus to town. Don't take no crap from anyone, Vale told you, and you and your brothers and sisters fought back, you learned to fight back years ago, but still the chanting continued, you couldn't fight them all, couldn't shut them up, what could you do? Don't wait to be hurt, don't wait for one of them to hit you, Vale said, go for them right away yourself—let them have it. Stones, mud, sticks, fists, feet. Kick 'em between the legs, Vale said. Don't take no shit from anyone. Vale with his kidding around and then his quick temper, Vale always a little dangerous, even before he'd been shipped away. Quick with his fists, quick to strike out. Of course no one ever sang that mocking song at him, not at *him*. He'd broken the jaw of one of the Krassov boys, at the age of fifteen; but it had been a fair fight, everyone said. Vale wasn't a bad boy, everyone said. Just a little quick-tempered, took after his grandfather, maybe . . . but meant no harm.

Your coat came from the rack at Goodwill, in that ugly little shop of theirs on Bridge Street. *Goodwill Industries of Yewville—Clothing Utensils Appliances Furniture.* Shame, shame. There go the Bartletts. Momma led you all into the store, making a parade of it, not embarrassed, never embarrassed, in fact enjoying herself. All of you washed and combed and wearing shoes though it was summer, and in fairly clean clothes—you were twelve at the time, you hated going there, knew what the volunteer workers' smiles meant, how sorry they were for you all, how contemptuous. Momma in good spirits, examining things carefully. Hard to please, Arlene Bartlett. Why does this cost so much, she asked, look at the collar— it's soiled; look at the buttons on this coat, they don't match, one of them is hanging by a single thread; look at this lampshade, it's been scorched on one side, it should be marked down more than it is. One of the children tripped on a cord and another was wailing because someone had pushed him and the boys were fooling around with the toys and Momma clomped around in her white rayon shorts, a green and white polka-dot top, wooden clogs on her feet and her toenails painted bright red. She smoked a cigarette and she hummed quite loudly, enjoying herself. She loved to shop, she loved a trip to town. She did not mind the saleswomen—they were well-to-do Yewville housewives, volunteering their services to Goodwill. Arlene didn't care that they pitied her or disapproved of her or were anxious about the kids' breaking things, she must have noticed their expressions but really didn't care, such things didn't bother her in the least. Two months pregnant at the time, Momma was—though none of you knew it yet. Her secret. So she was radiantly happy, clomping about the aisles in her silly shoes, hair fluffed out, looking good. Her breasts and hips were full, her waist rather small, and her wrists and ankles small; she looked good and knew it.

You stand in the coat and stare at yourself, big-eyed, looking pale, peaked. There you are—*you.* From behind you look like a child, people think you're a child, when you turn they see your face and think you're much older

152

than you are: no one knows what to think about you. At Cranberry Lake those boys thought you were sixteen or seventeen, and when the police came along they thought you were about eleven; at least at first. You want to grow up, you want to be an adult, as soon as you're sixteen you will leave home—will go to—No, you don't want to leave home. You can't. You don't want to grow up either. You don't want to be Nancy's age. Not ever. Last year you starved yourself and your periods stopped, you had the idea they would stop if you stopped growing, it had to do with your breasts growing too, you starved yourself until Momma began to notice, watched you at mealtimes, sharp-eyed Momma, nothing gets past her; but your periods did stop for eight months, and you can do that again any time you like, any time at all. You love to eat but you could stop at any time. You loved the lunch with Kasch but you could forget it entirely, you could forget him, you could do anything you want. You will leave home then. No: you will never leave home. You can't leave them, especially Momma, something bad might happen to her, to all of them. Grandpa might die—he will die. You don't want to think about it. His mind is off somewhere, he says you're his favorite grandchild but sometimes he calls you by your mother's name and sometimes just Dolly or Girlie, he groans in his sleep, he wanders off most of the day and could get lost, could freeze to death, he doesn't eat right, Momma says, he'll sicken and die and you can't leave home, not ever; you don't dare.

Evangeline . . . ? says Kasch.

You ignore him, you hate that name, wish you'd never told him about it, you find yourself staring at the small white tag on the coat—$595. You turn it over, there's nothing on the other side. $595. Jesus Christ. Hanging from one of the sleeves, a white tag with $595 on it, in ink.

No, it's hopeless. Ridiculous. You take off the coat, shaking your head. The hell with it. The saleswoman is surprised and seems hurt: the hell with her. I don't want it, you tell Kasch, let's forget about this, I don't need a coat, I have a coat. You take it off and grab your own coat and start to walk away, muttering to yourself. Jesus

Christ, a coat priced at $595, you are shocked and angry and want to tell everyone in the store to go to hell, what sort of shit is this, how dare they, you feel sick, you feel as if people are watching you and about to burst into laughter, a coat with fox fur, a coat with leather buttons, lovely rich dark material, would have to be shortened, it's hopeless, forget it, forget everything, you've got to get out of here. Behind you the saleswoman is saying to Kasch:

But it looked so lovely on your daughter, it went perfectly with her coloring and her hair—

You panic, gasp for air. You swing your legs away from him. Press your knees tight together.

No. . . . But wait, wait. I'm sorry.

Your heart is pumping crazily. You can hear your breath: you are really gasping, gulping for air. There isn't a thing you can do about it.

No, no, it's all right, all right, says Kasch. Goes to the bureau, pours himself another drink, stands there with his back to you. That wincing look of his means he's getting one of his headaches.

Wait, you say. I'm sorry.

The first time, in his apartment back in October, you'd been a little high when you got there, running up the stairs and pounding on the door, hadn't he asked you to come visit him at any time, hadn't he begged you? Spoiled and brattish, hair all touseled. You were sick of your friends—fed up. You ran halfway across town to the museum park to the cobblestone place where Kasch lived, ran up the stairs panting, triumphant. Too stupid to be scared. Kasch was unshaven, amazed to see you. Held your hand. Squeezed it. I'll get undressed, you said, I'm not afraid to get undressed, and you weren't—you were feeling so good. I'm not afraid of you or of anyone, you said. . . . But when he kissed you, you pushed him away: you burst into tears. All right, he said, all right, I didn't mean, I. . . . Afterward, you sat with him at the card table he'd set up for his meals, and the two of you drank beer and ate greasy salted nuts and tried to think of something to say. You know I love you, Kasch muttered, and
154

wouldn't hurt you, but you'd better not come here again. Don't you want me to? you asked, hurt.

In the hotel room overlooking the lake you almost love him, you almost cry aloud that you love him. But you don't. A terrible panic rises in you, your body twists and squirms like a cat's, you can smell panic about you, can taste it in your mouth. His kisses are shy, tentative, timorous, light as moths against your face, but you can't respond, you freeze and want to push him away. Brad kisses you, Brad mauls you; but you are accustomed to Brad. You don't care about Brad or the other boys. With them, too, you will suddenly and roughly push away, but you are not afraid of them, not so panicked, so despairing. They don't matter. You don't care if you hurt their feelings or if they get angry with you.

Maybe we'd better start back, Kasch says. If I get a migraine I won't be able to drive.

Then I can drive. I know how.

You don't have a license, Laney. Don't be ridiculous.

You lie there, still breathing hard. You are in your slip, he is in his underclothes. It seems that you've known each other a long time like this, the strain between you, your own absurd pounding heart, your dread and impatience with yourself. It's when I feel most alive, says Momma, you overheard her once, you were only a baby but you knew what she meant, you understood the tone of her voice; it's when I feel most alive . . . that, and being pregnant. God how I love it, I love it. I can't get enough of it.

He comes back to the bed, sits on the edge of it, the drink still in his hand. You don't even ask him for a sip; he would be angry. Stroking your cold hand, stroking the fingers individually. I must disgust you, he says. Must seem grotesque to you. You sigh, make a noise signaling impatience, the two of you have been through this before. . . . He holds your hand, you hope he will begin to talk about himself a little; when he's feeling bad, when he's a little drunk, he sometimes talks about himself; but you can't ask him directly. His wife, his divorce, twenty-eight years old he was at the time, something about a breakdown, something about a book he was trying to write, or did write; his parents' deaths, his years of travel-

155

ing, the West Coast, England, Europe. So old. He is so old. Yet no older than your mother, maybe only a year or two. He winces, his head must ache, you tell him to lie down beside you, why don't you both have a nap, you're both exhausted, it will do you good.

He lies beside you, all the length of him, and folds his arms across his chest. The Venetian blinds are drawn, there is a patchwork of light and shadow on the wall, the room is handsome, warm, all greens and browns, warm colors, the first hotel room you have ever seen. You will remember it all your life. The four-postered bed, the gilt mirror by the bureau, the astonishing bathroom—such luxury, it makes you reel—and Kasch's voice, gradually slowing, thickening.

Why were you unfaithful, I asked my wife, and she said she didn't know, but it wasn't *unfaithful* she had been—she wouldn't have used that word. She said. Was there a reason, I asked her, that you've been fucking him all these months, and she said no, not really, she had no idea, she didn't much like him, didn't take him seriously: he wasn't, she assured me, as intelligent and sensitive as I was. . . . So I said why, why did you do it, and she had no idea; were you angry with me, I asked, she said no, why should she be angry, a little impatient sometimes but that was natural, and anyway she understood why I was so thorough in preparing my dissertation—she knew it would pay off, the dissertation would be publishable, my advisor might even get it published at Harvard, wasn't that a possibility? No, she wasn't angry. She loved me. Loved me very much. . . . Then were you disappointed with me as a lover, I asked, and she thought about it and I wanted to kill her then, wanted to strangle her right then, and finally she said no; she was beginning to cry, shaking her head no, she'd taken her hair down, undid the twist or knot or whatever it was, she was very pretty and knew it and knew what she was doing to me, and she did love me, I think, otherwise why would she have wished to torture me? . . . no, she said, I wasn't disappointed with you, not at all. Then why, why did you go to him, why did you sleep with him? I don't know, she said. Did you want to hurt me, did you want someone to tell me and
156

then I'd be hurt? . . . No. No, not really. She was crying now, but it meant nothing. It was just something she did. Something that had to be done next. I asked her if she was in love with him and she said no, of course not; they were just friends; she liked his wife, actually, as well as she liked him. But isn't there the danger of you ruining their marriage, I asked, if she finds out?—the way you've ruined ours? She cried, she stood there and cried, she said she hadn't ruined our marriage or theirs, things could go on as they were, why did I have to be so angry, why make a fuss, she had slept with him because they had happened to meet late one afternoon at the library and he had taken her for a drink at the Wursthaus and that was the night his wife was teaching and I was working late, and his apartment was only across the way, a five-minute walk, so they'd gone there, there was nothing to it, a husband, a wife, somebody's husband, somebody's wife, it was all pretty much the same, wasn't it?—and nothing was ruined, she said, unless I wanted it ruined. And then it would be my fault. Mine. . . . I listened, I did not interrupt. I did not shout. I asked her calmly if she was attracted to him physically and she seemed annoyed and said no more than was natural: she would never have thought of him that way if they hadn't gone to bed together. So no. Not physically, not really. . . . Did she want our marriage to end, was that it, I asked, and she began to shout at me that I was being stupid, being ridiculous, I was the one who was ruining everything and talking about divorce, and if I loved her I would forgive her, wouldn't I— didn't I know these things went on all the time, in Cambridge and everywhere, everywhere? . . . But the marriage is over, I said, I began to shout, eighteen months and the marriage is over, *eighteen months* and you've been sleeping with him for three of those months, the marriage is over, you've ruined it, you've destroyed it, you've destroyed me— Afterward she told people I was crazy, she told people I was paranoid, I spied on her, I was puritanical and repressed and impotent and sick, she told people I had tried to kill her and threatened to try again. . . .

His voice thickened, slowed. He fell asleep. You lay

there beside him under the thin bedspread, listening to his deep, hoarse breath. Your brain broke into spangles suddenly, you slipped toward sleep yourself, you saw Christmas lights, a ghostly pale face in a three-way mirror, the irregular V of the Canada geese in flight, Kasch's eyes, Kasch's mouth, Momma's bleeding face, a white gravestone, an angel on a Christmas tree, stars and birds and glittering winking tinsel.

*Christmas Eve.* Drove up to Port Oriskany, two trips in one week, frayed frantic desperate shameless, bottle of Seagram's on the seat beside me. The use of, the occasion for, holy exercises, redemption. Laney's pity, Laney's sweet pungent odor, must let her go, abandon her to one of those brutes; I am a brute; drooling and pawing. My Lilith of the fields, the snowfields of Childwold. Unmanner of men. Must let her go: she can't make me other than I am now and must be forever, forevermore, forevermortal. . . . Lilith of the fields, of dirt. She's composed of it. Rubbed her wrist with my thumb hard and the tiny rolls of dirt appeared. From dust thou hast come and to dust thou must return. Hurry, hurry! Blessed be the name of the dust. Our dust. Ours.

Prayer, fasting, meditation. Life in time, in history: a failure. Must retreat. Where I live, what I live for. Experiment. Brave, noble. Will continue until I triumph, or I die. Kasch the lover, Kasch the ascetic. Kasch the drooling pawing self-pitying mess, Kasch the enlightened spirit, balding head haloed, weak watery eyes redeemed. . . . Read of a split-brain patient, left/right selves unaware of each other. "Selves." The right was mute, highly emotional, violent. The left was analytical, verbal, "civilized." They were strangers. They had never met. Ah, yet we think of ourselves as one person! We hug that delusion to our deaths! Not just the mad who are split but all of us, brains split as if with an ax, one side in authority, one side *the* self, and the other quietly waiting. . . . The split-brain patient walked about in his single body but sometimes fought little wars. One hand threatened the other. One hand did damage, and the other tried to restrain it.

*Doppelgänger* not a myth. Quite real. Kasch driving at seventy miles an hour, Kasch a poor driver, absent-minded, failed his driving test not once but twice—the only boy in high school to fail twice—but now an adult, one of the world's adults, speeding along the highway in the night. Kasch barking with laughter, glad to be alone. In a car you can do anything you wish: laugh, scream, sing Christmas carols, tell jokes, pose riddles, recite verses learned by heart long ago ("Th' expense of spirit in a waste of shame/ Is lust in action . . ." "I wandered lonely as a cloud . . ." "A sudden blow: the great wings beating still . . ." "Whan that Aprille with his shoures soote . . ." "Batter my heart, three person'd God . . .")

Kasch the happiest he's been for months.

Port Oriskany, county seat. Largest port on Lake Oriskany. Population 350,000. Served by five railroads, two airports (one quite small), a Greyhound bus line, a Trailways bus line, a ferry (in season) that crosses the lake's choppy waters to a small town on the distant shore. Principal industries cement, automobiles, steel, chemicals, fruit processing and canning, abrasives, cereals, and oil refining. Oriskany Community College, 5000 students. Some banking interests, investment houses, one good hotel, no good restaurants, central area emptying out, waterfront area wretched, old Front Street worse than I could have invented. Port Oriskany, port to hell. The air has a taste. The air stinks. Five above zero, cold enough to purify one's lungs, yet the air stinks, the wind stinks, here I am. . . . A derelict sprawled in a doorway: will freeze to death. Jesus. But I drive on by, I don't stop. Street nearly deserted. Christmas Eve, snow drifting across Northern Boulevard, Jacey's Bar & Grill, Howie's gas station, pawnshops, coffee shops, waterfront area now a slum, All-Nite Diner, Preston Steel, barbed wire, railroad yard, De Sales Hotel, gas pumps, oil tanks, traffic lights, Jax Bar & Grill, Superior Canning, water towers, Red Eagle Hotel, Danny's Pool Hall, Front Lounge. . . . Sunset, cocktail hour, Front Lounge waitresses in pants suits, television on above bar, have been here before, have lived and died and lived again, now in skin and bones of Fitz

159

John Kasch, waitress smiling perfunctorily, V-necked blouse, tight pants, rhinestone earrings, perfume that smells like something chemical, Merry Christmas, bar not crowded, tables almost empty, a children's choir singing on the television set, several girls at a table, Kasch leaning over the bar, elbows, knees bumping, glasses steamed, panic of blindness, will go blind someday, television now showing underwater suspense film, bartender switching from station to station, six, seven, eight men at the bar, three of them blacks, good-natured, Merry Christmas, in the Katha Upanishad it is said we travel from death to death so long as we are unenlightened, *Whatever is here, that is there; what is there, the same is here. He who seeth here as different, meeteth death after death.* Frances and Molly, pretending to be sisters, or did I miss the joke of it, Frances pulling sweater down over hips, tough little gal, curlyheaded too, drinks the martini as if it were a Coke, Molly quieter, elbows on table, pert smudged glopped-up face, eyelashes stiff with mascara, like spikes, hair dyed orange-red—or so it seems in this light: Molly subdued as if breakable or actually broken; Molly the obvious choice for Kasch.

Red Eagle Hotel, $10 for a double room; a bottle of Seagram's and two unwashed glasses; Molly so thin her ribs showed; noises from adjoining rooms, might as well interpret them as festive. Have you been here before, asked in gay innocence, has the cycle come round again, but she misunderstood and told me to go to hell, saucy and flaring, manner stylized as if on film, black stuff rubbed off onto her cheeks and the pillows and me; one moment hot-tempered and the next yawning, perhaps split-brained, like most of our species. Kasch, she said, what kind of a name is that: *Kasch,* I said, *cash, cache, catch, clash, crash.* Story of a life. Small wilderness of broken veins or capillaries on the girl's lower abdomen, dark violet tangle, someone must have slugged her hard. No comment from Molly. Story of a life.

How I've wanted this, how I've wanted you—why are you hanging back, dear? Come here, come closer! No one can see! . . . There's no harm to it. There's no harm to us.

Who's to see, dear? Who's to know? Anna?—never!

Why are you hanging back? You know you're not shy, girl! Not a bit! Not you!

My eyes ache, I can't see you, I don't understand. Something unfolding, like wings, wings unfolding to blot out the sun, the entire sky. . . . Best not to look directly at it, they say. Gigantic bird. Angel. Don't look: don't! Pearl! They say there are eyes covering its body, its entire body. Oh it's cruel, it's cruel, don't try to look at it, come to me, let me hold you, there's no danger as long as we're together. Don't you believe me? I'm not drunk! I haven't had a drop all day!

Pearl?

I asked did you love me and you said yes, you were laughing and bawling at the same time, a big husky girl like you, pretending to be shy. None of that, girl! Not with Joseph! I was frank with you, wasn't I, thought it best to speak out directly, more harm in keeping truth hid, I was never one of them sanctimonious hypocrites like my wife's family that you had the bad luck to marry into—you and me, ain't we something? Mooning around like this? It was Christmas did it, that rum punch going to my head, and the house overheated with all the children, noisy and crowded and lively, the way it should be at holidays— otherwise the snow would heap up and bury us all, wouldn't it? You said I was whiskery and whiskeyey, you laughed like somebody was tickling you, that quick doubling-over laugh, rowdy and silly and didn't care if the old folks were watching. Let them! Just let them! Anna and your husband and all that long-faced family, making a big fuss about Christmas services, had half a mind to forbid the kids to go, all that bullshit, you'd think by now, after so many centuries, people would catch on, eh? Just as well, let them hitch up the horses and plow through the snow, the house is quiet while they're gone, I don't mind a bit some peace and quiet in my own house. Morton would have died, though, if you told him what *you* thought!—poor stupid calf. Anna's give up on me long ago, long ago. She knows better than to nag.

I asked did you love me and you said yes and my heart it just sang, I was never so happy—never so happy! Thought all that was done: you know, over with for me, a woman loving me, that sort of thing. Not that I had any time for it. I didn't. I don't. You're something special, you just walked in the door with the snow on your head and shoulders, shaking it off, carrying all that stuff in your arms, a big smile on your face, cheeks red from the wind. . . . Well! Well, you know the rest.

Did you love me, I asked, felt like such a fool, my knees trembling, voice ready to crack, should we get married, I asked, should we tell the rest of them about it, about us? —my knees trembling like crazy. You'd think I was going to break a new horse, you'd think I looked down and saw a copperhead right there on the path, by my foot, or heard the ice cracking when I was halfway across the river. Why can't we love each other, why can't we see it through, I'm not afraid of Anna or her people, and what can that brother of hers do? Poor Morton! Twenty years older than you, ain't he? No children, either. *You* got nothing to worry about, *I'm* the one, eh? Yes, yes, I mean it! I surely mean it! . . . Haven't had a drop today, not a drop. I'm serious. Would I be talking like this if I wasn't?

Christmas is the worst time of all, the worst time. Too much going on. The kids run wild, the women go crazy with baking and cooking, us men sit around with nothing to do, s'post to be dressed up all day—the hell with that, Christmas morning and Christmas dinner is enough for me, and then if we go visiting—that's enough for me, thank you. Slipped out to the barns, checked the stock, went down to the river for a look-see, had to get some fresh air, the damn women want the house too hot, and all them kids under one roof. . . . No, they ain't no real nieces and nephews of mine, more like second or third cousins, something like that, makes my head spin to figure out these damn-fool connections; and of course Anna's got to throw the house open for her rag-tail relations, I don't mean you and Morton, honey, you're special and you ain't got no kids, and anyway we was just there at Easter, at your place —you made that ham with cider, that was the best I ever tasted, girl, don't you take no back seat to big bossy Anna
162

or her momma or that what's-her-name, the aunt, out in the kitchen loud-mouthing how things should be done, and *her!*—serving her people fried scrapple all winter, she was. Oh Anna ain't a bad cook, Anna's just fine, she loved you asking her about that stuffing, what was it, chestnut? —she loved that, don't you let her fool you. . . . Do you like dumplings? I got a taste for them, Jesus! Like 'em better than potatoes. They got to be made right, though. Beat an egg and mix it in, and maybe some nice fresh butter too, that's the way I like them, nice and rich. A man's got to eat, you know. . . . Shot a half-dozen pheasants last fall, wasn't even going to take the time off, Anna roasted 'em up just fine, though she was grumbling like always. Shot one of 'em out back of the barn, damn fool thing was just perched there on the fence, big as life, big cocky male, give me plenty of time to grab my gun. . . .. That was your bread, wasn't it, the honey bread, tasted so good? And the black pudding. Too much to eat, though —too much Christmas by the time you're through. Jesus! Gonna be carrying a belly big as Anna's old man if I don't watch out. . . . *You?* Never! A nice husky girl, just the right size, just *right*. Don't you talk against yourself, you hear? I don't allow that.

Should we get married then, I asked you, and you hid your face in my shoulder and didn't say a word, and I give you a shake, eh?—and you didn't say a word. You were crying. Well—! I'm the one with the kids, I said, and another on the way, look at me, am I afraid? I am not. I never started out with the idea of, of where it would take us, you know; never had a thought of it . . . or maybe I'd been scared as hell. . . . Pearl? What's wrong? You don't love him, do you? You know you don't. Feel sorry for him, maybe. He's a nice guy, hell, I been over there helping him out this summer, and never minded doing it either; it ain't his fault about that bad leg of his. Pearl? Honey? Where are you? I can see you, girl, where are you?

We were dancing that one time, you and me. Stomping and laughing. What was it except having fun, no harm to anybody, you said I was whiskery and whiskeyey, and poor Anna pretending not to notice. You had a drop yourself that night. I like a woman that enjoys herself. I don't like a woman that hangs back, or one that nags all the time, or one that's always sick and whining and sniffing. Your hair—I like the way it hangs loose, that's the right way to wear it. I like that color, honey-brown, could bury my face in it, otherwise it's cold, it's so cold with the wind coming off the river, and the winter goes on so long. . . . I never meant to hurt you, Pearl. Never. You ran outside and it was still snowy, must of been April by then, snow crunching underfoot, and neither of us with coats on, and I followed, you're damn right I followed, I wasn't going to stay put. Gave you a pinch, gave you a shake. Kissed you. You broke away, you were scared, but you knew who I was, you knew what I wanted. . . . Afterward you said you loved me, said you didn't love your husband, you were crying and acting almost crazy, and I told you be still, be still, wouldn't I take care of you? Never a doubt of it! Never!

I never changed my mind.

In the corner of your eye you can see it sometimes. It's best not to look. Pearl, so much has happened since we said good-by! I got so much to tell you! The thing I have learned is: don't give them a chance to get you. You hear? You're young yet, just a girl, eh?—plenty of time for you to worry about such things. I'm changed, I'm different now. See myself in the mirror and have the urge to cry out, it's such a surprise . . . such a surprise. You wouldn't know me maybe. Wouldn't recognize me. Pearl? Would you . . . ? Recognize me, love me? Now? Would you . . . ? But hell, you're just a girl; just a girl; don't pay no mind to me when one of these spells is on.

The thing I have learned is: if you give them a chance to get you, you're finished. Your life is theirs, they play around with you, stick needles in you, hook you up to their machines. Oh it's cruel, girl, you don't know how cruel! You don't *know*. I hope you never do, it was a good thing how Morton died, so fast like that, they said it was a stroke and then something failing—his liver, was it, or his kidneys—and he never lived more than a few days, so you didn't have to watch him suffer, I'm glad of that for you, you looked strong but you really weren't; not really. I wish I could spare you everything ugly, girl. I wish I had that power.

Poor Josef, do you remember?—Krassov. You wouldn't know him now. You'd scream and hide your eyes, that's what you'd do. Scared my poor daughter Arlenie. They stuck their needles in him and hooked him up to their machines and they've got him, he can't die the way he was s'post to, poor bastard. I sat with him, did I tell you? Sat with him in town until a nurse come in the room and pulled the blinds and snapped on the overhead lights and told me it was time to leave, visiting hours over, but how could I leave him, how could I just walk away . . . ? He wanted me to help him, you know. Wanted me to help him out of there. It was the hardest thing I did, walking away. . . . Now it's Christmas, I ain't got much heart for it, s'pose I should go out and open my presents, don't want to spoil the day, the children especially deserve a good Christmas, you know, it's got to be crowded and lively and warm, otherwise the winter is just too damned long.

Pearl? You know you're not shy, girl! Why don't you come closer?

There was Baby Dennie in the high chair, gurgling, giggling, face smeared with frosting from the Christmas cookies, bright dyed red, and the long-needled pine with the angel at the top brushing against the ceiling, and the living room floor awash with torn wrapping paper, bright red, bright green, silver, gold, big satiny ribbons and bows underfoot, and the honey twist all eaten, only a few crumbs and smears of confectioners' sugar left on the plate, and the knife fallen onto the floor beneath the coffee table, and Chuckie lying at one end of the sofa, a blanket tucked around him because of his bad cold and sore throat, looking peaked, maybe a little sick from all the Christmas cookies and molasses cookies and butterscotch brownies he ate that morning—and all before noon, even: and Momma in her easy chair by the side window, still unwrapping presents, taking her time, smoking, sipping coffee, nibbling at her piece of honey twist, Momma barelegged in spite of the chilly air that rises from the floor, her hair nice and brushed and shiny, the bleached streaks almost grown out now, Momma in her big fuzzy blue bedroom slippers and her blue quilted bathrobe, exclaiming over each present, and the kids playing at her feet, and Nancy fussing with the baby, and Grandpa Hurley trying to adjust one of the boy's things that came out of the package not quite right: an airplane with complicated parts. Why thank you, Laney! says Momma, looking up with a smile, taking the scarf out of the wrapping paper, Isn't this nice, just the color I need, why, it's some kind of angora wool, isn't it?—just what I need! Thank you, Laney.

The other night there was a telephone call, past midnight, and she talked for quite a while, you leaned down the stairs from the attic trying to listen, and in the morning you asked Nancy and she shrugged her shoulders and said she didn't know, maybe it *was* Earl, would that surprise anybody? If you're so nosy why don't you ask Momma yourself, Nancy said.

You undid the wrapping paper, careful not to rip it, and for some reason your hands trembled—just like a baby, to get so excited over a present!—and you couldn't believe it, drawing the tissue paper away, you had been mooning over this sweater at Menton's and here it was now, Momma's Christmas surprise, a lamb's wool cardigan of dark pink, very dark pink, and the buttons a pearlish-dark pink, and Momma laughed at the look on your face, she was so pleased. My God, how did you know? Jesus. . . . You took the sweater out of the box and examined it and held it up against you and ran your fingers over the soft, soft wool, and in the back of your mind you recalled the price, which was high, too high, far too high for a sweater, and you wondered who was going to pay for this and for the other things—the kids' toys, the leather bedroom slippers for Grandpa, the baby clothes and playthings, the electric football game, the new clock for the kitchen, the towel set, the mirror for Nancy's room, the turkey roasting in the oven; you looked over at Momma, now scolding one of the cats, which had jumped into a pile of things and knocked them over and gone a little

166

berserk from all the excitement; and you didn't ask. Thank you, Momma, you said. Thank you, Momma.

There was a long-needled pine this year, a fine handsome healthy tree, and two strings of bubble lights, bubbling away right now despite the snow glare from outside; there was the old faded crèche beneath the tree, pushed against the wall where the kids couldn't step into it, Baby Jesus in His crib with cotton batting beneath him, Mary and Joseph on either side, in long robes, and the three plaster-of-Paris Wise Men joined at their shoulders, and the manger animals—a cow, a horse, a sheep—made of rubber, newer than the other items and oversized, so that the sheep was as large as the three Wise Men put together. At the peak of the tree, as always, was an angel with tinfoil haloing her head like a small sun, and white satin wings, and a long white gown of some real material, like muslin. There were glass ornaments of all colors, some opaque, some transparent, some frosted, some with tiny things inside them like birds or butterflies or snowflakes; there were strings of crinkly tinsel; strings of popcorn from another year, now rather dusty; dangling aluminum icicles; tiny birds, squirrels, bears, reindeer; cutouts of Santa Claus and angels and candles the children had made at school; artificial snow scattered over everything. There were acorns with smiling faces painted on them, and decorated pine cones, things you yourself made—many years ago, at the grammar school. Doesn't everything look nice now, Grandpa Hurley said, blinking, as if the size of the tree and the number of the ornaments and the busy gurgle of the bubble lights were quite a surprise, something he'd never seen before.

The television was turned on, there were Christmas carols by a boys' choir, but no one listened; some of the little children were squabbling, Momma was exclaiming now over a ten-ounce bottle of Lilac Spray Cologne Ronnie had given her, and of course she had to spray a little of it on her throat and shoulders and the inside of her elbow, and everyone else had to have a chance at it, and one of the children sprayed the cat, and the lilac odor was mixed in with the odors of cigarette smoke, roasting

167

turkey, baby's formula, baby's diapers, medicine for Chuckie's throat, coffee, pine needles, Grandpa's unique smell that wasn't exactly pleasant but wasn't too bad either, tobacco and old clothes and stale food and something indefinable.

You jumped up to wipe Dennie's mouth with a tissue, since no one else was going to. You began to clear away some of the mess, stuffing wrapping paper too badly ripped to save into one of the big boxes, picking up bits of coffee cake from the rug. Noise! Commotion! Christmas! . . . You couldn't sit still for more than five minutes these days: your mind swerved onto Kasch no matter how you tried to keep it free. I must disgust you, he had said, I must seem ridiculous to you, I love you, I would never hurt you. . . . His hands, his mouth, his laborious breath. The sound of the whiskey bottle touching against the rim of the glass, lightly, almost inaudibly. I love you, I would never hurt you, I must disgust you, this has been a terrible mistake. . . . You came home and stamped snow from your boots and there was Momma looking at you, just looking, and not a word did she say, as if she knew everything—had been right there in the hotel room with you. You hid the expensive glossy brochure from the Rosewood Gallery, you said nothing about the bird cage, the wonderful omelette, the steak, the sudden, terrifying exhaustion you had felt most of the day. Momma I can't help it, you wanted to cry, going to her, feeling her arms around you, I'm so lonely, Momma please understand, I don't know why I went with him, I think I love him, I just want to be with him, lie next to him and the two of us could sleep —just lie beneath a cover and sleep and sleep—and never any shouting, never any slaps or blows or blood—never any nightmares again. I'm so lonely, Momma, I never knew it before.

You carried some of the boxes and wrapping paper out to the trash barrel and rinsed the breakfast plates in the sink and opened the side door and leaned out to get away from the noise: a fine clear sunny day, quite cold, must have been near zero. Snow heaped up unevenly, drifted across the yard, in strange delicate patterns on the broken

168

windmill and finely threaded against the front of the hay barn; last summer's hollyhocks and sunflowers and overgrown mustard weed top-heavy now with clumps of white, as if their heads were bowed, something weighed upon them and they must think, think, think. . . . There was a thin, cold, whistling wind from the mountains; it smelled of pine, of rock, of empty blue sky, of snow. You stood in the doorway staring, breathing in the air, thinking of the photographs, thinking of Kasch, his long thin legs crossed, his face pale and attentive in the mirror. I'm sorry, you whispered, I'm sorry—wait— But the image disappeared. You were staring at the old barnyard, at the familiar sagging roofs and doors, the chicken-wire fence around the chicken coop, belled out at its bottom for years, broken, useless, an eyesore, and there was Grandpa's kitchen garden of last summer, a wasteland of snow, a rough white desert where drifts careened this way and that way, no logic to them, a few tomato vines still attached to their poles, a few cornstalks not yet broken down. Out there with Grandpa one sweltering July you had squealed, having discovered a caterpillar in the young potato blossoms, and were going to kill it, disgusted by it, and frightened, and silly, and Grandpa told you not to touch it: No, no, Dolly, you see that one's got little grubs on it, see?—little bitty grubs hanging onto his tummy? They're eating him alive, that's what, those are some other bug's babies, and *they're* killing him, so you let them all alone, the whole bunch of them, see?—when they're done with him they move on to another caterpillar just like him and eat *him,* and we don't need to do nothing, y'see? So you let him alone, Dolly, just let the poor bugger crawl away. He ain't got long to live.

Leaf hoppers, aphids, squash bugs, tomato worms: hidden now beneath the snow, the hard crusted soil. Sleeping. Waiting. . . . Ain't got long to live.

I'm so lonely, Momma. I never knew it before.

Butch came running up the lane, tongue hanging loose. Paws all wet, big floppy clumsy tail threshing like mad, fringed with snow. Make sure he doesn't track up the house, Laney, Momma sang out behind you. This is

Christmas Day and I'm going to enjoy it best I can. Jesus, I *got* to enjoy it!

The telephone rang but it was just Aunt Esther, you couldn't hide your disappointment, that was cruel, cruel, Aunt Esther liked you so much, Aunt Esther was the nicest of the relatives, lived alone in Yewville and would have been happy to have you stay with her, be her little girl, you chatted with her a while and thanked her for the present she'd sent out, a very nice imitation-leather belt, just your size, and then she wanted to talk to Momma, and then to everyone else, saying Merry Christmas to everyone, and the children had to be rounded up, and Grandpa, who said the hell with it, why such a fuss, Christmas was like any other day, all this bullshitting embarrassed him, couldn't they tell Esther he was somewhere outside and couldn't be reached?—he hated telephones anyway, never learned to talk right over them. Another call came when you were helping set the table, but it was Jeannie and you couldn't talk—just exchanged a few minutes' news—her boy friend had given her a bracelet, Brad had given you a wallet, but you'd known that a while, it wasn't much of a surprise. Still another call came just before dinner: Aunt Carrie and Uncle Will, wanting to say Merry Christmas to everyone. Afterward Momma said in a strange voice that Vale wouldn't be calling—she knew—every time the phone rang she knew it wasn't Vale and it never would be Vale, and nobody said anything, not even Grandpa said anything, for fear it would start her crying. . . . I know he'll never call, she said.

For Christmas dinner there was turkey with corn-bread stuffing, which you had made yourself, and mashed potatoes, and gravy, but the gravy was too greasy for you, as always, in fact the sight of it in the dish could sometimes make you gag if you stared at it, so you had to be careful—Momma noted behavior like that and wasn't pleased; there were beets in sour sauce, a favorite of Grandpa's, and glazed onions, and Parker House rolls from the grocery store, in a little tinfoil tray that went right into the oven, and Grandpa complained about the taste of them, the white bread all doughy, he said, why
170

didn't Arlene make some real bread or at least let him, he knew how, he used to know how; but though he grumbled as always he ate three or four of the rolls, thickly spread with butter and rubbed around his plate, into the gravy and beets and mashed potatoes, and you tried not to watch him eat, or even to listen to the noises he made. You sat between two of the small children, to keep them apart, and across from Ronnie, who ate fast, ducking his head to his plate, scooping up food as if he were starving, probably not tasting it; you told him to stop eating like a pig, and he kicked you under the table, and you tried to kick back but couldn't reach him, and Nancy said they'd forgotten the sweet potato and apple scallop, she'd made it special, and there it was over on the stove, covered up, maybe it should be reheated; and the baby started to cry; and Chuckie was coughing so hard, it sounded as if his throat was all raw; and the phone rang again and half the Bartletts wanted to answer it and the other half wanted to let it ring, but Davy jumped up and ran to get it, and came back, saying it must have been a wrong number, whoever it was hung up when he said hello.

Grandpa was feeling good now, had a bit of rum on the side, had eaten every bit on his plate and wiped it clean, as he said he was taught, and over dessert he started telling stories, and you picked at your food, a little of this, a little of that, maybe you'd stop eating again, you hadn't much appetite, Momma complained you left so much turkey on your plate and hadn't even tried the beets or the gravy, which wasn't anywhere near as greasy as last time—you told her to leave you alone, you weren't used to eating at this crazy time of the day, what was it, only two o'clock? She said you were wasteful and a smart aleck and were going to get your mouth slapped, and Ronnie sneered, and Momma told him to shut up, and you and Nancy exchanged a look, rolling your eyes, and Momma saw *that* and wasn't pleased. But the icebox pudding was good, with macaroon filling, and there were three kinds of pie—sweet cherry, apple, and banana cream (though the banana cream was from a mix)—and chocolate wasps' nests, which were supposed to be your favorite from years ago, so you had to eat a few of them, though you weren't hungry at all.

Grandpa Hurley was telling stories: you remembered them, parts of them, but they were changed now, he made up new names and places and mixed people together, and sometimes couldn't remember what he was going to say, and you wanted to run upstairs, you'd had enough of Christmas, enough of food, plates, children, Norma stinking of cheap lilac cologne, Nancy's cigarettes, Baby Dennie's mess and bawling. Ronnie did leave the table, because the Arkin boy showed up, calling his name out in the yard, and Momma said all right, if Jerry didn't want to come in, that was all right, but Ronnie should be sure to wear his overshoes, for Christ's sake, and not go tramping along the road like last time, in his sneakers. And were they going to be shooting out back? Target practice? They'd better go way back in the woods, then, because she didn't want to hear the noise, especially not on Christmas Day.

Ghosts in the swamp, walking dead men with their throats streaming blood, the Death-Angel, gigantic snakes, bears, pumas, the strange giant-sized people who lived in the mountains. . . . Grandpa Hurley drank rum and talked and talked, and some of the children left the table and went into the front room to play, and some stayed to listen, and you sat there with a cigarette, half listening, too old now to believe, thinking of how he had frightened you in the past, and now he was frightening your little brothers and sisters, and even Momma listened or pretended to listen, and hugged herself and shivered; but then Momma believed anything, at least while it was being told, even the stupid television programs, the daytime programs, could make her cry. . . . There were the Peales, a clan of giants who lived in the mountains: the men were eight feet tall, the women almost that tall, their horses were the size of small elephants, they were outlaws, they came down from the mountains and burned barns under cover of thunderstorms, and stole livestock, and kidnapped children, and sometimes killed people for no reason at all. They were ugly, very ugly. They had fangs. Their side teeth were fangs, like a cat's. Their eyes were big and could see in the
172

dark. They all had black hair, and spiders lived in it. They rode big black stallions. They were wanted by the police, had been wanted for many years, but no one could catch them. Grandpa had seen one of the Peales once, riding a giant horse, in full daylight across the bridge, across the river, not far from the schoolhouse; it had been a long time ago, the man was Nelson Peale, the head of the clan, he'd killed thirteen men in a fight once and escaped on foot along a mountain trail and there was a thousand dollars reward money offered for him dead or alive; but Grandpa hadn't his gun with him, so he stayed hidden, he knew better than to let Peale see him. A long time ago, it was. Before any of you were born. Yes, right there on the road, right by the school. Giant man with black hair, crazy eyes, a shotgun across his saddle, stallion pawing and stamping, of course he was still alive, up in the mountains, the Peales would never die out, they were nasty as wolverines and bred as fast as rabbits; it was said they were building up their numbers and planned on moving back into the Valley someday. They wanted the good farmland, the good soil, for themselves. . . . Then there was Hamilton Boys, Grandpa had seen him when he first came here, in person, Grandpa ten years old and Hamilton maybe forty, in his prime, seven feet six inches tall, he was, that was an official fact, three hundred pounds, all muscle and bone, lived up the river near the Rapids, came here alone and cleared a farm for himself, working night and day, out in the field with his horses, like a horse himself, never asking any help or loans from anyone, and later on . . . couldn't remember when, or how it came about . . . later on there were some brothers of his, older brothers, who showed up and somehow . . . somehow cheated him of his farm; but then he was elected sheriff of the county, because everyone respected him so, and he worked alone, he carried a shotgun everywhere, and had a handgun stuck in his belt; he was sheriff for a long, long time, he drove all the troublemakers out of the county, he had shooting matches and always won, he could calm a horse by holding it and stroking it and talking to it, though he had once killed a horse, a mean horse, just by slapping it on the neck: he had broken the neck like a straw. Then,

173

somehow, it happened that things went wrong. . . . Something happened, what was it? . . . the Governor of the state, yes, he fired Hamilton Boys from his job, the Governor had accepted bribes from outlaws or from Boys's brothers, who were jealous of him and always wanted to kill him, to lead him into traps and kill him, but he escaped, and so they bribed the Governor and Boys was fired, and he went up into the mountains alone and became an outlaw himself . . . and he robbed banks and trains and rich people, and once he saved a poor black man and his wife from a mob that wanted to lynch them, that was right in Yewville, on the river, and Hamilton Boys saved them and rode them away on his horse. He gave money to a family that didn't have anything to eat, and it was Christmastime; he robbed everybody in a fancy restaurant except a man he recognized from long ago, who had been just a boy at the time, but Hamilton Boys remembered him, because he remembered every face he ever saw and never forgot a friend and never forgot an enemy: he threw posses off his trail by sprinkling his own blood along a false turn; he killed many men, but always in self-defense; he never shot anybody in the back though he had the opportunity often, watching them from behind rocks or from up in trees. . . . His secret place was just north of here, around Mt. Ayr. How did he die? Well, some people said he didn't die. Other people said he was shot in the back by one of his brothers, who had a pardon already made out in his pocket from the Governor; but there was also . . . it was said . . . the Governor had pardoned *him,* not the killer, and asked Boys to be sheriff again, but Boys refused, and left this part of the country and went out to Wyoming. . . . Yes, Grandpa Hurley had seen Boys himself. He would never forget the size of that man, and the size of the stallion he rode!

You cleared the dishes, you helped rinse them and wash them, you wanted to keep busy, you told Momma it was her day, why didn't she just relax, you and Nancy could clean up, you could hear Grandpa in his room, singing, he was a little drunk and would be lying on his bed, his shoes off, maybe leafing through last night's newspaper or some old magazines, and then he'd fall asleep.

. . . Those stories of Grandpa's, you said to Nancy, did they used to scare you? Nancy was daydreaming, her mind off somewhere. She looked peevish. What, she said, I wasn't listening, what did you say? Grandpa's stories, what about them? you said. Oh I wasn't listening to them either, she said, shrugging her shoulders. I got better things on my mind.

But there were serious stories too, believable stories Grandpa used to tell when he wasn't so excited, when there weren't so many people around. Years ago he liked to tell you about the times before you were born—about members of the family, people you had never seen, certain neighbors now moved away—his voice toned-down, gentle, his manner almost cajoling, as if these stories were less credible than the others simply because they were more human. You were very attentive: even when the stories were too long and you couldn't understand them, even when they became no more than a puzzling, teasing litany of names, you listened, lying in bed beneath the heavy covers, growing sleepy, or sitting in the living room on a snowy day, one of the cats on your lap, Grandpa sucking at his pipe and talking, talking, talking, his hands sometimes clasped behind his head, his flannel underwear sticking out at his shirt cuffs. You asked few questions. You didn't know what to ask. Were these people still alive? Where were they? Why didn't they come round to visit? Was that Uncle Herman he was talking about— jumping from the Alder River bridge on a five-dollar bet? —but how could it be Uncle Herman, so slow-moving and paunchy, how could it be *Uncle Herman* who had done such things? . . . And there was another son, George, who had flunked fifth grade twice in a row, but could help Grandpa with calculations about crops and prices better than anyone else, who could figure things out in his head without any intermediary steps, but could never explain afterward how he knew what he knew. He just *knew*. Stubborn even as a boy, flunking again at the grammar school, and once again—sixth grade being his last attempt —and some kind of trouble with the teacher, George doing something to her car one Halloween night, Grandpa

175

laughed and laughed, remembering it, though he had had to haul the car out of the creek himself with a team of horses. Your Uncle George: wasn't always so crabby as he is now. Joined the Army the week after Pearl Harbor, fought in France and Belgium and Italy, never a scratch on him, only a few bad memories he didn't care to talk about—yes, that was your Uncle George. Is. He's different now. . . . And there was Matt and Carrie, you seen those snapshots of Carrie when she was a girl?—real pretty, wasn't she, not tiny like you but more Nancy's size, a nice strong husky good-natured girl—her and Matt and your Momma were my favorites of the kids, got along real well and no trouble—'s a pity your Uncle Matt married the way he did, that woman always looking down her goddam pointed nose at the Hurleys, an' making Matt move so far away, them two kids of his are almost strangers now and grown up, ain't it a shame? But Matt was a real nice boy. A damn hard worker. Him and me dug the stock out one time, a snowstorm pret'in'ere covered the horse barn, I mean it drifted right up to the roof, just one night of it, a snowstorm in November for Christ's sake and nobody ready for it, Matt was the only boy left at home then and a damn hard worker, you should have seen him shoveling away, just wouldn't stop until the job was done. . . . A real nice boy, a good son. All my sons were good, though. Hard workers. Carrie too: real sweet strong gal. All my kids turned out fine. An' grandchildren too— real fine. I'm proud of you all, I *am*. I ain't like other people I could name, always whining and complaining about their kids don't have no time for them, or their grandchildren—you know what I mean? I ain't like them old buzzards at all. 'Course I might just be lucky, eh, your momma being how she is, a real fine daughter, even if she does fuss a little too much—gets the kids all fevered-up for Christmas, which I don't approve of . . . but she's a real fine girl, I don't give a damn what Carrie and them others say, your momma maybe has a little trouble now and then but she's—well, you know: she's what she is and that's that.

You brought him a pot of coffee, strong and hot the way he liked it. Instant coffee—not fresh-ground, which he used to demand—with a packet of sugar substitute and no cream at all. Thank you, thank you, he said, smiling, showing his discolored teeth, that's a real nice thoughtful girl, real nice, just as nice as can be. Did you have a Merry Christmas, Laney?—eh? Sit down, sit down! Right there! Just knock that junk onto the floor, that's the girl, push it right off—plenty of room on the floor—got to clean them newspapers out one of these days, your momma's been after me for weeks, wants to turn the vacuum cleaner loose in here. It ain't too dirty for you, is it, Dolly? Don't want to get your nice new sweater dirty just to please your grandpa. . . . That's a real pretty sweater, that sure is pretty. The nicest shade of pink, your momma knitted that for you herself, didn't she?—or didn't she?

Toes twitching inside his filthy woollen socks. Patches of stubble on his chin, where he had missed, shaving. He lay back on the bed, the pillows twisted behind him, ashes on the bedclothes, a big burn mark on the bedside table—did Momma know about *that?*—it looked new— lazy and cheerful and mumbling, just the right degree of drunkenness. Grandpa, you want to say, could I talk to you about something?—about someone? I'm so lonely! . . . But of course you don't say anything. You sit in his easy chair, you listen to him reminisce, you are grateful to be here, *here,* it's safe here and he loves you, he doesn't know you but he loves you, loves his granddaughter, loves all the children, one by one by one. . . . He is talking about a Christmas many years ago. He is sleepy, his eyelids droop. Grandpa, let me take that— And you get the coffee cup away from him, set it on the table; but not so that he really notices. A Christmas many years ago, but how many?—when all the children were home, all his children except for the oldest boy—when he'd had all that land and things were going so well, had money in the bank in Yewville then, did you know that?—yes, money saved up in a savings account, drawing three percent interest per year, everything going real well, roast turkey and roast beef and a suckling pig and a long-needled pine so tall, smelling so nice, and your grandmother still alive, and lots of people staying over on account of the snow, your grandma's brother and his wife, they didn't have any

177

children, they were a real nice couple, he helped his brother-in-law with his farm and never expected any reciprocation, and the wife was a real nice girl too, they all got along real well, liked to play gin rummy hour after hour in the kitchen, the wood stove blazing, that was the Christmas they were all together, they were all together. . . .

You sat there while he slept; you didn't mind his snoring. You were always thinking of— You were always thinking of— No, you were just sitting there. That Christmas, that Christmas Day. The pink lamb's wool sweater, and Grandpa telling you about the family, telling you things you had heard before, and the telephone ringing in the other room now and then, and your life held in secret, there, in that room, protected by your grandfather, though he knew nothing about you: remember?

*Four*

*EVENING, winter, unnoted day.* The moon is a stone, the sun fire, the earth dirt, the snow crystallized water, there are no miracles, there is no one to blame. Kasch has assets in paper pulp, in iron ore and copper north of Lake Superior, property along Main Street and fronting the Derby Highway is deeded in his name, not to mention shares in copper and manganese mined by the Heath Company of South West Africa, dating back to the forties. Kasch lies abed nursing his juices like a spider, poisoning himself, too lazy to go downtown to the Kasch Memorial Library to discover whether South West Africa still exists. . . . Tiptoeing along the corridor, portraits of Father and Mother benign on either side, Kasch well aware of the librarians' recognition, their considerate silence, knowing he is, of course, eccentric: the son, you know, Fitz John—the one who went away and did so well, the one who's a genius: but eccentric, my yes, like certain other members of his family. In the Kasch Memorial Library there is a Poetry Room, and behind glass in hardwood cases are volumes of poetry, some bound in aged leather, some spanking new, some hefty tomes—the *Complete Browning*—some slender insignificant pamphlet-sized productions, like *Riddles,* by F. J. Kasch himself, copyright 1965. But no: better forget. Impossible to retrace the steps of that life.

Could stroll downtown through the slush, to McNeil, Lillard & Topley; inquire about South West Africa, and about the possibility of signing the holdings, the stocks and bonds and time certificates and the property, over to someone else. . . . No, not a charitable institution. No, not
180

a member of the family. . . . But why, Fitz John, *why?* Do you want to destroy her completely?

I want. . . . I want. . . .
Here, look, my desperation, my devotion, this fragment out of my Sacred Book, proof that I want only life for her, the complexity and freedom of *life:*

I slip into you, I come to life inside you, Laney, a spirit hovering about your head, following you along the ugly un-redeemed Main Street of a dismal town called Yewville, you glance around as if aware of someone nearby, aware of something, your lovely stern gray eyes powerless to detect me: for I am cunning beyond all your suspicions. I slip into you, I fill out your young impatient limbs, I ease into the rhythm of your lungs, your heart, your most secret blood. . . . Is it you or I who pushes the door open, steps into the overheated air of the five-and-dime store? So familiar! *Kresge's Midwinter Sales.* Every aisle familiar, the odor of the lunch counter familiar, the worn linoleum floor, the bright signs advertising bargains, Women's Clothing, China-ware & Glassware, Kitchen Utensils, Women's Lingerie, Toys, Cosmetics, Sewing Supplies, Curtains, School Sup-plies, Candy & Nuts, Handbags, Gloves, Men's & Boys' Clothing, Lamps, Christmas Decorations Marked Down 50% . . . . You dawdle by the counter heaped with purses. All on sale, all marked down. Imitation leather, imitation alligator, unlikely shades of red, green, tan, purses with big brass buckles, purses with shoulder straps, plaid pouchlike handbags, handbags with drawstrings, handbags of imitation fur, so many, some of them already marred, scratched, one of the shoulder-strap bags broken, on special sale: $3.98 marked down from $7.98. *All sales final.* You finger the cheap items, you check the sales tags, you want nothing here but you continue to look, it's a habit, this looking, fingering, turning over and over items on heaped-up coun-ters, in sales bins; what are you looking for? . . . Across the way, against the wall, Girls' Clothing, short skirts, Orlon sweaters, belts with silver buckles, belts with tortoiseshell buckles, frilly blouses, see-through blouses, blouses of cotton jersey. Where is it? Where will you find it? . . . Nightgowns, pajamas, bathrobes. Some are made of flannel, some are silky, slinky. So alluring! A counter piled high with slips. Machine-made lace, pink and blue and white and black,

a slip like the one you were wearing that day, that day . . .
you lay in Kasch's arms and the two of you wept. . . . No:
it isn't true. You did not weep. *He* did but you didn't; you
never will. . . . You move on, along the aisle. What are
you looking for? Where is it? How long have you been
looking . . . ?

---

Desultory reading; Santayana, Yeats, Hegel. So familiar,
their words, read and reread, absorbed, forgotten, recalled. Am I a form of their voices, are they a form of
mine, what can be said that has not already been said,
said? . . . so often, and so vainly? Should one care that
his sexual life is (more or less) over at the age of forty,
should it seem a matter of much significance, a mere twist
of a gyre and all's changed, one is flicked off into eternity
anyway. Voices, voices. No spirits but in voices, in words.
I spoke to her before I saw her fully. I heard her frightened voice before I saw even her meager, frantic body.
Should my life matter, set beside hers? Failures, failures,
early success and early irony, my error having been (I see
now, now that it is too late) the determination to develop
my gift for words at any cost and to allow my other gifts
to atrophy, to plunge fiercely into the life of the intellect,
a warrior, a cunning warrior disguised in this quite unremarkable body. Not a life of reason, perhaps, but a life by
reason directed. No allowance for, no awareness of, no
toleration of accidents. Kasch becoming the father of himself. Kasch self-ordained. But there were, of course,
omens.

: P_____, the distinguished scholar and critic and "Man
of Letters," an amiable legendary scarecrow alcohol-dazed
in his seminars, brains scrambled, now and then a glimmer
of Self and a penetrating perceptive chilling observation,
whole paragraphs, pages of eloquent discourse, as if the
dying man before us were repeating something entrusted
to him, something sacred that refused to die with him: the
university authorities eager for him to resign, to disappear:
eager for something more sanitary and less legendary than
the way he did, finally die: collapsed in the Boston subway,
182

raving, in a coma for two weeks. Distinguished Professor of, Holder of the _____ Chair of American Literature, author of many books, many essays and reviews, many. Mourned by many, also; at least in theory. . . . And H_____, whose critical biography of Nietzsche I read with such passion, such elation, to whom I wrote a young man's letter of praise, fifteen pages long, embarrassing, silly, begging, frank, vulnerable, filled with impudent questions; H_____, who was kind enough to invite me to New York to visit him, H_____ in his late forties then, keen-witted, engaging, kind, charitable, patient, generous, not yet well-known. That came later, a few years later. Weekends in his big apartment, my presence not merely tolerated but actually—evidently—enjoyed; his wife's kindness as well, her sympathy, her interest in me; Fitz John the bright student, the brightest of the bright, a worthy disciple, a flattering acolyte, not yet a rival. Ah, how H_____ lived for ideas! How I adored him! Even today, even now. In a sense. The life of the mind—the *livingness* of the mind, the mind's creations—drinking late into the night and talking, talking, talking—respectful of my opinions, no matter how feebly expressed—reciting long passages from *Finnegans Wake,* from Rabelais, from—but does it matter, can it matter *now?* After the publication of my first book our friendship ended. Never had it been a "friendship," of course; but I didn't know that, hadn't known enough not to be hurt. . . . Not nearly enough. His wife told me on the phone not to attempt to call him again, not to bother to write, it was useless, he resented me, hated me, wouldn't listen to her if she tried to defend me, and she knew better than to try it—for hadn't she lived with him for years, hadn't she been through it all before? His "young friends" ended always by stealing his ideas and giving him no credit for them, or they deliberately rejected his ideas, or presented them in garbled, insulting forms. She had lived through this many times. . . . And there was B_____ the poet, not really a friend, an acquaintance only, B_____, warmly generous when it suited him and eerily mean when it suited him, an alcoholic also—an infant sucking, babbling, gurgling his exquisite jarring music—B_____ gloating over the death of a rival, a frail elderly woman poet,

183

toasting her virgin carcass at a noisy party in his honor, his admirers and flatterers ringing him around, his fourth or fifth wife, very young, very drunk, in close attendance. Omens, all. Amusing? No. Familiar? Yes, surely. Unfortunately. The life of reason, a life of words, a life "devoted" (as we used to say) to the arts: contaminated as if from within by something not merely nonrational, not merely irrational, but positively demonic.

And so, in the middle of my life, I have turned away from my own achievements, my own moderate success, I have left the world in which "Fitz John Kasch" has a certain value. It is rebirth I seek—I am not ashamed to say so.

But I am, at times, a little frightened.

Shortly after nine o'clock in the morning of December 28 there was a commotion downstairs, and Arlene hurried to see what it was: a U.S. mail truck in the driveway, two mailmen delivering packages to the side door, the kids running around, the dog barking. Arlene had Ronnie drag the dog out back, into the shed. "Why, what is this, what is all this?" Arlene asked, amazed and a little frightened. Must be Christmas presents, the mailmen said, held up because of the crush at the Yewville Post Office; was she Mrs. Bartlett, would she sign for the packages . . . ?

"But who sent them? Is there a card? Is there a name? . . . My God," Arlene said.

Twenty or more packages, identically wrapped in green candy-striped paper, from Ogden Brothers of Port Oriskany, the city's best store. The children were already ripping the paper off, tearing at the string, making a lot of noise. Nancy hurried downstairs, still in her nightgown, an old coat-sweater over it; what is it, what is it? she was crying. Christmas had come and gone and she was still waiting for presents from her husband, or a card at least. As soon as she ran into the kitchen, though, she knew Prentiss hadn't sent all *that*.

The children had opened the largest package first, and then were disgusted with it: a table lamp with a thick,
184

near-opaque shade, gold and black in an Oriental design. "Isn't that lovely! Isn't that lovely!" Arlene exclaimed. Another package contained a portable radio, cased in bright red plastic, with a leather handle and innumerable dials; the children switched it on at once, and it worked. Music blared. There were smaller packages containing toy dump trucks and BB guns and dolls, and several imitation gold bracelets and chain necklaces and gloves, and a tin containing an English-style fruitcake, and several women's sweaters, and fur-lined mittens, and a wind-up giraffe that clattered across the table and fell to the floor, and small, carefully wrapped figurines of the kind Laney used to collect—a bright orange butterfly, a delicate transparent swan, a sweet-faced sow and three tiny piglets; there was an electric football game, and the children groaned because they had one exactly like it; there was a lovely scarlet scarf with gold threads woven in it; there was a powder-and-cologne-and-soap set in a fancy cardboard box; there was a small hour-glass timer for use in cooking; an expensive-looking wooden salad bowl from Sweden; toy goggles; toy airplanes; toy jeeps; a pup tent; a large container from the Ogden Hospitality Shoppe, which contained tins of fancy biscuits and cookies and crackers, toffees, pheasant soup, canned Cornish game hen, jugged hare, leek soup, baby octopus, and several kinds of paté.

"It's somebody who knows us," Arlene said dully, and Nancy said, holding one of the sweaters up to her chest, "Of *course,* Momma, what do you think! My God! It wouldn't be somebody who didn't know us, would it?" and Laney, who had come downstairs to see what the uproar was about, went ashen-pale, and stood for a moment in the doorway as if afraid to come any closer. "What— what is it?" she said hoarsely. "Who sent all those things?" But there was no note, they couldn't find a note, the children made such a mess, there were wrappers underfoot and tissue paper everywhere, and Nancy was saying in a singsong nasty voice, "Good old Earl! Yeah, good old Earl! Ain't he something, though, don't take *no* for an answer, you got to hand it to him, Momma, he must be crazy about you," and Arlene made a gesture as if to

185

strike Nancy, who only giggled and hopped away. "Is it Earl? Did Earl send these things?" Laney asked. She was wearing a very old pair of blue jeans and a pull-over sweater she'd had since about the age of eleven, which now fit her rather tightly; her complexion looked grayish-yellow. "Are you sure—are you sure it's him?"

"Who else would it be," Arlene said tonelessly. Yet she was fairly excited; she couldn't sit down, kept walking round and round the table, picking things up, setting them down, staring at the marvelous gifts. What a surprise! One surprise after another! "Not that it makes any difference," she said. "In our relationship, I mean. No difference at all. No difference. . . . Goddam him, I wish he would leave me alone! The bastard! The miserable bastard! . . . I told him and told him, I *told* him we were through, I'd had enough of him and his loud mouth and his drinking and bullying, the son of a *bitch,* I told him, I never wanted to see him again, that's what I said, I was serious, I'm not going to change my mind. . . . Look at this, what the hell is this," she cried, snatching up one of the gold necklaces and examining it and looping it around her neck, "seventeen-carat gold, it says, *gold.* And look at this, Laney, the craziest stuff to eat, look, jugged hare, it says, and here's octopus, and here's some candies, here, you want some?—here."

Laney was examining the fur-lined mittens. They were just her size, a lovely cloudy blue on the outside, some sort of brown fur on the inside. So soft. Warm. Then she saw the tiny glass figurines. "Oh look!" she said. *"Look.* . . . Such little pigs, look, look at them, they must be for me!"

Arlene told everyone to search through the wrapping paper and the boxes once again to find the note, but no one was able to find it. "Oh damn it! Damn *him!"* Arlene shouted. "I just can't take this any longer. . . . He's driving me crazy, that's what; he just won't let me alone!"

"Christ, Momma, don't yell so loud," Nancy said, "they'll hear you over at the Arkins and come nosing around, and that's all we need."

"Shut your own mouth," Arlene said. "You been telling me what to do a little too often, girl, getting kind of smart-assed, aren't you? Moving in here with your two kids and never a peep from that husband of yours—and never a peep about when you're going to leave—"

"*Momma!*" Nancy and Laney cried at once.

"Well—well— Well, I'm under such pressure, I'm going crazy," Arlene shouted, grabbing at the necklace she wore and giving it a hard tug, as if trying to hurt herself, "I don't know—don't know—don't know what to *do* with my life—"

"Maybe these things aren't from Earl," Nancy said angrily. "How do you know who sent them? Could be they're a mistake, come to the wrong house—could be the mailmen delivered them wrong, and you so excitable and jumping to conclusions—got to figure Earl Tuller's crazy in love with you, huh, just like every other man you run into—"

"The address is *Mrs. Lyle Bartlett,* which is me! Me! Me and not you!" Arlene cried. "Put that sweater down, who says it's for you? All these things are going back! I won't have them in the house! I told him and told him—I begged him—he's got to let me alone, I said, I've got a family to take care of, I've got so many responsibilities I could die—I'm a widow, I have my father to take care of too, and this house is caving in, and—"

"Momma, please," Laney said, covering her ears. "Don't talk like that in front of the little kids."

"I'll talk however I want! This is *my* house, my house and my daddy's, I'm going crazy with all the responsibilities, and two full-grown daughters who always pick at me, and fight with me, and run around the countryside with God knows who, and don't love me, and are always criticizing me—"

"Momma, that's just *crazy,*" Laney said.

"Crazy, is it? You think I'm crazy? My own daughter speaking to me like that," Arlene said, beginning to cry. ". . . People telling lies about us, spreading all sorts of rumors, my life is my own, I tell them, I'm not hurting anyone else, who am I hurting? . . . Earl wasn't married, he was divorced. My girls are good girls, I tell them, not wild, not nasty, and what do I hear but Laney's doing this, Nancy's doing that, always rumors, I dread to pick

187

up the telephone, no telling what gossip I'll hear, and Ronnie hanging around with a bunch of smartalecks over at Marsena, and getting in trouble, I can't control any of you, I couldn't control Vale, God knows I tried, I should have been in the car with your daddy when he was killed, then you'd all be happy, no mother and no father and you could all run wild and have your boy friends or whoever they are come right here and live, you'd have a circus, wouldn't you, dancing on my grave, you don't love your mother, you don't respect your mother—Laney, come back here! Laney! —Look at her, she walks right out, turns her back and walks out on me, hiding away in that precious room of hers—I can't control her or you, Nancy, I'm not even going to try any longer—running all over the countryside and up to Yewville and God knows where, if it's not with kids your own age driving drunk on the highway it's with men old enough to be your father. I can't control you, I told and told Earl to leave me alone. I was a different woman now, I was going to lead a different life, he couldn't just crook his finger and I'd come running, no sir, *no*—those days are gone forever, I told him—but now look, look, just look at all these presents—I just know the store won't accept them back—"

"Look, Momma," Davy cried. He set the giraffe in motion again at her feet.

The other children, including Nancy, were eating cookies; Nancy had seated herself at the table, ignoring Arlene's outburst, and was going through the presents again thoughtfully. Her full, high-colored face showed some anger, but some pleasurable excitement as well; a cookie gripped firm between her teeth, she had discovered a frilly pink slip, overlooked previously, and was holding it up to examine it. Arlene saw that no one was listening so she reached for a cookie herself. She selected a chocolate one. "I just don't know what will become of us," she muttered vaguely. "But since nobody else cares, nobody else appears to give a damn, why should *I* . . . ? I'm tired of being the only person in this household with any sense of reality."

*New Year's Eve.* Stayed home. No more desperate trips to Port Oriskany. Kasch the pervert, Kasch the poet,

Kasch the coward. Either/Or, says Kierkegaard: either one lives aesthetically or one lives ethically. It is possible, I fear, to live a pig's life, to know nothing of either beauty or ethics. . . . I caught the girl going through my trousers, seeking my wallet. I grabbed her by the scruff of the neck. Shook her hard, made her squeal. She was very frightened. Bitch, whore, slut! I panted. I slugged her hard in the belly. No mercy. Afterward, when I had revived her, pressing a cold damp washcloth against her forehead and a damp towel against her belly, she said she was sorry, sorry, she asked to be forgiven, even tried to kiss my hand. I crouched over her, kingly and triumphant. In the end I showed mercy; even perverts are human. . . . On New Year's Eve, however, I stayed home.

In my head, my wombish spirit, a poem composed itself as I slept, salvation and redemption and damnation tease me hourly, these lyric ceaseless voices I cannot control—

*Childwold*
*Mt. Ayr*
*Sheep's Hill*
*Oxbridge*
*Woodside*
*Arthabasha Creek*
*Muirkirk*
*Yew Creek*
*Skane*
*St. Joachim*
*Merlin*
*Heron Creek*
*Cranberry Lake*
*Cochrane Mills*
*Wahamiss Falls*
*White Rapids*
*Kingescote*
*Eden River*
*Rouyn*
*Timiskaming*
*Manitowick*
*Marsena*
*Shaheen*
*Childwold*

> *Wolf's Head*
> *Frothing*
> *Black Squirrel Island*
> *Rockland*
> *Millgrove*
> *Flambrugh*
> *Moran Creek*
> *Kincardine*
> *Blind Man's Creek*
> *Chautauqua Falls*

I have no fear, I journey everywhere, up into the hills, into the mountains, turning back only when the narrow roads are impassable because of snow. A land glimpsed for the first time in the hard overexposed clarity of dreams: a land waiting to be claimed, to be possessed by the dreamer. Kingly and triumphant. The dreamer wakes, the dreamer steps forth.

\*

Sleep beside me, let us sleep side by side, chaste as brother and sister, father and daughter. Chaste as the dead. I will do you no harm—no harm! Unless I've told you too much of my life, my past. Have I? Cannot recall. The adultery, the charade of "talking it over," the rumors spread around Cambridge—Fitz John is, didn't you know, crazy, haven't you always sensed, paranoid, isn't it obvious, a potential murderer, don't his strange eyes give him away?—quite, quite mad. Can't remember what I said. Drunken monologue. Girl beside me, listening, too alarmed to speak. I love her. Loved. Don't dare see again. For her sake, for mine. . . . If we could only sleep side by side, holding hands, perhaps, good friends, loving friends! . . . wanting only the best for each other, wishing for the best. Or is she the daughter I never had, the daughter I crave? Her gray eyes, her soiled angelic face, her rosebud lips, bobbing curls. . . . Kierkegaard was a cripple like me, a vengeful dwarf, ugly, wizened, never a day without pain (like Pascal also: why is there so much pain in us, in genius?) which explains the cruelty of his pronouncement: Either/Or. But it must be Both/And! BOTH/AND! Both the girl and God, both time and eternity, both beloved and daughter, wife and sister, beauty and goodness. Both! Both!

190

A woman appeared at the foot of the stairs, I looked down and saw her silhouetted against the snow on the flagstone path, she called up to me, Kasch, Kasch? and my heart sang, I had never heard so melodic a voice before, I knew that my doom was upon me. Fitz John is a doomed child, they said. Whispered. Behind my parents' backs. They believed I was brain-damaged at birth—my mother had waited until her late thirties to "have a baby" —why, I don't know, can't know, don't wish to know: would you? I did not speak until the age of three, I did not crawl with the proper zest, I did not show the usual infant's curiosity in the phenomenal world, nor did I like being coddled and kissed and crooned over. They thought I was going to be "slow," a moron at the very least, and it would serve the Kasches right, wouldn't it, the two of them such snobs, such romantic outlandish snobs, throwing away old William Kasch's money like that, in handfuls, like twin gods of the countryside. . . . But there was nothing wrong with me except weak vision, which conferred upon everything I saw faint rainbows, a kind of blessing, an enchantment that the proper eyeglasses soon banished. Often, now, I go without my glasses out of laziness or sullenness, or because I have forgotten them, and the world dances prettily about me, the snow glares through the dusty windowpanes, the familiar mundane objects of my life take on a hushed iridescent halo, I glance out the window, blinking, and see someone striding across the park, walking a dog, maybe, or hand in hand with a lover, or alone . . . and my heart pounds with the hope that, the expectation that, the knowledge that. . . . But I am always wrong: no one comes here, no one knows me, in any case it would not be *she*.

Kasch, came the voice, Fitz John Kasch, wake up, it's time, come, come to me, I'm here, it's time for you, for me, time to wake—But I fumbled at my clothing, grabbed my glasses and put them on, atremble, and took so long getting downstairs that she lost patience with me: she had gone. Only the wind blowing across the hilly park, through the spruce and elms and low-lying juniper, only dusk, this perpetual midwinter dusk, mere emptiness, mere essence;

191

no human woman at all. Yet I smelled something light and fragrant, something perversely sweet. Must have been lilac. Lilac? And spring a small galaxy away?

Red-earthy wet, narrow rivulets aching. The pit of the belly aching. You were terrified the first time, your hands shook, you heard the whimpering in your throat: a small hurt animal. What was happening to you, to *you?* Momma had told you what to expect, Nancy had told you, your cousins and your friends and girls at school, you understood perfectly well, you had read about it, even, in the magazines your mother had lying around the house, you knew about babies, there was no mystery, you had seen the cats, the farm animals, you had lived with your mother and her pregnancies, there was no mystery, you understood the boys' nasty remarks, you caught onto the jokes and even laughed, you were not a child, you were not ignorant, no one could frighten *you.* Yet it began, began suddenly, one hour of one otherwise unremarkable day, the sensation of weeping, the pit of the belly aching, weeping, aching, a corresponding ache in the throat, as if you must weep for the loss of blood, for *this* blood, so dark, red-earthy dark, so secret. Your hands shook. Your knees shook. Now it is happening to you, now to you. To you. A sensation of lightheadedness. Euphoria. They said you were anemic, you were too pale, look, said the doctor in town, taking your hand and drawing your arm beside Momma's, look at the difference in skin tone, you see?— she's undernourished, her skin is the color of wax, we'd better take some blood samples. Anemic, lightheaded, feeling faint when you stood too quickly, so that you had to lower your head, whimpering, until you were all right again, the balance of blood restored. Iron tablets, red meat, liver, milk and cheese, green vegetables. You blushed an angry red when Momma spoke about your "periods," you detested that word, you could have slapped her right in the face, while the doctor stared in astonishment, how dare she, how dare anyone, you muttered something and Momma was angry, you went to wait in the car, how dare she, how dare they, it was a secret, it was
192

sacred, your body ached with it, carried along by it, how dare anyone intrude or even name what you were experiencing . . . ? The blood a blessing, fingers stained with it, clothing stained, sometimes too much of it, clots of it, what if you bleed to death? . . . oh my God, my God, don't let, please don't let. . . . Earth-wet, sluggish blood, a look of dirt, soil about it, fascinating, frightening, a secret not to be named. To yourself you whispered *It*. Now *it* is coming, now *it* is come. You ached with *it*. The cramps in your belly, in your loins, the heaviness in that part of your body, the attacks of dizziness, the fear that you would faint on the school bus or at school and everyone would gape at you and afterward everyone would know, the boys would make up songs and jokes about you, about *it*, and you would have to run away. Just relax, Momma says, don't be so tense, honey, that's what causes the cramps, you're all tight, wound up like a clock, Jesus, just touching you I can feel the tension, nothing will go wrong, Laney, just relax, don't be so afraid, it's nothing, it's really nothing, when I was a girl I had such cramps I had to stay in bed the first day and practically eat aspirin and Pa would give me a little brandy, he knew what the trouble was, he was so sweet, then after I had Vale it got easier and as the years went by even easier and now it's nothing, it's really nothing to me, I don't mind at all, I almost like it, I *do* like it, something about the certainty of it, I can't explain, but why are you so embarrassed, Laney, why are you so angry with me? Do you think you're the only one . . . ?

Barefoot, on your cousin Amos's old horse, soles of your feet out of the stirrups and placed flat on the horse's shoulders, riding along the lane, dreaming, whispering to yourself, you weren't going to stay home, weren't going to lie in bed, the heating pad on your stomach; you ran out, you ran out as always, you weren't sick, you liked to tramp the fields and your secret places in the woods, your secret paths through the underbrush, you ran along the river, you were Laney as always, nothing was going to keep you home, you showed up heat-flushed and dirty at your Aunt Carrie's and she made you lunch, scrambled
193

some eggs and breakfast ham in her big old iron skillet, and you played with the cats, you carried your favorite cat around until it struggled to get free, you saddled up Amos's dappled mare and rode out along the lane between the cornfields, Laney as always, Laney Bartlett, at the center of you, secret and aching as if it were angry, the narrow rivulet of blood continued, you could feel it seeping down from your body, tiny bubblelike drops, you weren't afraid, the pain was no worse than a mild stomachache, you could live with it, you wouldn't lie in bed and baby yourself and have everyone in the house know, and you didn't want Momma hovering around, you didn't want her sympathy; you were sure you hated her.

You rode to the end of the lane, you pulled at the horse's mouth and made her go down an incline, toward the creek; she was stubborn and lazy and didn't want to go, she was testing you, she wondered if she had to obey you, but you forced her down, her black tail flicking all the while, her head moving from side to side; she snorted, stamped, sighed, you stayed with her, talking to her, scolding. The noise of the insects on that day! . . . Singing like crazy in the marsh, in the high reeds and cattails and underbrush along the creek. And the birds, red-winged blackbirds, singing, calling raucous haunting calls, birds with tiny red and yellow patches on their shoulders, swaying on the reeds, excited by your presence. Nothing has changed: here is the swamp, here the creek that runs through your uncle's property, looking one way from this bank, another way from the other bank, looking different when you gaze downstream, different when you gaze upstream, but the same creek, the Yew Creek, always the same. The noise of its flowing, its passing, the splash, the spray, the waves breaking around the larger rocks, the sight of a frog jumping in alarm; you know where you are, you are safe, it's quieter here than on the river, it's quieter here than at your own place, where so many people live.

You stare at the water. Water and light, light-dappled, light-splashed. The creek flows from the mountains. You can see only a short distance upstream, the banks are overgrown, your vision is foreshortened, you stare and see
194

nothing except the water cascading toward you, you hear nothing now except the splashing, the low murmur, you feel only the sun on your face and back and the mare's rippling sides. Alive, alive. Everything is alive. You bring one knee up over the saddle toward the other knee; the pain is lessened that way.

Bankside bushes, sumac and willow, and vines trailing into the creek dry as corn shucks, mustard weed high as your shoulder, flies buzzing, bees everywhere, chicory, witch grass, small white butterflies, a water pipit walking on the other bank, a hawk cruising slowly in the distance, the hot deep blue sky, the minute seeping of blood. Boulders white-baked, moss baked brown in their crevices, water bugs, water spiders, the sky reflected in broken patches, the wind-stirred marsh grass, the vibrations you begin to feel, water pounding downstream, downstream, the great deep-chested breathing of the mare, the beat of the sun and the seeping of blood: you are amazed, you are lifted out of your pain, your fists clench in the horse's coarse hair and you hear your own voice, you hear strange singing words, not to be understood. What does it mean, why did you come here, what led you *here?*—a place, another of the sacred places you will remember all your life. Why this side of the bank and not the other, why your Aunt Carrie's farm and not someone else's, why today, why this hour, why Laney, when other children in the family have died, when the Childwold cemetery is filled with the dead? Here everything is living, everything is alive. The air rings with life. The light is so strong you can hardly see: cascading toward you, blinding you, plunging downstream from the mountains, from the future, making its way to you, to pass by you, breaking in the rocks a few yards away. Your vision goes out of focus. You are not dizzy, you are not lightheaded, you see the coin-sized splashes of sunlight, you hear them, you feel them burst in your blood, you lean forward to ease the pain, belly nearing thighs, back bent over the saddle horn, fingers caught in the horse's mane, lips moving. You are speaking. Singing. Whispering. You are speaking to the horse, to comfort her, to steady her, to apologize. You are speaking to the creek. To Laney. It's lovely, it won't hurt, nothing will hurt for long, it's what you must accept, it's normal, it's beautiful, it's alive, it's living, you don't own your body, you don't own the creek, you can't control it, you mustn't try, you must float with the current, the plunge of the rapids, you must close your eyes and move with it, everything is spilling toward you, around you, inside you, through you, your blood flows with it, you are rivers and streams and creeks, there is a heartbeat inside you, around you—

Beneath you the horse stirred impatiently, flicking her long stinging tail, heaving into life. A great body stirring, an alien life beneath you, a creature in its body as you were in yours. In you there stirred awe of it, of its restrained strength, the grace of its muscular sides and thighs, its hard hoofs. A heartbeat in the body, in both bodies, a pulsebeat in the creek, in the throb of the air, in the sun; ripples in flesh, snorting, neighing, whinnying, tiny dance of hoofs, eyes bulging from their sockets, deep brown staring eyes, again the impatient snap of the head, and you awoke and slipped your feet into the stirrups and stroked the horse's head between her ears, crooning to her, apologizing, allowing her to turn back, to return home.

Last summer of childhood, last July, girl and creekbed, bare heels and toes, sleep, let me childhide, Momma draws the covers up, Momma is singing, lovehide, lovewild, your fingers stained, the bedsheets stained. Just bleed, bleed, says Momma, nochrist, nogod, dark earthy-wet rivulets, secret, sleep, the creek carries it away, the words drown, you don't own yourself. The heartbeat continues.

Old Mrs. Krassov, Josef's mother, sitting in her rocking chair on the veranda, a new greeny-stiff straw hat perched on her head, shelling peas, fingers moving slowly, joints swollen, ugly, it's arthritis, it's a hell for her, ninety-one years old, shapeless fallen body, big-hipped, bluish-white veiny legs, thick cotton stockings, twisted, felt bedroom slippers with toes cut out to ease the pain of her corns, shelling peas all morning, face like a wrinkled glove, three or four teeth remaining in her jaws, a slow smile, grin, a look of recognition, cheerful mannish hello, *hello*. Why, Joseph, good to see you. Good to see you, boy.

In the tall, flattened grass there are snakes—harmless garter snakes—but you must be aware of copperheads—and in the mountains there are rattlers. In the riverbed, in the creekbeds, there are water snakes. Slow languid coiling motion. A mystery, their swimming, their movement, their life. Joseph's boy was playing with the Krassov's grandson in the small barn, sitting on the old plow seat, raising dust, rustling of what might have been mice, rustling in the hay, the children were bare-footed, are bare-footed, he heard a shriek, and another shriek, Mrs. Krassov was still talking, Mrs. Krassov was deaf, he had to back away from her, pleading, face gone white and pleading, no no no no, and then he ran, he ran, the shrieking stopped and then started again, by the time he got to the barn the Krassov boy was running toward him shouting— The children are bare-footed, they run everywhere in the tall grass, their browned feet are covered with scabs, their legs are covered with scars, you are not to blame. Shrieking, shrieking. Oh the terror of it! . . . Mrs. Krassov heard nothing, hears nothing, small milky eyes blinking in puzzlement, those eyes in the mirror, those dirt-lined creases in the skin, what has happened, Joseph?—what is happening? The shrieks grow fainter. The child, the boy, your son: he is not going to die. You know this. You know that the bite was a superficial one, the poison was mild, he did not die, is not going to die: a brief period of alarm, of fright, and that's all. You slashed at the wound yourself with a pocket knife. It bled, bled free. No one died. Your son did not die. . . . Which son was it? Cannot remember. One son and then another and another and . . . and which was it, that day at the Krassovs? The terror of it! The dread, that something so violent should ever happen again! Dear God no, no, spare my children such moments—

The shrieking again. Again, again. Old Mrs. Krassov looks up from the pan in her lap, blinking, astonished, deeply puzzled.

What is it?

Why?

Is it punishment for Pearl, for having loved her so? For having lost her?

Is it what must happen, what has happened once and must happen again, and again?

That voice, drawling and good-natured and mocking: you heard it and did not turn, did not show surprise.

You paused in front of the Montgomery Ward show window where the sales were advertised. Enormous red banners. SALES SAVINGS SALES HAPPY NEW YEAR TO OUR CUSTOMERS. SAVINGS LIKE NEVER BEFORE. Your face was burning, you hardly knew where you were, you stared at his moving reflection in the window, passing just behind you—you saw how he did not glance at you.

Snow, slush underfoot. Not cold enough for mittens, so you've stuffed yours in your coat pocket. Jeannie, beside you, is pointing out something in the window, querulous, her indignation exaggerated, as if she expects to be overheard. Shit, look at that, those shoes, you see those shoes? —with the ankle straps, the suede ones?—those goddam shoes were eighteen ninety-eight when I bought them and now the fucking things are marked down to ten dollars— how do you like that, for Christ's sake?

You turn to watch him walk away: the ruddy face in profile, the camel's-hair coat, a plaid scarf around his neck. Who's that with him?—a short, quick-stepping woman, hatless, blond hair puffed out and sprayed stiff, like wires, a woman maybe thirty-five years of age, not bad-looking. Who? Don't know. Don't recognize. He is talking to her, smiling and nodding, she is eager to laugh in response, too eager. They walk away. He doesn't see you, is unaware of you.

You feel faint. Jeannie doesn't notice; she is still angry about the shoes. What if the blood leaves your head, what if you faint here on the street? No! It can't happen! . . . Anyway, he's gone, he's gone. He didn't notice you.

Laney, Jesus, are you sick or something? What's wrong?

You are looking after him but there's no one there. Pedestrians, shoppers. Mainly women. Who? Who was it? No one. Would you have killed . . . ? Would you have run to the end of the driveway that night, would it have been possible, any of it, or was it a dream, raising the barrel and firing into his astonished face, into *that* face, you, *you,* under that spell, in that enchantment . . . ? No. Impossible. Never. Not *you.*

You begin to think that maybe it was a dream after all. Maybe you had been a little drunk one night and had bad dreams—wasn't that it? As for shooting Earl Tuller in the face: that just wasn't possible. Could never have been possible. Not him, not you. Not *that.*

On the seventh of January Mrs. Gordanier came to talk with Arlene and to look through the house, and Arlene had been sitting half-wrapped in a blanket, with Chuckie, who couldn't seem to shake his cold, watching television, midmorning and Arlene still in her nightgown and bathrobe and bedroom slippers, though wearing woollen socks because of the draft, her hair uncombed, face shiny and pale and rather plain, no eyebrows, no lipstick. She had been keeping Chuckie company because he was so quiet these days, not his usual self, hardly seemed interested in the television cartoons, and Arlene lay with him, lazily, dreamily, paying no attention to the nonsense on television but thinking her own thoughts and smoking and eating the last of the English toffees. It was January, the New Year's was past, she had not been very upset this year, didn't go out drinking like the other years, didn't make a fool of herself though Earl had called, and sent word, he was waiting for her, he said, he'd be waiting, he'd give her a while yet to make up her mind. She wasn't thinking of Earl, she never thought of Earl, it was the New Year's that was dangerous, that time of year, she felt so low, so beaten, so broken; she remembered the telephone call, the State Troopers, Lyle dead, instantaneously they said, what a blessing people said, if it had to happen at all: *He never knew what hit him, Arlene.* Shut up, she had cried, goddam you! Leave me alone! Leave me alone! . . . New Year's Day, around noon, the shame of him not being at home, hadn't been at home the night before, out drinking with his friends, men he'd gone to school with, bums, no good to their families, bastards, she knew them well, she knew how they dragged Lyle around with them, how they got him to spend his money. The shame of it, the shame, everyone knew and whispered about it, everyone told lies, the bodies had been so mangled no one could tell who had been in one car, who in another, it was not true he'd been with another woman, Arlene had never believed it, she knew the woman, the girl, and just could not believe it: Ginny Gallagher, *her,* running around with Arlene's husband! Never. Ginny was a nice girl, Arlene had liked her, had been friends with her for years, it was a pity about Ginny's husband but that was no one's fault, it wasn't Arlene's fault, she couldn't believe Ginny would hurt her like that, she didn't believe it, Ginny must have been in one of the other cars; but of course people lied. The New Year's was past, the bad time was past. She had gotten through it. No drinking, except with the family, over at Carrie's and that one night at Ephim's tavern and with Grandpa late one night, the two of them awake; she'd heard him fooling around in his room, singing to himself —how that man liked to sing—always had—*On top of Old Smokey all covered with snow, I lost my true lover . . . for courting too slow*—and then mumbling, talking to himself, maybe arguing with people long gone, long dead; and Arlene had knocked on his door and the two of them sat at the kitchen table, lights not on, sipping brandy, looking out at the yard, the snow, the strangely illuminated inky-blue sky, not talking much, just together, hour following hour, one bottle of brandy finished and another opened, not drunk, just warm and content and lazy and not wishing to sleep. She wanted to talk to him about Earl, maybe. About the children. About the house, the property, the taxes that were going to be raised. Jesus! There was Nancy's husband, a card from him finally, from Alaska. Alaska. Not clear what he was doing in Alaska. Had been training to be a pilot, a commercial pilot, maybe an airline pilot—was he still in training, in Anchorage? No explanation. Spoke of sending for Nancy and the children soon. As soon as things were settled. Soon, soon. Gone now for over a year. She wanted to talk to Grandpa about that, and about Laney, and about the shower stall in the corner of the kitchen, that awful drip, the awful rust, and about the roof needing repairs, and him, his health, shouldn't he see a doctor?—don't be mad, Pa, don't lose your temper, she would have to begin, dreading his rage— little things started him off now, any mention of his health had always maddened him—and she wanted to talk to him about Lyle, about the fact that it would be ten years soon, a full ten years, my God, how was it possible, how could time pass so quickly, her husband dead and buried for ten years, and Arlene still alive and young. . . .

But she said nothing, she said nothing, the Hurleys never spoke of such things, it was embarrassing to speak of anything like that, never a mention of God or death or love or the exact price of things, the exact price he'd gotten for a piece of land, or for a field he'd sold before harvest, unable to harvest it himself. The Hurleys talked about the preparation of food, about the weather, they gossiped, they told tales, they complained about their neighbors, they complained about their children, they were good-natured, they were good people, they liked to eat and drink, they didn't like to fuss. Arlene had never asked her father very much about her mother, because the subject embarrassed him: he'd make excuses to cut the conversation short, go outside, escape. She had never asked him about her oldest brother, John. When he wanted to talk he talked, no one could shut him up, he ranted, he argued, he mimicked the voices and mannerisms of other Hurleys, or of people Arlene did not know, people dead and gone now for many years. What about Lyle?—she did not dare ask. She was afraid the old man would stare blankly at her, not knowing who Lyle was.

She had been fifteen when they married. She'd dropped out of school at the age of twelve, being needed at home, and anyway hating to sit still and listen to the teacher going on and on about things nobody cared about, the history of the United States or the way you could multiply and divide big numbers; her girl friends had dropped out too, and all the boys, being needed for farmwork except in the worst of the winter; and then, of course, the school was closed anyway, because nobody could get through the snow. Lyle was in his mid-twenties but looked younger: handsome, small-boned, sweet. So sweet. There were other men, other boys, Arlene Hurley had been very popular, she'd had her pick, she liked to brag to Nancy and Laney how she'd had *her* pick at their age, but she had known enough to marry a man who was sweet, a man who wouldn't hurt her. Some of those others! God, how they turned out, a few years later married and with small kids and drinking so hard; Ginny Gallagher, in fact, her husband sent to state prison for killing a man in a knife fight, and other friends of Arlene's, girls like herself, in terrible trouble a few years later, when they were married women, mothers, and life had changed so much. . . . But she had fallen in love with Lyle Bartlett, who was so sweet, and everyone was impressed with the fact that his branch of the Bartlett family had moved to Yewville and owned a store, a hardware store; they were city people. Even Arlene's father, who hated most city people, seemed to be impressed. Three of his sons were farmers, and his older daughter had married a farmer, he was content with that, he didn't grumble much, in a way he seemed proud of his baby, his favorite child, who was marrying Lyle Bartlett whose father owned a hardware store on Erie Street in Yewville: it was something to brag about.

But the store hadn't been doing well. Not for years. Lyle's father knew who was to blame: the politicians, the people who had ruined the economy, foreign investors, foreign "influences," manufacturers whose products cost too much, Valley farmers who owed him money and wouldn't make good on their debts. It was a waste of time to take them to law, they simply hadn't any money: the court would find for Mr. Bartlett but no action was taken, it was useless to send a bailiff out when there was no money to be had, no money . . . and he couldn't force these people to sell their land, could he? Then there were rumors, always rumors, of deals made by courthouse people, of secret sales, bankruptcy sales, hundreds of acres sold for an airstrip that was planned, or a housing development, or an industrial park; these poisonous stories killed Lyle's father and his store was sold, the stock sold, even the counters and the appliances. Lyle was shaken but optimistic. He was not going to be bitter like his father, he said. He was not going to make the mistakes his father had made.

Slender, boyish, with curly fawn-colored hair and large gray eyes, so sweet . . . the sweetest man Arlene had ever known, until he changed. When the babies had started to come he had been a little frightened of them at first, afraid to hold them, embarrassed to feed them or change their diapers; but a good husband—a good man. She had loved him very much. Had been crazy about him. He had plans: he went into a partnership with one of his uncles, running a small grocery store in Yewville. Borrowed money. Worked hard. From nine in the morning until nine at night, sometimes on Sundays as well. They lived in town then, in a bungalow not far from the railroad tracks, on a street of small bungalows, and Arlene hadn't minded the trains after she got used to them, she loved her life, her husband and her babies; it was strange, she hadn't missed the farm much, didn't even miss her father much. There was another baby, and another. Lyle borrowed money without telling her, to invest in a project some local men were financing—drilling for oil in another part of the state, in the southeastern corner of the mountains; without telling Arlene he borrowed three thousand dollars from the bank. And the project was a failure, of course it was a failure, someone had talked these Yewville men into giving him their money and he'd taken it and there was nothing, nothing to show for it—no oil, not even adequate oil-drilling equipment. There was an exposé, even a few arrests, but what good did it do? Such fools! Stupid fools! How Arlene's father raged and crowed, how everyone laughed, these stupid fools suckered into giving their money away. . . . Their names were printed in the paper, everyone saw, everyone commented. What fools!

Lyle was at the store so often, and now they quarreled, the house was too small, so Arlene began staying out at the farm, sometimes just overnight, sometimes for a few days. The children loved their grandfather's farm. She loved it too: she could tramp around with the children, could go fishing with them, like a child herself, and there was always plenty to eat, and she loved to cook big dinners for her father and the children. There was sweet corn, there was chicken, there were fresh eggs and milk and butter and cream, good vegetables and good fruit, not the canned things poor Lyle tried to sell, that overcooked tasteless junk. A Loblaw's store had been built in downtown Yewville, the first supermarket in the area, and many of Lyle's customers went there, who could blame them?—Arlene inspected the store herself, amazed at the long wide aisles and the hundreds of things to buy, thousands of things, and there were stamps given away with purchases, green stamps, and prices were lower than anywhere else, even some of the fresh produce was cheaper than at the market, and much cheaper than it was at Lyle's store: who could blame his customers for leaving him? He got a part-time job at Vanderdeen's Auto Sales, working weekends in the used-car lot, he wore a suit and a tie and a smart-looking straw hat with a red band and he gave out cigars and did fairly well—people had always liked him, he claimed they bought cars from *him,* preferring him to the other salesmen. He began to drink more, he began to stay out late. He quarreled with Arlene but did not often hit her; she was grateful for that. Now she was staying out at the farm more and more often, and it was Lyle who would come out to spend a few days, always on his good behavior around his father-in-law, always rather eager to get away again. Years passed: the store was sold and Lyle worked full-time at Vanderdeen's and the family moved to Childwold and he lived there sometimes, and sometimes rented a room in town, and he was still small-bodied, slight, looking almost boyish at the time of his death, though he was well over forty by then and Arlene was thirty-four, no longer a girl.

He was dead, had died, it was best not to think of him. No one would love her as he had—he'd been so sweet, so tender! Her young husband was dead, she was nearly as old now as he'd been at the time of the accident, she really should not be thinking of such things, she wasn't morbid, she knew better, and anyway the man who had been killed wasn't the same man she had loved so much, she might as well admit it. . . . The straw hat with the red band, that ridiculous thing, how she'd hated it, how her father had made fun of it, mocking Lyle behind his back, making her feel ashamed she had ever married him: where was the hat now? After his death she'd put it away somewhere, out in the storage barn probably. Horrible, to come upon it sometime, to see it again. Horrible. But she shouldn't think of such things, she knew better. *She* was in charge of the household now.

Mrs. Gordanier of the County Child and Welfare Services Agency was a big-boned woman with a short hairdo, an alert jay-birdish look, all questions and no answers; not exactly Arlene's best friend. But Arlene showed her through the house just the same and tried to keep talking, tried to keep chattering, as if she weren't horrified by the bitch showing up when she did. What bad luck! Always such bad luck! Why did she show up today of all days, why at this hour, was something going on Arlene didn't know about, and her checks were going to be discontinued? Oh, the bitch! She could rake the Gordanier woman's face with her nails, could scream and scream and scream, it was unfair, it was so unfair, Chuckie sick and the kitchen a mess and the little boys' room upstairs smelling so bad because the mattresses were stained and it was too cold to air them out, and Nancy not dressed either, and her room cluttered, and the children underfoot acting like maniacs, the stairs littered with shoes, broken Christmas toys, towels, used Kleenex, crusts from that morning's toast. January seventh was so soon after the holidays, Arlene told Mrs. Gordanier, she hadn't had time to clean up yet, hadn't had a spare minute. Her son was sick and her father hadn't been feeling well and the furnace didn't work right, the upstairs rooms were always freezing, and that smell—that smell was from the furnace, it was acting up all the time now and nobody would come out to repair it. There was only the one toilet, downstairs, and it too was acting up, and the shower stall was filthy, Arlene knew it was filthy and was meaning to clean it one of these days, but she didn't think kitchen cleanser was strong enough and she was afraid to use toilet cleanser, it was so strong, she was waiting to get to Yewville to buy some special ammonia spray, somebody had told her that would do the trick . . . but the tile was so cracked, everything was so old, it would be a full day's job to get it clean. And that drip!—just listen to that drip. Her boy Ronnie had tried to fix it but without any success.

Dust balls, balls of fluff, tiny frail near-invisible strands of cobweb on the walls, up near the ceilings especially. Stains on the rugs, on the floorboards. Glasses and plates and silverware left in the oddest places. Arlene tried to laugh, surprised, wondering if the children had been playing games with her and she hadn't known—hadn't noticed. The bed wasn't made in her room but the spread was drawn up at least, and the things on her bureau set in order, not knocked every which way, which she had feared. There was a strong odor of cats in this room, which she noticed now for the first time: had one of the cats been bad here, just this morning? The damned things! Wasn't that just like them! One of them underfoot right now, the flabby-bellied white and ginger cat, ears laid back, hissing at Mrs. Gordanier. . . . Arlene laughed and gave the cat a gentle kick and showed Mrs. Gordanier up to Laney's room, the one neat room in the house, bed made and things in order, what a relief, the dotted-swiss curtains pretty, the pillows and photographs and the old doll pretty, thank God, though it was awfully cold up here, and the ashtray on Laney's bureau was heaped with cigarette butts and ashes, and there was the odor of stale smoke. Mrs. Gordanier stared at the photographs and pictures but said nothing. Arlene said, chattering away, that her daughter Laney was a sophomore in high school, she worked very hard and got good grades, fairly good grades, it was just a shame the bus ride was so long, the kids from Childwold spent hours on that damn bus, when they could be doing something useful. . . . It came out wrong, somehow it came out sounding all wrong. Just the word *damn* sounded wrong. Mrs. Gordanier only murmured something and turned away.

The television set? That was an old set, years old. Not a color set, either; just black and white. It must be down on her record, in her file, the television set . . . ? They had had it for years. . . . A new lamp, a Christmas present. A present from a friend. The car out in the driveway: another present. Toys scattered all over, the pup tent collapsed in the back hall, Davy and Mary Ellen and Louise giggling around the corner, and someone had let the dog in the kitchen, his tail was thumping against one of the chairs, Arlene knew that noise but Mrs. Gordanier didn't, she kept glancing around with that jay-birdlike look of hers, and Arlene was explaining about the Christmas presents and couldn't change the subject. . . . Jesus Christ, what bad luck! She could scream and scream, could tear her hair out in clumps, could tear Mrs. Gordanier's hair out, what did that awful woman mean by coming out here like this, spying on them as if they were white trash trying to cheat the welfare, as if Arlene weren't a widow with a big family to take care of, and an elderly father, and this ramshackle house. . . . The woman was asking her about Vale: did he have a job, was he sending money? He had a job, yes, Arlene said slowly, last she'd heard he had a job in Port Oriskany, on the waterfront, and he got checks from the government too, he was self-supporting; but he didn't send money home. No. He didn't have enough money to send any home. That was the truth—the truth. His health wasn't good, he had almost died, his face and his shoulder and part of his chest ripped open, eight months in the hospital, he wasn't quite well even now, they said he would regain his health but he hadn't, he was a good boy, a very fine boy, a hero—had been awarded a Purple Heart, did Mrs. Gordanier know that?—and he had a job and worked hard but didn't have enough money to send any home at the present time. And that was the truth. . . . That was the truth.

On the way out she asked Arlene about her health and Arlene said it was fine, just fine. She was never sick. The children got sick now and then, usually just colds, nothing serious, but Arlene herself was in good health. No need to see a doctor, then? No need, Arlene said slowly, puzzled. What was the woman getting at, what was she asking . . . ? Arlene touched her face unconsciously, but the marks were gone now, all gone, no trace of them except the scar in her eyebrow. That's good to hear, Mrs. Bartlett, the woman said, eying her frankly now, looking at the loose billowing gown Arlene wore while she buttoned up her own coat; that's good to hear.

Was that it! Was that it! Arlene was shocked, she started to say something, stopped, thought better of it. Was that it! The woman thought she was pregnant! . . . No, I'm in good health, Arlene said, forcing herself to speak quietly. There's nothing to report.

Afterward she shut herself in the bathroom, ran the faucets while she cried, cried bitterly, and not even the children pounding on the door could make her stop, or Nancy's frightened voice, Momma, Momma . . . ? What is it, Momma . . . ?


Through the scope he saw the man clearly but the man did not see him. Ha, ha! Crouched in the underbrush. Someone beside him—another of them—couldn't see because of the vegetation. Now on center, now off. Pull the trigger? Pull the trigger. Sometimes the animal died of shock, ran crazily, spewing blood and bellowing, ran until it dropped dead, you had to follow the bloodspots, blood-path, the small flies already crooning, rubbing their legs and wings happily. If living you took possession, you declared them prisoners, you flew away into the sky.

He went out with his buddies, he bought an Afro fantasy wig for himself, weird, wild, carrot-colored frizzy hair that stood out from his head at least a foot. People stared. People pointed. People were amazed. Fitzgerald's hair was tame in comparison, Fitzgerald had some style, but nothing like Vale. He wasn't jealous, though. The boys were friends and went around together, sometimes with Johnny, sometimes with other boys like themselves. They liked good times, they liked to laugh. They had promised themselves good times back here at home.

Vale worked part-time now for a friend of Fitzgerald's. During certain hours of the week he worked hard, but the rest of the time he had off. He had money, though, so he made a down payment on a new car, a black, low-slung Wolverine Special. Once in a while his body ached, the old wounds came alive and pounded away at him, so to shake the pain he would skin-pop for a day or two, as he'd been taught, but if it wasn't too bad he just drove around in the car and went out with his friends and drank beer. He had
208

a good time mainly. He didn't dwell upon the past. He even bought a handsome new suit, a suede outfit with a vest. It was the color of autumn leaves, a beautiful sharp rust-brown. He paid four hundred dollars cash for it. The trousers fitted him strangely in the crotch and sometimes itched, the material was rather heavy and made him sweat, but he wore the suit often because he looked so good in it. He caught certain glances from men and women both.

What a woman won't touch!—what a woman won't caress! He knew them all, he knew them ahead of time. Sighted in the scope, on center, right on center: should he pull the trigger or not? Maybe yes, maybe no. Maybe. Maybe not. It was up to him, it was his decision, he could do as he wished. Afterward he charged forward to make his claim. The dead lay scattered in fields at his feet, he didn't even have time to count them. That gurgling bubbling noise was their blood soaking into the earth. There were women among them, clawing at his feet. Too bad. No one's fault. He threw his gun away and pounded some of them to death with rocks, rocks in both his hands, it was the most effective method at close quarters. It was something to work up a sweat with.

He caught certain admiring glances from men and women both. "Rebuilt" face, torso, a set of teeth that sometimes made his jaws ache and caused him to worry that his gums might be shrinking—as one of the VA doctors had vaguely predicted; but handsome enough, handsome enough; real style to him, of the sort he'd never had back home. Just a farm boy back home, driving a souped-up fenderless car, in trouble with the police, charges lifted in the end—no witnesses—but they'd had him scared, the bastards. He hadn't known any better. Now he had style, now he lived in the city, he got along fine with his friends. Wide doped-up grin of Fitzgerald's, glistening brown eyes big as horses' eyes, the two of them converging on the enemy, one covering the other, one buddy protecting the other. Jesus, back in Childwold he'd hated niggers, hadn't ever talked face to face with a nigger, let alone been buddies with one! Now he was tight with Fitzgerald. They sometimes disagreed, but not often.

Johnny was second best, Johnny got drunk too often, maybe something had happened to his head; his reflexes were dulled and once he drove into a chain-link fence on Northern Boulevard. You couldn't trust him. He was a good friend, though, a good boy—a farm boy from Shaheen. Reminded Vale of, who was it, his sister Nancy's boy friend. No: husband. Couldn't remember his name.

Dropped by the college one night for the hell of it, alone, strolled through the corridor in his suede suit, no overcoat, because he was feeling nice and warm. Where was her classroom? Where was the bitch hiding? . . . but the room was darkened. Up the hall a class was in session, the door open, Vale drifted by and listened to a man's voice, listened to laughter, snickers, the resumption of the voice, something about interest rates. Vale stared into the classroom. Rows of desks, people in there, mainly men; the teacher a short, lively little bastard, writing on the blackboard so fast Vale couldn't believe it. Hey, said Vale, where's Miss Carlson? The man looked at him, big piece of chalk in his fingers, just looked at him, and the students looked at him, and Vale said again, Where's Miss Carlson, she used to teach down the hall, and finally the man smiled and said he didn't know, didn't have any idea; sorry; why didn't Vale try the registrar's office up on the third floor? . . . Though it would be closed probably; so why didn't Vale come back tomorrow and see? Vale thanked him and walked away and smiled, thinking of the woman, thinking he might go to her apartment building and look her up, maybe, maybe not, he hadn't hurt her, hadn't touched her, she had been talking very nicely to him and he'd been listening, and after a while he undressed her, so he must have touched her after all, and it came to him, the idea came to him, that he would surprise her and all the others: so he told her she was ugly, disgusting, he told her she made him sick the way she looked, what a pig she was, made him feel like puking, didn't she know *all women* shaved between their legs . . . ? The pig, the disgusting ugly pig, he had half a mind to give her a good hard kick there, to punish her; but she'd been so surprised and so frightened there was no need.
210

Maybe he would look her up sometime, maybe not. He would take Fitzgerald along maybe. Then again maybe not.

Gaping holes in the sky. Wind from the northeast, a hurting wind, a moon flickering and going out and brightening again; the air so cold it hurts, hurts. Shreds of cloud, the universe in tatters, great heaves and gasps of breath, why did I run out here, where am I, what year is this . . . ?

The noise in the trees!—*the Siddies,* a voice scolds, *come in to your supper before they carry you off,* then silence, patches of silence, decades. The night is busy with wind, with tides of air, the sky has come apart and is shifting in pieces above my head. Nothing can stop it. Her face, her fingers on my cheek, her scent, her voice—but her name, what is her name, her name?—*Joseph,* they scold, *hurry along! hurry! What are you about, staring at nothing like that?*

In love, he is; and already married; and a father. Back and forth the words rush, like a needle being threaded again and again, always something wrong, the thread slips out clumsily, horribly, the fingers are too big, too crude, something has gone wrong. The sky rears and tosses, the sky is frightening, he stares at the bright-glowing glowering clouds being blown across the mountains and can recognize nothing: how easy it would be to lose himself, on his own land! Even here, on his own land! The wind blows everything out of place.

Shards of cloud, shreds, tatters, strips, mother-of-pearl broken into fragments. The moon appears, disappears. Appears again. Stupid-faced, blank, pitiless. So bright! —Then darkened by a great tide of clouds. The pulse of it, the hurt of it: what language has he to tell of his hurt? At such times he does not even remember the woman's name.

Love, is it? This? Now?
*This . . . ?*

He wants you, hear him beg! sigh! puff! pant!—Wiping his fingers then on the bed sheets, thinking you don't notice.

He wants you, the sensation is like tickling: like electricity: a current darting up you, into you, so strong you almost cry aloud with the surprise of it.

,Do I disgust you, he said, and you began to laugh, your body shaking, you thought of the Gelfant boy, sixteen years old, gross pinkened cheeks, eyes that roll in his head, so merry, trotting along the dirt road past the school, fumbling at his trousers to frighten the girls: behind him his brothers and the other boys yelping, laughing, shouting encouragement. And you ran, you and the other girls ran, ran squealing, ran into the school, the boy's high rapid senseless piping voice behind you, not a human voice, Heyheyheyheyheyhey, the Gelfant boy they said should be put away except he was such a good worker on his father's farm: worked harder than two men, his father claimed. And the Zinner girl, so round-shouldered she was almost hunchbacked, freckled and old-young and ugly, warts on her hands, they said she was eighteen years old but she might have been forty, and then again she might have been four or five, judging from her voice and the way she shook her change purse ceaselessly, ceaselessly; waiting for the bus she crowded against you, seemed to like you, singled you out to be her friend, told dirty jokes, gloating, chuckling, Something bad is going to happen to you, her knowing sly look, her giggle, something is going to happen, whispering the words, always the same words, until you put your hands over your ears and screamed for her to shut up, she was crazy, everybody said she should be put away!—and she didn't seem to mind but hung around you anyway, always asked if she could sit with you on the bus, though she said one day, her feelings slightly hurt, that she would kill your cat with an ax if it wandered over onto their property just once more. . . .

Hear him, hear him: he's drunk, he wants you, he's crying, he can't see without his glasses, his face is so young, so helpless, you are afraid to look at him. He's drunk but he won't let you drink. You don't need to drink, you really don't like the taste of it, you can get along without it. Head between your knees, vomiting, the police yelling at the boys, disgusted with you, one of them giving you a hard pinch on your upper arm. Look at this

212

one! Look at her! Isn't this a pretty sight! . . . He wants
you, he loves you, you wish you could laugh at him, jeer
at him, scramble out of the bed and get dressed and run
away. Love: that word. The Zinner girl whispered Fuck,
always fuck, always always always, crowding up against
you, nudging you. Fuck fuck fuck. That's what they will
do to you—that's what will happen. You sat with your
cousin Jeannie and sometimes with Nancy in the old car
in the apple orchard, reading comic books and magazines
hour after hour, sometimes it was raining and you watched
the drops on the windshield and shivered, it was so cozy,
so secret; you read *True Romance* and *True Confessions*
and *True Love* and *True Story* and *Modern Screen Romances* and *True Experience* and *Real Romances* and
*My True Story* and *My Romance* and *True Secrets* and
*Secret Story* and you traded magazines back and forth
among your cousins, among girls at school, and Momma
of course read them sometimes but didn't want you to
know: you discovered her in the kitchen more than once,
the ironing board set up, the iron resting on its metal pro-
tector, Momma sitting at the table with a cup of coffee
and a cigarette, reading a magazine, irritated if you
caught her, angry, though if you made enough noise on
the stairs she would have time to put the magazine away,
to slide it beneath the stack of newspapers and magazines
on the floor by the refrigerator. "God Sent Me a Defective
Baby," "My Abortion," "My Shame," "He Said I Couldn't
Get Pregnant—But I Did!", "My Boy Friend Is a Sadist,"
"The Private Life of a Big-City Model," "My Boss's Wife
Committed Suicide—and I'm to Blame!", "Drugs, Liquor,
Prison and Love," "Starve or Steal—or Walk the Streets,"
"The Private Life of a Nun," "The Cincinnati Rapist,"
"My Father-in-Law Made Me Pregnant—To Spite His
Own Son!", "I Married a Homosexual," "I Believed His
Promises—I Was Only Eleven Years Old!" Diets to fill
out your breasts and hips; diets to reduce your weight
without starving; horoscopes, Christmas decorations and
recipes and advertisements for lingerie. "I was wild and
headstrong and learned my lesson," said the girls in these
pages, "I had not listened to my parents," they said,
brokenhearted, "I had not appreciated my husband while

213

I had him," they wept, they tore at their clothing, "I went after my boss and deserved the tragedy that followed"; they were a few years older than you in most cases, "Only faith in God kept me from destroying myself and my babies"; they were factory workers' daughters or maybe factory workers themselves, or farm girls like you, "The love of a good man is the greatest treasure on earth and I almost squandered it"; they were sometimes typists or secretaries or "executive" secretaries, or waitresses, or just housewives, or high-school girls gone wrong, "I came to my senses finally—and it was almost too late"; their husbands were usually factory workers but sometimes they owned small businesses or were professional men—doctors, lawyers, ministers—but the husbands' lives were vague, their work unclear, if there were money problems or unemployment or strikes or an inflated economy the girls in the magazines knew nothing of such things, they were to blame, *they* were sinful and selfish and cruel and ignorant, the very center of the universe lay between their legs, "My first kiss—and nine months later, my first baby!" and no one else was to blame, there was no larger world. You skimmed the stories, you studied the photographs, you traded one magazine for another, there were rapists and lying boy friends and perverted fathers-in-law and cruel bosses and kidnappers and friends but the girl was the center of the story, yes, you were the center of the story, just kissing and sinning and going wild with love and then the disaster followed and you wept or were beaten nearly to death or had an abortion or had a Mongoloid baby as punishment for your sins, but there were good men, there were also good men, they were husbands and fathers and kindly ministers, in the end you married them, you lived with them and had their babies, good healthy normal babies, "I don't deserve my happy marriage but I'm going to work the rest of my life to keep it." . . . You leafed through the magazines and tossed them aside and stared out into the orchard, your feet up on the car seat, your arms gripping your knees, knees pressed against your chest. You stared at the rain, at the dripping leaves and branches, at the green apples, at the
214

mist that often rose from the ground, you whispered to yourself that you were afraid, you were afraid, of what were you afraid?—you were baffled and angry and contemptuous too, but of what, of what?—you couldn't say, there were no words available, the magazine stories gave you no words, the girls were you and yet not you, they spoke to you but they lied, they must have lied, they must have deliberately lied.

Kasch, you said, Fitz John you are saying, softly, timidly, as if the sound of his name is outrageous, wait, please —wait—I'm sorry—I can't help it— I love you—

But he doesn't reply, he is asleep, his breathing is strained and slow, he's asleep or drunk, he's gone, you aren't going to see him again, you are greatly relieved, you are sick with the loss, you are triumphant.

There was a small *Private Residence* sign near the path but it was nearly hidden by snow so Arlene ignored it and went to the door of the carriage house and rang the bell. He lived upstairs, she knew. Did he have a dog? She halfway expected to hear a dog barking; in the country everyone had dogs and you had to be careful leaving your car if the dog didn't know you. She rang the bell again. No answer. Maybe it was disconnected, maybe he couldn't hear. She knocked. She tried the door—just a screen door, in bad condition—and it wasn't locked so she went inside and called up the dark stairs, "Is anyone home? Hello? Hello?"

She went up the stairs carefully; made sure she had hold of the railing. It was dark, dangerous, but at least the stairs weren't falling apart. "Hello," she called, "is anyone home? Mr. Kasch?" On the landing she knocked again, there was no answer, she put her ear to the door but heard nothing; nothing. Maybe he was inside, hiding from her. Maybe he was gone. He might have moved away—no one would know, no one would miss him. He might be dead: lying in there dead, alone, forgotten, like those hermits Grandpa would tell stories about, frozen to death in their shanties in the hills, or too sick to go out and dying of starvation, sometimes old couples, elderly couples, found together dead in bed, corpses partly decayed and melted into one another. Arlene shuddered. She knocked again but there was no answer.

She crossed the park to the museum, which she had never visited though she'd lived in this area all her life; just never got around to it. The day was surprisingly mild for February, mare's-tail clouds, sunshine warm enough to start the icicles dripping, a nice smell to the park, evergreens with waxy red berries, a walnut tree twice the size of theirs at home, damp-looking bark, everything vivid and fresh, new-looking. Beautiful.

The Kasch Memorial Museum: a cobblestone mansion with slate roofs, innumerable chimneys, impressive but rather gloomy-looking, Arlene thought, the windows had so many fussy little panes and were so narrow. Entrance through a courtyard. They hadn't cleared the courtyard of snow, had only shoveled a path through it; in the corners were ornamental trees of some kind in cement containers. In the spring, Arlene thought, it would probably be quite lovely. . . . An enormous carved-wood door, must have been of oak, with polished brass ornamentation: so heavy Arlene could hardly push it open. Inside, the foyer was rather dark. Arlene blinked, a little blinded. Had people once lived here? Here? It did not seem possible.

She must have been the only visitor in the museum. There was a uniformed guard sitting on a folding chair, reading a newspaper; there was a young clerk or attendant at the front desk, who looked up expectantly, half-smiling, when Arlene approached. It was very quiet.

There was no admission charge, which was fortunate, since Arlene did not intend to pay; she didn't have money to waste. But the place interested her: she read that the house had been built originally in 1820, was partly destroyed by a fire in 1860, and then rebuilt, enlarged, its core reinforced with concrete, its floors and walls a foot thick. Forty rooms. Forty rooms! . . . A registered National Landmark, leased to the county through the generosity of Sydney and Elvira Kasch.

Indian artifacts, arrowheads and axheads, drawings of "burial mounds," the "green corn festival," Indians dancing about a steaming pot, jet-black hair and faces that

216

appeared to be too red-tinted, rather mean, malicious look to them, unsmiling: Hurons, Mohawks, Iroquois, Tuscarora. Reconstructed bows, spears, headdresses, traps for wild game and for fish, leggings, moccasins, snowshoes, necklaces. Drawing of a portage: an Indian walking with a birchbark canoe over his shoulders and head, stooped slightly. Indian with a back pack and tumpline, a thong fastened at both ends to the pack with a wide section across his forehead. Indian on the bank of a rough-looking river, spear in hand. Gaunt, grim, unsmiling. . . . A model of an underground log cabin: a circular hole dug twenty to fifty feet across, its outside covered with brush and earth, its inside lined with cedar bark. Entrance through a smoke hole, down a log ladder. In summer, the notice said, they moved to wigwams. . . . Grandpa had talked about the Indians, always contemptuously. Everyone had hated them in the old days; now they were gone—out of the county entirely—Arlene had never even seen one. There was a reservation for them, somewhere to the west. Poor bastards, Arlene thought, no wonder they aren't smiling.

There were rooms of Revolutionary War and Civil War relics: muskets, handguns, knives, medals, flags and banners, aged crumbling maps and newspapers and broadsides beneath glass. Old sepia-toned photographs of regiments, of generals, of heroes. Arlene yawned. Boots, belts, uniforms, swords, helmets, gloves. In one of the rooms a reconstructed interior of a typical log cabin belonging to pioneers in the Eden Valley: it didn't look much worse than places Arlene had seen, had even lived in. Dark, poky, crowded with things, the cradle predominant, pretty gauzy material draped over it, even a doll inside. On the table of rough-hewn wood a single candle, burning. But not a real candle: Arlene saw that it was an electric light disguised as a candle.

Minerals in display cases. Topographical maps. More newspapers, World War I headlines, photographs, lists of the heroic dead. A small upright piano. A harp. Paintings of mountains, rivers, forests—watercolors by local artists. Amateurs, were they?—the paintings weren't very good. But Arlene liked the colors, liked the bright blue skies and

217

green pines. How wonderful, to be able to paint, to be able to draw. . . . She couldn't imagine how anyone began. What did you do first, did you sketch the scene in pencil and then fill it in, or did you just start to paint, as fast as possible, and hope it would turn out right . . . ? But she couldn't draw anything, could not even fashion a few lines together that would resemble a tree or a face or a house or a mountain; she had tried, as a girl. The lines were just lines, pencil marks. They floated on the blank white paper and were ridiculous. How did artists do it, how did their hands know what motions to make, how hard to press down, when to begin and when to end?

Then she saw something that drew her attention to it at once: a large map of the county, at least three by four feet. How interesting!—cities, towns, villages, hamlets, rivers, creeks, lakes, mountain peaks, highways, smaller roads, old trails, passes through the mountains!—why, it was all of Eden County, hanging there on the wall, blown up as if it were the entire country. She stood before it, staring. Where was Childwold? Where . . . ? At first she thought it was missing, it was too small to have been noted, then she found it, she murmured aloud her pleasure at finding it, and traced with her finger her own route to Yewville that morning. Along this road, that road, that road, and *that* road . . . across this bridge and that bridge and up the highway to Main Street and Bridge Street and Indian Trail . . . and now she was here, exactly here; *here,* where the tip of her finger rested. She smiled, enormously pleased. She didn't know quite why.

It crossed her mind that she'd been born and lived out all of her life, so far, within a few inches on this map. Was that good or bad? Did it matter? She was still smiling, there was something about the discovery of the map that excited her.

I've been happy here, she thought.

She went to the women's washroom and examined herself critically: the Persian lamb coat looked good, her jersey dress, blue-striped, looked good, her hair—just blond-tipped the other day—was in a style with bangs that made her look ten years younger at least. She was pleased with it; Nancy had done a good job. She had made

218

herself up that morning carefully, and her skin looked poreless, really nice, there were light spots of rouge on her cheeks, and her lips were bright red, and there was even a thin crescent of eye shadow on her lids. What could not be invented for a woman who looked like that! What future, what new life, what fate! If Earl saw her now he would really be sorry, that bastard. That cruel ignorant filthy-mouthed bastard. . . . But he wasn't going to see her; he wasn't going to get near her.

When she went to the carriage house again and climbed the stairs and knocked on the door, she was in luck: someone called out *Yes? What?* and in a moment the door swung open.

Trembling—
Shivering, he was so—
The agitation made his body ache, stirred the old wounds into life. Like too-hot water on the scar tissue. Began in his head, pulsed down into his body. Oh, the pain of it, the broken-headed pain. Pain pain pain.

Morphine, they had given him.

Pills, a pinch of heroin shot just under the skin, a few cans of beer, the Wolverine Special.

Then he was all right again, except for being in a hurry. He jumped in the car and backed it into the street and took off, tires screeching. He was in a hurry, in a hurry. Must get there. His head pounded with the need, all of Vale pounded with the need, like a gigantic heartbeat.

Warehouses, locomotives, railroad yards, granaries, Preston Steel, dairy bars, Swannie's Bar-B-Q, overpasses, drains, gates, walls topped with barbed wire, vans, asphalt, Esso, Exxon, Hi-Life Canned Goods, freighters and tug-towed barges and small fishing boats on the lake, a few sailboats in good weather, a constant wind. The wind blew across the lake. It blew from several directions at once. Vale noted the waves blown this way, that way, in a frenzy. He couldn't stay in one place for long, he backed the car around, headed across the bumpy sandy beach to the highway. Pain pain pain. Such wind. The sand was cluttered with debris—worn-out tires, mattresses, broken-
219

bottomed chairs, bottles, cans, dead gulls, dead fish. There was a fishing pier blocked off by barbed wire. *Warning: Area Unsafe for Swimming or Fishing. By Order of Port Oriskany Dept. of Health.*

He drove along the highway. There were voices in the car with him. Sometimes murmuring, sometimes teasing. Sometimes singing. When they sang, he knew the words; he sang with them.

> *She pushed a wheelbarrow*
> *through streets broad and narrow....*
>
> *On top of Old Smokey, all covered with snow*
> *I lost my true lover ...*
>            *... for courtin' too slow*
> *For courtin's a pleasure*
> *and partin' is grief*
> *and a falsehearted lover. ...*
> *You know I'm the one 'n' only one for you*
> *So why do you treat me so darn mean 'n' cruel*
> *Why break my poor old heart the way you do....*
>
> *... singing cockles and mussels*
> *alive, alive-O!*
>
> *The pony run, he jump, he pitch*
> *He throw my master in the ditch*
> *He die an' the jury wonder why....*
>
> *For courtin's a pleasure*
> *and partin' is grief*
> *and a falsehearted lover*
> *is worse than a thief....*
>    *For the thief will just rob you*
>    *and take what you have*
>    *but a falsehearted lover....*
>
> *And that was the end of*
> *Sweet Molly Malone....*
>
> *The Devil take the blue-tail fly!*

There was a farm labor settlement southwest of the city where you could always have a good time. There was a trailer camp, some tents, five or six taverns right in a row.

Vale drove down there but it was deserted—the workers didn't show up until the harvest season and it was only spring now, early spring. March or April, he couldn't remember. One of the taverns was open, though. He parked alongside a panel truck and jumped out of his car and ran inside, feeling good already.

Such joy, such elation! Blood pulsing so strongly!—with such certainty!

I examine the fragments that lie about me, I snatch them up in both hands, I am so happy, I am dizzy with happiness—has anyone ever deserved his happiness when it finally came to him?

There's no existing form of society that will suit the philosophic nature, says Plato, he speaks to me now, I remember his words well: why had I never grasped the glorious, liberating truth behind them?

I am in love, in love, in love. . . .

. . . Symptoms of a migraine beginning. . . .

No, no, please no. Not now. Not at a time like this. Twelve, fifteen hours of it. Pain like hammer blows, tears streaming down face, eyes shut tight: no. No.

I am in love, Kasch is in love, Kasch is redeemed.

The skull pounds. A fever. A throbbing halo of heat around the head, can actually feel it. Kasch directs himself to rise from the desk carefully carefully and go to the bathroom and soak the washcloth in cold water and return and lie down carefully not hurrying not hurrying a bit as if balancing an egg on that throbbing skull lie down carefully not on the bed not on the sagging mattress lie down on the cool floorboards with the cloth over his face. . . .

Forgot to pull the shades. Oh, God.

Don't dare move.

Headache, gravitational pull of earth, minerals in the skull drawn down, down, impossible to resist. I am in love. Who is in love? Minerals cannot love. I, I am in love. I am in love for the first time in my life.

Feet far away. Breathing regular. Tinges of pain, surprises of pain. Not overwhelming. Not yet. Have thought in the past, many times, *I'm finished, this is it!*—elated.

221

Relieved. When the pain stops simply stagger to your feet and go out and buy a gun and blow your brains out. That's it. That's all. . . . However, when the pain stops it stops. You weep with joy. You're sure it will never happen again.

In love, in love. Too much excitement.

Don't dare move.

Migraine headaches inherited from my mother, along with my cheekbones, body structure, eyes set too far back in their sockets. Elvira Kasch, Elvira Hendon. E. M. Hendon, her father, Hendon Packing, factories downriver, owned most of the village of South Yewville. Sickly woman, thirty-one years old when she married my father. He was only twenty-five. Both religious in slipshod non-denominational way: Unitarians, Christian Scientists, Rosicrucians. She walked weightless through the old house, a ghost, a vapor, tall and pale and elegant and sunken-eyed, a creature out of Poe, yet active in women's clubs, in local charities, organizer of fund-raising drives, banquets, outings. Father small, uneasy, prematurely bald. Close-mouthed. Nondrinkers, both of them; puritans; a household of copper and pewter utensils from colonial days, butter churns, an antique cradle used in Father's study to hold firewood, old fur rugs—bear, puma—old prints, broadsides under glass, family portraits, Fitz John the patriarch done in a shiny slick "Flemish"-tinted style, my namesake, God the Father of the Kasches with mutton-chop whiskers and a broad, rather piggish nose. Blood of my blood. Veins. Tributaries. A mistake to have attempted to forget them, deny them, transcend them. I *am* them.

The body must be an error, Mother said thoughtfully, it can't be explained, I've spent most of my life searching for an explanation, I've read all there is to read, or almost all. . . . Nothing can explain it, that we are trapped for a certain period of time in a fleshly vehicle. Cruel, cruel. Capricious. I've spent most of my life searching and I've thought very, very hard on the subject and I've come to the conclusion. . . .

And Father, at another time, eyes threaded with red and jowls quivering oddly, perversely, in that skinny face: Your mother and I probed the mysteries of life, our civic activities were a mere show, our true interests were else-where, elsewhere, but we failed, we failed, failed so de-spicably. . . . I know you must hate me, must hold me in contempt.

Yes, I said. Frankly, yes.

No, I said.

The two of us weeping quietly. Mother's death, that must have been. Father and son, son and father. Deny, transcend. Escape. Inherit. The mother gone, perhaps the headaches would disappear also . . . ? Unfor-tunately not. Headaches got worse. Frankly, I said, I am in love and I'm willing to gamble everything on that love. Frankly, I told Father's pitiful face, I love you and I de-spise you and I'm leaving home forever, to seek my true kingdom. I will never return. You'll have to ship my body back to get me home again.

Symptoms of migraine lessening.

But careful, careful—! No quick movements, no sudden gulps of air.

No thoughts of *her*. No thoughts of marriage, of mov-ing to Childwold, of love; not yet. Can't risk excitement. Can't risk—

Hope—

Can't risk.

An omen: a small bird (warbler?) flew against the window, fell to the ground, stunned, I ran downstairs to see, found it lying against the side of the building. Olive-colored with a faint yellow breast, black stripes. Canary-sized. Must have been a warbler. I picked it up, held it in the palm of my hand. Its eyes opened and closed. It was perfectly still. Don't die. Don't! Absurd, how excited I was. . . . Must not allow myself to get so excited.

Set the bird on a low-hanging tree limb, went back up-stairs, returned ten or fifteen minutes later and it was gone.

My imagination seizes that as an omen, a good omen: a sign that hope is not too outrageous.

The mind is freshest at dawn.

The night is a hellhole, filled with squawking brats and

223

calves and crows, their beaks jabbing; something opening its wing until your skull is pushed out of shape. A shiver, a shudder. Waking to tingling sensation in left arm, left leg. Numb. Cold. Paralysis. Feet far away—far away! No feeling. . . . Headache too. Never any headaches, a lifetime without them. Lasted a minute and then you slipped back into sleep and then you woke, the roosters were starting in, out in the barnyard and then a mile or two away at the Arkins and another at the McCords and another at the. . . . But the McCords are gone, the McCords are scattered. The Krassov place is empty. Sway-backed barn, a shame to see. Windows in house broken. Shame. Such good land. Shame shame shame.

The mind is freshest at dawn. The night is best forgotten.

Harsh, cold, clear. April sunlight. Windbreaker, wool cap, overshoes. Grunting. Can't buckle the overshoes. Frosted breath. Bleak countryside still, soft dark bark of pear trees, limbs rotted, broken in storms last winter. Cleaning-up to do—days of it, weeks. Hard work. Pitiless work, a farm. Clearing underbrush, plowing the hard earth, staggering in exhaustion behind the team. Great muscular legs, tails switching constantly. Poor beasts tormented by flies and no relief for them. Hell on earth. Hell's earth. That morning thunderstorm, the ruined lettuce, ruined tomato crop, wheat beaten down. . . . Still, hungry for noon dinner: mouth practically awash with saliva, that first whiff of ham and fresh-baked bread. What time is it? Still so early!—so early.

No horses now, no need to feed them, drench them. Horse barn empty. Used for storage. Kids' bicycles, wagons, sleds, broken toys, old furniture, old bedstead. Stock sold long ago. The babies won't even remember.

Network of nerves in the air, quivering. April sunshine. But cold. Is it April, so soon? Again. Again! Snow not yet melted. The rhubarb patch, the cornstalks, the grapevines grown wild in all directions . . . tendrils quivering in the air, strange, never saw such life before, fingerlike, pulsing and waving as if in water. He had a stroke, they said. And another. It was Pearl's husband, it was such a shock, I tried to pull her around to kiss her, wanted to shut her wailing mouth with my own, wanted to beat against her, to silence her, but she pushed me away. . . . Blame. Who's to blame. What a shame, they said, everyone said, the farm run down, the land sold off to strangers, what a shame, a widow, no babies, tornado warnings the day of the funeral, heavy black clouds and a warm wind, a terrible warm wind, and that outburst of rain, must wait at the church, don't dare leave, no basement to the church either, everyone silent, scared as hell, my Anna with eyes closed and lips moving, my Anna with her special connection to God. Pearl in black, not looking at me. I faced her fully. Before them all I faced her. Would have acknowledged her. But she did not see me, she would not be seated, stood with arms folded and head cocked to one side as if listening, almost a kind of smile on her face, queer, unnerving. She was a queer one, they said. After his death they said it more openly. She moved away, she remarried. She must be wondering why I didn't follow. Only a girl, thirty years old when he died and still a girl, that snorting laughter, that amazed look, stopping short what she had meant to say; stops and starts, clumsy-bodied. A shame. We weren't to blame though. How were we to blame? Anna said nothing. Anna prim, sarcastic, deliberately favored John to spite me. Never wanted my baby Arlenie to be born. But I showed her—showed them both. Showed them all.

My baby Arlene and her little girl, what is her name, little Curlylocks, my favorite, what is her name, what did they call her. . . . Sweethearts. Dolls, they are. Sometimes bad tempers but they can't help it. Shouldn't smoke that young. What is her name, Curlylocks, Dolly, used to sit on my lap, wanted to hear all the stories, loved to be frightened, just a baby. . . . If Anna only knew! But she couldn't stop me. Nobody could.

A stroke, he had. Paralyzed. Eyes bulging, tongue protruding. It was Pearl who found him. . . . It was his grandson who found him. One of the Krassov boys. A stroke, a heart attack, they said the liver was failing, they said there was nothing to be done except wait. Once they get you, once they stick those needles into you—! You lie there paralyzed and they hook you up to bottles and feed you through a straw or into your veins with a needle, they wash you in bed, I saw them at the nursing home, rubber sheets and attendants grunting, swearing, boys with sponges and soapy water in pails, my daughter had to wait out in the car. Josef, I whispered, can you hear me? Give me a sign. Give me a sign, please.

Mist along river, not yet burned off. Chilly wind. Must be careful not to slip on the path. . . . One of the children almost drowned here, who was it, could it have been Arlene? . . . almost drowned, nasty undertow, current had her 'way downstream in a minute. Fishing with Josef, Sundays. Blackberry wine. Liquor. A muskellunge, six foot if an inch, tough bastard but I brought him in, grunting and sweating all the way. No more muskies in the river now. The boys catch pike, rock bass. Nothing much. Little boys, don't know how to fish, haven't any patience. Scare the fish away. . . . Hunting with Josef and one of his sons and my three boys, up north of Kincardine, tracking deer, killing, skinning carcass and gutting it; damn cold that day, fingers and toes almost frozen. Blood freezing on hands. Odor sickening at first but you get used to it, in the cold air especially. Hard work, jointing the body. Stringy, tough meat. Didn't really care for venison but ate it just the same. Tracked and shot and killed and skinned and gutted: and ate. . . . That belly-shot, my foot must have slipped, never a mistake like that before or since, tracked the poor bugger for more than a mile, all of us, running and yelling, a little drunk, my boy Matt got to it first, poor thing lying on its side, a doe, front legs scrambling, hoofs in snow, powdery-fine, head wrenching from side to side, Oh God the pity of it, the guts burst out and so much blood, poor thing, poor thing, looked at us and tried to get to her feet, hideous sound, wheezing, racking breath, I couldn't shoot, I raised the gun and couldn't shoot, Josef's boy gave a yodel and straddled her, hunting knife in hand, stupid bastard could have been hurt by the hoofs, swaying drunk above her and the knife in hand and finally he slit her throat, never again, never, never again, so long ago, so long, long ago, never again: I told them I had no taste for it, for venison. And I didn't. Never again.

Josef, I said, do you remember? Give me a sign, I said.

Look, old man: hey! I can't sit here forever, my daughter is waiting for me!

Chunks of ice carried along, blue-glinting, in a frenzy. River high. Risen three or four inches from last year, they say. Cold wind. Should put ear flaps down. The river bounds the property, always did. Noise of it, crashing waves: always here. Sense enough to build on high ground, proud of that house, no flood ever touched it, look at those waves!—my God. Could fill the Valley. But no flood ever touched my house. . . . Seven decades, is it, hearing that noise. Washing, pounding, roaring. Crashing. Ice chunks from higher up, in the mountains; like something you would see at the North Pole. So cold! That wind!

. . . This isn't the summer river, this isn't the river we fished in. Don't know the name of this river. Blinding, the way the light breaks on the waves. So many pieces. Winking, glittering. Makes you dizzy. . . . Couldn't take a picture of it, that would be a lie. The moment after you took the picture it would be a lie. What river is this, where did I walk to? Still morning. Wind, waves, voices, that swelling roar, enough to fill the Valley. What if it floods? Enough to fill the world.

Dreamed of this river! Dreamed of it once. Years ago. Yes. That first heart attack. And the weeks afterward, hurting, moping, head jangling with what I saw. Got well and came out here, told no one, stood here on the path and stared and stared, years ago, it was the river, something about the river, called me to it. It was *this* river.

So close to dying that time! But I didn't die.

So close, so cold! Must get back to what it was like, must see it again, hear it again. . . .

Waves, light breaking into thousands of bits, millions of bits, like stars. A living network of them quivering, singing, calling: waves, wind, voices.

Must remember.

Must get back.


Grandpa . . .? Hey.

My sweetheart, my Curlylocks, come up behind me so quiet I didn't hear. Scared me a little.

Momma says breakfast is ready, you want to come

back? . . . Breakfast is ready now. She cups her hands to her mouth, talking loud because of the wind.

I don't want to go back to the house, not yet. Not just yet. I'm trying to remember something. . . . I'm not hungry, Dolly, I say; you just tell Momma I'll make my own breakfast a little later. I can take care of myself, you all know that.

Almost grown up now: mouth red, eyes too old, dressed for school she is, and not very patient with her grandpa. I see everything in their faces. . . . Momma says you'll catch cold out here, you'll catch pneumonia. There's buttermilk pancakes this morning, Grandpa. She says I better bring you back.

That makes me laugh, I can't help it.

Grandpa, what's funny?

Thinking of how I struggled to get her born, to get them all born: the babies don't know anything. Never will. Just babies, looking at me with their frowns and fussy-fussy mouths, trying to lure me back with pancakes, a kitchenful of children, a big crowded yelping house. They don't know anything. They can't know.

That's all right, Dolly. I'm all right. You go on back to the house and tell your momma I'm all right, like always, and there's no need to worry or fuss. Go on!

Playing hide-and-seek in the waves, in the light broken in the waves. Swimming, diving, swelling, subsiding . . . rising again to fill the world.

*Five*

A HALF-MILE long, that steep hill. Millgrove Street. Over the footbridge that runs alongside the railroad bridge, high above the river, along the new-laid sidewalk already beginning to crack, past vacant lots, the hill too steep to build on, down to the lumber mill and store—*Lewisohn's Lumber and Building Materials*—and the orange-brick Catholic church with the overgrown snowball bushes around the rectory, Millgrove Street continuing on and a smaller street easing off to the right, Cheektawaga Street . . . only a fifteen-minute walk from the center of Yewville, a ten-minute walk from the high school.

You sit in the window seat when your aunt isn't home, your shoes off, stockinged feet tucked under you, reading, dreaming, drawing tiny faces and geometrical figures on a notepad, looking up when a car turns off Millgrove and heads down Cheektawaga, a dead-end street, quiet, only six or seven other houses on it, small clapboard houses like your aunt's; quiet, quiet. So quiet. You read, you do your schoolwork, you sigh, you brood, you dream, you talk to yourself, you sing, you hum, you check the time: a present for your fifteenth birthday back in March, a wrist watch with a small neat face and a narrow black stretchband. So quiet, quiet. It is a luxury. It is a new-found world, smelling of floor wax and the pleasant sun-warmed mustiness of your aunt's front room and the subtle, almost imperceptible odor of her African violets and wax begonias and spider plant. Lovely. A paradise. You listen to the bell tolling down the street, at the Catholic church, you say aloud *I'm so happy . . .* !

Sometimes you start crying and can't stop.

Homesick, though you call every day or Momma calls you, to see how things are. And Friday afternoons you take the school bus back home; and stay until Monday morning.

Homesick because the house is so quiet. A tiny house, a bungalow, clapboards and shutters and shingles and a stovepipe chimney, a tiny lawn, only a few bushes and a small mountain ash out front and two scrawny crab apple trees in back, and the neighbors' houses up close, so that you can sometimes hear them when they talk loud or shout at one another. Neighbors so close! It amazes you. But your aunt doesn't think it's strange, she says they're nice people, everybody on the street gets along, she's lived here for twenty-five years, she says, and wouldn't ever move.

You're not lonely. You don't miss the farm. Your eyes sometimes flood with tears of gratitude; you're not really homesick. Why, Laney doesn't miss us at all! Not one bit! Look how pleased she is with herself!—so Momma teases you. Through a friend of hers who lives in town, and through your aunt, who knows lots of people because she works for an uptown doctor, you get babysitting jobs two or three times a week; over Easter vacation you made forty-five dollars, helping clerk at Kresge's; when school is out you will be working full-time there until September. When you're alone in the house you keep waiting for the telephone to ring, or you wait to hear the children screaming and shouting, running on the stairs, you wait to hear your mother's voice raised in exasperation, you wait to hear someone calling your name—but no, nothing: you are really safe, it has really happened. You add up figures, you multiply and calculate, you are very happy, already you've put thirty dollars in the bank, in a savings account under your own name; you want to give Momma some of your money, or Aunt Esther, but they say no, no, there's no need, there's no need. It's yours to keep.

The wrist watch is a present from Kasch; you were shy about wearing it to school. Your friends noticed. What's that, what's that!—a birthday present? From who? . . . Brad doesn't call you any longer, Brad is going out with a girl from South Yewville, Indian-black hair, eighteen
231

years old, the rumor is that she was married and something happened to her husband, a motorcycle accident that left him crippled and brain-damaged, so she divorced him; or maybe he was killed in Vietnam; or came back from Vietnam wounded and changed, and she divorced him because of that. You don't know her, don't care to know her. People tell you things but you shrug your shoulders. Such a shame, Laney, your friends say, don't you miss him?

Jeannie thinks she's pregnant. . . . Then, a few days later, she tells you it's all right: thank God, she says, and begins to cry.

Thank God, thank God. . . .

You are nervous about baby-sitting, you want to do well. You want the children to like you. The parents, the money paid to you, the savings account, the hours of solitude, the slightly panicked sensation when you realize how responsible you are, for the children of these strangers and for yourself, for your own life: in bed, in the little alcove room at the rear of the house, you fall asleep at once, exhausted. Your aunt is up early, before seven. You hear her in the kitchen though she takes care to be quiet. You lie in bed a while, not knowing what you are listening for—the creak of a tree limb against the roof, the hollow, bell-like sound of the wind in the old silo, maybe Butch barking downstairs, or the side door being slammed shut. But no: no. Those sounds are there, in Childwold, but you are no longer there to hear them.

Sometimes you cry, but not when your aunt can hear you. Sometimes you telephone your mother before going to school, or when you're at school, during noon hour. Hello? I'm just calling to . . . calling to say hello. . . . How is everyone? How is the baby? How is Grandpa? Your mother is always happy to talk to you, unless she's on her way out or busy with something there. It's Laney, she will say to someone at the other end. Hi, honey. How are you? . . . Such a fuss you're making, such a fuss, only twenty miles from home and anyway you see them on the weekends, and you wanted this, didn't you? . . . didn't you beg for this freedom?

Why, I'd be happy to have Laney stay with me, your

aunt said, you know I'd love that, Arlene. . . . I get so lonely sometimes.

Your aunt is really your mother's aunt. In her fifties, but so short and small-boned she seems girl-like, hardly more than your size, with light brown hair that is permanently waved every few months in exactly the same style. Never married. Clean, tidy, frugal. She speaks in a voice so soft you sometimes can't hear her; but she's a registered nurse, she has worked uptown for most of her life, everyone in the family respects her though they like to say they feel sorry for her—never married, the poor thing! And so sweet, too. A shame.

You can stay here as long as you like, she tells you. When is your mother planning on getting married . . . ?

The plans aren't definite yet, you tell her, looking away.

There are books Kasch has given you, and books from the library, and medical journals Aunt Esther brings home from the office. When you feel most agitated you read, you force yourself to read, a pencil in hand, and in a few minutes you forget everything but what you are reading, your face puckers with the effort to understand, to *know*. You want to know everything. There are books, so many books . . . so many books awaiting you. You want to know everything. You will.

For every *one* of the existing one million species of animal life on this earth, you read, there are hundreds now extinct.

You read and reread, you underline passages, you make notations in the margins; sometimes you try to decipher Kasch's notes, but his handwriting is too small. You read sometimes without comprehending. You read, you read and reread. The subject is life: life itself. You will never come to the end of it. . . . The forms of life are far more similar than they are different: you turn pages and see diagrams of a bird's wing, a man's arm, a dog's forelimb, a whale's forelimb. You read that life is unstoppable on certain levels. You try to understand, but the phenomenon seems not meant for understanding; you read of an experiment where a developing animal embryo is crushed to pulp and yet doesn't die—bits of tissue from a ten-day-

233

old chick embryo crushed and minced and filtered through a nylon sheet, then re-compacted and transplanted to the membrane of another growing embryo, and within a few days the scrambled eye cells are forming eyes, the liver cells a liver; kidneys, heart, brain, skin, feathers—still living, still growing into their invariable forms. Life is a flow, a powerful directed flow, not to be stopped, not to be stopped for long. You read, absorbed, shivering with excitement. You forget everything else. Life is organization, life is temporality, complexity, interactions that can be observed but not explained. There is always a direction to it—always a design. It insists upon its own fulfillment. It is the triumph of organization at the molecular level over a tendency toward chaos. But it is not to be understood, not even by its most scrupulous, faithful observers.

Momma, you say, seeing her in the front yard, digging in the flower bed, Momma, you cry, running up the driveway from the road on Friday afternoon, is everything all right? It's all right, isn't it?

Whyever shouldn't it be all right, Momma says, puzzled.

Deafening: the balls rolling down the alleys, the pins struck and flying, the men shouting, continuous roar of voices, bursts of laughter. So exuberant! Everyone so happy! The place catches at your heart, you feel your face taking on a wide vacuous hopeful grin. What can go wrong *here?* . . . A black-and-green marbled ball is sent down a nearby alley, the bowler stands poised, one leg gracefully twisted, his burly arm extended, dancerlike, even the fingers outstretched; the ball strikes the pins and they fly, they fly, it's a strike, is it a strike?—no, one pin remaining—one pin—only one pin—the bowler stamps his foot, shouts something unintelligible, his teammates shout, the pin is teetering but does not fall—does not fall. In the next alley another ball shoots down to the pins and they scatter, and in the next alley a ball is being returned, sent back in the ball return; and someone has put a coin in the juke box and music begins suddenly, somewhere overhead, but no one is listening; four or five men with bowling balls in satchels, bowling shoes in hand, pass close by you, now the man with the black-and-green ball strides forward and sends the ball violently down the alley and picks off the single pin and snaps his head as the pin flies, and turns back—shaking his hair out of his eyes, pretending disgust. In the next alley a black ball rolls fast toward the pins and strikes them and they fly with a clatter and. . . .

Twenty-five alleys. A Friday evening. Smoke, noise, beer, monogrammed shirts, men, a few women, constant traffic back and forth from the adjacent bar; you are alone, you are invisible, you are feeling absurdly confident.

He turns out to be that ruddy-faced man by the cigarette and candy counter, leaning against the glass top, talking and joking with the cashier and two men in bowling shirts, a cigar stuck in his mouth. Big husky goodlooking man, must have been very good-looking at one time, creases around his mouth from laughing so hard. Earl Tuller. Eyes shut, he is laughing so exuberantly, almost wheezing, at an anecdote one of the men is telling: something about backing a truck up a ramp. Earl Tuller, Earl Tuller, Mr. Tuller, could I speak to you in private for a moment, excuse me, please, are you Earl Tuller, they told me you were Earl Tuller and I, excuse me for interrupting, I wonder if—

Yeh? What?

Still smiling, blue-eyed, draws himself up to his full height, unconsciously tucking his shirt into his belt, seems polite, almost formal. You feel drawn to him suddenly; you like him, would be flattered if he liked you, if he joked with you as he does with other people. Mr. Tuller, my name is—

No, no, call me Earl; shit, my name is Earl.

My name is—

Voice too soft, can't be heard over the din. Earl leans forward, gives you a friendly tap on the shoulder, invites you into his office. Have a seat. Do we know each other? Straddling a chair, unembarrassed at his cowboyish style, big perspiring friendly face, neck as thick as your thigh.

You are narrow in face and body and manner, your voice is inappropriately cultured, he can still barely hear you over the hellish happy din. Then he realizes what you are saying.

What? *Her?* That bitch? . . . Look, pal, I don't know who you are or what you want, but I got *nothing* to do with that bitch, not one thing, wouldn't touch her with a ten-foot pole. . . . She says what? I'm bothering her, huh? Bothering *her?* . . . What are you, from the police? I don't know you; don't know who the hell you are. . . . A friend of the family, huh? Which means . . . ? Yeh, sure: you're her new boy friend. You're the new boy friend. Ha, ha! Congratulations! You can have her, pal. I wouldn't touch her with a ten-foot pole. It's a lot of bullshit, whatever she's been telling you . . . I don't care if the whole pack of them say so . . . took my car, didn't she, and traded it in and made money on the deal, I know exactly how much, I know that bitch through and through, she can maybe fool you for a while but she never fooled me. . . . What did you say your name was? Huh? Speak up, for Christ's sake! . . . Well, I don't know you and you don't know me and we got nothing to say to each other, we got no grounds for any conversation whatsoever, you go out to the bar and have a drink on me, have a drink on Earl, and that's that, no hard feelings, no bullshit, I got nothing to do with that woman and that's the truth and if she's been telling you different she's a goddam liar, always was, the whole family is just trash. . . . Look, I knew her husband. I know them all. The kids run wild, she's a slut, a whore, could be taking money for all I know or give a damn, I got nothing to do with her now, no telephone calls or nothing. If she's accusing me of threats or bullshit like that she'd better watch her mouth because I happen to have an attorney, I work with the best attorney in town, and that could be slander, friend, right? . . . No, I got nothing more to say, I'm busy, this is a busy night, it's a league night; you haul your ass out to the bar and tell the bartender Earl's setting you up for a drink, and that's that: that's that.

I'm sorry if I seemed rude, but it's very important that —that you understand—

236

Understand! . . . Why, there's nothing to understand. I already made that clear to you, didn't I?

That rustling sound.

Whispering.

Like paper, papers, something sharp and dry and thin.

Listen, just listen, no end to it, never-ending, never-ending, you start to run and the leaves tear against your face and you turn to run in another direction, panting, and the cornstalks are so high—reaching two or three feet over your head—you can't see, you don't know where you are, you don't know where you've come from. Help, you want to cry, help me, help, help please. . . .

Ah, they are feeding you; they must have found you. Lie still.

Jaws wired shut. You sip liquid through a plastic straw. It has no taste. Your tongue has been ripped out, something rubbery and cold has been inserted, the liquid slides harmlessly past it, there is no taste, there is no pain. A high humming in the ears, like the humming in the telephone wires in the winter wind. You aren't lost. You ran in the cornfield screaming, you ran and ran and the leaves scratched your face, you were bleeding from a dozen cuts, you didn't care, didn't have time to care, you wanted only to escape. That rustling, that whispering! That humming! Mmmmmmmmmm! Corn silk dried and brown and withered, big ears of corn knocking against your forehead, the tall straight stalks, rows and rows and rows, early September it was, the day you were lost, you ran through the field crying like a baby, a goddam little baby. Where's Vale, they laughed, oh where's the baby got to now? Why, he's soiled his pants! Soiled his pants!

They laughed and laughed and Momma hauled him away and cleaned him, he was a big boy, he was too big, wasn't he, to be bad in his pants.

Strapped in bed, lifted for the bedpan to be pushed under.

Sucking greedily through a plastic straw.

So hungry, so hungry!

Crazy with hunger!

You'll eat anything, you'll whimper and groan for anything, there's no shame to you, the life in you will leap out, you can't keep it back. Bought four candy bars, you did, unwrapped them one by one and ate them right there, on the sidewalk, a Milky Way, and a Tootsie Roll and a Mallo Cup and an O-Henry, licked your sticky fingers, so greedy, shaky with hunger, the girl who ran the snack wagon laughed, she had an eye for Vale, they all did, they all did. Tight blue slacks, zipper in front like a man's, bulging a little because of her tummy, plump and hard-looking at the same time. Joellen was her name, she said. You bought a ten-cent bag of peanuts and offered her a few and she popped them in her mouth from her cupped hand, chewing, smiling, wore a short jacket, so short it only came to her waist, pink imitation leather with pink imitation fur at the collar, big brass zipper and zipper pull, Joellen was her name, she had an eye for you like all of them. You asked her if she lived in the city, did she work at the snack wagon every day, hadn't the two of you run into each other sometime before, didn't you maybe look familiar to each other . . . ? You asked these questions and a few others. She answered them. It had all happened before so there was no need to listen, only to wait until the words got said. There was no need to worry that it could happen another way.

Help, you want to cry, help me, help, help please. . . .

*Are you prepared now for the culmination, for the absorption of the many into the one, where the eye goes not, where speech goes not, nor mind . . . ?*

The tremor in my hand communicated itself to the table, to the piles and piles of papers, a hissing, whispering sound, barely audible. Of course I am prepared! I have controlled all this, have I not? Am I not the One who controls the many . . . ?

I bear the world, yes, but I am far from lost in it!

*Are you prepared for the flaming forth of the divine indwelling spirit whom you have courted for these many months, faithful and desperate and greedy as any lover?*

The tremor filled my body; my teeth chattered. I tried to calm myself, fearing a migraine headache—that shameful lapse into mortality—and the danger passed, and passed, and passed.

Repairs on the roof, where the shingles are so badly rotted. That shower stall—! Impossible. Must be taken out, a new bathroom built, two new bathrooms. The furnace, which gives off such a peculiar odor, like oil, dust, something burned. The cellar so wet—bone-chilling—eerie. Planks on the dirt floor, to walk on. Naked light bulbs overhead, only two for the entire cellar. A secret nighttime world there beneath the floorboards of the house: went down with a flashlight to investigate the leaking and saw cringing in the slanted light stacks of lumber, piles of canvas, a hack saw, a hoe with a broken handle, barrel staves, pokers, a tar bucket and brushes, tin sheets, a nail keg, overturned, the rusted nails spilled out onto the ground, a snow shovel, coils of chicken-fence wire, old canning jars in a heap as if thrown down, their interiors scuttling with spiders. My hand trembled though there was nothing to fear, though the children were close beside me, pulling on my hand, my arm, my legs. So musty-damp, so tilted and careening in the weak halo of my light!—surely monsters dwell in that cellar and must be driven out.

And the stairs repaired: two of the steps are ready to collapse.

And the broken windowpanes replaced; and storm windows for next winter; and a new refrigerator, and a new stove—in time, in time, no need to hurry with everything, no need to get overexcited. The debts should be attended to first. Her debts. Years and years of borrowings, loans formal and informal. Can't remember most of them, she says. Two mortgages on the house but the payments are fairly low. Receipts, bills, overdue notices, a drawer stuffed with papers of an official nature mixed in with bits of string, rubber bands, loose thumb tacks, pencil stubs, the insurance policies smeared with glue that had dribbled out of a dime-store bottle of liquid glue, yellowing and torn birth certificates, a wedding certificate badly torn, bunches of report cards. . . . Everything is here somewhere, she says, around here somewhere.

One of the children is sick and must be driven to the doctor—to a doctor, not to a clinic; they must all be taken to the dentist sometime soon. The grandfather's breath is so hoarse and labored, I have heard it myself, have heard him in his room, alone, they say he isn't well but won't discuss it, gets angry if anyone crosses him at all these days, he has no appetite, doesn't sleep much, is out wandering for hours in the woods and along the river. . . . But he won't talk to me: just stands and appears to be listening, won't sit down, nods slowly and vacantly, maddeningly, never calls me by name, never really looks at me.

But why, why . . . ?

Doesn't he know I am prepared to love even *him?*

The woman raised her arms to me.

Blinded, I was, by her face: so blankly bright, uplifted and expectant. *Are you prepared, are you prepared . . . ?* Her expression shifted, her fine glowing skin puckered, one side of her face went suddenly dark, purplish-orange, and blood flowed from a slash just above her eye. I staggered toward her. I wanted to flee, but instead I staggered toward her, seized her hands, kissed the wound. Yes, yes, yes. Yes. I love you, I am yours, I am love in you, around you, through you. I am yours.

You love me then?

I love you.

Will you come live with me?

I want nothing else—I have never wanted anything else.

And you will never leave—?

Never.

Never

               never

        never

                  Never

                                  *Never.*

Rain. Days of rain. Washes everything clean. But there's mud, muck, a chill that never goes away, the new grass and bright new shoots are in danger of frost, the river is running high and hard and noisy. Hear it all the time now, asleep or awake. Like thunder. Like rocks and stones and pebbles being turned over and over, over, driven along beneath the surface of the water, gouging into the earth. Crashing, crushing waves . . . so cold, so cruel . . . voices in them clamoring to be heard but washed away, lost. Is there comfort in that, I asked him, leaning close to his ear so that no one else knew what I said; is there comfort in silence, in being dumb at last?

Give me a sign, a sign!

A sign!

The nurse came in chattering and pulled the shades and she smelled of perfume and I have always hated perfume on women and I told her to be still, to stop that monkey-noise, to haul her ass out of here until I was ready to leave.

She stared at me, her idiot mouth opening.

A sign, a sign. . . . One of them stared at me in the front office of that real estate place in Derby where I went in, muddy boots unbuckled, shouting for the bastard who had cheated me, a little drunk, maybe, but knowing my rights, knowing what justice was. Stared, stared! Let them. You'll kill yourself, Pa, you'll have another heart attack, my girl whines, oh Jesus, Pa, put her down, she's big enough to walk by herself, she's just taking advantage of you. . . . Put her down, put her down, you'll kill yourself, don't leave the bathroom door open, Pa, please, I tell you and tell you, Pa, don't I, please Pa, don't take the telephone off the hook and then break the connection when the phone rings, it could be an important call for us, it could be an important call for someone else on the line, Pa, you know better, why did you make such a mess in the sink, Pa, why didn't you wrap it in newspaper, there's plenty of newspaper on the floor, a pile on the floor to wrap garbage in, Pa, it stinks so, stinks up the whole house, in the sink all night and when I wake up the first thing I smell is that, don't you know any better, why do you want the gun in the room with you, what do you mean, boys chasing the cows, we don't have cows, you sold them off yourself, we don't have a single Hereford left, we don't have any horses, any sheep, any goats, any hogs, we have only a dozen scabby chickens and one rooster and a dog and two cats, you know all this, Pa, you know better, let me take the gun, Pa, a shotgun shouldn't be loaded in the house, please Pa, let me take it, I'll put it in the closet where you can get it any time, Pa, don't talk so loud, you'll wake the children, do you realize

241

it's three in the morning, Pa, I almost died when I heard someone walking down here, my God I couldn't imagine what, I thought it might be, I thought it might be Earl, my heart almost stopped, Jesus Christ you scared me so, Pa, let me have the gun, will you, what are you saying, I don't understand what you're saying, talk slower, Pa, please, and not so loud, what if the children wake up and run down here and see you like this, see us with this gun, let me have it, Pa, you know better than to scare me, don't I have enough worries right now, isn't there enough going on in our lives, you know there's nobody outside, Pa, just listen, that's only the rain, that's the rain, there aren't any boys trespassing in the barn, that was long ago, Pa, that was when I was just a girl myself, and nothing came of it, there was no need to be so angry even then, to chase them with the gun like you did, what if you'd hurt them, just boys, just boys who didn't know any better, it was a long time ago, Pa, give me the gun . . . give me the gun.

Yes, it was the rain. She was right. But I kept the gun anyway and it's here on the floor by the bed, sixteen gauge, good strong smell, I cleaned it just the other day. If they come for me, if they try to take me in the car. If they lay a hand on me. If they try to surprise me.


Rain and a gradual darkening of the sky and the wind getting worse and by noon it was like six in the evening and sheets of rain were being blown against the house and it got colder, it was April but it got cold, cold as January, the rain turned to sleet, there was an ice storm, a blizzard, April twenty-fifth and a blizzard, the sleet thrown against the house all day, roof, windows, doors, darting and dancing and rapping, rocking the house, the children ran wild, the electricity went off at two o'clock in the afternoon and never came on until the next morning at eleven, you felt like crying, you did cry, up there in your room, watching the storm, hardly able to see the barn, two sweaters on and a blanket wrapped around you and still you shivered, chilled to the bone. Years later you remember that ice storm: you remember thinking you would not come back home so often, you would stay more and more in town, at
242

your Aunt Esther's, gradually you would not come home at all, not to such a world.

Again the evergreens hanging heavy with snow, deformed and unbalanced; again the trees coated with ice, the old walnut tree badly damaged, one of its branches split and hanging against the ground; the sun white-glowing, glaring, anemic, pale, no warmth to it, no hope, only that frozen frigid glaring that could blind you if you didn't hide your eyes. Sparrows and juncos caught up in the wind, flying against the wind, dashed to the ground. What of the tulip shoots, what of the forsythia buds, that wind from the river, driving down from the north, so vicious, so whimsical, what will happen, the roads dangerous, the schools closed for the fourth or fifth time this year, what if your grandfather hadn't been close enough to get back in time, what if he'd been miles away, surprised by the storm, lost, weakened, confused . . . ? You cried because of the damage to the fruit trees and the tulips and the flowering shrubs, you cried because you were so cold, so miserable here at home, in this cramped silly room you had once loved, and because of your grandfather, and because you knew, you knew, that your mother and Fitz John Kasch would never be married: could never be married. You cried because you knew you would leave all these people before long; they would drive you away themselves, and never understand you.

Poor Fitz John! His father's son after all.
My father—?
Yes, of course: he had women, didn't you know? Everyone knew. He was so distracted, so pathetic, so shameless —poor Sydney! The first woman was just one of the secretaries at the office but after that he got courageous, he got imaginative and reckless, he went after country girls and even after migrant workers, he gave them ridiculous presents like clothes they had no use for, and bracelets and wrist watches and earrings, he gave them coats, shoes, boots with fur tops, he gave them money—which was all they wanted, of course; the little dears weren't stupid.

My *father*—? No, no, impossible. No. Really, it's im-

243

possible. You're just trying to upset me. I can understand your disapproval of—

No one disapproved, no one felt anything more than pity for him. He couldn't help himself. Your mother knew everything, her friends reported everything to her, she was greedy to know, to learn, she didn't condemn him, she believed it was her own fault, she had driven him to such lunacy, but she didn't feel guilt because of it: *what must be must be* was your mother's constant—I almost said *prayer*, but it wasn't a prayer, it was a command.

I can't believe—

Of course you can't. You didn't know them at all. You didn't know any of us at all.

Aunt Leita child-sized and child-cruel. Smiling, gloating. Hurt because I have not visited her for so long— pouty, waspish, frightening. I stare at her, awed, not knowing what she might say next.

Senility.

The old house on Mayberry Avenue, a noble wreck, the only one of the street's original houses now remaining; the area has been rezoned for commercial buildings, and already a string of gleaming façades has been erected, a mini-plaza—dry cleaner's, grocery store, carry-out Chinese food, drug store. She's bitter, she's lonely, she's senile. She watches me with that infuriating smug smile.

Breaking my heart.

Aunt Leita, I don't expect you or anyone else to understand—but I'm in love, I've fallen in love for the first time, really—my marriage was a mistake, a terrible error of judgment, I fell in love with a woman so much like me she could have been my sister, the two of us were—you remember her, don't you?—no?—but you claimed to like her, I remember distinctly your fussing over her and saying how beautiful she was!—But we were too much alike temperamentally, we were always in competition, even in our private conversations we were in competition, trying to outdo each other. But Mrs. Bartlett is totally different —Arlene is totally different—She's afraid to meet you but if you could offer some, if you could assure me that— She's a warm, marvelous person, my own age, her life has
244

been a very difficult one but she's so good-natured, so loving, so sane—

Aunt Leita smiling, smiling. Offers me more tea, though I have not finished drinking what I have: insipid watery herb tea, smells like alfalfa. On the marble coffee table between us there is a badly tarnished tray with a paper napkin outspread on it, a napkin that has obviously been used before, and a few chocolate-chip cookies from a box. The "girl," the maid, is a thick-waisted clumsy creature in her sixties at least, wearing bedroom slippers and a house dress with a rip under one arm, surprised rather than courteous when I rang the bell, not very articulate, out there in the kitchen with the radio turned up too high.

The house has fifteen rooms, or more, but Aunt Leita lives downstairs now, and some of the downstairs rooms are closed off. This room is a handsome one, as attractive as I remember: white-paneled walls, cushioned window seats, brocade drapes with thin white curtains behind them; an Oriental rug; plump cushioned chairs and sofas that look as if no one has ever sat on them. Parakeets in another room, at the rear of the house. If I look over Aunt Leita's head and out through the back yard I can see, beyond the three remaining elms, a revolving figure in the air, white, then white and red, a kind of miracle, the revolving sign from a drive-in restaurant on the other street: I think it consists of a white bucket with a man's face on it, grinning as he bites into a drumstick.

You don't know us at all, Aunt Leita says in her high, trilling voice. —Don't know anything.

Well, I say, laughing, stung, well—*what must be must be.*

Later, cleaning this place of my possessions, my vanities, the desperate debris that has shored itself at my feet, I think again of my aunt, my last living relative, and it hurts me to recall that smug vacuity of hers—as if she had no love for me, no recognition! No sense of our common humanity! As if she did not wish me well.

*Kasch* will be continued after all. Forevever. Silly woman, could she not see? The Bridegroom prepares himself. His heirs. God plays hide-and-seek in the dripping eaves, in the blink of sunlight, the yammering of the birds. I am preparing for a new life. I am preparing for new life. Kasch the son of, Kasch the father of. Fulcrum. Balance. Looking both ways: the pastness of the past, the ineluctable heady joy of the future. Could she not see, could none of them see? Kasch working hurriedly, throwing things into boxes, cartons. There is dust, there are mouse droppings, there are those disgusting little white bits hardened on the floor, the carcasses and husks of insects devoured by spiders; there are of course innumerable spider webs; but the spiders have fled. My exuberance terrifies them.

The girl drew her hands away from her face, the woman opened her arms to me. I see, I plunge forward, I fall to my knees. I am not worthy. But I am loved, though unworthy. I am loved at last. The curse is over, the spell is broken. . . . Should burn these books, tear the pages out one by one and burn them, no use now, no use, belong to my squalid past, belong to Kasch's larval stage, unnecessary now, a burden now, so much printed wisdom: what need, in her arms? What need anything else? My fragments are roughly assembled and swept from the table into a box, I will never glance at them again, I have grown beyond them, beyond all hypotheses, all verbalizing; scraps of paper, scrawled in various hands, enigmatic, dream-sketches, riddles, glimpses into other lives, Kasch's embroidery, Kasch's rosary, Kasch's prayer wheel, abandoned now that life itself begins. My love! My loves! The *Pensées* cannot equal you and so must be thrown aside, the works of Eckhart, the *Bhagavad Gita, Walden,* and Whitehead and Saint John of the Cross and *The Cloud of Unknowing* and. . . . And my own books, which I have not glanced at since coming here, and which I will not glance at now, will toss into one of the cartons with the rest—the poems I called *Riddles,* the slender, brittle, ascetic parable, *Golden Girls and Boys,* that read like a novel and was fairly well received, though misunderstood by everyone who commented on it; the study of Utopian and distopian literature that was published by a university press, and that I had never reread since doing the galleys; *Savagery and Mysticism,* an extended and deepened version of the study that was my doctoral dissertation at Harvard, lo these centuries ago, of which at one time I was ludicrously proud; and one or two other books, whose titles are as strange to me as if someone else had imagined them into existence, and I were entrusted now only with the chore of tossing them aside, out of harm's way. Should it surprise me, to realize that I have written so much, that I have published these books . . . ? It should, it should. For my mind is deliriously empty now. I am new, I am trembling with newness, I am like a child, I am innocent of past accomplishments as well as past sins, there is no connection, no attachment, I cast such things from me, reckless with the joy of . . . reckless with joy.

The fragments of my life are heaped together here at my feet. They are harmless now. I step over them, I push them into the corner of the room. . . . Soon, soon! The Bridegroom is hurrying to his Bride. *What must be must be.* I am equal to any fate. I am the author of myself. Someone seized my arm, her aged clawlike fingers digging into my flesh; someone broke down with love of me and fear for me and an old woman's babyish terrors; too late, too late for such emotions! Too late. My mother and father were the means by which I entered the world of being, it was through them I came to consciousness, now I am new, I am improvised, I am sheer joyful invention, nothing can stop me. My Bride awaits. My Brides.

Old woman, out of my way. . . .

Dawn. Mist. A chilly breeze. Fog along the river, in slow-drifting uneven patches.

Remains of the old dock swaying and creaking. Like a human cry—a high-pitched whimpering. The river's current is just too strong. Docks must be repaired every spring, after the damage from the ice. Otherwise let them go, abandon them, give up. It's better so—let the river tear them apart post by post, board by board. Flimsy things.

Let the river carry everything away!

No need for the shotgun. An old man's flurry, an old man's fever.

Those vivid dreams last night still with me: the farmland so bright, glowing, as if on fire with invisible flames. Such heat, such radiance. . . . The attic window beneath the peak of the roof illuminated, glowing, glaring, my darling, my Pearl, my sweet frightened girl in the window, leaning from the window, her arms outstretched, so lovely, her skin glowing, her eyes as they were in life—as they were in life.

Why are you frightened? There is no need. . . . I called out to her as if I weren't surprised to see her there; as if nothing was unusual.

The dream-river crashing and plunging at my feet. Waves high, bucking, pierced with light. Rude raw guffawing noises. Many rhythms, many pulses. Thunderous. Can't sort them out—can't hear them separately. Calling to me? Voices? The dead? No need! I put the shotgun back in the closet, did it without her hearing me, there is no need now, no need for that, I left the house in the dark, left them sleeping, and now it's dawn, dawning, fog and mist and drifting wet air, come again, again, the waves are a tumult, the dream-river beckons, breaks at my feet, and again, again, it breaks again and again, impatient, patient, a sign? So cold! Seeping into my shoes: so cold! A sign, a sign? My heart swelling with joy . . . with dread . . . with joy . . . Many-pulsed, tumultuous. The dream-river crashes out of the night alive at my feet, boisterous and bucking and alive, my own, my—

Beneath the cellar door on the stone steps that lead to the outside, crouched, hidden, shivering, giggling: here's a daddy longlegs going to get you! Going to crawl right down your neck! The crawl-space behind the furnace, the old potato bin that stinks, the piles of boards and canvas and old crates, Gonna bust your ugly mouth if you tell, gonna poke—peck—out your eyes, gonna knock out all your teeth, damn old crybaby, gonna knock your hindparts into the river! The car under the apple trees, the doors that won't shut, the stuffing that comes out of the back seat, Gonna rip your ass, gonna bust your ugly face up the side, chickenshit baby, the closet by the cellar stairs, the old wagon in the corner of the barn, the tunnel through the snowberry bushes, Momma's clothes closet,

248

the secret place in the old horse barn beneath the machinery, dusty oily smelly, Loony Laney can't find us, Big Fat-Ass Nanny, Momma's-Gonna-Slap-Slap can't find us, everybody's gone, nobody's home, the car's gone, Grandpa's gone, crawling, kicking, chortling, gurgling, ga-gaing, whinnying, wailing, chickie-chickie-chicking, slugs, slime, frogs, cocoons, daddy longlegs, the dead bullhead Butch dragged to the back door, Gonna make you eat it, stupid old crybaby, gonna lock you down in the cellar and let you cry cry cry there's nobody to hear, nobody to hear! . . . One of us butted his head against Jimmy, nobody's home, Momma's-Gonna-Slap-Slap-Slap, Big Mouth Ronnie's gone, let the baby cry, nobody's going to hear, I'm a boa constrictor gonna squeeze you to death, snuffling, sniffing, sniveling, you wipe your nose or I'll smash it in! Listen to the baby! Fucken cryen! . . . Running around the table, knocked one of the chairs over, somebody's knee got banged, somebody's face got smacked, haha! serves you right! red-hot burning face, eyes awash with tears, Gonna tell Momma on you and she'll rip your ass, gonna tell Momma and Nan what you did to Louise, a handful of pebbles thrown like buckshot, somebody screeching, what if the window is broke?—stupid shithead, stupid asshole—somebody rabbit-punched somebody else and it hurt, it hurt! There was a chase up the stairs into Nan's room and under the bed and somebody yanked the rug under to use as a defense, who's jumping on the bed, who's gonna get the shit kicked out of him, kicking, chortling, big-deal loudmouth, Chimpy-Chimpy-Chimpanzee, somebody slipped on the stairs, caught his chin on the top step, oh, my God look at the blood, the blood! Somebody got a towel, somebody ran in circles, jabbing, punching, butting his head, I'm a big bull, I'm a moose, I'm gonna smash you guys flat, the television was turned up loud, nobody's home, nobody's listening, look, look the vase fell over, what if it rolled to the floor, the panes of glass in the window were vibrating, somebody came stampeding into the room and around and out again and up the stairs and along the hall, slipping, sliding, gasping, screeching, giggling, panting, whinnying, stamping like horses, kicking and strutting, there was blood on the top step, somebody was gonna get it, somebody was gonna get his ass whipped like he deserved, there were kicks, there were jabs, somebody was shadowboxing and backed into the floor lamp, Butch was barking, Butch was yipping like crazy, the house shook, somebody was fever-hot crawling on the kitchen floor with a pillowcase over his head, bangbangbangbangbang, got you, you sonsabitches, you monkeyasses, acketyacketyacketyack, Get the hell out of Grandpa's room, make him get out of there!—grab hold of him, get his leg!—Gonna bust your face in two, you stop that crying, stop that crying before Momma comes back, you hear?—hey okay, hey okay, nobody's gonna tell, nobody's gonna tell—we better fix everything up— Grandpa's gonna come back here and give you guys hell, you know that? Somebody crawled to the back of Momma's clothes closet and sucked his thumb and fell asleep.

Grain elevators, chain-link fences, barges, tugs, cattails, knotweed, chicory, blacktop, telephone posts, Coulos Auto Service, Honey-Bee Drainage Service, Lake View Motor Court, traffic lights, moonlight, Lone Lee's Take-Out, barbed-wire fences, water towers, chimneys, No Trespassing, concrete, North Oriskany Car Wash, bulldozers, cranes, gas tanks. Mamma Mia Submarines, ramps, underpasses, Diesels, Greyhound buses, railroad tracks, Lots for Sale, Chuck's Harbor Inn.

What is this place, Vale asked, I don't know this place, who are these people?—but it was all right, Chuck's Harbor Inn was all right. Fitzgerald draped his long limp arm around Vale's shoulders and quieted him down.

This place's all right, Fitzgerald declared.

The tavern smelled of beer and smoke and people: a good smell.

Big as a barn, a long noisy bar and a back room jammed with tables, overlooking the lake. Vale knew the lake was there though he couldn't see it. The reflections in the windows were too distracting. Men and women, jammed in there together, were too distracting.

Do I know anybody here? Vale said.

Hush, said Fitzgerald.

250

That's right, said another boy, don't let him get too loud.

He ain't loud, Fitzgerald said. He's feeling good.

Do I know any of you? Vale asked.

Only a few people glanced his way. It was so noisy in here, there were so many conversations and outbursts of laughter, how could anyone hear him? They didn't give him a fair chance.

Do any of you know me? Vale cried.

Fitzgerald pressed something in the palm of Vale's hand and he washed it down with a beer, a bottle of Stroh's in three or four swallows. He must have been thirsty. He felt better at once.

Those sons-bitches don't know any of us, Fitzgerald said.

There was no provocation, he had done no harm, but one morning after his discharge from the hospital they came running at him, his own buddies, it took four or five of them to hold him down, though inside the screaming he was cool as ever, and was in control of the situation. His friends envied him, didn't they? Always had. With good reason. Vale Bartlett had style, Vale was calm and cold and deadly, no one crossed him, no one dared contradict him. He was well-known in the Valley, and in Yewville, and even in Derby. No one dared say anything about his family or his mother. They knew what would happen. Vale and his friends owned motorcycles and they drove up and down the highway and raced around the old track at the fair grounds and not even the highway patrol wanted to cross them. There was no provocation, but they jumped on him and held him down and hurt him, again they hurt him, cracked one of his ribs. His little finger was pulled out of its socket. I'll kill you, I'll kill you all, someone raged, and they jumped on him, they sat on his chest, they rubbed his face into the dirt. I'll kill you all, someone whispered.

During the explosions he had died, and been jolted awake to die again. He was not given a fair chance. His fingers were wet with something so they couldn't catch hold, couldn't haul him up. Once on his feet he would have run for cover; he was a fast runner and no one could have hurt him. He would have amazed them, running so fast. But he wasn't given a fair chance. The enemy was invisible. The enemy converged from three sides. . . . He died, pressing his face into the dirt. Whimpering. Slobbering. Something fled out the pit of his belly and he soiled his pants, like a baby, and his loins jumped and writhed with the need to discharge his life into the soil, the mud, the earth . . . faces passed rapidly through his vision, like playing cards being flipped, he saw girls he did not know, the variety of their faces and their expressions astonished him, he saw his sister Nancy's face, and Laney's, and his mother's, and the faces of his cousins, even his boy-cousins, and other boys whom he did not know, he saw the faces of certain friends, he saw doglike animals, whimpering and slobbering as he was, tongues dripping saliva. The wet earth came alive and was flesh and he felt his loins writhe violently against it, aching to be discharged, to be free of Vale, who was dying, who had been flung down like a worm-riddled apple or pear. Ah, how eager it was to fly out of him, out the pit of his belly, his penis hardened, shaftlike, helpless to stop what was happening!—his life, the living kernel of him, fled violently through him and into the mud and was gone. No sensation, no ecstasy: only a groaning whimpering threshing struggle. It wanted freedom from his dying body, it wanted to mate with and impregnate the earth.

Much later they held him down and wrapped him in a blanket to keep his arms against his body. Even so, he managed to sink his teeth into someone's wrist. Ha, ha! His jaws clamped shut like a snapping turtle's. . . . Something stinging and hot flowed into his left buttock, one of them had injected him with poison, but how could it harm him now that he was dead?

They pressed a glass into his hand. He drank.

Nothing was happening at Chuck's Harbor Inn so they drove back along the lake-front road. At first Vale thought the car was his, and he should have been driving, then he realized that the car wasn't his. He sat in the front seat, though.

On top of Old Smokey, all covered with snow. . . . I lost my true lover. . . .

Stopped for a beer at Darby's, small crowded dump of a place, Vale in his suede suit perspiring and irritated; he was overdressed, he was too good for this cheap crowd. Heard music somewhere. Music. No juke box in Darby's. Went to the men's room in the basement and saw, downstairs, more tables and a platform set up at the far end of the room, people jammed in, happy, loud, young people, strangers his own age, saw a boy of about twenty playing a guitar to the crowd, singing, trying to make himself heard over the din. There was a microphone but it didn't work right. There was a spotlight, just an ordinary lamp with its shade tilted sharply back. . . . The boy was very tall and thin, in a denim outfit, curly head bowed over the guitar, mouth working somberly over the words, Ain't gonna raise your flag no more, ain't gonna wear your uniform no more, his voice whiny, nasal, self-conscious. Kids from the college. A gathering of kids from the college. Vale pushed forward, unmindful of legs and feet in his way, and stood by a post listening. Ain't gonna fight your wars no more, Death, ain't gonna march in your parades no more. . . . Fitzgerald came looking for him just when the guitar player ended the song and there was a smattering of applause and another boy stepped up to the microphone.

What-all is this? Fitzgerald asked.

The boy looked quite young. It was disturbing, how young he looked. Even with a beard, even in a black turtleneck sweater, he looked much younger than Vale—reminded him of his brother Ronnie.

A free show, said Vale.

The boy began to read in a low, rapid voice. What was it? Something about fish dying in the lake. Vale couldn't catch all the words. He listened but could not make sense of what he heard. It angered him that the boy was up there at all, reading to the audience something that made no sense, and it angered him that the audience wasn't paying close enough attention.

Most of the noise came from the back of the room, from men who weren't college students. They were in their mid- or late twenties. There were three long tables set up in front of the platform and boys and girls at these tables were

253

fairly attentive; it flashed through Vale's mind that the boys and girls all knew one another, they were classmates, friends. One of them stood and yelled back for the men to be quiet, to be quiet, please!—and the bearded boy glanced up, frightened. Frightened in this place, in this safe snug hole. Vale's lips moved in contempt, he made a disgusted gesture, Fitzgerald wanted to leave but Vale didn't budge and after a while their friends came downstairs looking for them, and they got a table for themselves and ordered two pitchers of beer. This is a free show, Vale said, we got a right to watch it. The air was heavy with smoke. The ceiling was too low and the beams were exposed and the walls were only partly plastered, but something about the place was nice, Vale liked it, he felt curious about the boys and girls, he wondered who they were, who the girls were, if any of them had been in his English class and maybe remembered him.

Another bearded boy, wearing glasses. Took so long tuning his guitar that his friends began to tease him. He was fresh-faced, blond, kept smiling nervously, Vale's own lips twitched in sympathy. A girl stepped up onto the platform to help adjust the microphone. It didn't work right: kept picking up scuffling, rasping sounds. Vale stared at the girl. Tight-fitting jeans, a red sweater, hair that fell to her waist. Honey-blond. Pretty. Too thin. Her boy friend with the guitar was homely. Vale didn't like him. He adjusted the microphone again and still it wasn't quite right but he decided to go ahead anyway, mumbling something about the song he was going to sing, which he had written himself, suicidal forces, the fall of Saigon, the defeat of Empire, Black Plague, anthrax, conquest of the moon. Louder, someone said, we can't hear you. Louder!

A simple country tune, twangy and half-familiar. The boy's voice surprisingly strong. Vale listened, excited. For some reason he was excited. He could not follow the words of the song, could not quite put them together, but he recognized certain names, the names of places in Vietnam. When the song ended there was applause and, though he didn't join in, though he remained with his arms folded tightly across his chest, the response pleased him.

Another song. A love song. Vale caressed the left side
254

of his face, tenderly, slowly; he felt ripples, ridges, crevices, peaks and valleys and pits, spots that were smooth as a baby's skin, others that were tough as calluses. He had died, his face had been gouged out, but they had given him another face and here he was. The scar tissue on his shoulder and chest was different, still reddened, freakish-looking, but no one could see. Women caressed him, stroked him. There were women who would do that. They would do anything he asked. Anything.

"Vale Bartlett" was just something he wore, like this suit. He needed it to walk around in. He hid behind it, behind the face. Vale? they said and he answered to his name if he wished. Had been doing that all his life, without knowing what he did. He could tear the outfit off and jump up naked and surprise everybody, or he could sit inside it, hiding, until it was time to make his move. When he was nervous he was afraid it might happen at any time. If he didn't act quickly enough they would throw him down again and wrap him in a blanket and stick a needle in his thigh, but he thought he would probably act quickly enough, now he knew how things were.

Let's go, said Vale, and they followed the guitar player and the girl up the stairs, it was about midnight, a few people were leaving and Vale wanted to leave. On the sidewalk Vale told the boy he liked his singing. It was beginning to rain. Isn't it something, Vale said to his friends and to the boy and to the girl, who stood a few yards away, buttoning her jacket, that a person can make up things out of his head, put them into a song like that and sing them, I wish I could do that. . . . The boy smiled and thanked him. He seemed nervous. The girl smiled. In the street light they were less striking than they had seemed downstairs. The girl's hair was brown, not honey-blond. I know what you mean, I agree with you, Fitzgerald said. Used to be I sang a little myself. Had a guitar too. Not a fancy one like that, though. . . . This isn't very fancy, the boy laughed. Vale asked if the two of them would like to go for a drink somewhere, somewhere better than Darby's, but the boy said they were on their way to a friend's apartment, so Vale offered them a ride, but they said it was only a five-minute walk; no

255

trouble. Well I sure liked your singing, Vale said. I would like to hear it again sometime. The boy giggled, embarrassed, and the girl slid her arm through his and shook her long hair, smiling at Vale, smiling fully at him, he could see her teeth glistening. My name is Vale, he said. My name is Sally and this is Jake, the girl said. . . . Sure you don't want no ride, Fitzgerald asked, draping his arm around Vale's shoulders shining his aluminum hook plain. The boy started to say no but the girl said yes suddenly; yes, okay. It was maybe more than a five-minute walk, and now it was raining. So a ride would be awfully nice.

*I'll never be that old,* Ronnie thought.

The ugly sight was gone, the coffin closed, lowered into the hole. Puddles in the hole from the rain. *Hurley. Anna, b. 1901 d. 1941.* They would chip his name in now and the dates of his birth and death, and that would be that. Ronnie didn't miss him. He hadn't cried. He was embarrassed, angry and embarrassed. He didn't want to talk about it. . . . Anna Hurley, who was Anna Hurley? His grandmother. A face in some old snapshots, he couldn't even remember, didn't want to remember. *Joseph Hurley, Anna Hurley. May They Enter the House of the Lord.*

Why did Momma keep sniffing, why did she make so much noise!

There were birds in the berry bushes down by the fence, flicking and darting. No one else noticed. There was a jet plane overhead, far overhead, a long thread of white behind it, traced across half the sky; then it began to crumble and fade. Ronnie watched. He rubbed his fist against his nose.

Now it was over, now the fuss and commotion and embarrassment were over. But he didn't want to see his friends: they would act funny around him. Goddam it! Goddam them! He wanted to snatch up that stone on the path and throw it into the bushes, hard, and see if maybe he could clip one of those birds.

*Lyle Bartlett.* Daddy. White gravestone, looked stained; cheap. He couldn't remember his father too well, unless he tried. Maybe he couldn't remember him at all. What good did it do? None of that crap did any good.

The funeral parlor in town: Momma and the other women in hats, in shoes with heels. The men in suits. His brothers and sisters dressed up, looking miserable, looking scared and confused and stupid. Grandpa's eyes closed, lips closed; Grandpa in that dark suit of his; skin touched up with something like putty, to hide the cuts and bruises. Hair combed forward to hide the lacerations on the scalp. . . . Faint chemical odor.

Why the hell did she cry so much, why make such a fuss? He couldn't take it. He wouldn't! Yesterday she was carrying on and scaring the little kids, *my fault, it's my fault, I shouldn't have let him go out like that, I knew he'd have an accident, I knew something would happen,* and he and Davy, fooling around outside, staying close to the house, happened to look at each other for some reason and began to giggle. It was so funny! Jesus! Everybody carrying on, Momma wailing like that, poor Momma, she was so funny, Ronnie had to jam his fist against his mouth, he had to run away from Davy and climb up into the hayloft in the big barn and hide there, giggling, tears running down his cheeks, his stomach aching, oh it was funny, it was crazy, the way Momma cried. But what if the neighbors could hear her? They were a half-mile away but what if the wind blew in that direction?

He didn't miss his grandfather. He hadn't cried.

Everyone was acting strange, everyone was clumsy and embarrassed. Momma kept holding a tissue crumpled in her hand, a yellow tissue she brought to her nose again and again. She wore a hat with a veil. Her face looked puffy. There was her new boy friend next to her, looking scared, frowning and scared. Ronnie never did anything more than glance at him. There was Nancy, and Laney: Laney looking his way but not seeing him. She wore a dress, she wore stockings and shoes with heels, but no hat. She had been acting strange for a long time, as if she wasn't here, as if her mind was somewhere else. Sometimes she stared right at Ronnie without seeing him. *Don't tell anyone,* she said, just that morning, out on the porch where Ronnie was trying to scrape mud off his shoes, *don't tell anyone, not even Momma, okay?—but it wasn't ever any accident, it wasn't any mistake, he knew damn*

257

*well what he was doing, one morning I went after him and he was up there on the path, by the river, standing at the edge of the path, it looked like he was getting ready to step off and I wondered if I should call him, tell him no, don't!—I was scared as hell—so I ran up and he didn't like it any, me interrupting him like that. He knew every bit of what he was doing, Ronnie. He wanted to die! He wanted to die!* She spoke fast, so low he could hardly hear her. It was a secret between them but he didn't want it, didn't know what to do with it, he was afraid even to look at Laney, her face was so pale, dishwater gray, her eyes were wet and reddened and ugly, tears were caught on the lashes and ready to run down her cheeks. *He wanted to die!* she whispered.

Ronnie didn't care. He hadn't cried yet, except for a few minutes when he was alone. He wasn't going to think about it much; he wasn't going to think about anything much. He would get along all right. Just plowed the garden for the old man, and all the fuss Momma made about Grandpa being too feeble to work hard, taking on too much hoeing—somebody else was going to do it now.

*I don't care,* he thought. *I'll do it alone. . . . I'm never going to be that old anyway.*

Enchanted, enchained, inchanting, my love, my loves, afield in your arms, delicious flowerish liquor-laughter rising from all sides, Kasch dives and sinks and pops to the surface and dives plunging again, seeking, self-sought. Pilgrim. Many-armed. Many-limbed. His loves are many-eyed, glittering and winking. He is home at last. He is here.

The Bridegroom escorted to his bridal chamber.

Who is he? Will he stay? Will he stay with us?—the small voices cry.

Quiet, quiet!

Will he stay with us? Will he never leave?

The days lengthen, the sun takes hold of the sky, the summer solstice approaches. Will he never leave?

Never never never never.

One by one they throw their arms about him. Their

258

light gay laughter, their faces flowerlike, bright and blank, piercingly beautiful. One of them, more lovely than the rest, stands shyly aside, her gray gaze veiled, her lips parting slowly, slyly, to show the damp teeth, small white damp glistening teeth, ah! the surprise of it, of her! like a flower's pistil showing itself suddenly in that budlike mouth. Laughter, kisses, high shrill excited voices, angels' voices, angels crowding close. You are not drunk, not even with the music of their laughter, or the heated frenzy of their kisses; you see clearly for the first time in your life.

My love, my loves, my own, bring me to you, into you, let me lie in your arms, in your many warm warming arms, never leave me, never betray me, never expel me: never.

Surely Kasch has died and is entering paradise?

They are ringing him in. One, and another, and another. They are chanting. Wold, wood, world, wooed. Stay. Be still. Sweet, very sweet! The chill's past. The summer solstice approaches. Up the narrow stairs, the angels' voices ascending, her perfumed arms, shoulders, breast, belly, her strong wide hips and thighs, her slender ankles, the blue-veined feet, the small stubby toes, will you never leave, will you always love? Never. Always. The old hag broke your heart with her tea that tasted of grass and her stale store-bought cookies and her wattled shivering flesh that was not yours, not yours, not your mother, not your blame, she broke your heart and tittered and then, as you were leaving, she began to weep suddenly and her fingers closed upon you, clawlike, grasping, terrible: but it was too late. You escaped her. You were free.

Are free: taking her kiss on your eyelids as you ascend the stairs. Her breath tastes of wine, her shoulders and breasts of lilac, she stands at the top of the stairs and waits for you, her arms extended, her hands gripping your shoulders, her lovely mouth lowered to your forehead, to your grateful eyes. They close; she kisses the lids; never have you seen so clearly.

Your senses are filled to the brim, and over. You are afraid. You are on tiptoe. What you lived for, driven here into this corner, the faces dipping and floating about you in the darkness, the children's voices swelling, fading, subsiding, swelling again as one of the children—a girl no more than three or four years of age—scurries ahead of you, into the bedroom, switches on a lamp and ah, the surprise of that light, that warm, pale orangeish halo upon the wallpaper and the bed table and the bedclothes, the pillows!

Why did you wait so long to return, the broad-faced girl cries, holding an infant out to you: See? See? That's the nice man we met last year, that's him, do you remember, isn't he nice, isn't it nice that he's come back to us? We've waited so long, the winter has been so long, so cold; we've been so lonely!—But why did you wait all this while to return?

The infant blinks, his eyes struggle to focus on you. He waves his pudgy fingers; you lean forward to kiss them and they grope against your face, your nose, everyone laughs in delight, you touch the fingers lightly with your tongue, you blow on them and the infant laughs aloud, startled, delighted.

Why, why did you wait all this while?

Will you never leave, will you always love?

Never. Always.

Will you—?

Children dart into the shadowy corners of the room; a child scrambles beneath the bed. Another is turning back the bedcovers, carefully, reverentially, her shy gray gaze directed your way, her lips pursed trembling.—What pests, what nuisances! Go downstairs! Go away! Why, they've been drinking wine, they've been drinking hard cider, these pests!

You open the closet door and one of them is crouching inside, the hem of a dress over his face. He scrambles away on his hands and knees, giggling.

Away, away! Leave us!

Filled to the brim, your senses pulse and sway. You stand on tiptoe. Your fingers brush against the wall, you make your way like a sleepwalker, gaping, groping.—Away, away!

They scramble out of the shadows, they are thunderous on the stairs, the old house shakes with their gaiety. At the foot of the stairs the aged, ancient man crouches, too feeble to ascend. You will never leave, he calls. Never.

My love—

Surely my doom is upon me—

The roads lead into roads ever deeper, deeper, they turn, dip sharply, repeat themselves, a maze, a stupefaction, they sink between wooded hills, between cornfields, moist and sucking with spring rain they are earthy-wet, red-clayey, riotous with the singing of newborn frogs. Hills, fields, hollows, ditches, the river, the enormous barnlike house, the many-branched wind, the agitated vines, tree branches, clattering, Fitz John wake up, it's time, come, come to me, to us, we have been waiting so long, come, come now, now, the wood spirits sing, it's time for you to wake, time for you—Earthen-floored cellar, moist and oozing damp, shadows that scuttle with secret life, stairs that lead in all directions, corridors blocked off, rooms vacated and closed, the roof rotting, sagging, fierce large birds squawking about the chimney, alone you listen to them by the hour, beyond terror now, beyond desire: but no, you are not alone, you are never going to be alone again, the woman stands before you, waiting, she has been waiting all this time, she longs only to fold you in her arms and bring you to sleep.

In the distance the children cry out to you, the old man mumbles something you cannot hear, the winds poke about the house, many-fingered, curious. The woman laughs. Filled to the brim, she is, plump-breasted, her belly compact, her hips and thighs strong, her legs strong, firm, taut. My love! Lips moist, parted in a sly smile, between her teeth a seed, is it?—a tiny seed—a yew seed—you step forward and, trembling, bring your mouth to hers, your eager mouth to hers, you kiss, you taste, you eat: a tiny seed from a yew cone. Ah! Your hand is clasped, fingers are thrust through yours, a playful handshake, your eyelids tremble, your lips are eager, damp, someone brushes your hair away from your forehead, her cool fingers brushing against your heated skin. My

261

love! My love! You kiss, you taste, you eat. You hold them all in one embrace. The searing flame darts through you and rolls your eyes back into your head and it is over, it is done, your words are torn from you:

I love—

You hold them all in one embrace. All. Always. Forever.

I love—

I—

Exhausted, you sleep in someone's arms, you sleep as if felled with an ax, like a soft-bodied creature you are now, warm, warmed, asleep, a soft-bodied sleeper, spinal column on the outside of your body to protect you forevermore, her arms to protect you, theirs, their arms, their warm damp cheeks, their kisses. They are yours. They are you.

Waved over to the side of the street, to the curb. Jesus H. Christ, Vale whispered.

Uniformed, leather-booted, goggled; strode back to Vale and stared into his face. A stranger. License, please. Car registration, please.

Motor idling, parked by the Civic Stadium, waiting while his papers were being investigated, noted a wrestling match that Friday evening, Sourdough Kelly vs. The Psychic, main feature; "Mamma" Hernandez vs. "Black Angel" Jackie, second feature.

Was going under the speed limit, Vale said politely.

Holdup on Northern Boulevard, car description fits yours, but you're not the kid: he was seventeen, maybe younger. Exxon Station, Northern Boulevard. Manny Hendrix—know him?

No. Don't.

Two kids, actually. Boys. Shot Manny, got away with twelve fucking dollars, Manny's hurt pretty bad and might not live; just boys, kids. Little bastards.—White kids, too.

A hell of a thing, Vale said.

Happens all the time now, said the patrolman. Sorry to bother you. Okay?

Yeah, it's a hell of a thing, Vale said slowly.

When she returned she called out Laney, can I see you for a moment, Laney?—and you trotted over to her at once, you knew, you knew, you didn't look at her face to see what might be there.

Behind you the other girls were quiet, watching; in their gym clothes, a few of them without gym shoes and standing in their socks, staring after you. Laney? Is there trouble again, is something wrong with Laney—?

Miss Flagler touched your arm and you drew away, without speaking. You didn't look at her even then.

A call from the principal's office, she said awkwardly, you can take it right here, the phone on my desk; something about home, your family—

You knew, you knew. Three weeks after your grandfather's death and again, again: your insides tightened in readiness. Again? So soon again?—But no, it wasn't possible: you didn't know; you couldn't have guessed.

You can take the call right here, Laney—
All right. Thanks.
—I'll close the door so you can be alone—
All right.
You couldn't have guessed.

*Six*

JULY 4. The Marsena Volunteer Fireman's Picnic. "God, I hope I don't see many people I know," Arlene said faintly.

"The hell with them," said Wallace.

The wide grassy field behind the firehouse: swarming with people. Three enormous circus tents, innumerable smaller tents, open concessions, booths, announcements over a loudspeaker, recorded music played loud, screams and shouts of children running wild. Most of her own children were here, somewhere. Arlene would keep an eye out for them: she didn't want them to get in any trouble.

"Isn't it busy!—so many people," she said.

A Ferris wheel, a merry-go-round, dogs trotting loose everywhere between parked cars and trucks; a horse show, teen-agers on horseback; children passing with pink cotton candy on sticks; noise, noise; life. So many people! Arlene stared at the familiar sights, at the things she'd been seeing each summer for years, and a strange smile overtook her. So many people! So much to see!—She had made the right decision, then, to come out to Marsena for the day.

The biggest crowds were around the bingo tent and the beer tent. Flocks of pigeons, bold as you please, were pecking at discarded hot-dog buns and popcorn and other garbage, and when Wally made a feinting gesture at them they only flew a few yards away, alighting on a tent rope, wings flapping noisily; acted as if they were drunk, so nervy.

Firecrackers, like gun shots. Boys were setting them off

back in a field. Sunshine: heat. A boy who looked like Ronnie—was it Ronnie?—ducking with two other boys under a tent flap. A panting Irish setter scrambled after them. A ring toss, prizes of painted canes sprinkled with something that glittered: stardust. So many people! Hiram Tanner, an old friend of Arlene's, was spinning a wheel of fortune at one of the booths. He wore a smart brand-new straw hat with a bright green band and a pheasant feather stuck in the band; when he caught sight of Arlene he grinned and waved and even leaned over to see who she was with—but he didn't know Wally, did he?—or maybe he did. Wally was from town but lots of people seemed to know him.

Ah, the chicken chowder!—better this year, even, than last year. Served in big heavy mugs, with oyster crackers, thick steaming tasty chowder, globules of fat floating on the surface. Arlene licked her greasy lips. Where were the napkins? There were never enough napkins! Where was the salt? No benches, not even folding chairs, people just stood at the booth or in the path, eating. Wasn't it good? Better than last year? There was Judy Wrezsin dragging her two youngest kids, shorts and a halter, sandals, breasts bobbing, an inch or more of flesh about her waist, what a sight!—for a moment Arlene considered turning away so she wouldn't have to introduce Wally to Judy. How could that woman go out looking so messy, on a Sunday afternoon, on July Fourth of all days, didn't she give a damn any longer?—it was embarrassing. But Arlene called out and she came over, dragging the kids, her face brightened, she looked almost pretty, it turned out that her husband knew Wally from a while back—before he'd become a State Trooper, he'd worked on his father's farm out in the Rapids, hadn't he? —so they chatted for a while, Judy was really very nice, lots of laughs, Arlene had always liked her, Arlene had always discounted the nasty rumors attributed to *her*. She was really nice. For instance, she told Arlene two or three times how pretty she looked, right in front of Wally; your hair is perfect that way!—I love it; and that dress, how's it cut in back?—so pretty—you mean you made it *yourself?* —Jesus! Right in front of Wally, so that Arlene went red,

267

began to laugh like a young girl. Judy flabby, crow's-feet around her eyes, probably in search of her husband, those two little brats fighting each other between her legs, yet still she was nice: people *were* nice. Not a word of Arlene's bad luck, not a word, only a remark as she turned to go about missing old Joseph—he always loved the firemen's picnics so much, didn't he?—had the time of his life at them—it was sure a pity about him dying like that, so fast, such a terrible accident—or maybe it was for the best, who could tell?—her own father, as Arlene knew, was sick for such a long, long time. Arlene's eyes filled with tears, she squeezed Judy's arm to thank her, yes she was nice, they'd have to see more of each other, maybe drive up to Yewville for a day's shopping and have lunch there when the kids started school again.

An open field, a small crowd, kids between the ages of ten and thirteen, a "ski race." A fat man Arlene knew vaguely, couldn't remember the name, shouting through a megaphone. There were two teams of children, six on each team, jammed together with their feet fastened to long skis; it was a race, one-two, one-two, left-right, left-right, left— But one of the teams spilled down, shrieking with laughter; a child had gotten mixed up and broken the rhythm and his teammates capsized. The other team kept going. The leader, a boy who looked familiar—must have been an Arkin, with that face and chin and freckles— shouting Left-Right! Left-Right! Left-Right! Left-Right! The other team scrambled to their feet and readjusted themselves and started again, and people were cheering them on, and then something happened to the first team— a girl misstepped—and everyone fell over—and there was shrieking and screaming and groaning and laughter and the fat man hopped about teasing them, shouting Come on, now! Come on! Hey! Let's go! through his megaphone.

"Did you used to play these games when you were a kid?" Wally asked.

"I played all the games," Arlene said.

The bingo tent: mainly women. A few older men, a few boys. Sitting on long benches, out of the sun, pushing kernels of corn around on bingo cards; a growing excitement to the game, *Bingo* must have been near; the announcer's voice lively, urgent. A big crowd here too. The firemen were going to make a lot of money, wasn't that nice? They deserved it. A few years ago, wasn't it, that terrible thunderstorm, almost a hurricane, their picnic rained out and so much money lost?—but this year the attendance was higher than ever, going to set a record, wasn't that wonderful. They certainly deserved it. —Wally asked if she wanted to play bingo and she said hell no, didn't want to sit down and miss all the excitement, bingo didn't appeal to her, though some of the prizes looked good: out there in the center of the tent, on display, a pink wicker clothes hamper, a floor lamp with a fringed shade, a bird bath, some lawn ornaments, a child's sled, a dollhouse, an electronic football game, a set of stainless steel silverware, some china. And of course there were cash prizes too. As a girl Arlene had been crazy about bingo and she'd played three cards at a time with her girl friends, and once she won a hundred dollars—called out *Bingo!* so excited she could hardly see, jumping up and down, her girl friends excited too, and it was right— her card was checked and she really had bingo and the big prize was a hundred dollars cash and she just couldn't believe it and she never, never forgot the wild excitement of that day—though in the years afterward, when she played again, she never even got close to bingo. Word got around anyway that the game was fixed—not exactly fixed but almost—so she didn't take time to play now. Still, just remembering that day, how wildly happy she'd been and how people had congratulated her, made her feel good now.

She told Wally about it and he slipped his arms around her waist and squeezed her; he said he wished they'd known each other then.

Hot dogs, "foot-longs," hamburgers, chiliburgers, pizza-burgers, mustard and pickle relish and ketchup, corn on the cob, flies buzzing everywhere, recorded guitar music overhead, the sun quite hot. Arlene spotted June with two other little girls and someone's big sister, so it was all right but she'd better check anyway, ran over and asked if June needed any money, if she was having fun?—

gave her a dollar. Don't eat too much candy! Don't make yourself sick!

"That's a cute little girl," Wally said.

"She isn't bad," Arlene said. "Yeah, she's kind of cute."

"June, is it?"

"June."

She really felt good now, in spite of the heat. God, to think she almost hadn't come!—had very nearly spent the Sunday by herself. Wally had been around a few times and she'd talked with him, of course, couldn't just send him away, gave him coffee and peach upside-down cake one time, and had him stay for supper another time, when it was a pot roast and she knew it was tasty; but she had been reluctant to go out with him, even over to the tavern in Childwold for a few beers, her heart hadn't been in it, all the strain and fuss of taking up with a new man. Not again, never again. . . . It wasn't worth it. She'd been hurt so bad, her life turned around like that, such a surprise, such bad luck, always such bad luck, maybe there was a curse on her or something, that some men didn't love her enough and hurt her, and other men loved her too much, were a little crazy about it, and they hurt her too, damaged her life worse than the others. "God, God, God," she had moaned, thinking of Kasch and Earl, seeing them again in her mind's eye, again and again, hardly able to sleep for weeks after the trouble, moaning "God, God. . . . Stop them, don't let, oh please, please. . . ."

But why dwell on the past, on unhappy things. Why ruin this beautiful day. Why, why, no sense to it. Wally was sweet, so sweet. Why not go along with his mood, just be happy, why not be like everyone else . . . ? The beer tent was the most popular place of all. What a crowd! Wally had to elbow his way through to get their beers. Arlene waved to people she knew. She really did feel better. The sun was hot, her low-cut dress was maybe a mistake—she'd been inside so much this summer, moping around and brooding, trying to get her strength back, and so she was rather pale—what if she got sunburned? Shoulders especially. Arms and shoulders: God, what a disaster one summer, she'd been about Laney's age, went swimming and the day wasn't really hot and the sunshine was deceptive and she'd been so badly burned her skin had blistered, what a mess! Had to rub ointment on it for days. The sun was hot, she was sweating a little, but she really did feel better. The beer was so cold! So good. She was thirsty, Wally was thirsty. He finished his in a few swallows; went back for more. . . . Salted peanuts, potato chips, pretzels. The chips were a little stale. The beer was good, wasn't it?—beer on tap, from enormous barrels; delivered by truck that morning from Port Oriskany. Lots of jokes about the consumption of beer at this particular picnic. Big money-maker. Well, the Marsena firemen deserved to make money; they were really nice guys, most of them. And a few years ago the picnic had been rained out. . . .

That was the year, wasn't it, that the old man had died during a bingo game?—a heart attack and the other players didn't want to stop, bingo was near and they were furious, didn't want to stop the game; it got into the Yewville paper and was taken up by other newspapers in the state and the stories were sort of insulting, weren't they, making fun of hill people . . . ? Marsena, Childwold, the Rapids, Frothing: making fun of us. No, it wasn't that year; couldn't have been; must have been the year before. Anyway—

Wally saw some friends of his and he and Arlene went over to join them in a shady corner of the beer tent; they were nice guys, seemed to be nice guys, one of them a State Trooper like Wally, of course not in his uniform today, not with his pistol, just relaxed and having a good time. Arlene liked them very much. She gathered, as the minutes passed, that one of them knew Wally's wife, made some small allusion to her, frowning, shaking his head, as if to say it was a shame but—what the hell?—if people couldn't get along, if they were always fighting, if the wife tried to turn the children against the husband, well, what could you do? Arlene was rather pleased with her new dress; she knew the turquoise and orange colors became her, went well with the color of her hair. Her earrings were inexpensive summer earrings, white and orange dangles, her necklace matched, the beads like tiny seeds, really very pretty. She felt good. The beer went to her head and she heard herself giggling like a girl. From time to time Wally squeezed her around the waist or slid his arm around her shoulders, and once he even kissed her noisily on the forehead—he was in a wonderful mood, so sweet, so lively and funny, not a handsome man but attractive in his own way, big and strong and reliable, tanned face, hands, deep-chested laughter that reminded her of Earl, but he wasn't loud like Earl and wasn't bullying and nasty and crazy like Earl; that poor bastard.

Thank God they had been able to rent the old McInnis house, a five-minute walk along the road from Carrie and her husband—so they wouldn't be reminded of their bad luck, and wouldn't be reminded, even, of poor Grandpa; it was bad enough for Arlene since his death, waking up positive she'd heard him in his room sighing and grumbling in his sleep, or scolding the dog out back, or opening the refrigerator door in the middle of the night, or just wandering around downstairs as if he was lost. . . . The farm was his, the house was his, every room and closet and corner, she'd never realized until his death how it was his, it was *him,* and could never belong to anyone else. The children kept hearing him too, and even seeing him: Davy insisted that Gran'daddy had been in the little boys' bedroom one night, trying to tell them something, but his voice was faint and funny, and his words were all garbled; and Mary Ellen and even June crawled into bed with Arlene, saying they were afraid to sleep in their own beds; and even Nancy, who should have known better, started the children going again by swearing she'd heard his footsteps downstairs one night, she *heard* him, she did!—and got very snippy with Arlene when Arlene tried to calm her down. There's no such thing as ghosts! No such thing! Ronnie shouted. . . . And then Earl: the horrible thing that had happened to Earl. *There's no such goddamn thing as ghosts!* Ronnie yelled at them all.

So it was better for them to move out. It was the only thing to do.

Put the farm on the market, people told Arlene; maybe you'll be lucky and someone will come along and buy it, aren't there a few acres left?—eight acres?—and maybe
272

some of the farm equipment is worth something. Taxes are going up, being jacked up every year by the county, pretty soon all the old farms will be sold, nobody can afford them except the big corporations, the banks, it's the only thing to do, a woman in your circumstances: do you have any choice? But she couldn't sell the farm, she just couldn't. What a thing! Her father dead and buried such a short while, and his farm up for sale by his own daughter! . . . She couldn't do it. Couldn't. A pity Fitz John Kasch hadn't bought the land, and the adjoining land, as he had planned; talking so happily, so wildly, about buying back the two hundred fifty acres Arlene's father had once owned; a pity, wasn't it? But maybe he hadn't been serious about it, maybe he had not really known what he was saying, what his words were saying. *I want to . . . I hope to . . . I intend to . . .* Yes, it was possible he had not known what he was saying.

The McInnis house was an ugly old place with tar-paper roofs and no cellar but at least it was big enough for the family, and, to tell the truth, it was in slightly better condition than their own house, though Arlene would never admit it; and it was closer to the highway, only a five-minute walk, so that Ronnie could get the school bus there without much trouble. He would be taking the bus to Yewville this September for the first time, to the consolidated school. How fast time was going! The years, the years . . . ! Ronnie's voice already cracking, getting husky, the boy must have grown two or three inches in the past year, going to be Vale's size at least and going to have Vale's temper too. . . . Still, he was a good boy. He had taken charge so well, had known enough to telephone the police, to get things going right, he was a good boy, all the children were good; she was really quite proud of them, however much she fussed and scolded. Poor Judy Wreszin with that undersized little snot-nosed brat kicking at her, said to be a little slow in the head, what a pity! . . . but Arlene's children were all in good health. Laney was still too small for her age, never did eat right: maybe Esther would make her sit at the table and eat and not be up and running away all the time, like a nervous cat. Anyway she was in reasonably good health. . . . Now that Prentiss was back, Nancy was blooming: pregnant again. A surprise when Prentiss returned, not a word ahead of time, not even a telephone call, wasn't that just like a man?—a surprise, too, that he looked so thin-armed and boyish; Arlene had begun to forget exactly how he looked, or had started to mix him up with someone else. But he came back, he wept when he saw Louise and Baby Dennis, really loved them so, he swore he'd never be away from them for a day, even, the rest of his life—really sweet, that Prentiss, and just perfect for Nan when you saw the two of them together. Living now in Derby, Prentiss with a good job at the foundry, Nan busy with the children and trying to fix up their house, a cute place but awfully small; Arlene would have to get up there again soon, Nan would need help with the curtains. . . . Well, that had turned out fine. After all the worries, the tears, the threats, after all the nasty rumors spread by Arlene's so-called friends, Nan's marriage was turning out fine. . . . Thank God.

But poor Kasch! Poor Fitz John! She tried not to think about him, tried not to make herself unhappy. It did no good, thinking morbid thoughts, dwelling upon the past, turning over and over in her mind how things went, how they might have gone instead, how lives were changed, irreparably changed, in a few minutes. A certain choice made, no time to think, no time to think ahead: and that was that. If only Kasch had not been nearby when Earl showed up. . . . She would not have minded being beaten by Earl again, not even that, so long as he hadn't crippled or killed her, the bastard, the drunken loud-mouthed cruel swinish bastard . . . if only Kasch hadn't been out at the farm that day, if. . . . But. . . . Poor sweet Kasch, nervous about the mouth, his eyelids fluttering in her presence, nearsighted, undernourished, his voice so courteous, like someone on television, a sweet man, truly sweet, a gentleman, putting so much money in the bank for her, for the house and the children, offering to buy the farm, begging her to marry him, begging. . . .

*You're so beautiful,* he had said, staring. Those queer eyes of his behind the lenses of his glasses: too intense, too bright. As if he had seen into her head, into some-
274

thing in her that wasn't her at all, something he recognized but she knew nothing about; she felt only embarrassed and awkward when he spoke like that, stared at her like that. *So beautiful*. . . . She wasn't beautiful, that was silly. She knew what she looked like. Hadn't she lived with herself for forty years now, didn't she know all too well, it was just embarrassing to hear such things; but of course he had been sweet, he hadn't meant to make her feel self-conscious. He hadn't meant anything to happen as it had. And now. . . .

But why dwell on the past. Why, why, no sense to it. In another minute she'd be crying. And Wally was so sweet, one of the nicest men she'd ever met, he knew about what had happened and didn't care, didn't hold it against her as some men might; he never brought the subject up at all.

His friends left and he asked Arlene if she'd like supper somewhere, or did she want to stay at the picnic longer; he'd had a great time, he said, but wouldn't mind leaving now and driving out to Wolf's Head Lake, to the lodge there, having a fish fry, maybe, how did that sound? Arlene thought it sounded wonderful. She was hungry, she realized. Despite the beer and nuts and chips and pretzels, she was really hungry. . . . Yes, she said, it sounded like a wonderful idea.

"I'll take the river road," Wally said. "That's a real pretty way to drive."

You picked up the receiver and listened and there was a small clock on Miss Flagler's desk, a clock in a traveling case made of imitation red leather, you stared at it but didn't see the time, you stood there beginning to shake, listening, listening to Nancy's voice there on the other end, so many miles away, you had been through this before, hadn't you?—had lived through it before, many times, you remembered the clock and the traveling case and the bookcase against the wall stuffed with books and magazines and pamphlets, you remembered the sensation of cold inside you, the feeling that your tongue had gone numb again, again, hadn't you lived through this moment before, many times before? You were lying down and

275

someone stood above you, leaning over you. Laney? Dolly? It was Grandpa leaning over you; Momma sat beside the bed, her hand on your forehead, talking to Grandpa as if you weren't there. Grandpa's lips moved. You looked right into his eyes, right *into* his eyes. But he didn't see you. Momma said the doctor wouldn't come all the way out to the farm, maybe they should bundle you up and drive in, or maybe it would be dangerous, what would be best to do, Pa, what can I do?—I don't know what to do!—I don't know what to do! Grandpa touched your cheek, leaned over and kissed your forehead, you smelled the tobacco odor and his breath that wasn't nice, you reached up to grab his nose but your hand wouldn't move; it was stuck inside the covers, the covers were too heavy. What can I do, Momma said, oh God what can I do?—her temperature is a hundred and one, Pa, and that son of a bitch won't come out here—Grandpa backed away and you reached for him and began to cry and Momma held you, Momma sat on the edge of the bed and held you, It's all right, it's all right, honey, he was an old man, it's all right, I think it's all right, he was failing so, he was getting so thin, honey, Laney, it was the saddest thing, I never told anybody, it was the saddest thing, he told me one night—we were sitting downstairs in the kitchen, the two of us—just sitting—he told me he didn't think he could keep up with the younger men anymore, out in the fields; didn't think he could work a full day any longer. It was some other time in his mind, Laney, it must have been twenty years ago, but he was acting so embarrassed, it hurt him to tell me, he wanted me to explain to them that he wouldn't be working a full day the next day, would I be the one to tell them?—he was so ashamed, he almost couldn't get the words out! Poor Pa! Then he had no appetite these last few weeks, he said if he didn't work he didn't deserve to eat, wasn't even drinking much toward the end. He knew, he knew! He knew something was going to happen! I almost think—but—well, no—no, I better not say—Laney, it's all right, isn't it? Don't you think it's all right? He was getting so thin, his arthritis hurt him so bad, you know he never complained about anything, he said he'd like to be hit over the head
276

with a shovel if he ever carried on the way my mother did, scaring everyone, moaning and groaning and talking about dying, you know how he used to say that, and he never did complain, never said a word, oh poor Pa, he *never* said a word, kept everything to himself right till the end—

Grandpa stood close beside you. Merry Christmas, he said. Rolling his eyes, making a face: because Christmas was silly. Such a lot of fuss and commotion! You asked him did he like your present to him and he said yes, he liked it a lot, he liked it the best of all his presents, but Momma had to gather all the boxes up and sort things out because Grandpa just pretended to like his presents and sometimes they got mixed in with the wrapping paper and thrown out: one of his presents a few years ago, a nice chocolate-brown muffler, got thrown out that way and it was such a shame, real wool like that. Are you awfully sad, Laney, he asked you, standing close beside you in Miss Flagler's office, are you going to be lonely the rest of your life? Are you going to miss us? Cry over us? Don't! The hell with all that! . . . Your life is just getting started.

You were crying. When you put the receiver back it slipped and almost fell onto the floor. Miss Flagler would be waiting just outside the office wanting to know what was wrong, wanting to pity you; you didn't want to talk to her, you didn't want to talk to anyone. Momma? Grandpa? . . . I don't want to be lonely all my life, you said. I love him. I didn't love him. I wanted to love him but I didn't, I didn't know how. Is it too late? It's too late. . . . Momma, you said, don't be such a baby! He's just a friend, I could never love *him*.

You opened the door but Miss Flagler wasn't there. She must have gone back to the gymnasium, to the other girls. Thank God! You ran into the locker room, unbuttoning your shirt. Fingers cold, stiff. You couldn't see. There was your locker, you hadn't bothered to lock it, you reached for your skirt and sweater, you were in a hurry, such a terrible hurry. Years later you will half remember. Not quite remember. Too much hurt, too much confusion, push it away, aside, the hell with it, the hell
277

with pain—Isn't it all right, Laney? Don't cry, don't cry, you'll get me started again! Look, honey: we'll be all right. Haven't we always . . . ?

Vale pulled the guitar out from under his bed. It was dusty because he'd forgotten about it for months, had slid it under there and forgotten it, and now he remembered. He kicked off his shoes and sprawled on the bed and plucked at the strings, which were looser than before. He tightened them. Was that better? He strummed the strings and they cut into his fingers. He used the edges of his fingernails. . . . He strummed hard, harder. Fast. Then he picked at the strings separately, one after another, a tune he invented on the spur of the moment. A little song. Maybe he could make up words to go with it sometime. How did the tune go? He tried to play it again but couldn't get the notes exactly right. Music was hard to remember, music just floated out into the air and was gone. He would make up another tune then.

He sipped at his beer and cradled the guitar in his arm and strummed it for a while, softly; then he strummed it a little harder. He pulled at one of the strings, slipping his finger under it. When he released it, it made a twanging noise. That was funny. He laughed. He did it a few more times, then strummed up and down the strings, fast, impatiently, as if searching for something, trying to remember something. How did that boy's song go? . . . His mind flashed a face, two faces; he heard someone scream; but he just kept on with what he was doing, that was the only thing to do, the only method, let the flashes come, let the explosions come, be unmoved, don't even grimace, and eventually everything gets back to normal.

He strummed fast and hard, broad chords, sounded like a real professional, he began to sing nonsense words with the tune, really enjoying himself, one leg crossed and swinging in time with the music. It was fun, but when he stopped, the music stopped; and his fingers hurt. Still, he thought he'd practice for a while, for a few minutes anyway. . . .

*The Devil take the blue-tail fly!*

Kasch, thou art translated.

How fell, how fallen? Wold wald weald weld wild wood. Accident. Essentially. A tenth of an inch's difference and no reverse, no regain. Accident: essence sprayed out onto the cinders. No scooping it back up again. Perhaps in my madness I tried? Tried to scoop the brains back up again, squeeze them into the broken shell?

---

## THE PILGRIM

*Beware, beware!—desire springs forth*
*Beware, wishes fulfilled!*
*Death: Triumph: Death*

---

The infant's eyes blink and come into focus and his pudgy fingers open, reach for you, he makes a startled gurgling sound and everyone laughs in delight, you laugh in delight, you bend to kiss the fingers, they close upon your nose, they fumble and slip away, you laugh, you touch the fingers with your tongue, you blow gently upon them and the baby laughs suddenly, amazed. *Why did you stay away so long? Will you never leave?*

A rock dropped in the midst of struggle, clumsy grunting sobbing cries, graceless, adults stumbling like giant children, oh give it here! Here! Give it here! And then—

---

## A MELON FOR BREAKFAST

Scent so powerful, my head snapped forward—musk-melon—taste & eat—senses filled to the brim—beauty, beauty, beauty—springing out of the earth, these fruits, these souls. Taste. Eat. My eyeballs rolled in my head—oh love, love!

When will—?

The shape, the odor, the several clinging seeds, slimy-slick, a little soft, bruised—these fruits, these head-shells —skulls—Can it be! What! I! He! This! Where—? What has—?

When will—?

Never.

---

How fell, this fall; but how, how so rudely fallen? All innocent. Innocent, all. The three of us wedded but innocent; must be forgiven. *She* must be forgiven. To stop him from his ravaging, to stop the smashing of my poor face, to stop, stop his wheezing, the terror of his bulk, bellowing bull-sized breath, fists, fury, only to stop—her screams, her weak blows—only to stop him, stooping as she did to pick up the rock, dropping it so that it glanced against his leg, fell to the ground, and I—not she—never *she*—I, I bent to grasp it in both hands—silly whitewashed ornamental rock—and so—and—Again, again, again. Translated.

Wrestling in mud as befits lusty earthy lovers. Bold. So bold! Hesitated only a moment when I first heard him, could have hidden in the house—could have crept into the cellar, pressed my face against the wall, arms outstretched to embrace the clammy oozing rock, could have hidden for days, for years!—but bold, madly bold, rushed outside to confront him. Him: them: it. Fate. And so quickly did one cry this and another cry that, so quickly did this, that, one and then the other and then the other—poor Kasch never knew what it was splashed onto his hands. The world shifts into such patterns as God breaks out of the clouds; in an instant slipping into us, bold mad devouring creatures, yet godly, are we not?—for surely God dwells in us at such times. Our strength is not our own.

Kasch enters the bridal chamber. Kasch seeks his Bride. Flowerlike among flowers she hides among the children. Why did you stay away so long? Why so cruel? Must pass the old man at the foot of the stairs, step lightly over him, pay him no heed. Dead! Translated! The chanting is a heartbeat: Childwold, childwold. Ringing you in. Must be careful, careful. Must never hurt. Never hurt. A single embrace will contain them all.

I wish to be executed as swiftly as possible.

In both hands raised and in both hands brought down, smashing, so hard, so hard!—never such strength in me before—surely God entered me at that moment? But if God entered, God left. Kasch left. There is no one. Nought. Kasch is molecules, atoms, particles, nought. Kasch the poet, Kasch the lover: battered to death by Kasch the murderer. He is gone, gone. Scooped up and buried along with his lusty rival. I am so very sorry, my friends, so very, very sorry, oh my friends, what have I done, what was done through me, through the brute agency of me, I am in perpetual mourning now, my insides cringe and slither in mourning, my guts are afire with sorrow; oh my friends, I am punishment enough for Kasch, I am a suffering reed, a frail trembling membrane, nothing more, I am so sorry, my friends, when will you see fit to extinguish me? For there is immortal life, I have discovered: nor are we out of it.

Self-defense. Second-degree manslaughter. The judge a young-old version of his father, friend of a friend of Father's, pitying, aghast, prim, one glance at me and he saw my innocence, my wreckage. Not guilty by reason of temporary insanity. . . . But it was self-defense, was it not? Such hurt, such terror, to assure the self's hellish survival?

*I demand to be executed as swiftly as possible.*

(Suicide, they say, is against the law. Yet everyone in this place, in this place they have imprisoned me, conspires to break the law: giggles and schemes and bribes and dreams of death by scissors, razor blades, forks, tweezers, rope, twine, pills, nails, thumbtacks, strips of bedsheet, electrical outlets, drowning in basins, in tubs, in toilet bowls, choking by way of oversized clumps of meat, wads of newspaper, washcloths. Ha, ha! To the most ingenious go the prizes!)

---

Laney, Evangeline, do you forgive me? Do you even remember me? I betrayed you with her; I had not the courage for you. Years pass. Our lifetimes pass. My dear, my lovely girl, my daughter, did I ruin your life, did I poison your childhood? . . . Kasch, they say, they scold, be good, be content, take your dosages, eat your meals, rest, mend, think little of the past, of those people, their pastness is irrevocable. You will live and live and live. . . . But there is no Kasch. Where is Kasch? Nought. Zed. If she does not think of Kasch, where is Kasch?

---

I slip into you, I stir your limbs, your sleep. I awaken behind your lovely eyes. But what world is this? I recognize nothing. Where are you, Laney? Where have you gone? I have lost you. Do you exist? Did you ever exist? You have left Childwold, I sense that: but where have you gone? You stir, you wake, you come to consciousness, heaved upon the sands of consciousness; but where are you, why have you gone so far? The books you read are not my books, the language you use is not my language. You are no longer recognizable! You are no longer mine!

---

Stern bulging elks' eyes, we had; grunting straining ludicrous bodies. We fought over your mother, he and I. He had hurt her, was hurting her, would not release her; I rushed forward to my doom. The clumsiness of martyrdom! If only we had seen ourselves, if only we had had the grace to break into laughter . . . peals of helpless, helpless laughter. . . . But there was no seeing, there was no grace. There was no laughter. There was no time. A queer sullen inertia to us, despite our frenzy. The stupidity of brute action: a corresponding stupidity in the body, in the very marrow of the bones. Futility. Waste. They are right, they are right, the saints who teach contemplation, who shy away from action! They are right.

What is done cannot be undone.

So we stumbled in our dance, he and I. There were words, there were curses, shoves, lunges, outcries, threats. A blow to my jaw that was an astonishment. Pain beyond pain. Incredulity. Do such things happen, do such things really happen? I hadn't known. . . . Vision darkened, head ringing, how crude, ludicrous, not possible, couldn't be, can't be, staggered and was struck a second time, glasses knocked off, a voice that must have been my own, begging no no no please, my God please, do such things happen . . . ? Doubled over with pain, blinded, blind, the woman screaming, the rival turning to her: no mercy!

Nose and cheekbone cracked, blood welling in my mouth. Must spit, spit. My glasses gone. Can't see. Blood-veined haze. Beneath the porch the dog was howling as if mad. Again and again and again, both hands gripping the rock, suddenly hammering, pounding, can't stop, can't stop, until I was stooped over him, grunting, sobbing, until the flame passed out of me, the rock slipped from my fingers, blood-smeared, brain-smeared, clumps of flesh and hair stuck to it.

No mercy.

_____

She led me away. A disheveled woman, a stranger. Face ugly, white, contorted. Stranger. The flame had passed out of me, now I had only to grope, to make my way carefully, feet sinking in the mud. Moist red-earthy wet. A spring day. Blood welling in my mouth, beginning to choke me, must spit it out, spit it out. Why did the dog howl? Why were the children crying? She too wept; she washed my face and wept, wept. Beyond their sorrow the land was silent, all of creation was silent. It is silent still.

. . . warehouses, granaries, Preston Steel, dairy bars, brickyards, underpasses, clouds, freighters, railroad tracks, box cars, pigeons, Babs' Bar & Grill, Red Eagle Motel, diesels, Trailway buses, guard rails, water towers, concrete, chimneys, loading docks, Atkinson Shipping, gas tanks, oil drums, Standard Hydraulics, barbed wire, *No Parking,* Civic Stadium, gates, fire escapes, awnings, Eastport Tavern, vans, asphalt, chain-link fences, bull-dozers, chain saws, fire hydrants, ramps, spires, Eden Savings & Loan, Jacey's 24-Hour Fine Food, milkweed, thistles, billboards, tires, telephone poles, ditches, cattails, grass, crabgrass, witch weed, wild mustard. . . .

Hello . . . ? Is anyone there . . . ?

A movement at one of the first-floor windows: quivering and pale as a candle flame. He appears and then steps back at once. . . . Hello, you cry. Like one of those egrets you've just seen in the marshland along the highway, you stand motionless, staring; listening. Your voice is not so strong as you would like.

Hello . . . ?

That ruin of a house, worse than you could have imagined: chimney crumbled, front porch tilting crazily to one side, roof covered with moss and trumpet vine. The big barn caved in, saplings and enormous weeds growing in the barnyard, in the old haystack. A nightmare, a wreck! Everywhere there are weeds, sky-high triumphant weeds, only a few tiger lilies and wild rose and sunflowers remaining; from all sides the din of crickets and other insects—you have forgotten how loud they can be. What tiny arrogant cries! Sawing, rasping, cracking, chipping, grating, scraping little cries . . . ! You have almost forgotten how loud these insects are.

. . . Is he watching? You can't see anyone. The place seems empty, there is a feeling of emptiness about it, a sense of desertion. Starlings strut about the room, fearless. The upstairs windows are boarded up with cheap plywood panels: one of the downstairs windows, broken, has been clumsily stuffed with newspaper and old rags. Or is that an old curtain? The material looks familiar.

Hello . . . ? Please, I only want to. . . . I won't stay very. . . .

You stand in the driveway, you come no closer to the house. All those *No Trespassing* signs! You'd better not go out there, they told you, stay away from that one, he's crazy, you don't know what somebody like that could do, look at what he did once: he could do that again, couldn't he? Go berserk and kill someone? He never answers the door, they say. Hides in the cellar or the barn if someone drives up to the house. Bought all that land and doesn't do a thing with it, doesn't even hunt or fish or set traps, nobody knows *what* he does . . . people leave him alone. He pays his taxes and bills by mail, has an account in a Yewville bank, buys groceries and supplies at one of the new markets at the mall, where he thinks no one knows him. He isn't crazy, they say. He's just mean. . . . But he must be crazy, they say: a man living alone like that, never seeing anyone, letting himself go, hermits are always a little crazy, you see them walking along arguing with themselves, not even aware of other people; of course he's crazy. They all are. They all have money too . . . most of them have money . . . hidden under mattresses or in pillowcases or in the pigpen or in the well. . . . There was a crazy old hermit once off the Marsena Road, had three thousand dollars cash in a fishing tackle box hanging down in a net into his cistern, the cistern was dry, and when he died nobody even knew about it for weeks or maybe months and by the time they checked on him of course the body was picked nearly clean and bones were dragged into the damndest places in that house and you can imagine how surprised we all were, finding that money! . . . three thousand dollars cash, and the poor old bugger living in such filth. . . .

Is that a movement at the window? You start to smile, you start to wave. But no: must be your imagination.

And then he does appear, suddenly. Cringing, pale, wraithlike. Silent. Utterly silent. Ah, it's true: what they've told you is true. His hair is colorless now, might be pale, pale blond or silver, his beard is straggly, a light, metallic gray. His face is gaunt and narrow.

It's Laney, do you remember . . . ? Laney Bartlett . . . ?

With your mother you drove halfway across the state to the hospital, several years ago, to see him: but they told you he wouldn't see any visitors, refused to speak to anyone, even the staff, he was dead, he insisted he was dead, and never looked anyone in the eye, never seemed to hear what was being said to him. No, it was impossible; visitors outside the immediate family, in a case like this, really impossible. He thinks he's *dead?* your mother had wailed, very nearly seizing the nurse's arm. *Dead* . . . ? But can't you talk him out of it, can't you fix him up, why couldn't you just—couldn't you just stand him in front of a mirror so he could see himself, you know, and—wouldn't that work? . . . And again a year later you drove out alone, you had your driver's license now and the use of a car that belonged to a friend at college, and still he refused to see you: he was much improved, they said, would probably be released in a few months if there were no relapses, but he refused to see anyone, he was adamant about turning away the few visitors who did come, he had no interest in any living human beings, he said. *No interest in any living human beings.*

You wrote him a note and the nurse took it to him.

You waited. In the coffee shop, in the waiting room, in the foyer. On the front walk. You waited, prowling around the public areas of the hospital, admiring the flower beds and vegetable gardens tended by the inmates; you overheard snatches of conversations; you examined yourself nervously in a washroom mirror, wondering what he looked like now, after so many months, and what you would look like in his eyes. But there was no reply to your note. . . . He doesn't want to see you, the nurse said.

So you drove back to Yewville.

It's Laney, you call out to him. Do you remember . . . ?
He steps away from the window again.

You are blinking rapidly, you've lost him, you come a step closer and stop, not knowing what to do. He was at the window but he turned away, disappeared, you lost him, what should you do next . . . ? Cockleburs on your skirt. Eyes stinging. Was he really there in that house, was that really *him* . . . ?

No, the place is deserted.

Starlings, grackles, cowbirds. Crows. The high shrill screaming of insects. Great battalions of clouds, like chunks of rock, of ice, blowing down from the mountains. Kasch? In all this? Lost, in this? The roof of the house is going to cave in. One of the three largest branches of the walnut tree is dead. Something scuttles through the underbrush alongside the house. . . . I am here, I am Laney, don't you remember me? Kasch? Don't you love me any longer?

Something is crying, whimpering. The wind. The birds.

The insects. Must be careful of poison ivy, careful of snakes, in this high grass. Buttercups, Queen Anne's lace, heal-all, goldenrod, blue chicory flowers, insect-riddled blossoms. Eating. Devouring. Cloud into cloud, bud into blossoms into ragged shredded petals, bagworms in the apple orchard, in the pear orchard, half the trees marked with their ugly gray tents—why doesn't someone burn them down? Sow thistle grown nine or ten feet high by the barn. Is there no one to cut it back, no one to tear it out by the roots? The old silo, the old windmill. Fallen. Rubble. Those hulks of cars, rust-hulks, skeletons hidden in the grass. The old chicken coop: caved in. No chickens, no rooster. No cats. No Butch: they have another dog now, a brown floppy-eared spaniel, just a puppy, a Christmas present to the youngest children from Momma's boy friend. He isn't allowed out of the yard, he whines and yelps, lonely for the children when they're at school, stuck in there all day long for fear he'll run out into the street where it's so busy, cars and big trucks at any hour. Too much traffic there in the city, rattling the house, making the windows vibrate. Here it's silent: you can hear the silence pulsing beneath the noise of the insects. . . . Kasch? Is it really you? Here? After so long? But why? Am I here, calling to you? Waiting for you? Kasch? My love? Are you really here, are you still alive? Is that you, hiding in there, in that ruin of a house?—hiding from me? Kasch? Bearded, gaunt, sickly-pale, hair colorless as dead hair, eyes in shadow, dry bitter mouth in shadow, is it Kasch, here, is it Laney, here, shading her eyes, waiting for a sign?

A sign, a sign . . . ?

# CURRENT CREST BESTSELLERS

☐ BORN WITH THE CENTURY      24295   $3.50
by William Kinsolving
A gripping chronicle of a man who creates an empire for his family, and how they engineer its destruction.

☐ SINS OF THE FATHERS      24417   $3.95
by Susan Howatch
The tale of a family divided from generation to generation by great wealth and the consequences of a terrible secret.

☐ THE NINJA      24367   $3.50
by Eric Van Lustbader
They were merciless assassins, skilled in the ways of love and the deadliest of martial arts. An exotic thriller spanning postwar Japan and present-day New York.

☐ KANE & ABEL      24376   $3.75
by Jeffrey Archer
A saga spanning 60 years, this is the story of two ruthless, powerful businessmen whose ultimate confrontation rocks the financial community as well as their own lives.

☐ GREEN MONDAY      24400   $3.50
by Michael M. Thomas
An all-too-plausible thriller in which the clandestine manipulation of world oil prices results in the most fantastic bull market the world has ever known.